THE CENTAUR'S WIFE

ALSO BY AMANDA LEDUC

Disfigured: On Fairy Tales, Disability, and Making Space

The Miracles of Ordinary Men

THE CENTAUR'S WIFE

AMANDA LEDUC

Random House Canada

PUBLISHED BY RANDOM HOUSE CANADA

LIBRARY AND ARCHIVES CANADA CATALOGUING IN PUBLICATION
Title: The centaur's wife / Amanda Leduc.
Names: Leduc, Amanda, author.
Identifiers: Canadiana (print) 2020025586X | Canadiana (ebook) 20200255916 |
ISBN 9780735272859 (softcover) | ISBN 9780735272866 (EPUB)
Classification: LCC PS8623.E426 C46 2021 | DDC C813/.6—dc23

Text design by Emma Dolan
Cover art and design by Emma Dolan

Printed and bound in Canada

www.penguinrandomhouse.ca

10 9 8 7 6 5 4 3 2

Penguin
Random House
RANDOM HOUSE CANADA

For Jess, always and forever

To survive is an astonishing gift. The price of that gift is memory.

—D.A. Powell, *Tea*

PROLOGUE

In the beginning, a horse fell in love with a woman. Because magic was strong in the ground there, the horse dug himself a grave on his mountain and slept in it, buried in the dirt, on the one night a year when the stars are at their brightest. In the morning, he climbed out of the dirt as a man and made his way down the mountain. He stole clothes from a line when no one was looking and learned human language by watching men and women in the market square. The mountain's magic was still with him, so he learned quickly, and by the time he reached the woman's village you would never have guessed that he still had the heart of a stallion.

He'd been beautiful as a horse—black-maned and black-skinned, a white star in the centre of his forehead—and he was beautiful as a man, black-skinned and tall, a shock of white in his dark hair. The woman fell in love with him almost right away. He seemed wild to her but also familiar —she sensed a power in him that she wanted for herself, a different set of eyes with which to view the world. They courted and were married before the moon changed. The entire village came out to the wedding. After the music and the dancing were over, the villagers left them in the wedding tent—bright-eyed and flushed, two very-nearly strangers who were surprised to find themselves alone.

The woman was so beautiful he was afraid to touch her. She had lilies in her soft blonde hair and designs painted up and down her arms. The designs asked for happiness, health, children, an ever-loving husband—all of the good things anyone might wish a bride. The husband felt the symbols reach out and touch his stallion's heart for the smallest of instants—felt them *know*, and pull away. A draft blew through the room, then the air cleared again.

In less than a month, the woman was pregnant. The pregnancy was hard but not unbearable, and the husband was so besotted with his wife, so fearful for her safety, that he carried her almost everywhere they went. In time she grew so big the villagers began to prepare for triplets. A neighbour fashioned a cart like a rickshaw, so when his wife became too big for him to carry, the husband could pull her around like a queen. Sometimes he gave the village children rides when they asked. Sometimes, when his wife was in pain, he did not.

She was pregnant for longer than usual. As her belly grew enormous, the rest of her became a shadow. When her time finally came, the panic in her blue eyes made the village midwives nervous, and so the elders sent for one of the doctors who travelled the countryside. Sometimes women left when children came into the world, and they weren't about to let that happen. The doctor was also a woman. She was kind and gentle, with hands that were as strong as those of any man in the village, except perhaps the wife's own husband.

The wife had gone into labour in the morning and struggled all that day and into the next. You could see the babies in her belly, trying to break through this last membrane, their sharp little fists and heels making bumps beneath her skin. But try as she might, she couldn't push them out. After the second morning, the doctor placed a hand inside the wife and felt legs where a baby's head needed to be.

"The first is breech," she said, "and I can't turn it. I'll have to operate."

No one in the village had ever seen an operation of any kind, and people crowded around the door and the windows. Everyone was worried. Would the babies survive? Would the wife? No one could bear to look at the anguish in the husband's face.

But the doctor was the best, or so they'd been told, and she did not seem worried. She numbed the wife with drugs as best she could, then took her scalpel and made the first incision, quick and clean. Blood beaded up and ran down the wife's belly.

As she worked, the doctor hummed a wordless song to calm the wife. "Three cuts," she said, and smiled. "Three doors into the world for three special babies." Her second incision pierced the fascia. The crowd had gone quiet, the only noise the doctor's humming and the soft sounds of tissue giving way.

At the third cut, her scalpel gently slit the uterine wall. She did not stop humming. She set down her knife, pressed down and pushed in and scooped out the first baby.

The house went still for the smallest of moments. And then the screaming started.

The babies—and there *were* three of them—were red and squalling, one darker, two pale, all with the wife's blue eyes and a perfect, plump little torso atop the body of a tiny horse. Each leg, slick with mucus, ended in a dark little hoof. A tiny girl, two tiny boys. The midwives all ran for the door. *Monsters!* they cried as they fell outside. *They are monsters! Heaven help us. Get them away!* When the villagers tried to rush inside, the husband roared with fury and blocked the way.

The doctor—whose hands didn't shake, even now—laid each baby on the table, one by one. Then she turned back to the wife, still humming, and stitched up her wound as though nothing had happened. The wife, whose eyes were wide with terror, looked from the doctor to the babies and back, over and over. She didn't look at her husband, who stood silent by the closed door. When she tried to speak, the doctor hushed her.

"You've been through so much," the doctor said. She paused in her stitching and laid a hand against the wife's cheek. "I think you should sleep now." Perhaps the words were magic, perhaps it was the touch of her hand, but the wife fell asleep almost right away. When her breathing was untroubled and her stitches were done and the wound bandaged, the doctor moved to the crying babies and checked them over. They had strong lungs, she saw, and two hearts—one above, and one below—beating in sync.

"Lies will always come out," the doctor said. "Even lies with the best of intentions." She didn't look up from the babies.

The husband didn't say a word.

"You'll have to leave," the doctor said, "with the children. They won't let you stay here."

The husband swallowed hard. The doctor raised her head and watched him as the things he couldn't say caught in his throat. "You aren't from here," she said. "You should take the children back to your old life."

"My wife," he said, finally. "What about my wife?"

The doctor, whose own mother had once been called a witch, knew of ground magic and could guess what had happened. She checked the babies over a last time—they'd all fallen silent—and considered a moment before she spoke. "Your wife won't come."

The husband shook his head. "No, she will come." She loved him. Wasn't he still a man, despite his stallion's heart?

The doctor looked at the babies again—they were beautiful, in their strange, ungodly way—and sighed. Life and death went everywhere with her in her travels, hand in bloody hand. "If you do not leave tonight," she said, "the villagers will kill them." She'd seen enough of this to know—a deformed limb, a child born without a face. A child with no arms who'd been left outside to die in the snow. "They will kill you, too, if you fight them. If you love your children, you need to take them away."

She could hear the pounding of his heart now, like a drum announcing its own end. He said, "I won't leave without her."

But when the wife woke up and saw the babies, she screamed with rage and hit the husband with her fists. "Kill them," she told the doctor. "What monsters are these?" Who was he, this man she'd called her husband? He looked like a man but he wasn't. She'd been deceived. Everything she'd known was a lie. She had no husband now. "Get them away from me," she said, and she covered her eyes in terror and disgust. "Get them away."

When they heard her scream, the villagers began to pummel the house with shovels and sticks. The doctor swaddled the children as best she could, and when she placed them in the husband's arms, he gathered each child numbly to his chest. He could barely understand what was happening.

The doctor put goat's milk in a couple of bottles, tucked them in her own satchel along with her provisions, and slung it over his shoulder. "It's not a lot of food," she said, "enough for a day, maybe two. Protect their heads," she added, and then she swung open the door and stepped outside.

Such was her power—even now, after delivering these monster children—that the villagers fell quiet.

"They are leaving," the doctor said, pitching her voice to reach all of the crowd. "They will not bother you anymore. Let them go."

"They're monsters!" someone cried. Inside the house, the wife began to wail. "We don't want them here!"

"They are going and will not come back," the doctor said, and the husband slipped out into the space that her words made. The villagers looked at the bundles in his arms and shrank back, and they let him walk past them and vanish into the darkness beyond their fires.

The man headed back to the mountain from which he'd come, grief and anger struggling in his heart. He fed the children the goat's milk and soothed them when they cried, then found and milked more goats. When they reached his mountain, he climbed as far as he could, to where the magic of the mountain was the strongest, and he dug them a grave there, in the reddish-brown dirt beneath three weeping willows. It was not a night bright with stars, but he hoped the magic would still save them. The mountain—his home for so long—would save them. The magic of the trees around them, the roots that they pressed into the soil—all of these things had brought him to his love once, and they would do so again. They would make his children whole and human.

When the night deepened, he lowered the babies into the grave and, when they began to wail, settled himself in beside them and held them close. He pulled enough dirt over them to bury them almost but not quite. The babies, comforted by the closeness of his heartbeat, went silent. When he slept, they slept too. In his dreams, he stood beneath the sky and begged the mountain and the ground: *Make them like me. Give them what you gave to me.* In the dream he saw them all, two-legged and free, running in the village with the other girls and boys. Their mother smiled at them as they played—everyone whole now, everyone happy.

In the morning, though, when the father pushed aside some of the dirt, he saw that the babies were unchanged. And when he stood up and looked down at himself, he saw his old black stallion chest and legs, though his arms were still the arms of a man and his human head still ached with grief. Because, as the mountain knew, he had a stallion's heart but a man's love and longing. Like the babies, he belonged neither to one world nor the other, but somewhere in between. He wept then, for the first time. When he was done weeping, he woke the children, who'd grown bigger overnight, and they crawled out of the hole to him. They stood on spindly legs and looked around at the morning, as though they had new eyes.

So it came to pass that the father and his children spent the rest of their days on the mountain. After a while the father stopped dreaming about his two-legged children running in the village, and eventually—long years later—he dreamed less of his wife. His children grew happy and strong; they'd known no other life. Though sometimes a rage would break in them and the father would be reminded of his wife, his human love, whose anger had erupted like a volcano, whose rage still burned bright at his betrayal. Other times, the fierceness of their anger would remind the father of himself, and the dark things he harboured, the grief that never went away. He tried to be gentle with them when they raged, but the children grew wary of their own anger, the same way they grew wary of their father's love for them and the way he so jealously guarded their home.

When their father died, after many more years, they buried him beneath the three willows and wept over his grave, then slept there, sprawled beneath the stars. The next morning, when the sun came up, new beings pulled themselves out of the dirt where their father had been, beings that also had the heads and arms of humans and the strong bodies of horses. When the children looked at all of these new siblings, they saw the mountain's own glimmering anger in their deep and darkened eyes, and understood that though the mountain had taken their father back and given the children companions so that they would not be alone, it had also not forgotten their father's betrayal in leaving the mountain so long ago. It had given them a gift, but also a warning.

And that is how the centaurs came to be.

PART ONE

Heather is sleeping when they come, the meteors, raining from the sky. The twins, born only the day before, lie in a crib next to her hospital bed, their fingers laced together even in sleep. Greta and Jilly. Jilly and Greta. B is rumpled in the corner chair, snoring softly. Heather opens her eyes in the seconds before it happens, something having jolted her awake. Some dark dream or memory, her father tumbling down the side of that mountain so long ago. She lies silent, eyes open. The clock reads 5:00 a.m. In that tiny flash before the world ends she thinks about crawling out of bed, sliding out the door in her slippers, and running far away.

But then she hears a whistle, so loud the walls tremble. A whistle, and then a great crash outside. The ground shakes. Heather turns to look out her window—so slow—and all she sees are flames.

B is awake now and moves to the window like a ghost. The girls are crying; someone outside in the hall is screaming. Heather hasn't moved from the bed. B looks outside and then back at her. She can see that he thinks he's still dreaming.

"The world's on fire," he says, too confused to be afraid.

Heather swings her legs over the side of the bed and joins him at the window. Walking hurts. She can hear people running in the hall, more crashes, more screams. She stands beside B and watches giant balls of fire rain down from the sky and smash into buildings, cars, the orderly trees that line the roads. The smell of burning metal permeates the room.

The rock—is that what it is?—that slams into the hospital hits close enough for them both to feel the heat of it. They run to the babies and scoop them from their crib, and then they slip out of the room, bent and shaking. *Basement!* someone shouts. *We all have to get to the basement!* There are many people moving through the halls, and even more crying out from their hospital beds. *Help me. Help me, please.*

Basement, she thinks. *Basement. Basement.*

The elevators don't work, so they stumble down the stairs, B breathing hard beside her, his hand on her elbow as she limps as fast as she can go. The babies crying, the screams of everyone else ringing in her ears. Another crash outside, another flush of heat that trembles through the wall. They climb down and down and down.

At last, they find themselves in an old stone foundation. The air is damp and musty here, but also hot with panic. People jabber and weep, shout into their cell phones. *I can't hear you. I don't know what's going on.*

Heather collapses softly against a wall and tries to breathe. B huddles beside her.

"Are you all right?" he says, pitching his voice low so it can find her in the din.

She can't speak; she only nods.

More people keep coming from the stairs. They are screaming and sobbing, some of them bloody. Another crash above them and everyone shrieks; the lights flicker, go out, come back on again. She thinks about the people hooked up to machines, the people they left behind. Soon there is hardly room to sit, bodies pressed so close around her she fights the urge to panic.

Breathe in, she thinks. *Breathe out.* She closes her eyes and tries to imagine the mountain air, but all she can picture is fire on the mountain too.

The mountain. The ones on the mountain, and fire.

Is he there? she wonders. *Is he all right?*

When she opens her eyes, B is crouched in front of her, Greta silent in his arms, her eyes wide and searching. "Look at me," he says. "Heather—it's all right."

"It's not all right." She wants to scream out loud, but whispers. "What's going on?"

"I don't know," he says. He reaches his free hand out and once more grasps her elbow. "But we're here. We're okay. Everything will be okay."

She wants to scream again at this; she only looks at him, then nods. *Breathe in, breathe out.* She holds Jilly close and breathes in her crumpled newness—the soft velvet of her bright-red head, the folds of skin at her neck.

Mine, she thinks. *Mine.*

Another crash above them, and the lights begin to flicker. The room fills with screaming.

"Calm down," B calls out. "Everyone—calm down."

She feels a hinge of disbelief in the air. She feels people turn their faces to his voice.

"Calm down?" a voice calls. "*What do you mean, calm down?*"

"There's nothing we can do right now," B says. "We just have to wait."

"Wait for what?" Another voice, this time from what sounds like the opposite side of the room.

Beside her B stands up and clears his throat. "I don't know," he says. "But I don't think it's safe to go outside."

There is a moment of silence in the room—she feels them all look up to the darkness above. Crashes—fainter now, but still there.

"Is it an earthquake?" someone says.

"Maybe," B says.

But Heather shakes her head. "Not an earthquake." She thinks of the fire raining down from the sky.

"Well," he says, then he speaks so everyone can hear. "Whatever it is—we can't go outside. We just have to wait."

"What if we're trapped?" someone else says. "How do we get out?"

"We'll get out," B says. "We just have to be patient."

There is another crash, louder than all the ones before it. The lights go out, and do not come back on.

This time there are no screams—only a whimper that reverberates around the room. Nothing else crashes above them. People check their phones again, lose calls. *Hello? Hello?*

The girls fall asleep, eventually. The sobs of those around Heather gradually soften and go quiet. Above them the wind wails cold and lonely. A tornado, maybe. Or some other kind of madness.

B tries to stretch his legs out in front of him, but there's no room. "I hate closed spaces," he mutters. Gone is the man who was so steadfast only a short time before. There's a vulnerability in his voice that reminds her of the night they met—drunk ramblings at the bar, the sweetness of his palm in hers as they stumbled down the street. They'd gone to the same high school. She hardly remembered him. She hardly remembered anybody. Everyone in the city was a stranger to her, even the people she'd known all her life.

The sweetness of his palm. That sudden rush of animal power as they fell together in the park, the dirt on her knees, the faraway-ness of the stars. She looked up and saw the mountain's deeper shadow in the dark sky—she felt its power pour down around her as she came, in a rush of rage and longing, and then it was gone and she was only sweaty on the grass, B once more sweet above her, mildly surprised.

He held her hand as he walked her home, and after he kissed her at her door she went inside, sure she'd never see him again. A nice boy, but what was there to talk about? They'd shared one thing, and that was enough.

He sent her texts—she didn't remember his name, had him listed only as *B*. She ignored the messages until the day, weeks later, when she found herself staring at a pregnancy test in the dim light of her bathroom.

She would get an abortion, obviously. She was thirty-seven, single— it was the only thing to do. Except that she didn't and one day passed and then another, and she stopped drinking and made an appointment with her doctor and bought herself the vitamins that she recommended. Then she went to her mother's house.

Everyone has to grow up sometime, Heather, was what her mother said.

She knew that they were two before the doctors did. Twin girls. She wanted them; she was afraid of them too. She worried about premature births, about a delivery like her mother's—prolonged and difficult, brain damage from oxygen deprivation in the birth canal. She dreamed about two girls who came into the world with a gait just like hers—rollicking, uneven, one side of each tiny body unable to function quite like the rest. Muscles that didn't stretch quite the way they should, feet twisted from a brain that gave weak signals. Their twinned futures slices of bullied days on the schoolyard. *Cerebral palsy. Cerebral loser. Stupid fucking spaz.*

She didn't want them to grow up without a dad. And so she looked up B's last text and sent him a message, and then there was coffee, and then dinner, and sometime after that there was a shy proposal and she said yes because there was nothing else to say, and then there was a wedding. She looked surprised in the photos, not quite sure how she got there, her belly big under its covering of grey lace.

His name is Brendan, but to her he is only B. She reaches over, takes his hand, takes her turn at being reassuring. "Everything will be okay," she says. Her eyes have adjusted to the darkness and she sees him smile a little.

Then Jilly starts to cry. Greta, in B's arms, lets out a wail. Heather feels the fear in the room spike again, mouths around them open and ready to scream.

In front of her, low to the ground, a fox materializes out of nowhere. Its blue eyes open and blink at her.

Blue eyes, like the sky. Two tiny bodies suckling against her orange-grey fur.

Heather catches her breath, looks around—no one else seems to notice the fox. She watches it stand up as its babies gently fall, then carry them one by one over to the wall, stepping lightly around the people huddled on the floor. No one moves. No one notices.

In front of the foxes, the wall shimmers and then disappears. Beyond it, the green reaches of the mountain, a flash of bright blue sky. No fires. The fox turns to look at her.

She wants to gather up her own babies and run to the wall, through stone and onto mountain grass. She can hardly breathe.

B's hand on her elbow, again. "Heather." His voice is urgent. "Heather, please."

The babies are now wailing at the top of their lungs. She looks at the portal again, at the foxes who wait, and then back at B.

"There was a fox," she says, and the babies—and the wails of the people around them—quiet. Like magic. The silence that comes after this is puzzled, unsure. The foxes at the wall cock their heads and look at her; the mountain beyond them shimmers grey-green and blue.

"What fox?" It is a child who asks. Heather shifts so that B can put Greta in her lap. She gathers both babies close, takes a breath. The entire room is silent now, waiting.

They are listening only because they are tired and frightened and there is nothing else to do. She glances at the wall again, but the foxes are gone, and so is the portal. And so she begins.

"There once was a fox on the mountain," she says. An old story, one that her father had told her when she was small. "She wanted babies of her own more than anything else in the world. But she didn't know how to get them, and so she asked the mountain how."

When they were born, her daughters tumbled from her like firecrackers—their hair bright red, their voices loud enough to fill the room. She was too tired to cry, too tired to think, too tired to be anything other than relieved. The nurses cleaned the babies up and handed her one girl and then the other, and she held them against her, skin to skin. They were perfect. Their mouths opened like tiny birds. They rooted against her collarbone, her breasts, and the nurses helped to turn them, one mouth against one nipple, one mouth against the other. It hurt when they latched on, and Heather hissed, fought the urge to fling them both across the room, see their tiny skulls crack against the wall. Did it show?

"It will get better." Had the nurse seen the storm in her face? Maybe she said this to all the mothers. The nurse nodded to B, weeping with joy by the bed. "You have help. You'll be just fine."

"They're so beautiful," B said, and he reached over Heather's shoulder, cupped one tiny head in his palm. "They're so beautiful."

Already, she was so tired of him. It felt hormonal but she knew it went much deeper—beyond the emergence of these tiny bodies, beyond the relief and the sudden flush of power: *I did it, I did it, now I can do anything*. She wanted to run screaming through the hospital, climb the walls, jump off a mountain. She was almost certain she could fly. And she hated the way he wept, the way he seemed so happy. Ten months ago she had had hardly any idea who he was, and now she was married to this man in a way that went even deeper than the ring she'd let him put on her finger.

Greta and Jilly. Jilly and Greta. They were perfect. She loved them, and it was an iron cage that settled over her heart and clanged shut in a way that reverberated right down to her toes. She had been free before, and now she was chained to them forever.

The next day, meteors rained down from the sky.

When they climb out of the basement long hours later, the hospital is gone. They clutch the girls—B has Jilly now, while Greta sniffles in the crook of Heather's arm—and climb the stairwell until they step out into a tired orange light that reveals a city turned to rubble, littered with dust. It could be late afternoon, it could be evening. The air is hot and dry and smells of burning. The sky is thick with cloud and smoke. Their fellow basement dwellers emerge the way they do—squinting, shielding their eyes from the light or the wreckage, maybe both. There are no human sounds, not even sirens.

"Were we attacked?" someone quavers. No one knows what to say.

There is a toppled building to their left, half of an office tower shaved off in front of them across the street, the ground littered with downed trees and fallen branches, shards of broken glass, power lines dancing in the wind. On the far side of the office tower, smoke rises in a steady plume. She wants to go and see what's burning, and the answering vision comes to her in a flash, like so many others have through the years. A crater, a hunk of molten rock, the area around it so hot it's hard to breathe.

People are moaning in disbelief. "What happened?" someone says. "What's going on?"

Heather glances around—so many people spilling out into the dim light, all of them looking around with the terrified eyes of children. She has no stories left to calm anyone.

"Your phone," she says to B. "See if it works now."

He's one step ahead of her, thumbing at his phone with one hand and holding Jilly with the other. "No signal."

A woman beside her—her scrubs splattered with blood, dirt smeared across her face—pulls her own phone out of her pocket and taps it. "I can't get a signal either."

One by one, people tap their screens and hold them up to the sky. Nothing happens.

"The cell towers," someone says, finally. "They must be down."

Heather bundles Greta tight in the folds of her hospital gown and moves farther out into the road. She's in bare feet. It's taken her this long to notice.

"Heather," B says. "Be careful."

"I'm always careful," she says. "I just need to see what's going on."

He holds out an arm. "Give me Greta."

Heather shakes her head. "She's fine."

"You're not wearing any shoes," he says, carefully. "I don't want you to fall."

"I'm not going to *drop* her." She's angry at the way his words have brought her own fears to the surface. "I'm fine."

Behind B, the crowd is starting to disperse—shell-shocked and terrified, some people wailing again. Others still wave their phones in the air. She turns away from B and steps forward, picking a path through the rubble. She feels his eyes on her uneven gait.

I can keep her safe, she thinks. *Fuck you.*

When she gets to the end of the street, everything is exactly as she envisioned it. The crater has demolished an apartment building and spans almost a block. Small fires burn all around. The others from the hospital join her—B beside her once more, his hand shielding Jilly's face.

He nods to Greta. "Cover her. She shouldn't be breathing this in." By *this* he means the tiny flecks of ash and dust that dance around them. They float almost lazily, as though they have all the time in the world.

"She *is* covered." She draws Greta deeper into her gown nonetheless.

"Heather." B's voice is sharp now. "Heather, come away from here. Please."

She turns and walks away from the crater, stopping at first by a small house that is seemingly untouched except for the roof, which is smoking. Greta snuffles in her arms, a tiny pig gone to sleep again. For a moment she imagines the story she'll tell the girls years from now. *You both could sleep through anything. Even the end of the world.*

She opens its door and steps into the house and hears B calling her name in a voice that belongs to someone else—to the person that told everyone to calm down in the basement. He's trying to take charge. He's worried for *her*.

She moves down the entry hall and into the kitchen, where mugs of tea are abandoned on the counter, flecks of ash and soot floating on the surface. The patio doors have blown open—ash is everywhere in the house and, as she steps outside, onto the patio, spread thickly over back-yard grass. She cradles Greta and watches the smoke rise out of a hole in the backyard, a much smaller crater than the one she's just seen. Smoke drifts over the half-buried bodies by the wreckage of the pool. An arm attached to nothing, just lying curled on the blackened grass. The air here smells like a barbecue that's gone on too long.

Beyond the fence at the end of the backyard and the squat brown house on the other side, beyond the street that lies in rubble on the far side of that—*Deadwood Street,* she thinks dizzily, how fitting—over still more roads and paths that lead out toward the forest (*Miller Road, Longwood Avenue, Larkspur Crescent*), beyond the smoke and the glittering fires that burn all around, the mountain rises, cool and green. Untouched. There are no fires burning there, as far as she can see.

The relief makes her dizzy; her knees buckle and she almost falls.

"Give me Greta," B snaps, from behind her. "Give her to me now."

When she hands him the baby, his face softens right away. "There's a TV in the living room," he says. "No signal there either." She can hear the faint scratch of static and is surprised there's power at all. Others are filtering out into the backyard and come to stand beside them.

What happens now? she sees everyone thinking. *What happens now?*

The ones on the mountain—she knows they're there—see them too. They stand untouched, their marble arms and glossy flanks just as she remembered from that day on the mountain when she was a child, while Heather and B stand with the girls, their lives flecked with ruin.

No one goes up on the mountain now. She's the reason why.

She'd been a strange child. Dark-haired and quiet, her limp sometimes imperceptible and other times visible from halfway down the street. She had a crutch when she was tiny but then, when she was a little older, only her own unsteady feet. Her mother worried about shoes and braces; her father said it didn't matter.

"No one else walks like you, Heather-Feather," he would say to her. "That's something to be proud of."

When she was a baby, her family had moved from their house under the mountain's shadow to a house in the city proper—at the end of the last street before the mountain fields. A house that backed onto thick forest.

"We've moved for her. We need to be close to good schools," her mother always said, though Heather knew it was for her mother too.

The mountain made her mother nervous in a way she couldn't explain. So instead she focused on the things that she could know: how far away the schools were, how long it would take Heather to walk there.

"I don't want her to have to walk too far," her mother said. "I don't want her to get tired."

"Heather's a trooper," her father had said. She'd been born two months early; they hadn't been sure she'd survive. "The more she walks, the stronger she'll get."

"I know *that*," her mother said. "But what will the children at school think?"

The children at school thought she walked funny, and told her so. They imitated her when they thought she wasn't looking—the uneven circle of her hips, the slow swing of her leg. They laughed.

School became another place for her to practise being alone. The stories she told herself on the playground were like the stories her father told her at night before bed; the stepsisters who cut off their toes so that they could wear the glass slipper, Hansel and Gretel with no happy ending.

"The witch has a crutch," she said to her father. "Like the one I used to have."

"But you don't need the crutch anymore," he told her. "And the witch was only pretending." Then he told her about the mermaid who drowned herself in the sea.

"Stop telling her those stories," her mother would say. Her mother, who had fallen in love with a dark-haired boy who worked outside and sang to trees. They were older now, with bills and a house and a child. No more romantic nights beneath the stars for them. Most days she felt foolish when she remembered who they used to be.

In the city, it was easier for Heather's mother to pretend that Heather's father was merely *eccentric*. He might go for long walks at night; he might go closer to the mountain than anyone was supposed to go. His whole family had been like that—dreamers, fantasists, people who told you a good story but forgot to put food on the table. In the city this could all be kept secret; that was the point of being city dwellers now, not outcasts who lived in a strange house under the mountain. He could tend the municipal gardens. She could teach at the school.

"Stop telling her things that are *sad*," Heather's mother would say. "Heaven knows she gets enough of that already."

But Heather wasn't sad; not really. The world was deep and dark and wonderful. Sometimes, like when she was at school, she did not like to be in it, and sometimes she *did* cry, but that was okay. Her father made it okay.

At night he went for long walks through the fields close to the mountain, sometimes for hours, always alone. He rarely slept. His fingernails were almost always black with dirt, but his hands were lovely—strong hands that tamed the flowers on the city boulevard as easily as they coaxed colour from the gardens at their house. He talked to the flowers and sometimes, he told Heather, they talked back. It had been so long since he'd been unhappy that Heather forgot that he'd ever been sad.

It was good, the doctors told her mother, to indulge him from time to time. If he was happy, let him be happy. Let him believe stories were true.

"One day you'll come walk with me too," he told Heather when she was ten. "We just need to wait until you're a little older, Heather-Feather, and a little stronger. That's all."

She grew; her legs grew too, though her right leg remained shorter than the left. She was not able to do all of the things that the other kids could do—she couldn't run as fast, she was a tentative climber—but to keep him hoping, she told her father stories of the games they played at school, the hikes the kids took in the city parks. *I came in third in the race in gym today.*

She kept the stories that he told her close, and thought about him walking far and wide under the moon. *Once upon a time there were twelve princesses who danced late into the night. Once upon a time there were foxes who could talk, and witches who lived in the woods and granted wishes if you were brave enough to find them.* They were only stories, yes, but wasn't it nice to imagine a world that had so much dancing? Wasn't it nice to imagine a world where mermaids were real, where she might win a race, where maybe one day it wouldn't be difficult to walk a straight line?

Sometimes, if she was lucky, her father took her out into the city parks at night, and together they counted the stars. Three billion, one hundred and twenty-six million, four hundred and twenty-five thousand

and one. They were like snowflakes, he told her. No two were the same. She carried the words inside her heart.

Then he died, and she didn't have words anymore.

✳

The survivors gather in another of the nearby houses, closer to the wreckage of the hospital. This one is larger, and there are no burned bodies in the backyard. They shuffle in and collapse on the couches, on the floor. Someone picks up the cordless phone beside the couch and dials 911 and nothing happens. There is no dial tone.

"So the TV stations and the cell towers are out. It can't be everything. Can it?" a young girl says. Eighteen, maybe nineteen, something like that. Her hair is white-blonde and choppy, her Doc Martens boots just like the ones Heather wore as a teen.

"If the stations are out," Heather says, "it's because the satellites are out."

"Maybe it was just our stations, though. Our satellites. Maybe other cities are okay?"

"If our *own* satellites are out," Heather says, gently, "this isn't the only place where this has happened." She watches the man standing beside B take all of this in. Watches him remember that *yes,* there are other places, there's an entire rest of the world. *Surely the rest of the world is okay. Surely this was just us—one catastrophe, contained.*

She closes her eyes and sees the large crater, looks down inside, sees the hunk of rock that's even now cooling and fusing hard to the dirt. The pictures in her mind tumble fast—fiery rocks in other cities, in the oceans, across the continent.

"The whole world is burning," she says. Her voice is low, but they hear her.

"What do you mean, the whole world?" the man shouts.

The blonde girl has gone rigid. "How do you know?"

Because I'm just like my father, she wants to say, only that isn't right. *Everyone thought he was crazy too.*

How to explain it? It was just there after she came down from the mountain alone those years ago: these flashes in her head of things that would happen in other parts of the world. Some kind of connection that hadn't been there before.

The kids had called her crazy at school after it happened, after he fell. *Crazy. Just like your fucking dad.*

"I don't, not really," she lies now. "Maybe that's just how it all feels."

Another man goes to the TV in this new house and kneels down in front of it, reaches forward to the screen as though sending out a prayer. He presses the button—nothing.

"It's a digital TV," Heather says, weary. "No satellites, remember?" Everyone else is silent, looking at the floor.

"Does anyone have a radio?" B asks. Several people reach for their phones.

"He means a radio that isn't digital." She looks at B. "What about the cars outside?" she says.

B hands her the baby—Greta? No, Jilly, she's been holding Greta this whole time. She follows B outside, walking carefully, trying not to notice how he glances back at her, nervous. She thinks about her slippers—burned away, perhaps, or buried under how many cubic tonnes of hospital rubble.

The car in the driveway—it's a minivan, with animal crackers scattered over the back seat—is locked, but B goes back into the house and fetches a wire hanger. He straightens it, then shimmies it down through the window.

"Couldn't find the keys," he says when he sees her staring.

"I didn't know you could do that."

He looks up as the lock clicks open, manages to grin at her. "I'm surprised I even remembered."

He hot-wires the ignition, then turns the radio dial through static. Heather walks around to the passenger side and climbs in beside him. When a voice breaks through, they both jump.

"Satellites have gone dark. Police are asking everyone to stay calm. Evacuation orders—"

"Evacuation orders?" B mutters. "Evacuation where?"

"It was a meteor shower." It's the blonde girl again, at the passenger window. She kicks at the rubble scattered over the ground. "That's what they're saying." She points down the street to another car, where a group of people huddle around an open door. That radio is louder. *State of emergency*, she hears. *State of emergency.*

It sounds ridiculous, all of it, like something from a movie. But the pictures that run through her head will not stop. Cities that are burning. Faces locked in screams. The voices over the radio confirm what she already knows. No one has heard from the other side of the world in hours.

"How long do you think we were in the basement?" Heather asks as she slides back out of the car.

The blonde girl shrugs. "Hours? I'm not sure."

"It's after six," B says. "Someone had an analog watch. We were under the hospital for most of the day."

Heather thinks then of her mother, who is already dead—who did not live to see the twins or this. Four months ago—alone in her bed, her heart just giving out. A peaceful death, if unexpected. A murmur, the doctors told Heather after it happened. Undiagnosed her whole life.

Heather hadn't cried. She didn't cry when the girls were born and she isn't crying now, even as the people around her wail anew at the scale of the disaster. Instead she walks across the sidewalk, then stands there for a moment, looking at the dusty grass. Soon B is beside her, reaching for the girls.

She lets him take them, then sits carefully down on the ground. When she is sitting and stable, he hands the twins back to her, one by one. She unlatches her bra beneath the hospital gown and shifts Greta so her tiny mouth latches on. It still hurts. B goes back to the car—he's found a better frequency, less static. The blonde girl stands in front of her. When Heather looks up, she sees the mountain looming large over her shoulder.

The girl squats and reaches out to touch Jilly's head. "What are their names?" she says.

"Jilly. And this one's Greta."

"I love their red hair. What's your name?"

"Heather."

"Heather. I'm Elyse." She sits and wraps her arms around her knees.

Greta stops nursing and Heather shifts the baby to her shoulder to burp her, the baby's bright head lolling softly into the dip of her neck. They are so calm, her babies. Already they seem older than they are. "So you were in the hospital too."

Elyse nods. "My friend just had a lung transplant. She was hooked up to a machine." She clears her throat, digs the toe of one Doc Martens into the dirt. "Her mum was there too. She wouldn't leave the room."

Heather thinks about this.

"I'm supposed to have the same surgery," Elyse whispers. "I was supposed to go into the hospital next month. But what's going to happen now? *There is no hospital.*"

Greta burps and Heather lays her back down in her lap, then picks Jilly up. After she latches on, Heather lays a hand on Elyse's shoulder and squeezes.

Elyse seems very young now. "Did you hurt your foot? When everyone was running to the basement?"

Heather blinks at this, and then remembers. "No," she says. "That's just how I walk."

"I'm sorry," Elyse says, instantly. "I didn't mean—"

"It's okay."

Her eyes follow Heather's, up to the mountain. "Yanna and I were going to hike the mountain after we'd both recovered from our surgeries," Elyse says. "The doctors said we wouldn't be able to do it and we wanted to prove them wrong."

"They don't let people up the mountain." A phrase she's learned by rote. "It isn't safe."

"I know," Elyse says. "I've heard the stories too."

A faint siren peals into the air and everyone falls silent—Heather, Elyse, B over by the radio, the group near the other car. The sound grows, leaps from the air and burrows deep into their ears and hearts, their veins, their memories. Jilly pulls away from Heather's breast and starts to cry;

Heather covers her ears and Elyse covers Greta's. Heather and Elyse press their foreheads together, smell the sour reek of each other's fear. The siren cannot be any louder than this but still it comes.

Then there is a great shudder of tiles on pavement and the siren stops. They look up to see two fire trucks and an ambulance in the middle of the street, people spilling out like ants from the top of a hill. Their clothes stained and dirty, their faces bloody and bruised. They stare at the wreckage where the hospital used to be and despair leaks out over their faces. Who knows where they've come from, but clearly they were hoping that this city would be different. Their faces reveal more than the radio news—destruction behind them, wherever they've been, and destruction in front of them now.

Heather looks up at the mountain, and again it tells her nothing.

A dark-haired, dark-skinned woman steps out of the driver's seat of the ambulance, wearing scrubs. Her eyes are brown and bright, slightly frantic. She's fine-boned, like a bird—a small brown sparrow—but when she speaks she seems much taller. "Who's in charge here?"

"No one," B replies. Heather almost laughs. He walks over to her after he speaks, bends down to pick Greta up and rests her against his shoulder.

They are parents, Heather realizes again. She's a *mother*.

The woman nods. Another woman, tall and blonde, has climbed down from the passenger side of the ambulance and comes to stand beside her. "Is the whole hospital gone? Are there salvageable supplies?" She raises her voice and Heather watches little shimmers of movement around them as people step toward her, hope flaring in their eyes. *Maybe she knows. Maybe she understands what's going on.*

"How many survivors?" the dark-haired woman calls out.

"We don't know," B says. "We've only just come out of shelter."

She looks at him with something like confusion in her face, which quickly softens into sadness. "We've been driving for hours," she says. "The whole day. There are fires everywhere."

Everywhere. They already know this, but still the shock rolls through them like a wave. Heather finds herself staring at the ground. What comes next? She has no idea. There are no flashes to tell her.

Then two scuffed greyish runners appear in front of her, peeking out from dark-blue scrubs. The small woman kneels and places a delicate brown hand—the nails blunt, the fingers slender—on Jilly's head. The girls are both sleeping now, incredibly.

"Are they all right?" she asks.

Heather nods.

"My name is Tasha." The woman peers into Heather's face. "Are *you* all right?"

Heather laughs for real this time—sudden, hysterical. "Are you a doctor?"

"Yes." The other woman sits back on her heels. Her hand feels warm and dry on Heather's forehead, but at her touch, Heather sees a darkened room, hears weeping so loud it's almost a scream. Her nostrils fill with smoke.

"What happened?" Heather whispers. "What happened in that other fire?"

Tasha pulls away as though burned. She stays crouched for a moment, opens her mouth to speak and then closes it. After another moment, she stands, wipes her hands against her scrubs, and moves on. She touches other faces, asks everyone's name.

Heather sits on the curb until B takes the girls from her. He leads her back into the second house, where they find a spot on the living room floor, bedding down among strangers with blankets from somewhere far away.

She sleeps beside B, the girls snuggled between them, but she is not there. She is on the mountain. Only clouds and looming green ahead of her.

He isn't there. She cannot see him no matter where she looks.

MOTHER FOX

Once there was a fox on the mountain, and she wanted babies more than anything else in the world. But she didn't know how to get them, and so she asked the mountain.

The mountain told her, *You must go down off the mountain and into the grasslands where the sun shines and casts no shadow. Once there, find a rock and pry it up from its resting place so that the earth beneath the rock sees the sun for the first time. Say to the rock:* I am ready to bring you into the world now, *and turn in two circles. If it thinks you deserve them, the rock will give you your babies.*

The rock doesn't know who I am, the fox said.

Everyone knows who you are, said the mountain. *You're the Fox. You have red hair and a long red tail. The trees recognize you. The ground knows the way your footsteps feel different than the Deer's. The rock will know you too.*

But how will the rock know I deserve babies? the fox asked. *How will it know I am worthy?*

To this, the mountain made no answer.

The fox went down the mountain anyway. She was quick and light and small, and knew how to hide when larger creatures—bears, a wolf, an orange-brown coyote that grinned at her through the trees—got in her way. She found the grasslands with no trouble. She even found a rock. After she lifted it, she turned herself in two careful circles, then sat and spoke the words.

I am ready to bring you into the world now.

But when the fox looked down at the earth beneath the rock, she saw only dirt and worms. The fox was confused. There was no mountain around to tell her what to do next. So she walked farther through the grasses and found another rock and lifted it. She turned herself in two more careful circles and spoke the words again.

I am ready to bring you into the world now.

Again, only dirt and worms.

The fox, puzzled, went back to the first rock. She reached out a paw and touched it. It was warm, which surprised her; she'd never touched warm rock before.

The sun warms me, the rock said. It didn't actually speak, but the fox heard it anyway. *The sun warms rocks differently on the mountain.*

I am ready to bring you into the world now, the fox said again, thinking that perhaps the rock hadn't heard her.

I know, the rock said. *The babies were waiting for you when you turned me over.*

But, the fox said, not understanding, *I saw only dirt and worms.*

Can't worms also be babies? the rock said. *Don't they also deserve to be in the world?*

I don't know anything about worms, the fox said. *I don't know what they eat. I don't know how to keep them safe.*

No one knows at first, the rock said to her. *But everyone can learn.*

The fox, understanding, was ashamed. She sat back on her haunches and looked at the rock for a while.

I am ready to bring you into the world now, she said again.

The worms crawled out of the dirt to her, and she was very happy.

— 2 —

When the meteors come for them, Tasha is at work in the sickly green of the ER, dealing with the normal crises of an ordinary shift. Then there are bangs and screaming, and fire everywhere. She is standing by the charge desk one moment, and the next she's crawling out from beneath a pile of chairs and pieces of ceiling and scattered patient charts, the fire alarm screaming through the space between her ears.

Where is Annie? She looks around and sees only bodies, some of them sprawled motionless, others struggling to stand. Blood like a slow red wave. The fire alarms go on and on.

Have they been bombed?

Tasha pushes herself up, shaky on her legs. She touches the side of her head and her hand comes away sticky—blood, something else. There are other fluids on the floor. Bags of saline, bottles of hand sanitizer cracked and leaking onto the tiles.

Someone appears in front of her, grabs her by both arms. Mouth open, no sound. Brown eyes. Blonde hair. Annie.

"Speak up," Tasha says. "I can't hear you."

A frown, and Annie's mouth moves again. "Tasha," she hears, faintly. "Tasha, look at me."

Tasha's hands start to tremble. She balls her fists and closes her eyes, takes one deep breath. "I hit my head," she says, looking at Annie again. "What happened?"

"I don't know," Annie says. "A bomb?"

Who would want to bomb them? That makes no sense. Then the ground shakes beneath them and Tasha feels the idea of a bomb move out of both their minds and become something else. It was like that with Annie, sometimes. They felt things at the same time, understood crossword puzzle clues at the same moment, even when they were on opposite sides of the house. They'd made a silly Sunday game out of it over morning coffee—finishing their respective puzzles in unison, the two of them flushed and triumphant.

"Earthquake," Tasha says.

"Tsunami," Annie says. The seashore is so close; the water would rise up to cover them all. "We need to get away from here."

Annie grabs Tasha's hand and they run to the nearest exit, and from there to the ambulance on the ER ramp. Two fire trucks come screaming up the street as more people stagger out of the hospital, patients in rumpled gowns, nurses and doctors and orderlies in scrubs, their arms filled with blankets and bandages and boxes.

"*We don't have time!*" Annie screams. "We need to go."

Tasha turns back to the hospital. She does not want to die—not after what she's survived. But they can't leave yet. They need supplies. They need to figure out where to go.

She looks back toward Annie and sees people climbing into and onto the fire trucks, drivers in yellow jackets pushing people up.

Then a ball of fire arcs over their heads, so bright everything turns iridescent. It smashes into the hospital. Tasha falls to the ground, all

sound

gone.

The world explodes.

A hand on her arm. She lets Annie pull her up, stumbles with her to the ambulance, gets in the passenger side. The heat is almost unbearable. The two red fire trucks pull away in the smoke. Annie throws the ambulance into gear and they peel down the ramp and onto the road.

They've left people standing, but she can't hear the screams.

＊

As a child, she'd had night terrors—long twisted minutes with half of her in one world and the other half in the next. Endless dusty hallways with no corners and snarling demons who lunged at her through the wall. She'd bolt upright in her bed and scream, still asleep, strike the demons across the face only to have them multiply and pin her to the bed.

The demons came from the ground, like all wild things. They slithered up through the floorboards of the house and through the windows, pretending to be birds. They wrapped their talons in her hair and choked her with their feathered wings, then slid scaly down her arms and held her fast to the bed. Sometimes the terror in her chest would become its own thing, unfurling from her ribcage like a bat. It would smile with pointed teeth and press down into the bleeding skin of her stomach before launching itself into the air. The darkness from her ribcage would overwhelm the sky.

In the morning her mother might have a black eye, her father a puffed lip from where Tasha had hit them in the night. Her mother would hold Tasha close and murmur stories in her ear—dancing octopuses, starfish that gathered treasure and hid it beneath the sand, mountains, far away, that were so tall they reached the moon. Her father made them oatmeal and toast, weak tea with lots of warm milk and extra sugar for Tasha. Sometimes after a troubled night this would be enough to restore her and she was able to go to school. Other times she'd be too tired and they'd keep her home.

The doctors told her parents that the terrors would go away. They said this when she was seven, and again when she was nine, and after the night of her twelfth birthday, when she screamed about birds that burned holes in the ground, they shook their heads and said she was still a child and it would pass. Her mother turned the fire-birds into a story, but the terrors did not go away. In high school she found comfort in science and stayed up late into the night reading biology textbooks—blood and kidneys, heartbeats, brain. Night terrors, she read, were thought to be linked to epilepsy in some cases but not in others. There were questions around whether night terrors were congenital. Her grandmother had sleepwalked as a child. As the doctors said, most children outgrew night terrors before they hit their teens—and if they didn't, nine times out of ten, the terrors became easier to manage. Medication to help you sleep without dreaming. Strict diets that helped to facilitate an easier transition into delta sleep.

Her terrors did become less, but also more—fewer instances, longer dreams. Once or twice she woke up and found herself on the lawn. The second time this happened it was snowing; with Tasha's permission, her parents installed a lock outside of the door to her room and locked her in. The demons did not hold her down against the bed anymore—they just taunted her alone in a locked room.

Her years of studying late into the night prepared her well for medical school, then residency. She was alert when other students struggled to get by; as a resident she was eager to plunge into a trauma case at two-thirty in the morning when everyone around her was bleary-eyed and cautious. She did not need stories to help her through the night now, not when there were bodies to disappear into and heartbeats to measure. Mountains that reached the moon were not real, nor were starfish that hid treasure, nor were fire-birds that fell screaming from the sky and bone-bat things that crawled out from your ribcage.

On the first day of her residency she'd seen Annie in the hospital cafeteria, clad in her scrubs and sitting with three other nurses. Tall and blonde, like the princesses in some of the stories that her mother had told. (There were never any dark-haired, dark-skinned princesses, but she'd been too busy trying to sleep to wonder about that.) Annie looked up with something like recognition as Tasha approached, and Tasha felt her chest expand into a world bright and soft. The winged thing that unfurled from her ribcage this time was only made of light.

They were married in a year. Their parents surprised them with the down payment on a house. When she was finished her residency, offers came from other hospitals far away but Tasha turned them down so they could stay in the house by the ocean. They thought about having a child. She had terrors so rarely now they felt like the stuff of legend.

But demons are demons and don't forget how to find you. When they came for her again, their hands were filled with fire. That time, they took her parents.

This time, they took everything else.

Billowing smoke, shaking ground, and groaning road. Great gaping holes around them as they drive past bodies tumbled over one another, past the wreckage of houses and tall apartment towers. The sky continues to fall around them in great flaming chunks. The ragged breathing of children and their parents fills the ambulance, too many people on board, but still they screech to a halt when they see someone standing in the mess. It doesn't happen often enough.

"Where is everyone?" Annie asks at one point. Tasha has no answer. Sound has come back to her, slowly, along with a heightened sense of colour. Everything outside feels like it belongs to a different universe.

"What are we going to do?" Annie whispers.

"Keep driving," Tasha says. The world still shakes off and on, but not as often. Water from the ocean has not followed them.

Not a tsunami after all. Something else entirely. Everything feels like a dream.

"Tasha," Annie says, sharply. "Don't fall asleep."

"I'm not," Tasha says instantly—but she *is* drowsy, drifting alongside Annie, closing her eyes against a world so sharp it almost hurts.

"You hit your head," Annie reminds her. "It could be a concussion. Don't fall asleep until I can check."

"Annie, I'm okay."

"You don't know that."

It's all right, she wants to say. *Annie, it will be all right.*

But the words don't come. They drive on, and the world continues to burn.

✳

Meteors, catastrophe, impact event. The radio bursts in the ambulance are infrequent, and always catch them off guard. The entire world, it seems, has been caught by surprise. They stop for gas at one abandoned station and leave a pile of bills on the counter. The next time they fill up, Tasha slides money across the counter to a weeping sixteen-year-old boy.

"Come with us," she says, but he only shakes his head.

"My parents," he says. "No one's picking the phone up at home. I don't know where they are. I don't know what's going on."

Sometimes the road is blocked and they have to turn around to find another route inland. They keep driving north, away from the sea, just in case. Eventually they have no room for more people and when they see someone they don't stop. As they drive through miniature dust storms, they hope there are no people lost in the murk.

Once, as they prepare for yet one more blind push through the dust, Tasha grabs the edge of the seat beneath her and holds her breath. They hit a bump that could be a body; she crosses herself, even though she hasn't done that in years. When they're through the dust, Annie, almost hysterical, pulls the ambulance over to the side of the road.

"What was that?" Annie asks.

"I don't know," Tasha whispers. "A body? Do you want me to check?"

Annie shakes her head. "Not that," she says. "*You.* Are you praying?"

Laughter catches her off guard; Tasha hiccups, almost chokes.

"Maybe," she says. "I don't know. I'm just trying to hang on." She reaches over and opens the door, then steps down onto the ground and looks back toward the dust storm, which is already clearing.

There is no human body on the road. Instead there is a bear—a small brown bear, likely a cub. Tasha takes a breath and walks over to it. As she gets closer she can see that half of the cub's snout is smeared with blood, the other half burned away in strips of red and blackened flesh. There is skin and fur under the bear's claws from scratching itself bloody in a frenzy to soothe the burning.

They might have hit it, she thinks. It might have died before.

"Tasha." Annie is leaning out the driver's window, calling. "Tasha, leave it alone. It might be diseased."

Beyond the bear, on the other side of the road, is another body. That one is human—a woman, the bottom half of her burned beyond recognition, her top half serene—as though she's only sleeping. Tasha takes one step and then another, and then she's standing over the body, trying not to cry. The yellow ribbon in the woman's brown hair is bright and cheerful against the tumbled grass. She is a halfway creature, a mermaid of the ash and fire.

"*Tasha!*" Annie shouts. "Tasha, we have to go."

Go where? She turns back to Annie and the ambulance, to the fire trucks that have pulled up behind them and are waiting for her too. Should they go back to the coast and see what's left to salvage? Or do they see what lies ahead?

"Tasha." Annie's voice is softer now. "Tasha, just come back in the ambulance, please." There's a sliver of panic in her voice that Tasha recognizes. It's the same panic Annie tried so hard to hide two years ago, after Tasha's parents were killed in the fire and Tasha could not function. *Where are you? Don't leave me alone.*

She takes a breath, then walks back to Annie.

"Here," she says. "I can drive."

"Are you sure?"

"Yes. I'm sure."

Annie is too tired to argue. She slides out of her seat reluctantly and yet also with relief; she's asleep almost as soon as her seatbelt is buckled. Tasha starts the ambulance and pulls back onto the road. The bear cub and the woman by the side of the road disappear.

From the driver's seat, things look even sharper, brighter, more intense. She spots more dead animals by the side of the road, others that flash quickly across the road in front of them—a deer, a fox, a skittering raccoon—and disappear into the trees. As they crawl farther north, the sloping greenlands on either side of the road give way to trees and clouded sky. Green trees, burning woods.

North. They keep on going north. She's not sure why, but the road takes her there. Turn here, turn there, keep driving. Far ahead of them are the mountains her mother told stories about. Maybe they'll reach the mountains and climb up to the moon.

She isn't surprised when a blurred grey line appears on the horizon that thickens and darkens and sharpens into peaks. Soon foothills roll around them like an earthquake that won't stop, the houses dotted among them all collapsed or on fire. As they drive on, the houses coalesce into a city.

Or what's left of it. She reaches up as the winding road becomes a city street and flicks on the siren. The fire trucks behind them follow suit. The sound wakes Annie, who sits up and leans forward.

Tasha feels sad in a way that she hasn't before—even with the bear cub, even with the burned woman. She drives the ambulance down streets that are too empty, streets where some houses remain untouched while others are caved in and smoking. No one comes out to watch them pass, to beg for help. It is early evening. The sun, or what they can see of it, has begun to climb behind the mountain, and the houses cast thick, smoky shadows over the road.

"Where is everyone?" Annie asks, again. No one answers.

They reach the end of the road—stopped short by a giant crater that spans the block. Tasha grunts in frustration and backs the ambulance up, then turns down a side street. The houses are silent and still.

She heads, though she can't say how she knows to do so, toward the wreckage of a building that looks like a hospital. The side street leads her to a wider boulevard where the high rises are, or used to be. Here, finally, people come into view. They stand scattered on the street—clustered in groups by the side of the road, gathered around a few open cars.

For a moment she badly wants to cry. No one here will be able to help her.

She turns the key and feels the engine shudder to a halt as the siren quits. Annie reaches over, takes her hand. For a moment Tasha stares down at their interlocked fingers as though they belong to a stranger.

"We'll be okay," Annie says. Her Annie.

Tasha gives the smallest hint of a squeeze and pulls her hand away, then climbs out.

These people look haunted, like everyone else they've encountered on the road. A tall man with red hair, a blonde girl in a black leather jacket and scuffed lace-up boots. Other men, women, and children staggering about.

A dark-haired woman in a hospital gown sits on the curb, two bright-haired bundles in her lap.

The woman raises her head and looks straight at Tasha. She looks lost too—but there is also something else, something unpredictable and bottomless in her expression that makes Tasha shiver.

She takes a breath. The air is thick with ash and smoke here too, but it feels sharper than the air that she knew by the sea.

All right, she thinks. *I'll be sharper too.*

"Who's in charge here?" she asks, and they tell her.

THE GIRL MADE OF STARS

Once upon a time there was a star that tripped and fell while dancing in the night sky, and tumbled to earth as a girl. When she woke up, the girl did not know who or where she was, only that the darkness above her, speckled with bright spots of light, looked familiar. She had no clothes or name, and when she came to the nearest village, the men and women thought that she was a witch. Since she did not know what a witch was, she couldn't correct them. They threw stones at her until she ran from them, bruised and afraid.

She found comfort in the darkness, in being alone under the stars. The animals of the forest were kind to her, and brought her things to eat—nuts and berries, roots from the ground that she washed in the river. She did not know how to speak to the animals, but they listened anyway. At night, she washed her hair in the river and sang wordless songs to keep herself company. In time her hair shone as bright as the moon.

The girl slept during the day, under the cover of trees. At night she walked bareheaded beneath the sky; eventually she made her way to the mountains and up among them. She grew to know the trees around her by name—their *real* names, not the names humans give them—and for a time she was happy, or as happy as she could be while knowing that she wasn't where she was supposed to be.

One evening, while making her way through the mountain woods, the girl came across a boy—a young man, really, creeping quietly through the underbrush, tracking a deer. She was frightened—she remembered the stones—but the boy had a kind face, and he hadn't seen her, so she followed him in silence, curious to see what he might do.

When the boy lifted his knife some time later, the girl understood his intention and cried out. The boy, surprised, whipped around to face her and threw the knife before he could help it. The blade caught the girl's long hair and pinned it to a tree, driving deep into the wood. Unable to free herself, the girl looked into the boy's eyes and saw the villagers and their rocks, but also the trees the boy had climbed as a child, the rivers in which he'd washed his own hair and sung his own songs.

She opened her mouth, but she had no words.

"I'm sorry," the boy said, and he reached for the knife. "I didn't see you."

The girl did not understand this, but if she had, she would have told him that the people in the village hadn't seen her either. She stayed still as he pulled the blade out of the tree. The deer was gone now, safe somewhere in the trees, and for that the girl was grateful.

"Are you lost?" the boy said, but the girl didn't understand this either. Instead she walked away from him, up the steep mountain path. The boy followed her because he could.

The boy did not know what he was starving for, in truth. But neither did the girl.

As he followed her, the girl became restless and worried. She began to run faster, but the boy kept up—they climbed higher and higher, each one of them afraid of and afraid for the other. The boy chased the girl right up to the peak, so high they could see clouds far below. At the edge, the girl turned back to face the boy.

He held out his hand. "I won't hurt you," he said. "Please believe me. Please say you believe me."

But the girl had no words and could not speak. She took a step back and the ground crumbled beneath her feet. The boy reached for her but he was too late. She fell and her hair fanned about her like moonlight.

Oh, the girl thought. *I remember this feeling.* She fell down and then up, into the bottomless expanse of the sky, her moonlight hair shining with a different kind of light now, a light fresh and made of stars.

The boy did not see this. But then, he hadn't seen the real girl anyway. He'd only ever seen his dream of her.

— 3 —

They are tiny, Heather's babies, made of magic, like the stars. They are perfect. They are awful. They gurgle and whimper, feed from her, and cry. After that day under the hospital they show their true selves— they do not sleep, ever, unless they're attached to her and she is moving. Up one street and down the next. Greta and Jilly, Jilly and Greta. Their tiny curled fists, the squished wrinkle of their faces. The unholy pitch of their screams.

Heather straps them to her chest and goes for long, dizzied walks amongst the trees near the mountain. B does not come with her. He is helping the other survivors. He has become someone everyone recognizes—the people from the basement, who turned reluctantly to him at first and now follow his lead; the people from the ambulance and fire trucks, who know him as the first person who spoke when they arrived.

No one's in charge here, he said, but he was wrong.

He doesn't like that she's taking such long walks with the babies, but he likes it less when she tries to help. The babies won't stop screaming, and she finds it hard to pay attention to anything or anyone else. Finally B just tells her to take them away, and she goes.

There are so many dead. Some remain only in pieces—an arm here, a buried bit of skull that could have belonged to a child. Three days after the meteors come, she is walking through the city's central square—there used to be a park here, but it is now a field of rubble—when a man and a woman enter the square a few paces ahead of her, carrying tools and wood. They stop in the centre of the square and drop things on the ground, and she pauses to watch. First they pound a wooden post into the ground with a sledgehammer. Then they nail a sheet of plywood to the post. They loop lengths of string through a hole in the top left-hand corner of the plywood and tie the ends around several black markers.

ANNALISE BOWEN, the woman writes on the plywood. *FREYA BOWEN. KARLA BOWEN.*

DOMINIC HOLLINGSHEAD, writes the man. *AMY GREEN.*

The woman holds out a marker to Heather, but she shakes her head. She hasn't slept in twenty-six hours; she hasn't bathed in four days.

The man comes toward her. "Who are you missing?" he says. His tone is the kind you might use with someone talking loudly to themselves at the bus station.

Heather steps back and shakes her head. "No one," she says. "I'm missing no one."

The woman's face spasms and she turns away. The man only nods. "Tell everyone you see about the board," he says.

She nods, avoiding eye contact with the woman, and walks away from them. Ahead of her, the forest beckons, calm and green.

On her way back, she notices that B's parents' names are now on the board. When she sees him later that afternoon, he doesn't mention it.

At first they sleep on couches and mattresses with the others from the hospital basement, refugees in their own city. As the days plod on, Heather and B steal time to go up and down the streets, jimmy locks, slide into bright kitchens. They pad across gleaming hardwood hallways and ash-covered kitchen floors, looking for something that could become a home. Their own apartment is gone.

"Find houses near the city centre," the doctor has told them. Tasha. "Everyone should stay close, at least for now."

Sometimes, while she's walking the babies, Heather searches for a house alone. She slips into houses with unlocked doors and stands in silent hallways, trying to imagine herself in the space. Herself, her husband, her girls. They are a happy family. Look—this house even has a white picket fence.

She's making her way through one of these houses when a sound behind one of the doors catches her ear—scratching and thumps, a tiny groan. She pictures a raccoon locked in a closet and grasps the handle, opens the door.

A teenage girl and boy fall out onto the dull hardwood floor, all tangled arms and breasts and rapidly shrinking penis. Scrabbling for clothes.

"Sorry," Heather says, faintly surprised. The door leads to a tiny bathroom. There's barely enough room for one person to stand up in there, never mind two.

"Do you mind?" the girl snaps.

"Is this your house?" Heather says.

The boy mumbles, "I don't think it belongs to anybody. At least, no one that's come back."

Heather glances again at the bathroom, and then at the rest of the house. From the front hallway you can see through to the glass wall in the kitchen. The backyard grass is already high enough to reach the door. "Why the bathroom when you can have the whole house?"

"Dunno," the boy says.

A long moment stretches between them.

"Condoms," she says finally. She feels a thousand years old. "Make sure you use condoms."

"What are you, the birth control police?"

Isn't that obvious? she wants to say. Instead she just looks at the girl. "You don't want to get pregnant. Not now."

The girl raises her chin. "I'm not stupid."

What a gift—to be young and horny as the world ends. "Lock it after I leave," she says as she heads for the door. She fights the urge to turn back and touch their faces.

✳

She and B find a house two streets down from the wreckage of the hospital. There is a high chair in the kitchen, a baby carrier in the hallway, a car seat in the garage even though there is no car. There is an art station in the kitchen, with fingerpaints and pencil crayons. The pencil crayons are scattered over the floor, as though they were dropped in a hurry. Maybe these people got away. Maybe they all got into a car and drove away in those hours when she was sitting scared beneath the hospital.

Before they move in, Heather packs away all of the family pictures. A mother, a father, a daughter, and two sons. The pool out back is filled with rubble from the wreckage of the house behind them. Boston ivy flanks the backyard fence, tendrils of it already reaching out over the destruction. Within days of them moving in, the pool is crisscrossed in green.

The girls share a bedroom in this new house. B finds a bicycle abandoned on the street and scavenges odds and ends from the other empty houses—winter coats, a garden shovel, all of the canned food from the kitchen next door. There are some diapers in the house, but B takes his bicycle and brings back as many packages from the store as he can. One trip, another, another.

"We'll replace everything if they come back," he says. Heather tries to imagine a world where this mother and father and their three children make their way back to the mountains.

When she closes her eyes, she still sees fire in other cities. She sees burned vehicles and blackened bodies inert at the sides of the highway. She says nothing about this to B.

She feeds the babies and puts them down to nap and picks them up and rocks them when they keep crying. They are angry, red-haired monsters filled with colic and rage, and then they are sweet, impossible fairies—always one or the other, never anything in between. She walks beneath the maples and the oak trees, wearing thick socks and jeans tucked into rubber boots that are too big. They are the only shoes here that will fit over her twisted foot.

She ventures as close to the mountain as she dares. The sun is weak and feeble these days, filtered through a grey sky choked with cloud. But in the woods, the world looks the same. The green trees, the whispers of a grey-green mountain that stretches high above them.

He is not here, he is not here.

As she walks the girls, she tells them stories. Sometimes she yells the stories over their screams, the urge to throw them headfirst onto the ground and watch their tiny necks snap so strong she can taste it. Cinderella and her mice. Rumpelstiltskin and his fire. *ONCE UPON A TIME THERE WERE A KING AND QUEEN WHO LONGED TO HAVE A CHILD.*

The only thing she longs for now is quiet, and sleep.

The forest is calm, its greenness doubly rich against the backdrop of the destroyed city. *Once upon a time there was a girl who lived in a village and looked after the geese for the queen.* When they are also calm, the girls stare up at her and snuffle like little pigs. Their eyes are newborn blue, but flecked with greenish-brown. In a few months they'll go hazel, just like B's.

She is so tired. She walks them and walks them, and when the girls scream, she thinks about unwrapping them, pulling them away from her chest, and laying them on the marbled green forest floor so the wolves can take them, so the fox will come back and find her and show her the way up the mountain.

She doesn't unwrap them. She doesn't let them go.

*

The first earthquake comes—a small one, just enough to shake the pictures on the walls. The girls are finally, briefly, asleep, tucked between Heather and B on the bed. At the first rumble, they both reach for one of the girls, then stumble down to the kitchen and squeeze under the table. They stare at each other as the girls wail, as they wait for more disaster to rain down around them.

Nothing happens. After an uncomfortable hour, B gives Jilly to Heather and climbs out from under the table to look around outside. When he comes back, he's relieved. "All clear," he says. "But maybe I'll go see how the others are. I won't be gone for long." His voice is thick with the determined cheerfulness that's begun to characterize him, to characterize their city. *We'll get through this. Everything will be okay.*

After he leaves, Heather crawls out from under the table and lays both girls out on its surface. They immediately start to wail. She puts her hands over her ears. Outside, the sky is grey and brown, the air heavy with rain that doesn't come. B will come back soon—and then what? They'll eat, maybe, or the girls will continue to cry and Heather will take them for another long walk beneath the trees. Maybe they'll go together to the looted grocery store down the road and see what remains on the shelves. Tomorrow they will do it all again.

The girls are red-faced, screaming, furious. She pulls her hands away from her ears and then reaches for the dishtowel, thinking if she muffles their noise just a little maybe the pounding of her heart won't be as bad. Then she balls the dishtowel in her fists. *No. No. No.*

She won't do it.

She won't.

The kitchen has a screen door and she bangs out through it into the backyard—stumbling as though there is no air left in the house.

The bouquet sits on the bottom step, blood red and lushly green. She registers the flowers just in time to jump over them, landing hard. She crouches frozen for a moment, then turns around and stares at the bouquet before reaching to pick it up. The stems soft and fresh against her palms. The deep-red burst of amaryllis, the dark-green grounding of satin leaves. Everything smells of the mountain.

She is weeping so hard she cannot see.

When B comes back, the babies are still crying on the table. Heather hasn't moved from her place by the steps.

"Where did those come from?" he asks. He's carrying shopping bags—he went to the store after all—and he must have walked right past the girls to find her. She clutches the flowers and lies instantly.

"I don't know."

He stares at her. "Yes, you do. I can see it all over your face."

"They're just flowers," she says, weakly.

"If they're just flowers, you can tell me."

She looks away.

"Why is someone else bringing my wife flowers?" he says. There's an edge to his voice she's never heard before. "Heather, what the fuck is going on?"

"It's nothing," she says. She gets up and takes a step toward him. "B—really. They're from an old friend. That's all."

He drops the shopping bags. "What *old friend* of yours has time to go and find tropical flowers in this goddamned mess?"

The wails from the kitchen intensify, and they both look to the house. When they turn back to one another, Heather nods. "My father used to bring me flowers like these on my birthday," she says. "We had a tropical garden when I was growing up." She doesn't talk much about her father; maybe this will soften him. She isn't sure.

He doesn't move. "How come your old friend knows that and I don't? I'm your husband. I should know these things!"

"I know," she says, her voice low. She puts a hand against his chest, tries to soothe him. "We just—we haven't had time. Everything happened so fast." The girls are still crying. "B—I have to go to the babies. I'll throw the flowers out. They don't mean anything. Really."

He sighs, then bends and picks up the bags. "I would have gotten you flowers. But there weren't any." He pulls out a container of cupcakes— the icing thick and white, the expiration date one week ago—and hands them to her. "They're stale, obviously. But they're also full of preservatives, so at least we don't have to worry about mould. Happy birthday."

She chokes on a bit of laughter. His eyes relax.

"You don't have to throw the flowers away," he says, softly. "But who gave them to you? That's all I want to know."

She can see it in his face: *I know all of the survivors here. Which one is bringing my wife flowers?*

"Does it matter?" she says. "They aren't in my life anymore."

"It matters to me," he says. "How do they know that you're here? If they aren't in your life anymore, why bring you flowers at all?"

She looks at him, then nods. She grasps the bouquet in one hand and throws it back into the yard—the amaryllis bounce on the surface of the Boston ivy and then half sink into the green. "You're right," she says, and she walks past him into the house.

✳

They go into the kitchen and B puts down his grocery bags and scoops up the girls. Heather takes the shopping bags and unpacks—the cupcakes, some cans of tuna, a few cartons of batteries.

He looks at her, shrugs. "We'll need them," he says. "Who knows if the power's going to come back on."

Heather nods, then moves into the front room. B follows with the girls, their faces splotched with red. Their eyes follow the dusty sunlight that filters through the window.

He stands and rocks the babies. They don't usually fall asleep for him the way they do with Heather, but they are beyond tired. When they go quiet, Heather takes out the pencil crayons and draws the mountain on the living room wall. The mountain, the flowers, the clouds.

B sits gingerly on the couch, still holding the girls. They don't wake up. A miracle. "I didn't know you could draw," he says.

She doesn't look back at him. A dark-red whorl of amaryllis appears at the base of the mountain.

"Right," he says, softly. "I remember now. You carried a sketchbook around with you at school."

She pauses. "That was twenty years ago. You remember that?"

"I remember you," he says, simply.

She thinks about this for a moment, and then sketches them in, lightly—four small figures at the base of the mountain. Two tiny bundles, three heads of flaming red hair. One dark.

"If this *old friend* isn't in your life anymore," he says, again, "how come they know how to find you? We've only just moved in."

Her hand trembles; he doesn't notice. "I don't know." She sounds so much calmer than she feels. "Maybe they just—maybe it's just a way for me to know that they're okay. There are—" she swallows, thinking anew of B's missing parents—"there are so many missing. Maybe they thought I'd be worried."

When she looks back at him, he's staring down at the babies in his lap. "You can have friends, you know," he says. "Even friends who were old boyfriends. I'm not a monster."

"I know that," she says. "It really doesn't matter. They're not in my life anymore."

"Why not?"

He is so wary with her, and yet so hopeful too. "Because *you* are."

The girls wake a short time later and immediately start screaming; she takes them from him and carries them outside, heading into the forest, one foot in front of the other.

When she returns, B is gone and the flowers sit in a jug in the front window.

✳

The next day, before Heather leaves for the first long walk of the morning, Tasha comes to visit them. Annie and Elyse are with her, and so is B, holding a shovel, his pants smeared with dirt. Elyse has a blue surgical mask over her face. Heather blinks and thinks back to their moments together after climbing out of the basement. Lung transplant, the girl had said. Her friend had just received one; Elyse had still been waiting.

She hasn't slept again, and for a moment as she stands in the doorway, she isn't sure what's going on.

"What do you want?" she blurts.

Tasha steps forward and takes her hand. Heather lets her. "We came to ask if you wanted to help," she says. "With the cleanup, and the consolidation of supplies."

"I tried to help," Heather says. "B didn't want me."

B flushes. "There are things you can do now," he says. "I'm sorry."

What for? Heather thinks. *What's the point?* Above them, the sky is reddish-brown, the air warm and stretched and waiting. "You've already been consolidating," she says. She pulls her hand away. "The stores are practically empty. Did you think we wouldn't see?"

"People have been looting," Tasha says. "We needed to get there quickly so we could stockpile things for us all."

"The food's going to run out anyway," Heather says. "It's not going to last forever."

"Maybe not." Tasha is calm. "But we can make it last longer if we're careful about it, and smart. We don't know how long it will be before help arrives."

Help. Heather blinks at this notion. When she looks at B, she sees again the determined cheerful slant of him. Her face hardens. "What if help isn't coming, Tasha—did you ever think of that?"

"We can help ourselves," Tasha says. "There's so much we can do. We need to make sure everyone has a safe place to sleep. I need people to help me build a clinic as best we can, and we need people to help catalogue and organize supplies and figure out a rationing plan. We need to build greenhouses. We need people to grow food." Her voice softens. "Brendan says you used to have a garden. Maybe you could help us with that."

"My *father* was a gardener. I can't do jack shit." The words are out before she can stop them.

"You could plant flowers," B says, and she realizes that this is his idea. "It's a small thing, Heather, but it will help."

"What am I supposed to do with them?" and she motions to the twins bundled across her chest. "They don't sleep. You *know* they don't sleep. That's why you sent me away the first time!"

"You can walk them around the town," he says. A pause. "And then you wouldn't have to walk so far into the forest." He flushes, but just a little. "I don't want you to fall out there with no one else around."

She's so angry for a moment she almost can't see—she stares away from them all, into the overgrown front yard of the house next door. "I'm fine," she grits out, eventually. "I'm careful with the girls. I'm their fucking mother."

"No one is saying that you aren't careful," Tasha says. Even though that is exactly what B is saying. Not careful with the girls, not careful with his heart. *Why is someone else bringing my wife flowers?* "All we're saying is that it's safer for everyone to stay together."

Heather takes a deep breath and closes her eyes. When she opens them again, she looks straight at B. "I'm fine," she says again. Maybe a little too loudly. "I won't go as far into the forest, if that makes you happy. But until you can find another way to make them sleep, I'm going to keep walking."

"Do you want someone else to walk them from time to time?" Tasha asks. She takes a step closer to Heather, puts a hand on Greta's tiny head. "Aren't you tired? Are you getting enough sleep?"

"Is anybody?" Heather takes a step back and Tasha's hand falls. She can see that Annie is irritated, but Tasha doesn't blink.

"Let me know if you want me to do anything for you," Tasha says. "I know none of this is easy." Behind her B looks defeated.

"Where are those flowers from?" Annie says. She's stepped back onto the front path—she must see the flowers in the window.

"They were a gift," Heather says. "For my birthday."

Annie looks back at her, then at Brendan. "Where did you find tropical flowers?"

As if on cue, Jilly wakes up and starts to cry; Heather backs away from the door and reaches for her boots. "I will help when I can," she says, finally, because they're not going to go until she does. "Now can you leave me alone?"

✳

After this, she walks in the forest a little less and in the city a little more, just enough to ease B's suspicions. She watches the townspeople as she walks—first they clear the debris from the centre of town, take what they can from the wreckage and pack away anything useful they can find. The strip mall near the central square is relatively undamaged—she watches person after person carry box after box inside.

Time inches slowly forward. The days seem twice as long as she remembers days to be.

On one of her morning walks she sees that someone has grouped the generators from restaurants and other businesses together behind the mall. By the time she returns from the forest there is a chicken-wire fence around them, complete with a makeshift padlocked door. All day long, the generators hum intermittently. The key to the enclosure hangs at Annie's waist.

More days go by, and there is no news. Tasha sends volunteers on scouting missions but none of them come back. Other people pack their bags and leave late in the night—some in cars but more of them on foot or on bicycles. Mothers and daughters, fathers and sons. Whole families. They don't come back either.

The vines grow thicker over their backyard pool. Soon they cover it completely.

When they've been in the house for a little over a month, a man comes back to the house next to theirs. He knocks on the door one morning right before B is leaving to go to the strip mall. Heather, bleary-eyed and grumpy, gets the door.

"Hello," the man on the doorstep says. He looks faintly surprised. "You're not Denise."

"No," Heather says. She fights down a rush of guilt. "They haven't come back."

He nods. "Probably better for them, in the long run."

No one says anything for a moment. B emerges from the kitchen and comes to stand behind her.

"I live next door," the man says, and waves his hand in the direction of the house to their left. His voice sounds hollow, almost robotic. "I'm Joseph."

"Brendan," B says. He steps forward and reaches across Heather, takes the other man's hand. "This is Heather. And this is Greta," he points, "and Jilly." He looks over to the house. "Everything all right?"

"We were away," Joseph says. "I just got back."

"We?" Brendan asks, and Heather wants to kick him. "Your family?"

"I came back alone," Joseph says. That hollowness again. He jerks a thumb at the house. "I have chickens in the backyard. Surprised to find them still alive, to be honest." Then he laughs. It is not a nice sound. "I guess the natural world outlives us all, anyway."

Chickens? Heather thinks. And now she can smell it, the faint scent of acrid chickenshit under the thickness of ash and dirt that still falls through the air. She hadn't noticed any chickens. But she hasn't noticed much. The babies. The walking. The boxes carried into the strip mall.

The pink bicycle in Joseph's driveway, lopsided against the garage.

"Anyway," Joseph says, "I'll have eggs for a while. Don't know how long—until the feed runs out and they all die, I guess. I'll bring over my extras, if you want them."

"Thank you," Heather says, finally. "We'd be grateful."

Joseph looks at her again. This time he seems to see the babies—really *see* them. "It's fine," he says, abruptly. Then he jerks his head in the direction of the city centre. "Who put them in charge? Tasha—right? Annie? Where's the City Council?"

"Dead or gone," B says.

"So—what—we just let them hoard the food? Is that what's going on?"

"They're *rationing* the food," B says. "We don't know how long everything will have to last."

"And gas?" Joseph says.

"People were taking gas," B says. "But we're saving it now for the generators. I'm sure you could get some if you asked for it."

Joseph laughs. "No need for that," he says. "My van was destroyed when the meteors came. Surprised I made it back alive, to be honest."

"Do you want to help with the rebuild?" B says. "I'm just about to head in now."

Joseph blinks.

"B," Heather says. She fights to keep an edge from her voice. "He only just got back."

"We need all the hands we can get," B says, not meeting her eyes.

"Maybe," Joseph says. "Not now." Heather can almost see the words in his head. *What's left to rebuild?* He steps back down the path. "I need to sort out my house first."

Later that night, lying exhausted on the bed, B says, "Maybe we should think about chickens." He's only half joking. "Maybe we should start a farm."

"We don't know anything about farming," she says. "We'd starve."

He shrugs. "Maybe we'll starve anyway." He reaches for Jilly. They both do this now, she's noticed—reach for the babies when they should be reaching for each other.

"It's not a bad idea," Heather says, relenting. "But I wouldn't know what to do. I'd be useless."

"You could learn. So could I."

"Do you really think we'll starve?" She stares at him over Greta's coppery head.

B pauses and then shakes his head. "We won't. We can't. Tasha won't let that happen."

"Tasha can't feed everybody."

"So what do you want me to say?"

She flushes. "I don't know."

"We'll ration the food until help arrives. They must be mobilizing the army. I don't know." Jilly starts to whimper and he sits up, rocks her softly. "Maybe they'll send in a train."

"Send a train where?"

"I don't know! Jesus, Heather—it's like you want them to fail. Like you want *us* to fail."

"I don't," she says. "I don't want that."

"How can I be sure?" he says. "You don't tell me things and you disappear for most of the day. It's like—" he looks straight at her—"it's like I don't even know you."

What to say? They *don't* know each other, not really. They've been thrown together the same way they were thrown into this house. But he will be hurt if she says this.

"I'm so tired," she whispers. "I want the girls to be quiet. That's all I want. And that only happens when I walk them. I don't have space for anything else."

He looks away. "I'm sorry. Forget I said anything."

Heather sighs and sits up. "I walk them and I tell them stories," she says. "The stories calm them down. The trees calm *me* down. That's all."

He relaxes, but only a little. "Do you meet your old friend on your walks?"

"I told you they're not in my life anymore," she says. "If you want to know me, start by believing that."

He doesn't believe her. She reaches for his hand, twines her fingers through his own.

"I'm trying," she says. Her voice shakes. "I know none of this is what you imagined, what you wanted. But I'm trying. I promise."

He looks at her, then squeezes her hand a little and tries to laugh. "I don't think any of us imagined this," he says. "I'll try to remember that too."

✳

As the days pass, she again ventures closer to the mountain on her walks. She tells the girls about Cinderella and Snow White, the twelve dancing princesses, Hansel and Gretel. Mermaids who grant wishes, people who sleep for five hundred years. Sometimes as she sings to them she feels the trees listening; more often than not they walk in silence or to the rise and fall of wailing.

She sees her foxes twice in those early weeks. The first time they are a sudden flash of white and orange against the emerald green of the forest, blue eyes that blink at her through the leaves. The babies cluster around the mother; bigger now, their eyes alight with curiosity.

The vixen turns, and Heather follows, moving as fast as she can through the trees and the underbrush, pushing spiderwebs away with her hands. The foxes stop at the foot of the mountain and turn back to stare at her. Three pairs of blue eyes in a line.

She cups a hand around each baby's copper head. She doesn't move. The foxes blink. She draws a breath and turns back toward the city. They do not follow.

The second time, she's walking down the middle of a city street. The girls have been screaming with colic for hours. It's late afternoon, the weak sun readying itself to disappear behind the mountain. The girls' screams rise up around her. Each step that she takes pushes them deeper into sweaty, red-faced rage.

She is heading for the forest, but the wilderness meets her sooner than expected. Vines crawl up the sides of the houses that sit on the last street before the mountain. Grasses have overtaken the sidewalks here. She crosses the field that leads from the town to the trees and it feels narrower than she remembers. She's not imagining it. It's as though the trees have picked themselves up in the dead of night and crept closer to the city.

The foxes are waiting for her at the edge of the field, where the trees start. She can't tell the mother from the babies—they're all the same size now. They don't move, even when she marches up to them and unwraps each shrieking baby from her sling and lays them on the ground. They stop crying. They blink up at her and then reach out to touch the foxes' whiskers. One of the foxes steps over the babies and Greta grabs for its tail.

"I can't do this anymore," Heather whispers.

Beyond the foxes, the portal yawns open. It is a shifting mass with blurred black edges, a doorway that will take her to the summit. The mountain and its clear grey stone and bright blue sky. The scent of mountain air. The scent of something else.

Of someone else.

The portal creeps over the foxes until only their eyes are left, a shimmered black nothing that spreads over the ground and reaches out toward the girls' soft hair.

She snatches them up, breathing hard, then turns and walks back across the field and down the street toward the city. She's so intent on the ground in front of her, she doesn't notice the vehicle until someone calls her name.

"Heather."

She looks up and sees Tasha beside her, in the ambulance. She stops; the ambulance stops too. It feels like Tasha's been calling her name for a while.

"Heather," Tasha says again. "Are you all right?"

The babies stretch toward Tasha and coo.

"I'm fine," Heather says. She glances back over her shoulder. The foxes are still there, watching her, but the portal is gone.

Tasha follows her gaze and then looks back at her. She does not see the foxes, that much is clear. "Do you want a ride back?" she asks.

"I'm fine," Heather says again, louder this time. She starts walking, and after another moment Tasha drives slowly past her.

When she looks back over her shoulder a second time, the foxes are gone.

A story always starts, her father told her long ago, from the end of something else.

The weeks go by, and help does not come. Instead they build greenhouses from materials taken from the abandoned hardware stores. Heather walks the babies through the square and to the outskirts of town, past people who plant seeds into garden plots, past others who sometimes gather outside and pray for rain. There is no rain. Yet somehow the grass grows high and the vines begin to climb the walls of the houses.

There is no army, there is no train.

During the day, B is determined and cheerful, shouting orders in the square, helping people push abandoned cars off the streets. Sometimes, as she walks by, she sees him hunched with Tasha, Annie, and the others. They have impromptu meetings everywhere—at bus shelters, on picnic tables out in front of abandoned restaurants. He tells her that they're planning for the winter.

"We have to be prepared," he says. He's lost weight. So has she.

When the girls are a few months old, he starts to come for her at night, in the pockets of time when the babies aren't wailing. He traces his hands over her face as though he's convinced himself that he knows Heather in ways that even she doesn't fathom. (Maybe that's true. She knows her body and yet she doesn't know it like this—as a thing that someone could want, a thing that someone might treasure.)

He is gentle with her, at first, and then not. He is a man reaching up from a well. His hands in her hair, between her legs. His cock inside of her like its own story, searching for some kind of happy ending. She holds his face between her hands and lets him take whatever he wants.

When they finish, they lie together until the girls start to scream again—sometimes minutes, sometimes a little longer.

One night, in those scant seconds of time before the babies start up again, he asks, "Where did you go?" He is stretched out behind her on the bed, his arm over her stomach. "Just now."

She pretends to not understand. "I'm right here."

"No, you're not," he says. He isn't angry, or accusing. He is just tired. "You never are."

She says nothing. He is silent for so long she thinks he's gone to sleep.

"I love you," he says, finally.

Yes, she thinks, *he does*. She reaches for his hand and squeezes it. "I love you too."

Then the babies start up again; she pushes his arm away and slides out of the bed.

THE GOOSE GIRL

Once there was a girl who looked after the geese for the queen. In the mornings she brought the geese out of their enclosure and let them run around the yard; in the afternoons she would herd them down to the royal pond and let them paddle in the water and eat the water plants. Before dinner, the queen would come to the pond and visit the geese, bringing them lettuce from the royal kitchens, which she fed to them, piece by piece, her royal gown dipping into the scummy pond water each time she bent forward with a morsel in her fingers.

The geese loved the queen. They loved her more than they loved the goose girl, the tender of their home and protector of their eggs. Each time the queen got up to leave, they would follow her back to the castle, a line of waddling white bodies that made the castle staff—and the towns-people, when they saw them—chuckle. The queen would let the geese trail her until she reached the castle door. Then she would turn and smile at them and tell them they could go no further.

"You belong in the pond," she would say. "That is your table. You do not belong at mine." Then she would close the castle door.

Each time this happened, the geese would wait in a cluster until the goose girl came to fetch them. She would coax them home with bread, even though the queen had forbidden this—*Geese should eat roots and stems,* she said, and she wasn't wrong—and herd them back down to the pond and from there to their enclosure. It was the goose girl's job to make sure the geese were safely tucked away at night so that the foxes wouldn't eat them. Each night she walked the geese up into their coop—a larger, more elegant one than had been built for the chickens—and made sure they were settled in their nests before closing the coop door and locking it tight.

Every night, before she closed the door, the geese asked her the same question.

"Why can't we eat at the queen's table?" they said. "Why won't she have us, if indeed she loves us so?"

"The queen eats bread," the goose girl told them. "And bread is not good for you."

"But you feed us bread," the geese retorted.

"I feed you bread only when you will not listen," the goose girl said. "If you come with me when I tell you to, I will not feed you bread anymore."

The oldest of the geese was a matriarch named Dorrie. When she heard this from the goose girl, she shook her head. "But if you give us bread until we listen," she said, "then what's to stop us from ignoring you all of the time? You are the goose girl, but you make no sense. Why should we listen to you at all?"

"Who keeps you safe?" The goose girl was growing annoyed. "Who takes you out into the sun each day, and brings you down to the pond so you can splash in the water and attend on the queen? Who makes sure that you're protected from the foxes? You are ungrateful, goose, and it is very unbecoming."

"I am not ungrateful," said Dorrie. "I want to know why I am not good enough for the queen's table when the queen's royal gown is good enough for my pond."

The goose girl looked at Dorrie, then sighed. "Only the queen can tell you that," she said. "Would you like to ask her yourself?"

"Yes," Dorrie said. "I would."

The goose girl made sure that the rest of the geese were locked safely in the coop, and then took Dorrie back to the castle. When the soldier at the door saw Dorrie, he shook his head and refused to let them enter. In response, Dorrie reared up and beat her wings in the air. She was the largest of the geese, and her wings stretched six feet from tip to tip. She beat the guard over the head so hard that he fell; when other guards came running, Dorrie squawked so loud the entire castle heard her.

"Let her in!" the goose girl shouted, and this time the guards obeyed.

When they got to the dining hall, the queen was already standing.

"Dorrie," she said, in her most regal voice. "Dorrie, what's all this?"

"I want to sit at your table," Dorrie said.

"Silly goose," the queen said. "Geese do not sit at my table—that's why you have a pond."

"The world is larger than my pond!" Dorrie cried. "The world is larger than my coop, than the yard, and larger even than your castle. I am not a silly goose."

The queen looked down at Dorrie, then sighed. "Very well. Come here, Dorrie, and sit down." She pulled a great chair out from the table and motioned for Dorrie to take it. Dorrie climbed in without difficulty. She wrapped her wings around the silver fork and knife at her place and looked up at the queen.

"That is better," she said. "Where is the bread?"

"There is no bread," the queen said. "We are having goose for dinner." Then she slit Dorrie's throat with the knife she'd been hiding up her sleeve. Dorrie could do nothing except watch her blood spill out onto the tablecloth. When her eyes finally closed, the queen nodded to her servants.

"Clean that up," she said. Then she went back to her meal.

The goose girl, unnoticed, slipped out of the dining hall and away from the castle. She crept into the farmyard and unlocked the coop and brought the geese out, one by one, and told them what had happened to Dorrie.

"I won't feed you bread anymore," she said. "The world is much larger than bread, and far more delicious. You deserve to know that for yourselves."

Then the goose girl and her geese took leave from the kingdom, and were not heard from again.

E stajfan runs alone. He's always run alone. In the mornings he's gone
before Petrolio and the others are even awake. His gallop down the
mountain is a whirlwind of light and sound, a tangled fall of dark trees
and leaves—in the bitter winter wind, in the summer with the rush and
hint of morning sun to come. He jumps and he lands and he lunges and
jumps again, his arms spread for balance, his muscles tensing and releas-
ing over and over again.

It feels good to be alive in these moments, possibly because he knows
it could all change so quickly—one hoof snagged and down he would
go, a foreleg snapped, tumbling in a different way, the weight of his body
the thing, in the end, that will kill him. But he doesn't stumble. He runs
and jumps, and always his hooves land exactly where they should. He
doesn't break.

When the mountain meets the ground, he keeps on running. He runs
until he reaches the edge of the mountain forest and can see the houses
and their already overgrown yards through the trees. And then he stops,
and waits.

The ground magic is different here, where the earth is flat. It used to be louder, but it has been muffled by the human houses and human roads, by the pipes that run underground and disrupt the dirt.

It's getting louder now, day by day.

The trees are moving slowly south—half an inch this day, half an inch the next. He feels them stretch their roots beneath the soil and inch forward the way caterpillars inch along their branches. The way that vines are inching over the houses. The way that slowly, slowly, the human city is sinking back into the green.

No one has noticed this yet, he thinks, except perhaps for Heather.

They will notice soon enough.

He hears her footsteps on the sidewalk long before she comes into view. The city is so quiet now. There are cars, but only rarely—there is no power, so the houses do not rumble and shake. There are noises now and then from the centre of the town, but nothing like they used to be. It isn't hard to hear the ground bring her close to him. That gait—*tap-TAP, tap-TAP*—that belongs only to her.

He sinks into the trees as she comes into view. She will go into the forest as far as she is able, and walk amongst the trees with her girls. She tells them stories, or she weeps silently as they wail to the sky.

She is looking for him. He knows she is always looking for him.

When he was younger, he ran only at night. He ran down the mountain and past the city nestled in its shadow—beyond the foothills, beyond the rivers. He ran through the flatlands—keeping always in the shadows and away from human roads. When he needed to hide, the ground told him where was safe.

Their father had also been restless. Gone from the mountains for days at a time as a horse, and gone for days at a time in his new life as an in-between thing, hiding the way that Estajfan would eventually learn to do. He came back to the mountain with clothing and toys and all manner of human paraphernalia—pots and pans, books that he shelved on a struc-ture he made from dead trees. At night he told his children stories of their village, even though Estajfan had known, from the time he was small, that they did not belong there. Not as a family. He knew their father went back to the village and roamed it at night when everyone was sleeping. The toys that he brought them, the tools that he used to build things on the mountain—all of this came from the village and smelled of the past.

After their father died, Petrolio had wanted to fling these things off the mountain. But Estajfan couldn't bear to let them go. He wanted more of it—the touch of the human world, the things they made. His longing for their father was so great it brought him down into the world their father had forbidden them to see—down into the midnight darkness of the flatlands, past these squat human houses all bursting with things. He crept through the trees and watched humans make their way down cobblestone streets. The gas lamps on the sides of their roads, the chugging power of the trains.

When he came back up from his first run, Aura met him on the mountain trail.

"Da told us not to go down," she said.

"Da isn't here anymore."

"You want to honour him. So do I." Her voice was thick with pain.

"Our whole life has been the mountain," he said. "But what if it can be more than that?"

"They'll hurt you," she said. In the moonlight her blue-green eyes seemed frightened and huge and her blonde hair shone white. "They won't understand."

"How do you know that? Have *you* ever been down?" When she didn't say anything, he felt his bones soften in shock. "You have?"

"Not really," she said, quickly. "Only in dreams."

"Dreams," he repeated, looking at her. He didn't dream, and neither did Petrolio, but he knew enough about dreams to understand that they weren't real. "So you don't actually know what the humans would do."

"I know what they did to Da," she said. "I know what they did to us. That's enough. It should be enough for you too."

It wasn't. As the years went by he went down more and more. He stole children's toys and items abandoned around a country farm.

He stole picture frames propped against the side of a darkened house. When he brought them back up the mountain, it felt as though their father was still alive.

Their father's eyes had been mossy brown, like the eyes of the new centaurs birthed by the mountain. Centaurs who looked and talked like them but were comfortable in their bodies in ways that the three of them were not. The new centaurs didn't cry. They didn't laugh. They had no interest, whatsoever, in the world below them. A world that moved so quickly—gas lamps that gave way to electric lights. Trains that soon ran beside highways and cars. Subways. Children who so soon became adults. Every time Estajfan went down it felt like a jump into the future. He brought back a music player that ran on batteries, a handheld mirror that was one thing the mountain centaurs adored. Sometimes he caught Petrolio with it, and teased him, but the mirror unnerved Estajfan a little. It was the same feeling he got whenever he saw his face in the stream— his father's face, his mother's eyes. He wished that no part of him had reminded their father of her.

This had been his life. It was not enough, but it had been bearable.

Then, the girl and her father on the mountain.

Today when Heather comes she is already weeping, the babies squalling and squirming in pain. He watches her stride through the field and into the trees. She passes so close he can smell the dampness of her hair. Beneath that, her sweat and fear and sorrow. She is thinner than she was a week ago. In the night, when he creeps among the houses in the dark, he hears the whispered worries of the people in the city. No one has come to help them. There has been no news.

I can't do this anymore, she'd said those months ago. *I want to be up on the mountain with you.*

He'd told her again that the mountain was not her home. *It's barely even my home,* he said. He could tell that she didn't believe him.

You've lived there all your life. It's the only home you know.

He tried to make her understand. *It is an in-between place*, he said. *For an in-between thing.*

Rigid with anger, she'd gone back to the city.

The next time he saw her, she was pregnant.

I think it would be better, she said, *if we didn't do this anymore. You're right. I belong here. You belong there. I was stupid to think otherwise.*

He didn't think she was stupid. He wanted to tell her that. But in his head, he heard his sister.

They'll hurt you, Aura had said. *They won't understand.*

And so he let her go.

After the meteors came, he stood vigil in the forest, day in and out, until he once more heard her footsteps on the streets of the city. Unmistakably hers. *Tap-TAP, tap-TAP.* He shouldn't have been able to hear them, but he did—the ground, he knew, was giving him a kindness. Only then did he make his way back up the mountain.

Now he comes down every day and waits for her, though he stays hidden. The trees bend around him, obscure him in leaves.

With her babies, she is not an in-between thing, even though she might wish to be. She does not belong on the mountain.

He sees the fox tempt her at the edge of the forest. He sees the portal open up. He is ready to yell when she unwraps the children and lays them before it, ready to come crashing out and scoop up the babies. She grabs them just in time.

When she walks past him again this time, oblivious to the centaur hidden in the trees, he lets out a breath and a prayer.

On the way back up the mountain, he encounters Fox on the mountain path.

"You shouldn't have done that," he says.

Fox only shrugs. "You cannot control what she wants forever."

"You aren't offering her what she wants!" he cries. Through that portal is the mountain's deep gorge and a long, heedless fall to the ground.

Fox licks her lips. "The world is no longer a place for in-between things," she says. "If you decide to speak to her, you would do well to tell your human that."

"No longer a place?" he says. "What does that mean?"

Fox blinks. "It means you have a choice to make."

＊

Farther up the mountain, his sister waits for him.

"You need to stop going down," Aura says. "You can't help her, Estajfan. You can only make things worse."

"They have no home. Their home has been destroyed."

"What can you do?" Aura says. "Nothing. You need to stay here."

He turns to her, incredulous. "I expect that from the mountain centaurs. Not from you."

She flushes. "Estajfan, we aren't meant to be down there. With them. It's too dangerous."

"Dangerous?" he almost shouts. "Aura, they are going to starve."

"You don't know that," she insists. "Fox says they're storing food."

"Do you think that food will last forever?" he asks. She's never been down off the mountain. She hasn't seen their cities, their malls. The cars that used to scuttle along the roads. Their bicycles, their buildings. Their mirrors and their music players, their batteries, their gas lamps, their electric trains.

They are magic, he wants to tell her—a different kind of magic from the mountain. Raw and selfish and angry, yes, but magic all the same.

"They're planting gardens," he concedes. He doesn't want to fight with her. He thinks of the magic in the ground around the city—how much louder it is now, how gleeful its rage. "But I don't think that's going to help them."

Aura doesn't meet his eyes. "We don't belong there," she says.

The mountain centaurs sang when fire rained down from the sky. They raised their arms and cheered.

Why not? he wants to say. *Why can't we belong anywhere we want to go?*

"We don't belong on the mountain either," he says instead, and walks on past her.

✳

Aura had been with him that day, years ago, when the girl and her father had come up the mountain. The two of them had been alone and basking in the sun, and suddenly there were human voices coming closer, carried to them on the wind. They shrank into the trees and watched the father and the girl climb up and stop in a small clearing on the path. Watched them sit down and open their packs and begin to eat.

Aura moved toward the humans first. That is what happened.

He still doesn't know what alerted the father to their presence, whether it was Aura passing through a shaft of sunlight, a sound. But he looked up from his meal and straight at her, no longer quite as hidden in the trees. Then the girl looked up too, and gasped.

He can close his eyes and see the scene in detail all these years later. The shock on their faces. The joy and the terror. Aura was close enough to touch, and the moment the father *realized* this, he stood and reached out, likely expecting something magical to happen.

"Hello," the father had breathed as he took hold of Aura's wrist. She jumped back, startled, but he tightened his grip, turning to the girl. Estajfan couldn't hear what he said to his daughter, but he watched betrayal bloom over her small face. As the father turned back to Aura, she yanked her hand away with such force the man pitched forward and wobbled, unsteady on the mountain rocks. And then he lost his balance and tumbled over the side of the mountain.

Estajfan was almost in time, lunging for the man's outstretched arms, his fingers brushing the father's fingers, but he was gone, no time for screaming. They heard the impact in the trees so far below, then nothing.

The girl stood frozen. He felt as if she could reach into his chest and know everything there was to know about him—the longing, the fear. Her shoulders began to heave and she opened her mouth. He was terrified that she would scream, that the mountain centaurs would hear her and come running and toss her off the mountain too. He scooped her into his arms before she had a chance. Then he was running down the path, the girl's tears hot against his shoulder.

He ran until they were at the base of the mountain, until they were in the forest, until they were outside the girl's house. It took a long time. It took no time at all. He bent and put her on the ground; he expected her to collapse, but she stood firm.

"How did you know where my house was?" she whispered. It was dark now, and her face was a collection of shadows.

"I didn't," Estajfan said, because it was true. The house had called to him, alive with the girl and her memories. He'd never forget where it was.

"What's your name?" she said.

"Estajfan." A light came on in the dark house. "Don't ever come up the mountain again," he said. "You, or anyone else."

The girl nodded. He could see that she was still shivering—still waiting to scream. Somehow he knew that she wouldn't tell anyone about it—Aura, how her father had died. He thought of Aura, whom he'd left alone on the mountainside.

"Forgive me," he said, finally. And then, "Forgive him."

He saw the girl's fists tighten and he turned around and ran for the forest.

The scream, when it came, reached him anyway.

※

Before the man fell, Estajfan had never dreamed. The first time it happened he woke up screaming, to find the mountain centaurs massed around him, silent and suspicious. Aura had come running too. "It's all right, Estajfan," she said. "It's just a dream. It will go away."

She was wrong—the dream came back. It was always the same: the mountain, the father, the fall. The look of hurt on the child's face. That tiny slice of time when the father's fingers brushed his and then were gone. That tinier sliver when Estajfan had hesitated. These humans, climbing up into his home without asking. Touching Aura like she was something they owned.

Expecting magic from them, like it was something they were owed.

He didn't dream of the girl. He didn't need to. After her scream followed him back up the mountain, he felt her every day—a presence down below, a shadow that moved through the halls of her home. He knew that she was hurting. Though her pain dulled in time, every now and then her grief would spike, the swell of it so huge that Estajfan would have to stop and close his eyes.

She had gone silent, lost her words. He could feel the worry of everyone around her. No one knew what to say, what to do.

He did not know what to say, or do. As the anniversary of the father's death approached, her silence grew loud and desperate. He felt her mind whirling up here, looking for him, as she trudged from school to home and back again.

He woke on the morning of that first anniversary with a pain in his chest that wouldn't go away and the remnants of a dream—this time of the girl, standing at the edge of a cliff. He paced the mountain path alone, wandering lower and lower, until he reached the spot where they'd picnicked a year ago.

The flowers were as bright and red as ever. Beneath them, he saw the father's knapsack, toppled on its side and crusted over with dirt. Animals had long ago eaten whatever food had been inside.

He picked flowers until his arms were full, then slung the knapsack over his shoulder and made his way down the mountain.

✳

Before he reaches their home on the mountain, another centaur stops him. Mossy green-brown eyes like his father's. Hard like the mountain in everything else. A female palomino with white-blonde hair, like Aura's.

"The humans are ending," she tells him. "You should not be going down the mountain anymore."

"I can't leave them alone," he says.

The mountain centaur shrugs. "The more you try to stop what is happening, the more it will hurt."

He's so tired of hearing them say this. They could all go down. They could help the humans find food. They could—he thinks of the way Heather's father's face erupted in joy at the sight of them so long ago—carry flowers right into the houses. The humans might be frightened at first, but beauty could bring them happiness too.

Don't they deserve that, at least?

Doesn't Heather?

"You should stop thinking about what the humans deserve," the centaur says, "and focus on what *you* deserve."

"No one deserves what's going to happen next," he says. He's unsure what that is, exactly, but the rage deep in the ground makes him uneasy.

"I don't know what's going to happen either," the centaur says. "And I don't need to know. The mountain has given us what we need. Stay here, and let that be enough for you, too."

She isn't being unkind—none of the mountain centaurs are *unkind* to him and his siblings, exactly, but they don't understand him, and they don't care to.

That night he climbs to the top of the mountain and sees the palomino standing with another centaur. Watching for what, he doesn't know. The stars pinwheel over their heads in a slow, constant circle. Estajfan goes to the three old willows and lets his heart reach deep into the ground.

Da, he says. *Show me what to do.*

His father has been dead for more years than he can count. And the mountain, if it has any wisdom, refuses to give it.

On that first anniversary the girl had found him in her backyard, half hidden in the trees. He'd dropped the knapsack at her feet and held the bouquet out to her.

"What are those for?" she said. The first time he'd heard her voice since her father died.

"They're ... for you," he said.

"Flowers aren't going to bring him back." But still she took them from him. She was thinner than she'd been a year ago. And taller, as though grief had stretched her out. She sniffed the flowers. "Why are you really here?"

"You've been silent," he said. "I was . . . worried."

The girl cleared her throat. "How would you know? Have you been spying?"

"Spying?" he said, confused. "I don't know what that is. I can feel your silence." He took a step closer. "Why aren't you talking?"

The girl shrugged. "I don't have anything to say." She put the flowers gently on the ground and then picked up the knapsack and sniffed it. "It still smells like him," she said, surprised. "I thought it would smell like the mountain."

He looked up at the house. He could feel her mother in there some-where, sleeping. "Your mother worries about you," he said.

She mulled this over. "Does she worry about you? The other . . ."

"Centaur," he said, giving her the word. "Sometimes. She's my sister. She always worries."

The girl smiled faintly. "I don't have a sister. No one worries about me except for my mom."

"Everyone worries about you. I can feel that, too." He spread his hands. "If I could take anything back—"

"It wasn't your fault he fell." She looked down at the flowers, cleared her throat. "The flowers he grew are dead now. My mother wouldn't let me take care of them. She said the greenhouse was too close to the mountain. She's afraid I'll go back up."

"Will you?"

The girl looked straight at him. "I miss the mountain. I was afraid of it, but I miss how it made me feel—strong." She dropped her eyes as she whispered. "Was he right?"

"You are not meant for the mountain," he said. "The mountain will not save you. You do not *need* to be saved." Her head went up at this, her gaze puzzled and hopeful as she tried to understand. "But," he said, relenting, "I can bring you flowers, if you want."

He could tell that it wasn't what she wanted, but she nodded. "What's your name?" he asked her.

"Heather." She looked back down at the flowers, then swallowed hard. "How come I'm the one that survived?"

He thought of the way she made her way through the halls at school. The uneven, inexorable stride. And then he thought of his father, building their life on the mountain alone. "Maybe you were ready to survive," he said. "Maybe you've always been ready."

"My father used to tell me stories," she said. "No one's told me stories for a year."

"A year," he repeated, slowly. When she looked at him, he only shrugged. "Humans are like the stars that fall in the sky," he said. "Everything about you is so quick, and then gone." He cleared his throat. "I can tell you stories. My father used to tell us stories too."

"I would like that."

They stood for a moment in silence. Estajfan cleared his throat. "What kind of story would you like to hear?"

She moved forward until she was standing directly beneath him.

"Tell me where you come from," she said. "Tell me about where you live."

In the morning he wakes with a jolt, the air around him hushed and still, another dark dream about that day receding. The mountain centaurs are gone and he is alone on the summit.

The air is clear here. It is so easy to believe that life on the mountain can continue exactly like this, forever.

The red-haired man, he knows, is the father of her twins. Each day he tries to rebuild the city while Heather walks through the trees alone.

She tells her daughters stories. She tells stories to herself. She doesn't say his name.

She is safe, at least for now. She said that she doesn't want to see him. But he can keep her safe. Even if he can't help everyone else.

THE DOCTOR

The doctor is invited to the mother's second wedding. She toasts the beautiful blonde bride, the humble, happy farmer with his homely face and capable hands who is her new love. There is wine and good food, and the villagers are happy to see the doctor again, though there's no denying that they're also uneasy—they need her, but she reminds them of monsters. But there is nothing to worry about this time around. The new husband has lived here all his life—he went to the village school, spent his summers tending fields with his father. Great swathes of corn and acres of strawberries, row upon row of giant orange carrots and great purple beets. This was the kind of magic the villagers relied on. This was magic they understood.

The mother and her new husband invite the doctor to stay with them. She sleeps in the old back room, the one with the fireplace, which they've converted into a bedroom with a view of the gardens. The table is gone. The floors are new, pale wood, smooth under her feet, scrubbed and sanded clean.

The mother seems quieter now, her blonde hair slightly dulled. The doctor isn't sure why she didn't give the house to someone else, or even burn it down, but she doesn't say this. Instead she toasts them at the wedding and wishes them nothing but the brightest kinds of happiness. She dances with the village boys. They laugh at the clomp of her boots, but she's a good dancer, better than most. When the night ends, she stumbles back to the house alone and falls into bed, leaving the mother and her new husband in the wedding tent.

In the middle of the night, the doctor wakes and hears footfalls outside her door. At first she thinks it's the newlyweds—they've forgotten something, or maybe they need another blanket for the tent. But the steps pause and then someone softly turns the handle. The doctor leaps out of bed and grabs her satchel, searching for her favourite scalpel, polished and sharp. She finds it and holds it in front of her as the door swings open. She says a wordless prayer. She doesn't believe in the gods, but the night is cold and she is alone and the gods, in this moment, are better than nothing.

Solid darkness enters the room. The scalpel slips from her hands and clatters to the floor. "You," she says.

The husband—the first husband—cocks his head at her. His face is the same: the anguish hasn't left him; the shadows are still there. He is quiet in the same way that the mother is—a silence that came in the wake of the children. This is not the first time that he's been there—the doctor can see that right away. She's also sure that the mother doesn't know he comes at all.

He is so much bigger. She wants to stare at the rest of him—the great black legs, the gleaming flanks—but that would be impolite. The doctor has been many things in her life, but she's never been rude. She keeps her eyes on his face.

"Me," he says.

How much pain fits in a word? She wants to cup her hands and catch it, throw it away from him the same way she's disappeared so many other hurts. But there is no way to fix this. She can't help it—she looks at the rest of him, at the body she doesn't know.

"I took them back," he says. "To my home. I tried to save them."

How terrible, she thinks. *The babies all dead.*

He sees this in her face and shakes his head. "No," he says. "I asked the mountain to make them human so I could bring them back. Instead," and he indicates the new body she's trying so hard to ignore, "it matched me to them."

The doctor doesn't know what this means, *the mountain*, and she doesn't want to ask. She takes a step closer to him. "So the babies survived?"

He smiles. "Yes," he says. "They are alive, and they are beautiful."

The rush of happiness almost makes her dizzy. She steps forward again and takes his hands—at first she isn't sure that he'll let her, but he does. She is a tall woman in a nightshirt, sleeping in an almost-stranger's house. The events of a year ago feel like a dream.

"You shouldn't be here," she says. "They'll come back soon."

"I saw her. In the wedding tent. With her new husband, and the villagers. I saw them all."

The doctor doesn't let go of his hands. "You've built a new life for yourself. She has to do the same."

"The mountain is very beautiful," he whispers. "I think—I know that she would love it."

The doctor shakes her head. "That doesn't matter now. *This* is no longer your life." She looks up to meet his eyes. "Your children need you. You can't leave them alone."

"They're so much like her," he says. "So impulsive, so angry."

"And you've never done an impulsive thing in your life? You've never been angry or sad enough to tear the world apart?"

He smiles again, a little. "Perhaps."

"I would love to see them again."

He shakes his head, pulls his hands away. "They are on the mountain now," he says. "They will stay on the mountain. It is safer for them there."

"I won't hurt them," she says.

"You are of the human world, and that world will hurt them if it gets too close. I can't let that happen."

The doctor lets it go, and backs away. As she does, she steps on the scalpel and bends down to retrieve it.

"Were you going to attack me with that?" he asks, amused. "It looks sharp."

It is. The doctor's father made a set of these for her after she'd finished her schooling. It is its own work of art—polished steel, the handle traced with tiny stems and flowers. Her hands are steadier when she works with this knife. It is her favourite tool.

This is the one she used to cut the mother open a year ago, here in this very room. She watches the first husband remember this and look away from her.

"I'll go now," he says. "You're right—I shouldn't be here."

"Wait," the doctor says, almost without thinking. She reaches into her satchel, finds the drawstring bag where she stows her knives for safe-keeping. She slips her favourite tool into the bag and removes the others. "Take this," she says. "This knife brought you your children. Look at it and remember—from pain, also life. From death, another life."

He hesitates, then takes the bag. "Thank you," he says. He ducks back through the door.

She runs after him. "Wait. Please."

He stops and turns to her, the old pain back on his face. Something else is in the air now too—a heaviness, a dislike that radiates from the walls. She swallows. "Promise me you won't come back," she says. "If they catch you here, no one will understand." Half man, half horse? They'll shoot him before he can speak.

But he only smiles. "I never *mean* to come here," he says. "It just happens. The house draws me in, the way the mountain drew me back."

The house draws me in. The thought makes her shiver.

"What do I call you now?" she says.

He shrugs. "I am the centaur."

When he's gone, she bolts the front door again—How did he get past it? Does she even want to know?—and crawls back into bed. There, she lies silent and thinks about this, over and over. Outside she can hear that a few of the young ones are still up and drinking. They laugh, they sing raunchy songs. She would smile if she didn't also feel that the house was watching, that it has been watching her this whole time.

When the sun finally rises, her relief is so great she almost weeps.

The new bride and her husband come back later that morning. They are happy to see her and ask her to stay another night. She politely refuses.

"Were you uncomfortable?" the bride asks, concerned.

"No—it's just that I must be going." She shoulders her satchel. "I have patients to attend to in other places."

"I'm glad you could come to the wedding." The mother is as beautiful as all newly married brides, but not as beautiful as she'd been at that other wedding, nor as happy.

This is all right, the doctor thinks—her new griefs will also be smaller. (Surely the mother's new griefs will be smaller.) She shakes the husband's hand. She hugs the bride.

"Thank you for letting me stay in your home," the doctor says. "I hope you'll be very happy here."

It isn't a lie, not exactly. But as the doctor walks away from the village and into the hills, she thinks about this, hard. She does wish them happiness. But she suspects that the room where she slept will always feel hollow—along with some aspect of this new marriage. You can't plaster over that kind of grief.

As she moves along the path that winds through the trees and will take her back out onto the road and from there down to the sea, the doctor thinks that maybe she'll give this village to someone else to tend. She knows others who'd be happy to add this cluster of homes to their rounds. They'll visit the new bride and her husband and bring their children into the world and never recognize the sadness in her face for what it is. The villagers will keep the secret. The village takes care of its own.

Or maybe she'll keep coming back. Maybe the stories won't let her go.

The doctor travels for days, ministering to all along her way. She sleeps when she's tired and eats when she wants to—there are many little villages along this stretch of road, and she's never short of company. Sometimes she pays for lodging, but more often she stays for free. People like to have a doctor in their debt.

It is a gift, she tells herself over and over. *It is a gift to be able to do this.*

She believes it. She means it. But at night, she dreams of that empty room in the house she left behind.

—5—

Her first night in the city, Tasha sleeps on the floor beside Annie, in a house just down from the destroyed hospital. Strangers lie beside them—no one wants to be alone. The girl, Elyse, sleeps on the couch, her breathing laboured. When Tasha wakes up some hours later, in the early hours of the morning, Elyse turns to her, pale and worried in the dim light.

"Was it a dream?" she whispers.

Tasha sits up and draws her knees to her chest. "No dream."

Her words wake Annie, who puts a hand on Tasha's arm.

"Did you sleep okay?" Annie asks.

"Yes," Tasha says, knowing what she means. If a night terror was going to visit her, surely it would come now, with the end of the world. "I slept fine." More than fine. She slept like the dead.

Maybe they *are* dead, she thinks, even as the people around them begin to stretch and stir. Maybe this is a terror that finally makes sense.

"What happens now?" Elyse says.

Tasha takes Annie's hand and kisses her palm and is rewarded with a tired smile. "Now we figure out what happens now," she says.

When she stands up, everyone turns to her, waiting.

✳

"We'll be all right," she tells everyone as she leads them out into the streets. "Everything will be all right. We'll take it one step at a time."

First, we must help the wounded. She and Annie stand for hours that day in front of the hospital wreckage, tending the injured, making sure everyone is bandaged, setting broken bones. There is morphine in the ambulance and they use as much of it as they need. She doesn't think about saving it until later.

Next, food. She and Annie—trailed by Elyse, who won't let them out of her sight—find a convenience store two streets over. No one else is here except for a young man who sits slumped at the till. When they walk in, he blinks as though he doesn't quite believe they're real.

"People will need food," Tasha says. She uses her doctor voice— calm, certain, and unhurried. He nods. She wonders if he's been here the whole time. She pulls her wallet from the pocket of her scrubs and empties all her cash onto the counter. Thirty-five dollars. "If people come in," she says, "let them have whatever they want. I will pay you for the rest of it later."

He is young, nervous. He doesn't ask her how she's going to pay for the rest of it; he just nods and takes the money. When she turns back to the door, one of the firemen who came with them from the coast—his name is Kevin, and his yellow jacket is smudged with soot—is standing in the doorway.

"There's a grocery store nearby," he says. "People are panicking."

When they get to the store, people are crying and shouting, appealing to a man who stands in the front of the registers with his hands up to hold them back.

"The system is down," he says. "I can't ring anyone through."

"The sky fucking fell apart!" someone shouts. "When do you *think* the system's going back up?"

Tasha pushes her way to the front of the crowd. "Hello," she says to the grocery store clerk. "What's your name?"

The man looks at her as if she makes no sense, but says, "Alan."

"Are you the manager?"

He looks around nervously. "One of them. I don't know where the other ones are."

"I'm sure they'll be here eventually," Tasha says.

Even though she hasn't asked, he says, "The tills won't even open when the system is down."

"That's okay, Alan. We all understand. But people need to eat."

"There are restaurants," he says, feebly. "They have generators. After the hurricane a few years ago the power went out and they were packed for like a week. I remember." He looks at Annie, then behind her, then back at Tasha. "I can't—I don't have the authority to do anything. It's not my fault."

Another voice shouts. "This wasn't a fucking hurricane! Half of the city is gone!"

Tasha ignores the other voice. "I know it's not your fault." She reaches out and puts a reassuring hand on Alan's arm. "But we have to work with what we have right now, Alan, okay? Some of these people don't have houses anymore. We don't know what's happening. When you add that to being hungry, it's a lot. People just want food. We can pay for things later, when the system goes back up."

When the system goes back up. This is another thing you learn in the ER—that hope is like a kind of lying.

"There's no power," he whispers. "How are people going to cook?"

"We'll find a way," she says. His shoulders relax. She beckons to Kevin. "Help everyone get what they need," she says, and then, leaning close to his ear, "Make sure no one takes too much." She turns and heads for the door.

Outside, Annie looks at her. "You'll need to eat too," she says.

"I'm fine," Tasha says. Above them, the sky is grey and brown.

Next, we need places for everyone to sleep. When the cell towers are still down late into the afternoon, she gathers the paramedics and the other firemen who came with them, all pale with fatigue but alert—and sends them to survey the houses still standing near the hospital. Asking for shelter when people answer the door. Forcing open doors when no one answers.

She also asks everyone to put their phones away and stop checking for reception. For now. Just for now.

Help will come. Help will come. Until then, we'll help each other.

Help will come.

Help will come.

She says the words over and over until they mean absolutely nothing.

✳

Later still on that long day in the city, Annie says to Tasha, "You need to *sleep*. And not on a floor."

Annie is also tired, Tasha wants to point out. Elyse, who has followed them everywhere today, says, "Should we go back to the house we were in last night and snag the bedrooms?"

Tasha and Annie glance at each other. "There are a lot of houses," Tasha says. "Let's find another one for the three of us."

Elyse's shoulders slump in relief. They both see it, and say nothing.

Annie is the one who finds them a townhouse one street over from the wreckage of the hospital. The front door isn't even locked.

"Hello?" Annie calls as they step inside, but no one answers.

Everything is peaceful and quiet. Their footsteps echo on the floor. The windows are dusted with a layer of fine brown dirt, and Tasha makes a mental note to clean them as soon as she can.

The bedrooms upstairs are neat. No children live here, at least none who are small. Both the master bedroom and the smaller one overlook the destroyed backyard. A fence is blown in on the right-hand side. A maple in the garden is split in half, its carcass bent and leaning against the small bedroom's window.

There's a couch in the master bedroom. "I can sleep on that," Elyse says.

Annie shakes her head. "You take the other room." She slides an arm around Elyse's shoulders. "It'll be more comfortable. We'll be right next door, Elyse."

Elyse looks away, her lip trembling. "I'm not—I know I shouldn't be scared—"

"I'll sleep on the couch," Tasha says. She smiles at Elyse, at them both. "You and Annie take the bed until you're comfortable, Elyse. Everything's going to be okay."

Elyse looks down at the floor. "I'm sorry," she says.

"It's fine," Tasha says. "None of this is going to be forever."

She waits for Annie to protest, but she doesn't say a word.

Over the following weeks, they mobilize their resources. They go to all the restaurants, most of them in ruins, and move the working generators to a spot behind the strip mall. They clear the wreckage of the hospital, searching for supplies. Some of the eastern wing is still standing, along with the front stairwell where people had climbed out from the basement that first afternoon.

Elyse goes everywhere they do. She can't exert herself too much, so they ask her to sit in a chair in front of the rubble and count and pack what they salvage into boxes. Cotton balls and tongue depressors, scalpels wrapped in plastic. Water from burst pipes has crept over what's left of the floor, and their shoes squelch as they crouch down in doorways to peer further into the wreckage. Tasha's sneakers are soaked through. She can tell by the wrinkle in Annie's nose that hers are too.

They find other things—a baby's bonnet, a suit jacket smeared with dirt and blood. A watch lying face up in a puddle, the digital face blank. A silver earring shaped like a goose. After a while Elyse gets restless packing boxes and moves around the wreckage, popping random things into a yellow bucket Annie found.

"Look," she calls. When they turn, she holds up a Get Well card, the lilac ink now smudged. *"For Sharon. Get better soon—love, Edgar."* She stares at the card before dropping it in the bucket. "I hope Sharon and Edgar survived."

Other things they discover: a torn cerulean purse; a zip-lock bag filled with salted peanuts; a day planner with soaked pages that have softened into one misshapen hunk of paper. A loop of child's teething beads. A soggy romance novel. Twenty empty pill bottles. Six more solo earrings, and one diamond ring.

"We should have a lost and found," Elyse says. "We could keep it somewhere central. Maybe by the sign in the square?"

She heads deeper into the darker hallways, where Tasha and Annie have already been, and Tasha calls out, "Don't go any further."

Elyse stops, turns to them. "But—there might be more stuff in those rooms. And what if there are . . . people? Shouldn't we be looking?"

"We've looked. You don't need to go in there." Annie's voice is firm.

Elyse's face trembles. She closes her eyes. Annie goes to her, puts an arm around her shoulder. "If anyone was still alive under the rubble, we would have heard them by now," she says. "They would be trying to make noise. Have you heard anything?"

What's left of the hospital is silent and dead.

On another day, they search a school. It was empty when the meteors hit and sustained little damage—but the pipes have burst here, too, and books bob softly in the hallways. They squelch through the corridors and take what they can.

"Won't the kids need these things when they come back?" Elyse asks, after they've trudged outside yet again with their arms full of books and dropped them on the grass.

Tasha and Annie glance at one another.

"I think," Tasha says, carefully, "we can assume that won't be for a while."

Elyse stares at her. "But—you said help will come."

Tasha nods. "And I think it will. It just might take longer than anyone expects."

Elyse nods at this, slowly. "There must be places that weren't hit as bad."

"Of course," Tasha says. "But they might be on the other side of the world. We need to take care of ourselves, and prepare for the future as best we can. If for nothing other than to keep people busy. I don't want anyone to worry any more than they have to, and the best thing for that is to give people something to do."

"Okay," Elyse says. She goes back to organizing the books.

It *is* helpful, the repetition—bottles in boxes and boxes in boxes and this food goes here and let's gather blankets and keep them all in one central place so that no one stops to think about the fact that there is no one in the pharmacy, there is no one at the bank, there is no power, there is no news from elsewhere.

She and Annie have help, for which Tasha is more grateful than she can say. Kevin from the fire trucks, other paramedics from their old seaside city. Brendan, with the red hair and the girls and the dark-haired wife, Heather. Alan from the grocery store. Other people who open up their homes to strangers and share their food. Still others who defuse confrontations that break out in the streets. There is so much fear in the air, so much fighting. But slowly, slowly, the survivors come together.

On the nights that she can't sleep, Tasha sends Annie and Elyse home and walks the city with other insomniacs—foraging, she calls it. Never looting. It isn't just her own survival she's thinking about. She's thinking about everyone else. That's how they're all going to survive—by thinking about everyone else. She goes up and down the night streets with others that she trusts—Kevin, and Alan, and Zeljko, the youth from the convenience store—and together they search for anything that might help them survive.

She hardly sleeps. But then, she's used to that.

One night when she comes home in the early hours of the morning, Annie is waiting for her, just inside the front door. "Hi," she whispers, and Tasha closes the door behind her and then Annie pushes her up against the door and Annie's hands are in her hair, Annie's tongue is in her mouth, Annie's hands are pulling hard at the zipper of her jeans. Her skin feels grimy and dry but so does Tasha's—they slide against one another like paper dolls, crumpling together, falling to the floor.

Tasha makes a sound deep in her throat, then lifts her head and bites Annie's ear. Annie puts a hand over her mouth. "Shhh," she says. "You'll wake Elyse."

Tasha laughs into Annie's palm. She slides a finger deep inside of Annie and watches her wife shudder in the dark. Then she pulls her hand away.

"More," Annie whispers.

Tasha only shakes her head. "What about Elyse?" she says, but her mouth is on Annie's shoulder now, her fingers slick and hovering over Annie's face. She sticks a finger in Annie's mouth and Annie sucks it.

And then it is gone, the desire, the shock of its absence rushing cold into the room. Tasha pushes herself up, sits back against the closed front door. Annie blinks at her, surprised.

"I wasn't serious," Annie says. "Not really. I mean—it's not like we haven't had to be quiet before."

Before. Once upon a time in a seaside city long, long ago. They'd had silent sex in the guest room in Annie's parents' house a hundred times. The laughter building in them, ready to burst.

Before. It hasn't been that long, but it feels like it. Tasha pulls her knees up and sighs a little. Then she takes Annie's palm and kisses it, folds Annie's fingers over the kiss. "It's late," she says. "And it'll be another long day tomorrow. We should go to bed."

This time Annie is the one who pulls her hand away, her fist balled tight, like she's a child afraid the kiss will disappear.

Elyse is on the couch when they go upstairs to their room. They climb into the bed without speaking and wind their bodies together—Annie curled inside and Tasha behind her, her arms sliding around Annie's slender torso. Her golden-haired princess, all dirt and sweat.

Another evening, Tasha's alone on her rounds, driving the ambulance in widening circles, looking for places they might have missed. Just as she decides to turn for home, she once again sees the dark-haired woman, Heather, coming toward her from the mountain, carrying her babies.

Their red hair shines even from this far away. Tasha stops beside her.

"Heather," she calls. The woman keeps walking, her eyes on the ground. "Are you all right?"

Heather lifts her head, startled, then nods. "I'm just tired," she says.

What happened in that other fire? Tasha wants to reach out and touch her. To crawl back to that moment in front of the hospital, when she touched Heather's forehead and heard the high-pitched sound of screaming. The taste of starlight at once impossible and unmistakable in her mouth. Where had that come from? What did it mean?

"Okay," she says instead. "Well—Annie and I are in a townhouse by the hospital. The one with the blue roof. If you need anything."

Heather shrugs. "Okay," she says. "Thank you."

"Where were you walking?"

Heather's face is still shuttered, but she says, "I was just in the forest for a little bit. The trees relax me."

"I was just curious. I don't care where you go." Then, tentatively. "Maybe I could come with you sometime?"

Heather doesn't say anything, but since she's still standing there, Tasha asks, "Remember that first day, by the ambulance, when I touched your face? What did you see?"

Heather sighs. "That there was a fire," she says. "Or—there had been a fire. And you were alone." She looks back down at the ground. "Sometimes I see things like that. Other people's—memories. I know it sounds ridiculous."

"I saw you," Tasha says, and Heather's face softens in surprise. "Or—I heard you. When my hand touched your face, I saw the mountain and clouds, and I heard you scream. What happened? Did someone fall?"

Heather stares at her for a long moment. "My father," she says, eventually. "My father had an accident on the mountain. He died."

"I'm so sorry." Tasha feels her eyes blur with tears.

"It's all right," Heather says. "It was a long time ago." Then, still looking at Tasha, "Your fire wasn't a long time ago, was it?"

Tasha looks away from Heather, out through the windshield of the ambulance and up the street, which is slowly being overtaken by green.

"No." She sniffs, then wipes at her nose with her hand. "My parents, two years ago. They died in a house fire."

"I'm so sorry," Heather says. When Tasha turns back to her, there's an understanding deep in Heather's eyes. Tasha wants to fall into it. She feels tiny, like a child.

"I try to forget," Tasha says. "Or—not forget, I'll never forget, I just—concentrate. On something else. You know?" Then she takes a breath, uncomfortably aware that she's starting to babble. "How did you see what you saw? And why did I see your memory? That's never happened to me before."

Heather lifts her shoulders a little. "I'm not sure," she says. Now her face is—not unfriendly, exactly, but warier. "I should get back," she says. "I've been gone a long time."

"Do you want a ride?"

"No, thank you."

"Well. You know where we are if you . . . need anything."

"Yes," Heather says. "You said that already."

Tasha flushes. "Right," she says. "Well—I'll see you around, then, I guess." Heather only nods and starts walking. After a moment, Tasha puts the ambulance in gear.

To her right, the mountain. She's heard the rumours about it. Strange animals in the trees. People who disappear. The stories the city people tell about the mountain comfort her, in a weird way. They remind her of the stories her mother told her as a child. The mountain and its secrets have endured—they will survive long after all of humanity is gone, whether by disaster or illness or old age.

This mountain, the one closest to them, rises pristine and untouched into the clouds. Did Heather's father fall from there?

Then Tasha shakes her head. *We can endure,* she thinks. *Maybe Elyse is right—maybe help* will *come. We just need to be smart and care for each other and focus on concrete things. The things we know to be true, and not the things we imagine.*

There's a spark of something in the city. She can sense it. It isn't hope yet, but it's close.

✳

When she gets back to the middle of the city, there is yelling in the square. The area in front of the name boards is chaotic, frenzied, filled with rage. Half the people left in the city, it seems, are milling about in the streets, angry and frightened.

Tasha pulls the ambulance up as close as she can, then jumps out, shoving the keys into her pocket. "What's going on?" she shouts, making her way through the crowd.

Kevin stands in front of the crowd, his arms spread wide, holding everyone back. Behind him, in front of the name boards, stand three people—a woman, a man, and Annie.

The woman has one arm locked around Annie's neck. The other hand holds a knife against Annie's throat.

"What's going on?" Tasha says, again. She clenches her fists and fights to push a long-ago dream memory away. Fiery birds burning holes in the ground. A woman who screams and screams.

"*What's going on?*" the woman shouts. She looks right at Tasha. "The food is disappearing—that's what's fucking going on! You think we're stupid? You think we don't *know* you're going to take off with the gas?"

"I don't think anyone's stupid," Tasha says calmly. She holds out her hands and takes a step forward—and then, when the woman moves the knife and Annie winces, stops. "We've been collecting and saving what we can. So that *everyone* will survive. That's all."

"So it's *looting* when everyone else does it but it's fine when it's done by a fucking stranger?" The man steps forward and jabs a finger into Tasha's collarbone. Tasha can't remember his name.

Tasha spreads her hands farther, steps back from him. *I have nothing. I have nothing.* "I haven't accused anyone of looting," she says.

"*She did!*" the woman screams, jerking her head to Annie.

"They were." Annie speaks through gritted teeth. "They climbed over the enclosure. They were trying to get at the gas."

"So what if we were?" the man shouts. Wendell. That's his name. "Who the fuck do you think you are, anyway? You don't even live here."

"I'm nobody," Tasha says, and she means it. "But I do live here now. And so does Annie. We're just trying to help."

"Well, guess what," the woman says. "You're *not* helping. Do you think hoarding all of the food in that godforsaken mall is going to help us in the winter? Is hoarding the gas going to help other people come to the city and help? Is it?"

"Help is coming," Tasha says. "We just have to be patient. We just have to look out for each other. I know this is hard."

"*Do you?*" the woman screams. She flings Annie away from her and moves toward Tasha, brandishing the knife in her face. "My home was destroyed. I haven't slept in three days. I don't feel safe. And no one is coming. No one is coming to help."

Tasha doesn't flinch. "Many of us don't have homes anymore." She ignores the ripple of unease that goes through the crowd behind her, like a great beast slowly waking from sleep. She ignores Annie, stumbling forward to stand in the crowd. She reaches tentatively for the woman's shoulder, but the woman shies away. "But we're building a new home, together. One that can last for as long as we need it."

The woman laughs, then sobs. She turns around and throws the knife at the boards—it goes deep, splintering an unknown name in two. "We're fucking stuck here," the woman says. "We can't leave because you won't let us have gas to go. How far do you think any of us is going to get on foot? I've seen the vines growing over the roads. And we're going to run out of food. Whatever you think you're building—it isn't going to last. We're all going to starve."

"We're not going to starve," Tasha says. Then she says it again, louder. "We are *not* going to starve."

"Maybe not now," the woman says. "But if help doesn't come, we'll all be dead by the end of the winter." Her eyes burn. "And if *that* doesn't happen, the mountain will drive us all mad anyway."

Tasha's breath stills, for a moment. "What?" she says.

"You're not from here," the woman snaps. "You don't know—but we do. Just wait. We'll stay here and starve, and people will start disappearing. They'll get lost, or they'll walk too close to the mountain and bears will eat them. Bears—or other things. Monsters that hide in the trees."

"Monsters aren't real," Tasha says. She keeps her voice soft. "That's only a story. And I won't let anyone go up the mount—"

"You don't have anything to do with it!" the woman cries. "We all know—but you don't. You haven't lived in the shadow of this mountain. You do *not* understand."

Tasha feels the crowd behind her shiver, as if they were on the edge of unleashing a wail. "Heather goes near the mountain. She's fine. No monsters at all."

"Heather?" the woman sneers. "The one with the crazy father who *died* on the mountain? It's because of her that we all stay away! She's the last person you should be talking to. She's already nuts."

"She's not *nuts*," Tasha says, severely.

"Bullshit. She says she went up the mountain, but she walks like *this?*" The woman acts out a limp, staggering around. "How's she supposed to get up the mountain? She's a liar. Don't believe a word she says."

Tasha glances around. The people from her city look confused, but everyone else looks uneasy, like these are things they've been whispering about for years. She locks eyes with a man who stands beside Kevin. He shrugs.

"We've all heard things about the mountain," he says. "But they're only stories. You know, the kind parents tell to keep their children in the house. *Johnny went up the mountain and was never seen again.* That kind of thing."

"They aren't just stories!" the woman cries again. "You know they aren't."

"And Heather?" Tasha presses.

The man shrugs again. "Every village has its idi—" he sees Tasha's expression, catches himself—"someone eccentric, right? That's all it is."

Tasha grits her teeth. *Maybe she goes there to get away from all of you.* Then she stops and stills herself. *They are all terrified*, she thinks. *They are all dancing on the edge of so much.* She reaches into her pocket and pulls out the keys to the ambulance, then drops them on the ground in front of the woman. "Take the ambulance and go. The last thing I want is for people to stay here and sink into despair."

The woman stares at her. "You're not serious."

"Do I look like I'm making a joke?" Tasha turns to face the crowd. "Anyone can leave here," she says. "You can take the ambulance right now and go. Try to find another place that maybe hasn't been hit as hard. Send help our way if you can." She turns back to the woman. "If you don't want to stay, then I want you to go."

The woman looks, briefly, hurt by this, but again her anger flares. She bends and grabs the keys. She shouts. "Anyone who wants to come—get in."

The woman throws open the driver's door and climbs inside. She turns the key, and the engine rumbles to life. The man who was standing beside her runs around to the passenger side, then gets in. And suddenly other people are scrambling into the back, tossing a few of Tasha's carefully gathered boxes out onto the ground to make room. The woman in the driver's seat yells, "Stop! We might need that!" Then she looks straight at Tasha. "Fuck you!" she shouts, and she rams the pedal to the floor.

People scream and jump out of the way just in time as the ambulance speeds down the street and around the corner, out of sight.

Tasha turns to Annie. "Are you all right?"

"I'm fine." Annie brushes at the grime on her pants.

"What happened?"

Annie shrugs. "You heard her. I confronted them trying to break in— they ran, and I chased them to the square. Then she pulled the knife."

Tasha nods. Her hands tremble, even as she continues to hold them tight in fists. The crowd is slowly dispersing around them.

How many, she wonders, already regret that they didn't jump in the ambulance too? "Where's Elyse?"

Annie runs a hand through her hair. "Back at the house. I was just out doing a final walk around the mall."

"Don't walk around alone anymore," Tasha says, thinking of the crowd. A beast gone back to slumber.

"Me?" Annie says, incredulous. "Tasha, she was yelling at you."

She's already turning away, heading back to the house. "I'll be fine," she says, and Annie doesn't answer.

✳

The next morning they're awoken by Elyse, who starts coughing so hard when she gets out of bed that she falls over.

Tasha is on her feet right away. Annie reaches for the towels they've stacked by the nightstand just for this. She lays them over the mattress, mounts the pillows, and covers them with a towel too.

"I'm sorry," Elyse rasps, as she climbs onto the bed and lies face down over the pillows.

"Don't be silly," Tasha says.

Annie starts counting, and with each beat Tasha slaps Elyse's back, working up and down her ribs, dislodging the buildup in her lungs bit by bit.

As Elyse coughs mucus out onto the towel, Annie swaps one towel for another. She doesn't stop counting.

Eventually, Tasha's efforts start Elyse coughing in earnest, and she eases off and steps back from the bed, raising an arm to wipe the sweat from her forehead.

After she's coughed herself out, Elyse lies silent on the mattress for a few minutes. Then she turns over, sits up, and reaches for her shirt. "Thank you," she says. Annie gathers up the filthy towels.

Tasha thinks about Elyse every time the wind rises, kicking up dust and debris. Once upon a time Elyse had wanted to be a doctor too. The new drug she was taking, the surgery—these were going to help her climb a mountain.

If help doesn't come, Elyse will be lucky if she lives out the year.

"Let's have another session tonight," Tasha says as they all start to get ready for the day.

Elyse shrugs. Already she's trying to put it behind them. "I should be good now," she says. "I'll help Annie in the pharmacy. I won't be a bother, I promise."

"You're not a bother, Elyse." It's what Tasha says every time. It's what she says to everybody.

Elyse shrugs at this, too, and goes out the bedroom door.

✻

The people who took the ambulance don't come back. Tasha tries to forget them, tries to focus on the city. They keep stockpiling all the food they can find. They build greenhouses, make garden plots, plant as many little seed packets as they can. The days are long and unrelenting.

There is no news. Sometime after the knife incident, others break into the strip mall in the night, steal gas and food, and drive away from the city.

Even though there is very little rain, the grass grows high, vines climb over the houses, and weeds fill the road. But the bean, pepper, potato, and tomato plants they grow yield vegetables that are stunted and unappetizing—if they yield anything at all. Tasha goes from one greenhouse to the next, adding fertilizer collected from the garden centres. Nothing works. The vegetables do not get bigger, and they all taste the same—bland, with a faint tang of metal, of burning.

We're all going to starve, the woman had said. Celeste, Tasha had found out later. She had lived in the mountain city all her life. Her words run on repeat through Tasha's head while she tries to sleep.

We're all going to starve.

We're all going to starve.

✻

"How much do we have in the supply rooms?" It's late summer and Tasha has begun to ask this question once a day at least. She and Annie are sprawled on a mattress on the floor of their makeshift clinic—a little store in the strip mall that used to be a butcher shop. They've dedicated one of the generators to keeping its fridges running, to safeguard the medications they've scrounged.

Tasha spends most of her nights here now, in case someone needs her. Sometimes Annie joins her, though mostly she stays at the town-house with Elyse. When Tasha sleeps alone, she dreams of birds who burn holes in the ground. A bat made of human flesh and ribs. She wakes screaming, slick with sweat.

"We have enough," Annie says. "If we're careful."

"How much is enough?"

Annie sighs. "If we're smart, enough to last us until spring. Maybe a little longer. We'll be eating crackers and canned tuna and nothing else by the end of it." She circles Tasha's right breast with her hand, thumbs her nipple. Moonlight glints on her wedding ring—silver, identical to Tasha's. The only thing that either of them have left from their old lives, except for each other.

"Tasha," Annie says, slowly, "help isn't coming, is it."

Tasha raises a hand and holds Annie's palm to her chest. "We just have to be patient. We'll figure it out."

✳

In September, one of the city residents suggests that they plant clover in the gardens to enrich the soil.

"Next spring, we can till it in, and it'll release nutrients as it decomposes," he tells them. His name is Joseph. He doesn't trust Tasha. He doesn't trust anybody.

Joseph often goes out of town on his bicycle, searching for news. Sometimes others join him and sometimes he goes alone. On bikes they are still able to weave their way along roads choked with grass and vines.

They bring back supplies—bags of rice and lentils, dented cans of tomatoes and beans. More often than not they bring only stories: death in that city, death in that town. Looting and fire and terror and fear.

One night when Joseph returns, he half staggers into the clinic, his shirt spotted with blood.

"Jesus," Annie says. She loops his arm around her shoulders and brings him to the back room, then settles him down on the mattress. As she strips him of the shirt, Tasha pulls on a pair of gloves. A four-inch slit gapes down Joseph's side.

"What happened?" she asks.

The front bell sounds and they all look up—it is only Elyse, coming in carrying a bag of chips.

"I—I didn't know if anyone had eaten," she falters when she sees them.

Tasha waves her in. She looks back to Joseph. "Tell me what went wrong."

"Ambush," he says, hissing as Tasha swabs his skin with disinfectant. "Pushed me off the bike and took all of the supplies. Swiped at me when I got up and ran after them. I didn't have a lot—I guess that was a good thing."

"They didn't take the bike?" Annie says.

"No." Joseph manages to laugh. "There's so much green shit on the roads, even the bike is practically useless."

Tasha shines the beam of a mini flashlight on the wound. It isn't as deep as she'd feared. There is bruising and swelling around it, but the edges are clean and no ribs appear to be broken.

"No more going out alone," Tasha says. "That's an order."

Annie snorts, softly. Tasha half expects Joseph to snap at her, but he only says, "I don't know how much longer we'll be able to go out anyway. The roads are impassable."

Tasha wipes the cut with disinfectant on a small sponge, working as gently as she can. "When was your last tetanus shot?"

"Tetanus shot?" he says. "I think the kids got theirs—two years ago?" His face clouds over. "My oldest hated needles. I got a booster of some kind at the same time so he could see it wasn't the end of the world." A sharp intake of breath—at his own words or the action of her hand, she isn't sure. "It might have been tetanus. I don't know."

Elyse opens her bag of chips and passes it to Joseph. He reaches in, silently, and grabs a handful, crunching as Tasha cleans the wound.

When she's done, Annie hands her a small tube from a satchel that sits on the counter. Tasha's own personal medical kit. It's one of the first things she put together when they arrived.

"Surgical glue," Tasha says when she sees Joseph stare at it. "It's safe, I swear. If the cut was deeper, I would stitch you." She closes the wound, then covers it with a bandage. "No biking for at least a week," she says. "Also, keep it dry for at least two days. No showers, no long, luxurious soaks in the tub."

He doesn't laugh. "What are you going to do when the winter comes? When no one can leave the city?"

"Anyone can leave," Tasha says. "I'm not stopping them."

"That's not what I mean," he says. "What if something happens in the city? What if you aren't enough? I see the way people look at you now. Half of them hate you and half of them look like they think you can fucking cure cancer. What are you going to do if the food runs out?"

She sits back on her heels. "I've always tried to be truthful. I never said—"

"*Help will come,*" he mocks. "You've been saying that for months. I'm not an idiot! You're making it so that people don't *want* to leave."

"I'm trying to give everyone hope," Tasha says around a sinking feeling in her gut. "I'm trying to give everyone something to do. Is that bad?"

"Is having something to do going to save them in the winter when we run out of food? What happens when we run out of the water-purifying tablets that you stole from the store?"

"I didn't *steal* them, I *collect*—"

"You know what I mean! What happens when the sun sets at four in the afternoon and doesn't rise till ten and people scare themselves by telling ghost stories about the mountain? You think everyone's going to be calm and happy and *satisfied* when we're in the dark all the time?"

"No one's going to tell ghost stories," Tasha says, trying to keep her voice light. "We're just going to survive."

He snorts. "You really have no fucking clue, do you. You're *already* telling them a fairy tale. *Stay here, work together, everything will be okay.* When in the end we're all going to become ghosts."

We're all going to starve. We're all going to starve.

"We'll find a way," Elyse insists, her voice surprisingly loud. "Annie and Tasha will help us find a way."

Joseph rolls his eyes. "Sure, kid, sure."

She bristles. "I'm not a kid. If you hate it here so much, why did you come back?"

Something dark washes over Joseph's face. "The mountain called me back. I had nowhere else to go." He laughs a little. "Whatever. You know what? You let Tasha and Annie find a way for you, Elyse, and tell me how that goes. As for me—I'll do just fine without you, thanks very much."

Tasha stands up, brushes her pant legs off, and tries not to sound hurt. "Just be careful with that cut and you won't need any saving. If you do, you know where we are."

Joseph, looking not a little ashamed of himself, puts on his bloody shirt and heads out the door.

"We could go," Annie says after he leaves. "You and me and Elyse. We could take one of the fire trucks and drive away from here right now. A fire truck would make it through."

Tasha sighs. "Where would we go? What's better than here?"

"I don't know," Annie says, "but it's better than starving to death surrounded by madmen."

"No one's mad," Tasha says. "They're just afraid. That's all."

"So then what did Joseph mean by the mountain calling him back?" Elyse says.

No one has an answer.

✳

The next day, Tasha slips out of the clinic alone and makes her way to the forest. She has come often since that day weeks ago when she saw Heather and the twins. She's found that the trees calm her down too. And there is something oddly addictive about the mountain—how small she feels in its shadow, how insignificant. The world has changed so much as to be almost unrecognizable, but the mountains endure.

For the first time since she started walking in the woods, she spots Heather, up ahead of her, telling stories to the babies. A genie and three wishes. Fairies who come to steal babies from their cribs.

"Come with us," said the fairies, "and we'll give you halls of golden toys and warm fires to sleep near, and so many good things to eat." The babies were cold and defeated by the rumbling of their stomachs, so they held out their hands and the fairies scooped them away.

"Where do the fairies take them?" Tasha calls out, softly.

Heather whips around, then relaxes a little when she sees it's only Tasha. "Somewhere better," she says. Shadows play over her face. To her girls, she says, "But don't worry. You're safe with me and Daddy. Everything will be okay."

Tasha takes a step forward.

Heather takes a step back, then holds her ground. "Is something wrong?"

"No." Tasha comes to stand in front of her. "Sorry. I just—I found I like to go for walks out here too."

The babies crane their heads to look at Tasha. "They still don't sleep," Heather says. "I have to walk them all the time."

Tasha nods. She has heard this from Brendan. "They're what—five months old now?" she says. "If it's colic, they should grow out of it soon."

"I guess," Heather says. Up close, she is a shadow of a shadow, her eyes frantic and bright. "I feel like that day will never come."

"I can imagine."

Heather laughs. "Can you?"

Tasha shrugs.

Heather turns and starts walking again—not an invitation, not quite a dismissal—and Tasha falls in step behind her. They walk for a long time in silence, stepping carefully over the forest floor. They're not on a path— not exactly—but as Tasha follows Heather's lead, she begins to see a faint impression that tells her someone has been this way before. They come to a break in the trees and set out across a small field matted with tall weeds and grasses, tangled wildflowers. Milkweed with seed pods the size of her hand. Queen Anne's lace that reaches her shoulders. Sunflowers that are taller than she is. The greens are so deep they're hard to look at, too strong for the eyes. It's intoxicating, but it makes Tasha uneasy.

The babies watch Tasha with bright, interested eyes. One of them—Greta?—smiles at Tasha, then stretches her hand out to the milkweed. Without looking, Heather gently intercepts her baby.

"Why won't you talk to me?" Tasha asks, at last.

"I don't talk to most people," Heather says, some amusement in her voice. "Surely everyone has told you that by now."

"But—I heard you scream," Tasha says. She feels ridiculous, but presses on. "I heard you scream, and you saw me after the fire."

"Why do you want that to matter so much?"

"Shouldn't it matter? What does it mean?"

"You tell me. You're the doctor."

"Oh, stop with that!" Tasha shouts. "I just want to know. I want to understand." She takes a couple of steps ahead of Heather and throws an arm out to the vegetation around them. "Why are plants growing like this out here when we can't grow things in our gardens or the greenhouses?"

"How am I supposed to know the answer to that?"

"I don't know!" She's embarrassed by the loudness of her voice. "No one else comes out here except for you. And me. No one else goes to the mountain. Instead all I hear are stories about the mountain from people who struggle to believe that coming together as a community will help us get through the winter. And yet everyone's perfectly happy to believe that the mountain is home to monsters, or whatever. None of it makes any sense."

Heather keeps walking.

"People do tell me that you're crazy," Tasha says, baldly. She watches Heather's shoulders stiffen. "They say that you went up the mountain and when you came down you were never the same." She wants to take the words back instantly.

"By people," Heather says, "do you mean my husband?"

Tasha feels shame creep up her neck and stain her face. "No."

Heather glances at her. "You're lying," she says. "Or maybe he's not the only one who says that. That's all right. What else did he tell you?"

"He didn't say you were crazy," Tasha says. *That was other people.* "He just said that something happened to you when you were young."

"What else do people tell you about the mountain?"

"More stories," Tasha says. "A friend of a friend who disappeared on the mountain years ago. Monsters who live in the forest trees. Shadows people see when they're drunk. That kind of thing."

"Stories are never just stories, Tasha. You of all people should know that."

She blinks. "What's that supposed to mean?"

"You don't know?" Heather says. She sounds amused and also exhausted—a touch manic, a sliver hysterical. "You tell stories to the people every day."

She thinks of Joseph, and looks down at the ground. "What? I do not."

Heather sighs. "Tasha. Of course you do. 'Everything will be okay if we stick together and help each other out—'"

"Everything *will* be okay," Tasha says, fiercely. "That's not a story—it's the truth. We just have to be there for each other."

Heather snorts. "This city is not good at that kind of thing. I could have told you that when you got here."

"But you didn't," Tasha presses. "You barely talk to me at all."

"It's all I can do to hang on," Heather says, her hands going to her babies' heads.

"Were they there for you? The people in the city?" Tasha asks, softly. Even though she knows the answer.

Heather casts her a sidelong glance, but keeps on walking. "Who wants to be there for the village idiot?" she says. "Especially when they can make the village idiot into a story herself?"

Tasha thinks again, oddly, of fiery birds burning holes in the ground. Octopuses who gather treasure. A prince gone to find a woman locked in a tower. "My parents told me stories when I was young to help me overcome something," she says. "To give me hope, to help me *hang on.* And then I got older, and I didn't need the stories anymore. But the stories that people tell in this town feel different. These aren't stories that help. They don't inspire hope—they inspire fear. I can't let that happen. Everything that we're dealing with is bad enough, and stories that scare people are only going to make it worse. Why are people afraid of the mountain, for real?"

Heather cocks her head slightly to the side. "You know why," she says. "My father died there, a long time ago. Mothers tell their kids that people disappear on the mountain. That way they avoid it, and no one gets hurt."

"Are there trails up it?"

Heather shrugs. "There used to be. They're overgrown now. The city made them off-limits."

The forest suddenly feels still and heavy. The light has changed—the sky clouding over. "What about the monster stories, though," Tasha asks. "Creatures that hide in the trees? Ghosts who lure children away?"

Heather doesn't answer.

"None of it makes any sense," Tasha continues, frustrated.

"Why does it need to make sense?"

Tasha trips on a whorl of green and almost falls. When she straightens, she says, "Because people are already on edge! And when they tell each other these stories, they feed their paranoia. People talk about monsters and they talk about how we're all going to starve. People have no hope."

Heather nods. "You've been talking to Joseph," she says. "Look, Tasha"—and her tone is almost kind now—"everything is unfamiliar. Even the city that some of these people have known their whole lives. They're telling stories to make sense of it—to try and understand it. That's all."

"But what good will stories about monsters do?" Tasha presses. "That doesn't help people gather food or ration supplies or believe that we'll be able to take care of one another. If anything, it makes it worse."

They step out of the trees into another tangled meadow. There's a greenhouse here, half swallowed by wildflowers and grass.

They both stop to stare. Tasha is confused. She turns to look at Heather. "Did we build one all the way out here?"

Heather walks to the greenhouse, puts her hand against the clouded door.

It's old, Tasha realizes. It's not one of theirs.

Heather grasps the door and pulls it open. The babies coo and stir.

Tasha can smell the flowers before she sees them. When she steps up beside Heather, her eyes fill with colour—the blue rustle of a jacaranda tree growing tall in the middle of the greenhouse. Pink and orange and red lilies that burst at their feet, the twining shocks of white and purple orchids that reach up through the tangles of green. The deep, dark red of amaryllis.

"Where did this come from?" Tasha says. "Why is everything—why is everything growing?"

"I don't know," Heather whispers.

"Did you build this? Is this where those flowers came from, the ones in your house?"

"I—no. Not me." Heather shakes her head. "My father built this greenhouse. A long time ago."

"Did he plant all of this?"

"Yes. But I thought everything died after he did. I haven't been back here in years."

Tasha stares into the greenhouse, tries to focus. The colours swim together. "Well, it isn't dead now," she says. "You're sure this isn't where your flowers are from?"

"I have no idea," Heather says. She is staring at the amaryllis.

"Why are things growing here when they aren't growing in the other greenhouses?"

It's Heather's turn to snap. "I don't know, Tasha! Why are there vines growing over the houses when nothing grows in the gardens? Why are the goddamned sunflowers six feet high and the tomato plants turning yellow?" She falls silent and they both stand for a moment, breathing in. It smells sweet in here, and fresh. Everything feels new and also secret, as though it hasn't been disturbed in years.

"Jilly," Heather hisses suddenly and Tasha snaps back to herself. The baby looks at them, her hand caught in a plant hanging down by her face.

Two green half moons are clamped around her fist. Tasha reaches for the plant and pulls it open. Jilly's hand is unharmed, though covered with a sticky, greenish-white residue.

Tasha wipes the baby's fist clean with her sleeve. She pulls a bandage from her side bag and wraps it around Jilly's hand just in case. "Don't let her put her fingers in her mouth until you've washed them."

Heather nods. Then she puts her hand around Tasha's. "Thank you," she says. "I know I don't say that enough." She swallows. "We'd best get back." She turns toward the city, not waiting for Tasha to follow.

Tasha pulls the greenhouse door shut, then runs to catch up. "If stories are never only stories," she says, "then why do you tell the twins about fairies stealing babies from their cribs?"

Heather laughs—a high, clear sound that makes Tasha shiver.

"That story wasn't for them," she says. "It was for me."

THE JEALOUS BIRD

Once there was a bird who was jealous of the sun. No matter how high the bird flew, the sun was always higher, and it made the bird angry.

"Why should the sun fly higher than we do?" he said to his fellow birds. "We work so hard to stay in the air but the sun sits up there and does nothing. It's not fair."

"The sun has always flown above us." The bird who said this was much older than the jealous bird, and had seen much more of the world. "This is how it has always been."

"Why should something stay the same just because it has always been that way?" said the jealous bird.

The old bird said, severely, "The sun is higher. We are lower. The sun warms us when we're cold and sends us light to see worms in the grass, and asks of us nothing in return. You should be grateful for this, not angry."

"I will be grateful when the sun sees how much higher I can fly!" cried the bird. He threw his head back and crowed, and many other birds, massed around him, threw back their heads and did the same.

"You cannot fly higher than the sun," the old bird warned. "It is foolish to even try."

But the jealous bird would not be swayed, for he knew a secret his mother had told him long ago: the birds themselves had come from the sun.

When he was a fumbling chick in the nest, his mother had said, "You have sunlight in your wings. All that we are comes from the sun. We are the same. Before the world was born, when we all spun round in the sky together, the sun's fire was also your own."

And so the bird gathered all those who were set on fire by his words and told them they would fly to the sun and reclaim their place in the sky. "We have the sun in our feathers," he said. As one, they spread their wings and lifted from the trees.

The birds flew high, and then higher still. They flew so high the air became thin; some birds gasped, but kept on struggling; other birds gave up and dropped back, far down to the ground. The jealous bird and a few close friends kept flying.

They flew so high the air was hard to breathe; they flew so high the sun began to burn their wings. One by one, the birds burst into flame and fell, screaming. When they hit the ground, the earth went black with mourning.

The jealous bird's wings burned too, but he held his mother's words deep inside and pushed on. He flew until the sky curved, until the great dark belly of the universe came into view.

The sun, the bird saw to his surprise, was still so far away. But the sun saw him, and knew who he was instantly.

"I have been waiting for you," the sun said. "I have been waiting for so long."

"I'm here to take my rightful place!" the bird cried. He puffed out his chest and waited for the sun to come at him, full of anger.

But the sun only smiled. "How long have I been here?" it said. "I have watched the world spin for millions of years. I have waited alone in the dark sky for company. You and your kind were content to fly amongst the trees and dream without daring to reach—to make me into a monster—when all along it is I who've been waiting for you."

The jealous bird, shocked by this, almost fell. "You have always flown higher than we have," he said. "Had I known that you were lonely, I would have come much sooner."

"The kindness of your heart is not what brought you close to me," the sun said. "You are here because you thought you were better than the best. I am here to tell you: you are."

The bird was filled with joy at this. But then he thought of his friends who had fallen back to the earth and burned. "Does that mean my friends are weak?"

"Your friends are not weak," said the sun. "But they did not believe. The world is so much bigger than the tops of your trees, and in the depths of their hearts, they were not sure. You understand that now, yes?"

The bird looked back down at the world from which he had come, and then at the sun. "Yes," he said, and he no longer sounded jealous.

"Good," said the sun. "There is still much to learn."

And the jealous bird, no longer jealous, caught fire in truth this time, and shone as bright as any star had ever done.

— 6 —

The girls smile at two months—both of them at the same time, their mouths curling up as they watch one another. Their eyes follow her everywhere. On the rare days when sunshine filters through the front window, Heather spreads a blanket on the living room floor and lays them down. They stretch their arms to the ceiling. She whispers silly things into the soft cups of their ears.

On the rare evenings when the girls aren't colicky and he is home from scavenging, B lies with her in the living room and makes funny faces at the babies. He calls them *beautiful* and *gorgeous* and *Daddy's favourite flowers*. He picks them up and twirls them in the centre of the floor until their faces split with smiles, and then he goes into the kitchen and makes dinner for them all. His eyes say *beautiful* and *gorgeous* to Heather when he's too tired—and they are both of them almost always too tired, now—to say the words.

He brings her wildflowers from the southern edge of town; tall daisies and tulips, irises and snapdragons. She throws the dried amaryllis into the backyard and this time B does not bring it back; the next day it is covered by Boston ivy.

B says he loves them in the food that he cooks, in the way that he dances with and sings to the girls. His voice soaring high and sweet, sounding so much younger than she feels.

At night he reaches for her again and again and weeps his hot tears into her hair. This, too, is a kind of love.

It's a miracle that any of them survived. This family they have—a miracle.

The girls shine with a sticky magic that pulls her toward them, a force that feels older than love. Her children. The dark matter of her mind and heart is in constant, uneasy orbit around their flaming heads.

They are three months old, then four, then five.

She grows thinner. Everyone does.

Summer has given way to autumn. Daylight gives way to the dark. Heather and B go to bed earlier and wake up when the light comes, turning themselves toward the remnants of the sun. The sky is grey-tinged, with faint rust at the edges. There is no power in the city save for the generator that keeps Tasha's clinic refrigerators going.

The girls have finally started to sleep for stretches at a time without wailing. Three hours here, five hours there. Still Heather walks them, and sometimes B comes too. He carries one twin, she carries another. Sometimes they even hold hands—the way they did before the girls came, when she was pregnant and life spooled in front of her, boring but safe. They walk up and down the streets and nod to the people they see. Everyone knows who B is, and they call out to him and smile.

One day, B finds a battery-powered radio in a heap of rubble and brings it back to the house. At night they put the girls down, then turn on the radio and search for news, all of which is ominous. One city has been hit with an unknown sickness—the doctors gone, the food almost nonexistent. *Please, somebody help. We can't do this much longer.* A voice-over at another station complains of what they call *the greening*—the vines that crawl up to choke the buildings and the vegetation strangling the roads.

It's a fucking referendum OF THE TREES, people! This from a man who identifies himself only as Nate. *If you haven't noticed the way the trees are taking the world back, you haven't been paying attention! Hoard your matches! Don't be burned—make sure you DO THE BURNING!*

B doesn't like Nate. B doesn't really like the radio at all. Inevitably he is the one who goes to bed while Heather sits at the kitchen table with the volume low and searches for other voices.

Every night, B reaches for her when she finally comes to bed. His hand between her thighs and then his cock, his tears against her shoulder, his frustrated grunting in her ear. She looks out the window and up to the mountain. She does not make a sound.

"Where have you gone?" he whispers. "I feel like I'm fucking a ghost."

Once, when she is feeding the girls dinner from jars of mushy peas and puréed carrots they've hoarded down in the basement, B comes across a station that is playing cello music. The notes burst into the kitchen, mournful and dark. The girls stop fussing, instantly. The only music they've ever heard is their mother singing to them in the forest. She watches, transfixed, as their eyes register the sound, as they twist their heads around to find where it is. B watches them too. As the music becomes more urgent, they break into open-mouthed smiles, and then they are laughing with joy in a way they've never done, and suddenly Heather is laughing too, then crying, and B comes to her, gathering her into his arms as she sobs into his dirt-encrusted shirt.

"It's okay," he whispers. "Heather, we'll be okay." After the cello trails away, the girls stare at her, and then at B, uncertain.

That night she is the one who reaches for his cock, his face, his lips. She straddles him in the darkness of their bedroom and rocks in utter silence, the only sound the creaking of the mattress, B's laboured breaths.

He laughs as he comes inside of her, soft and incredulous.

In the days after this she often turns the radio on. She lets the girls roll around on the floor as she looks for the music again. She finds the cello once or twice, here and there a violin or trumpet. She never finds anyone singing.

She burns through one pair of batteries and then another, and then B takes the radio away.

"We have to make our supply of batteries last," he says. Even B has given up hope of someone coming to the rescue.

The next day, Heather goes to the strip mall, to where Annie is taking inventory in the clinic, which is filled with tired mothers and sniffling children. Tasha is nowhere to be found.

"Batteries," Heather says by way of hello. "I want more batteries, Annie."

"Everyone wants batteries," Annie says, not looking up. She is border-line skeletal now, as they all are.

"I just want a couple," Heather says. "I won't tell anyone."

Annie laughs. "A secret like all the other secrets you're keeping?"

Heather blinks. "I'm not keeping any secrets."

Annie snorts. "Sure. Sneaking off to that greenhouse by the mountain is what, exactly?"

Inside of her, a sudden bloom of irrational betrayal. "How do you know about the greenhouse?" She knows the greenhouse does not belong to her. Tasha can talk about it with anyone.

Annie rolls her eyes. "You're not the only person sneaking away from work, it would seem."

"I have children to take care of—"

"And I have an entire *city* to take care of!" Annie slams her palm down on the counter. "Do you care about that? Does Tasha?"

"Annie, I don't know what you're talking about."

"I *know* you go to the greenhouse," Annie hisses. "I know that Tasha goes there too."

"Tasha?" Heather asks, now thoroughly confused. "Alone?"

"Everyone is working so hard," Annie says. "Tasha most of all. She won't sleep, I can barely get her to eat—but she disappears into the forest and goes to a fucking *greenhouse?* For what—so she can pick some fuck-ing flowers that no one can eat?"

"Maybe she just needs some time alone," Heather says.

"*Well that's too bad!*"

Heather and all the people in the clinic stiffen in shock.

Annie flushes, shakes her head. "Come with me," she mutters to Heather. She leads her into the back of the clinic, but then stops and uses the keys at her belt to let them into a small room, a tiny space with a window that faces west. When Heather follows her in, Annie closes the door behind them. The walls are stacked to the ceiling with shelves, which are full of boxes and bundles and who knows what else. Annie turns to face her.

"Why do you go to the greenhouse?" she says. "Why does Tasha?"

"I don't know why Tasha goes," Heather says. "But it reminds *me* of my dad—he's the one who built it."

"You know *something*," Annie presses. "I see the way that Tasha looks at you."

"Look, Annie—why don't you ask her?"

"I do, but she doesn't tell me." Something in her flat tone reminds Heather of B. "She acts like we're meant to be here when we could just as easily go anywhere else." She reaches up, yanks a box down from a high shelf. "I was there for her," she says. "The whole goddamned time after her parents died. She wouldn't have gotten out of bed if it hadn't been for me. I didn't complain. I didn't say anything. Because I *love* her." She stares at the box in her hands. "I thought about leaving her. A hundred times. But that's not what you do, is it—not when things get bad. And now the world *actually falls apart* and where is she? Playing the lone saviour and taking off whenever she can to a fucking greenhouse?" She swipes an angry fist across her forehead and fixes her gaze on Heather again. "Why do the people here talk about you?"

Heather clears her throat. "The batteries, Annie?"

"Is it the mountain? Everyone says that no one has been up there except for you. What's the big fucking secret?"

"My father died on the mountain," Heather says. "After he fell, the city made it a law that no one could climb the mountain."

"You went up with him?" *You,* her face says. *You, with your twisted feet?*

Heather nods.

"Why?"

"I wanted him to believe that I was strong, that I could keep up with him. It was the only thing he wanted for me."

"So what's the big deal? What's up there?"

"Nothing, Annie. Nothing is up there."

"Then why do people keep talking about it? What did he do—jump?" As soon as the words are out of her mouth, Annie freezes, a look of horror on her face. She won't meet Heather's eyes, and begins to fumble through the box, then grabs a small package of batteries and holds it out to Heather.

"He fell," Heather says, not taking her eyes from Annie's face. "He didn't jump."

Annie nods. "I'm sorry," she whispers. When Heather takes the batteries, Annie moves past her, head down, and goes out the door.

Alone in the closet, Heather stares around her at all the boxes. She shoves the batteries in her pocket and reaches for another box on the shelves.

"You shouldn't be in here," a voice says. When Heather spins around, she sees Elyse, pale and thin in the doorway, breathing hard.

"Annie let me in."

Elyse shrugs. "You shouldn't be here now," she says. "All of this is private."

"Private?"

"We don't know what the winter will bring," Elyse says. "We all need to go without so that everyone can have a little. Annie and Tasha know what they're doing."

"No one knows what they're doing," Heather says. She brushes past Elyse, doesn't wait for an answer.

The next day, after B leaves in the morning, she finds where he stashed the radio and plays it once more for the girls. The cello music bursts forth from the speaker as if by magic. Their smiles are bright, their laughter uncontrolled.

The town that had the sickness does not broadcast anymore.

✳

When the last pair of batteries dies, she walks the girls in the forest more. They are five months old now, and she works to carry both of them. Their eyes are now bright and curious, ready to take in everything around them. Ravenous monsters. They reach out for the trees and brush their tiny hands across the bark; they reach forward to the deep-orange flowers that twine through and hang down from some of the trunks. She's never seen these orange flowers before. She guides their hands away.

Everything in the forest now feels poisonous to her, even the plants that she knows. Still, she walks. She tamps down the tangled grass and roots and holds her hands out to brush the branches away. They reach the field with the sunflowers—husks now, disrobing for winter. They walk across the field and into the forest on the other side and eventually reach the greenhouse.

She opens the door and the smells spill out. The orchids, the lilies, the jacaranda tall and blue in the middle of it all. The air in the greenhouse still feels hot and heavy, waiting for what, she doesn't know.

The amaryllis bob at her, fiery red and sweet. The girls reach out their hands.

She is twelve years old and she and her father are going up the mountain to celebrate her birthday. It is a secret—no one knows, not even her mother. Her mother thinks they are going into town to see the flowers Heather's father has planted in the square, and then to a movie and dinner. A father-daughter date.

"Have fun!" her mother calls, and waves to them both from the door. They walk to the end of the street and turn left as though they are heading downtown. Then they double back along the street parallel to theirs and make their way to the base of the mountain.

Everyone has heard the stories, but Heather's father isn't afraid.

"Who died?" he has often said to his wife and daughter. "No one knows *anyone* who has actually been up here. I'm the only one who's even been close to the mountain in years."

"People have disappeared," her mother always says. "You know they have."

"But who?" The last time he asks that, they are in the kitchen after dinner, washing dishes. Heather is supposed to be taking a bath, but she has crept back along the hallway and stands listening by the kitchen door. Her father reaches for her mother's hand and strokes it. "We'll be fine. I found a path—it's man-made, you can tell. I've been smoothing it out these past few months, making it ready for Heather. The incline isn't that steep. It'll be just like walking the hills in the park."

"You can't *seriously* be thinking of taking her up with you."

"Of course I'm serious," her father says. He catches sight of Heather, peeking around the kitchen door, and smiles. "Heather is stronger than you know. The climb will be *good for her*—it's good for her to touch the world. You don't want her to grow? To overcome her fears?"

"I want her to be who she is!" Her mother's voice rings out in the small room and Heather flinches, shocked. More quietly, her mother says, "I don't want her to climb the mountain just to prove something to you." She notices where her husband is looking, and turns to see Heather now standing in the doorway.

Her father says, "Heather, do you want to go up?"

Of course she wants to go up. She nods. She expects her mother to object again, but she only sighs and goes back to her dishes.

The next day, she forbids them to go.

The day after that is Heather's birthday.

On their way to the mountain, they stop at the greenhouse and check the plants. They cross the field and plunge into the trees again.

"The trees are coming closer!" her father says. She gets the feeling that he says this every time to himself—a private joke, a long-held wish. She knows how badly he misses being among the mountain trees.

At the foot of the mountain, they find the path. It is just as he described—old and somehow new, ready for her. The slope seems to go on forever, a long stretch of green eventually lost in the clouds.

"Why don't we live on the mountain if you love it so much?" she asks.

"Your mother wouldn't like it." He smiles as he says it so she knows he isn't mad at his wife. "She thinks it's better for us to be in the city. She doesn't like the stories. She used to, but she doesn't like them anymore."

"She can probably climb better than I can."

"You climb just fine, Heather-Feather," he says.

"But what if I fall?" she whispers.

"You won't fall," he says.

She wants to believe him; she wants to show him that she can. But the climb is difficult. As they go higher, the drop at the edge of the path calls her like a song. She fights to concentrate: one foot down, and then another. Her legs shake, but on she goes. She is surprised to see tropical flowers blooming off the mountainside, but her father just behaves as though he'd known all along they would be here.

He sings as they climb higher—little ditties to make her giggle. More flowers appear; she breathes in the scent of them, feels her lungs expand with mountain air. She lets go of her fear, just a little.

"That's it, Heather-Feather," he says. His smile is so lovely it makes her want to cry. "I knew you could do it. I knew it."

Her legs hurt, but it's a good kind of pain. She wants to drink from the mountain streams. Or cut her palm and mark the stones with her blood. Here, her father isn't eccentric, and she is no longer strange—instead they are magic, instead they belong.

This is what he meant, she thinks. *The magic of things that are possible.* Her chest expands with sunlight, with hope. *I'm climbing,* she thinks. And still they go higher. *I'm above the clouds.*

They stop for lunch, perched on rocks that line the path, red amaryllis around them. Her father pops a cherry tomato whole into his mouth and she laughs; the sound echoes.

He grins. "How's your leg, Heather-Feather? I told you you could do it. See how strong you are?"

As she opens her mouth to reply, she sees a sudden flash of blonde in the trees behind him.

✳

They stay at the greenhouse until the girls begin to fuss. These days it doesn't take long—they want to *move,* her girls, they want to see and feel and taste the world. To put it in their mouths.

She opens the door and, just before they leave, she turns back. She stands in the doorway with a hand on each of their bright heads and closes her eyes. She feels her legs rooted firmly, feels the vines whisper around her ankles, feels the way the ground slopes ever so slightly upward here, reaching for the sky. The air smells of flowers, but it is fevered by the city's grief and despair. She lets herself think of it—that long moment when her father lost his footing on the path, that even longer instant when he was falling backward, his eyes and face alive with terror. The chasm of grief that cracked open inside her.

She waits for the air to change—to smell of starlight, to carry to her the deep, wild musk of the mountain. It doesn't come. He never comes. She walks in the forest every day, and every day the answer is the same.

The girls whimper, which saves her. She opens her eyes and stumbles; she was *leaning* into the greenhouse, into that old despair. She clears her throat and wraps her arms around the girls, then turns to make her way back to the city. To find the blonde girl, Elyse, standing there.

"Jesus," Heather says. "You couldn't say hello?"

"Sorry," Elyse says. She doesn't sound it.

Heather clears her throat. "What are you doing here?"

Elyse shrugs. "I heard there was a trail."

"Did you follow me?"

Elyse doesn't meet her eyes.

"It's a greenhouse," Heather says, pausing on each word for emphasis. "What's the big fucking deal?"

"Nothing," Elyse says, quickly. "There's no big deal."

Heather rolls her eyes. She moves forward past Elyse; after a moment, the blonde girl comes after her. "Aren't you afraid, out here all alone?"

Heather can't help but laugh. "I've spent my whole life alone," she says. "It feels normal to me."

Keeping pace with them, in the trees, is an orange-grey blur of fur and tail. Elyse does not notice. The fox follows them all the way back to the city; Heather concentrates on putting one foot in front of the other and pretends the fox isn't there.

＊

Her father is singing when the creature steps out from the trees. A palomino, though Heather won't know that word until much later. Golden hair and blue-green eyes and sleek and muscled arms, a golden cuff that shines softly on her wrist. The body of a woman, the strong chest and legs of a horse. The creature takes another step, and then another, until she stands in front of them. She looks young but also old, as though she's been on the mountain forever. Her small breasts are bare.

Heather's own breasts are larger, even at twelve, and her arms instinctively go up to hide their roundness.

"Hello," her father breathes. The tone of his voice makes Heather think of church.

"Hello," the creature breathes back. She sounds excited but also afraid. Her voice is sweet and clear and strange. Heather feels frightened but also electric—*The stories*, she thinks. *The stories are true.* She glances at her father and she can tell he's thinking the same thing. He gets up from the rock and takes several small careful steps forward, then reaches out and puts a hand around the creature's wrist.

"What are you?" her father asks.

The creature blinks. "I am . . . a centaur," she says.

"Centaur," he repeats. Then he nods. "Help us," he says. "Help my daughter."

The shock of his words is like slimy ice in her veins. Her father turns to her and smiles reassuringly, reaches for her with his other hand. "You made it all this way, Heather-Feather," he says. "Now just think what you'll be able to do when your legs don't hurt anymore."

The creature tries to pull her hand away, but her father won't let go. The ground around them rumbles, shakes.

It *breathes*, Heather realizes. The mountain is *breathing*.

"Please," he whispers to the creature. "I know you can heal her. We've come all this way."

The creature jerks her hand away so fiercely her father stumbles backward, his foot catching on a rock. Everything happens so quickly.

The other creature, the dark-haired one, reaches out for her father from the trees, but he misses, and her father falls.

✳

It is cold now in the city, late autumn, and still the wild things grow. The city sinks in green. In the mornings the survivors line up at the strip mall for rations. One packet of oatmeal per person, one capsule of vitamin C. A handful of shrivelled, mushy beets, of tiny green tomatoes. The people in front of and behind Heather in line grumble but she doesn't complain. Joseph might bring them eggs today. He likes the babies.

She drops the groceries at home and walks the girls to the forest edge and back, over and over. *Rapunzel, Rapunzel, let down your long hair.* She lays them on the forest floor and rests with her back against a tree while she continues the story—the prince who scales Rapunzel's tower and makes love to her, secretly, in the dead of night. Rapunzel's own twins, growing in her belly, giving her away.

"The witch discovered them and took Rapunzel away to a desolate land," she says. "In despair, the prince threw himself from the tower. He landed among thorns, which blinded him, and he wandered the land, lost, for years."

They laugh at the way she tells this story, stretching her arms above her head to show the tower.

Despair hits her, and she imagines their faces as she leaves them for the fox, for the wolves. For other creatures that might come and take them away.

Their tiny bodies in the air as she flings them off the mountainside. As she flings herself off the mountainside.

She holds them close and breathes them in. "But she found him," she whispers. She buries her face in their sweet skin. "She found him, years later, and her tears made him see."

✳

After her father fell, she told the doctors and her mother about the mountain—the way they climbed, the way they stopped, the way the mountain breathed, the way she'd understood almost instantly that the mountain didn't want them there.

I felt it, she said. *I felt the mountain come alive.* No one believed her. They thought her father had jumped.

She was recovering from trauma, the doctors said. She'd just seen her father die. (On that, it seemed, everyone was agreed.) It wasn't unusual for people recovering from trauma to say strange things.

"Her world does not make sense right now," the doctors told her mother. *Reactive psychosis,* caused by grief and stress. It would pass. "Give her time to heal."

Instead Heather shut her mouth and refused to say anything else. Through the search partway up the mountain, before the team had to turn back in defeat because of bad weather; as people put on bright-orange jackets and walked through the mountain trees for hours, calling her father's name. Maybe he was lying crumpled on the ground somewhere and couldn't get up. Maybe he had crawled until he couldn't crawl anymore and was too weak to answer when they yelled for him.

They came back to her with more questions.

Did he really fall?

Nod.

Did you see it?

Nod.

Heather. Are you sure *he didn't jump?*

Shake of the head.

What happened?

Silence. There was nothing she could say.

After the search teams gave up, the city council passed a law to ban people from the mountain. They let the fields leading to the mountain grow wild, allowed the forest to creep in.

Her mother held a funeral but Heather didn't go. How could they bury her father when there was no body? It made no sense.

None of it made any sense.

"Why won't you *talk* to me?" her mother said when Heather was home from the hospital, but Heather couldn't—or wouldn't—answer.

Her mother packed his clothes away and carried them to the basement. When Heather found the boxes, she brought them to her room.

The house seemed so much larger without her father inside of it. The walls echoed with the absence of story.

People stared at Heather wherever she went. Rumours and whispers grew. He jumped. He was angry, and sad, and he jumped. The wolves on the mountain found his body. There wasn't even a scrap of clothing left.

Eventually her mother started to tell stories too. He was charismatic and intoxicating, and she'd fallen so deeply in love, but he was also unstable and sad. He jumped. Of course he did. She should have known, she should have *said something*, but she wanted so badly to believe it wasn't true. She'd loved him; she had hoped that would be enough. It wasn't. It never had been.

"Heather is my worry now," she would say to the friends who sat up with her when everyone thought that Heather had gone to sleep. "She's so much like her father. I can't lose them both."

Was she like her father? Heather wondered. Probably. He hadn't jumped. She wouldn't jump, not even in the midst of all this hurt. But there had been magic in her life when her father was alive, and now it was all gone. No more walks under the stars, no more journeys up the mountain.

"I can't believe he took you," her mother said, over and over. "What if something had happened to you, too?"

Help us, he had said to the creature. *I know you can heal her.*

So she hadn't been perfect, or strong. Not really. Not enough.

She had nightmares for months. She twisted so violently in bed she started sleeping without sheets. Her father, there and gone. His hand reaching and just missing the centaur's fingers.

Just think what you'll be able to do when your legs don't hurt anymore. Because climbing halfway up a mountain hadn't been good enough, hadn't ever been good enough, no matter what he had said.

That long, tumbled run down the mountain—her face buried in the centaur's neck, his arms firm around her, one hand cradling her head.

No one else walks like you, Heather-Feather. That's something to be proud of. Until it wasn't. Until he'd wanted her to walk like everyone else.

The silence inside of her built like a wall. The doctors and counsellors couldn't get past it. Her mother couldn't get past it. At night, she crept out of the house and took long walks through the fields, keeping close to the tree-bordered edges so that no one could see her. Close to the mountain, then closer still. To her father's greenhouse, now filled with weeds and dead things.

See, Heather-Feather. See how strong you are?

The anniversary of her father's death dawned fresh and bright—the spring sun warm, the air still cool. She floated, silent, through the day. Three hundred and sixty-five days. How many more would they live without him?

In the evening, outside her window, the sudden smell of mountain flowers. She scrambled out of bed and pushed the window open. A shape, just there, hidden by the trees that lined the back of the yard. She shimmied awkwardly out the window, jumped to the ground. She wanted to weep, but couldn't. Tall, dark shape against trees and sky. He came to her and dropped something at her feet—the knapsack. It still smelled of her father, even after all these months. The moonlight glinted on a golden cuff around his wrist. He was a tall mass against the shadowed trees, all wild hair and dark wiry arms. She hardly even noticed the flowers.

"You," she said. "It's you."

✳

Sometimes when the girls and B are asleep she slips out of the house and stands silent on the overgrown street. She smells the grass, the night air, the thick stench of the city. Everything smells now, even in fall.

Everything tastes of despair.

She walks back to the house and goes inside. As she pads softly down the hall, the girls do not wake. She slips into the bedroom, slides in beside B.

She is almost asleep when he asks, "Where did you go?"

"Just outside, onto the street."

A long pause. "You shouldn't go out at night alone."

"It really wasn't far, B."

"You were gone for a long time. Next time, wake me up so I can go with you."

"I don't need you to go with me."

The anger in his voice is dark and surprising. "You're always going, that's the point."

She doesn't answer, just lies silent beside him and imagines one long running leap out the window, a flight up the street, into the forest, through the trees. Up the long slope of the mountain, the air thin in her lungs. She steps out of her skin and deep into its dirt, and then she is no more.

The girls grow bigger and more restless by the day. She walks to the strip mall to retrieve her ration of oatmeal, she cooks eggs given to them by Joseph over their backyard fire. Tasha sends people out to hunt. B joins with some of the other men—Kevin and Alan, and Annie goes too. They take hunting rifles into the forest, bring back what they can. A deer they butcher in the old town square, squirrels they skin and roast over backyard fires.

The Council, people have begun to call Tasha and the rest. *The Council will know what to do.*

Heather hardly pays attention. She changes the girls and throws the dirty diapers into the ravines that line some trails along her mountain walks. She sets buckets out to collect water whenever it rains and boils it in their backyard firepit to make sure it's safe to drink. She walks the girls beneath the sky. She whispers his name until her throat hurts.

He does not come for her.

She is walking by the greenhouse when nausea creeps up and then explodes, a heavy crampish feeling that does not go away. Her breasts hurt. Her whole body feels swollen.

She is so tired. She stops and lets the girls down on the forest floor and smiles, with effort, as they reach for her.

She's known for a while what's been happening to her—the subtle but unmistakable changes in her body, the unrelenting fatigue. *You're starving*, she told herself. *That's all it is. You're starving, you're unwell. You should go see Tasha, and see if she can give you something for despair.*

But what kind of medication is there for this level of sadness? So one day passed and then another, and she did not go to Tasha, she did not go to Annie, and now she is here, in front of the greenhouse, the girls laid out on the ground in front of her as another life blooms inside her.

She sobs aloud, then catches her breath. Colours swim—bright-red flowers that cover the greenhouse, dark, husky berries that sway up from the ground. She leans her forehead against the cool glass of the greenhouse and closes her eyes, reminded of her father. Soon the snow will come in earnest and bury them all.

She doesn't want to bring another child into this mess. She doesn't want to die, frozen and starving.

She picks some berries and brings them to her mouth. *Belladonna.* Belladonna, oleander, poison oak in the shade beyond the greenhouse. Her father had loved poisonous plants the best.

The babies coo; she barely hears them. The berries won't kill her, just make her sick, and maybe that will do the rest. Her father was right, all those years ago. She isn't strong enough. She never was. The world smells of amaryllis and lilies and orchids and the jacaranda tree and the sweetness of the berries in her hand and then something else. A sudden dark shadow comes toward her, rippling the leaves. A shape that smells of mountain and snow and crystalline air but also of sunlight and flowers, of animal and darkness.

"You," she says, as he comes out from the trees. "It's you."

*

After he brought the knapsack, the centaur returned to her night after night. She snuck out after her mother was asleep. Out the back door and into the trees. If her mother suspected anything, she didn't ask. Or she didn't want to know.

Instead of flowers, Estajfan brought her stories. They walked through the silent fields and the cicadas stopped to listen. The crickets went still, like they knew him.

He told her about the time that he and his brother—Petrolio, the name like a flower on the tongue—ran down the mountain so fast they almost fell. The rage that their father had been in when they'd returned—how he'd yelled at them, how he'd wept. How he'd been so sure they'd been killed.

Don't go down the mountain, his father had said, and they raced each other anyway.

Estajfan told her about the other centaurs—how they'd grown from his father's bones, how they'd pulled themselves out of the earth. They had no names, he said, because they didn't need any. He told her fairy tales she hadn't heard before—stories about octopuses who guard treasure in the deeps, mountain deer who kidnap and raise a human child. Fairies who lived in the salt mines beneath the mountains, long ago, who coated themselves in salt crystals before mating. That one sounded familiar—an old wives' tale her father once told her, about elders who threw salt across a doorway to ask good things into a woman's life.

"Stories are never just stories," her father had said. "There's always a kernel of truth hidden deep within the words."

In turn, she told Estajfan about walking late at night. About the twelve dancing princesses, the goose girl, the queen. She talked through the silence that surrounded her, her words like a knife, cutting a web that had grown thick and hard.

She entered ninth grade with no friends except the one she met late at night. She read fairy tales at lunch and drew dragons in her notebook.

Dragons, Estajfan told her, had lived on the mountain long ago. They'd disappeared before the horses were there.

"Were they dinosaurs?" she asked him.

"I'm not sure," he said. He knew many things and yet often seemed like a child—fascinated with mundane human objects like combination locks, a cafeteria tray heaped with food, the money humans passed to one another.

She brought him things for his collection—picture frames, a baseball glove. Her first job was at a bookstore and instead of saving her wages for college she bought paint and pencil crayons and thick sheets of creamy paper and passed them to him in the dark. "So you can draw, if you want to."

"Draw?" he said.

She showed him what she meant—spreading the paper on the ground, the moon just strong enough to show the pencil lines. Four legs, two arms, a tangle of hair in dreads. He smiled when she finished.

"Is that me?" he said.

She was suddenly too shy to say yes, so she just shrugged. "I'm guessing you all look the same," she said, and he laughed.

"Mostly we do." He took the pencils, the paper, and the drawing with him up the mountain.

The years went by. She graduated high school and decided not to go to college after all, telling herself that she didn't want to leave her mother alone. It was mostly true. She got a full-time job at the bookstore, and started to send out her illustrations. Bears with long teeth. Unicorns and strange birds. Dark forests with shadowed beasts among the trees. Her illustrations began to be published. She illustrated a picture book, and then a volume of fables. She stopped working at the bookstore, and moved into her own apartment. She walked the trails up to the mountain in the dusk to meet Estajfan. Every birthday he brought her flowers, which bloomed in her windows for months. Fifteen years went by like that.

She drew centaurs, over and over. She drew her father falling, his face rigid with terror. Estajfan's fingers just missing his. Her father's broken, mangled body somewhere down far below. No one saw those.

She drew herself, a wide-eyed twelve-year-old, one leg shorter than the other, her feet twisted and bent. Her mouth open in a silent scream.

She drew herself now. Her father's eyes, her father's smile. The uneven legs and lopsided shoulders that were entirely her own.

Once upon a time there was a father and daughter who went up a mountain together, and only one person came down.

One night she showed Estjafan these pictures. He was gentle with them. When he looked at her afterwards, there was something in his face that made her ribcage tighten.

"Could I keep these, too?" he asked. She wanted to say no, but she nodded.

"Did you ever find him?" she asked.

"I didn't look," he said. "Heather, I'm sorry."

Everything went hot and blurry. "You didn't try to find him? You just left him to rot?"

"I didn't want to see it," he admitted. "I didn't want to remember what I'd done to you."

"It was an accident."

In the dark, she saw him swallow. "When I reached for him, I—I hesitated."

The world skittered in and out of focus. "For how long?" she said, finally.

"I don't know," he whispered. "He was already falling."

She closed her eyes. "Why did you hesitate?"

"You weren't supposed to be there," he said. "Neither of you. He touched Aura like he had a right to do it. Like we were . . . property." A long pause. "And what he said—I saw your face. I saw what that did to you."

She swallowed. "He deserved to die for that?"

His eyes were dark, bottomless pools. "I'll spend the rest of my life being sorry."

She tried not to imagine it, but the thoughts came anyway. The animals that had nibbled on his flesh. The maggots that ate his eyes. Had he died right away? Or had death come later, in the dark?

"He deserved somewhere to rest," she said. "He deserved at least that much."

Estajfan took her wrist and she jumped. It was the first time he had touched her since he carried her down the mountain. "I don't think I should come to see you anymore."

"Why did you come in the first place?"

A long pause. "I didn't know why," he admitted. "And then I did."

What was it that he'd said years before? Humans are like the brightness of comets in the sky. She was thirty-seven years old—older than her father had been when he died. Time was going so quickly. Time was not going at all.

She held fast to his hand. "Don't go," she said.

"Heather," he said.

He so rarely said her name.

✳

It's the first time she's seen him in the daylight in years. She's forgotten how big he is, how magical. A story made flesh.

"Heather," Estajfan says. They stand together in the forest, near the greenhouse. The weak sunlight glints on the golden cuff on his arm. The girls lie gurgling on the forest floor between them. It is warmer than any November she remembers. "I won't let you starve."

He's brought her a small sack of things—cherries, nuts, and apples.

She closes her eyes and lets the nightshade berries drop onto the ground. "And what about another baby?" she asks. "You're going to feed us all? See us through the winter, when snow buries everyone in the city?"

"I'll find a way," he says. "I promise."

I promise. He had promised to stay on the mountain. He had promised to leave her alone.

"I don't think we should do this anymore," she had said just over a year ago. Two pink lines on a pregnancy test, dinner with B in the immediate future. "I need to live my real life."

He had nodded, had accepted it all without question.

Now he is here again, in front of her.

Everything has changed.

"What am I supposed to do?" she says. Half to him, half to some-body—anybody—else. The girls start to fuss. "How am I supposed to have a baby? I'm barely eating enough as it is to feed myself and the girls."

"I'll bring you more food. Things are still growing on the mountain."

She stares at him. "Why are things still growing on the mountain if they aren't growing in the gardens? Or the greenhouses?"

He looks at her, but doesn't speak.

"Estajfan."

"I don't know," he says, carefully. "I can guess, but I'm not sure."

"Well—*guess*, please."

"Haven't you already guessed for yourself?"

You are not meant for the mountain. Perhaps humans are not meant for the world now either. She takes a deep breath. "So—what—the *world* is starving us now? There's nothing we can do?"

"There are always things we can do," he says. "I will not let you starve."

"Stop saying that!"

He is taken aback, hurt. "What else do you want me to say?"

"I asked you to go *and you went.* I walked these forests for *months* after the meteors came, waiting for you to come back, and you never did. Not once."

"I came." His voice is almost a whisper. "I came every day. I watched you through the trees. But you had your husband. Your girls. Your *real* life."

"Well. The world got in the way of that, too, I guess." She bends and picks up Greta, puts her in her sling, and then does the same for Jilly. "You won't be able to feed us forever. Even I know that."

"Maybe not forever," he says. "But maybe for now is enough."

She would laugh, but she's too tired. "Humans don't live in the *now*, Estajfan."

He bends and snips a lily from the greenhouse, then reaches forward and tucks it behind her ear. "Then maybe," he says carefully, "I'm glad I'm not human."

*

It isn't easy, carrying the girls and the sack of fruit back from the forest, but she manages. The fox follows her and she pays it no attention. No one sees her slip into the house and put the food away. But B discovers it all later that evening, as she plays with the girls in the dark living room.

"What's this?" When she looks up at him, she sees that he's holding an apple in each hand. "Where the fuck did this come from?"

"I found it in the forest," she says.

She doesn't expect him to believe her. She is not wrong. "Oh sure. Apples and cherries. Just lying on the ground?"

"I found the sack," she says. "Maybe someone left it there?"

He looks at her, scoffs. "Do you think I'm a moron? A fucking idiot?"

She flinches, thinking of the children who mocked her at school. *Moron. Idiot. Fucking spaz.*

B stops and looks at her—*really* looks at her. He is gone with Tasha and Annie every day now, preparing for the winter. He is so thin. "If I find out that you've been fucking someone else off in the forest—"

She throws the first thing she grabs—a paperweight they keep on the living room table. It catches him on the side of the head with an audible *thump,* then shatters on the floor. He stares at her with horrified surprise, a hand to his head.

The silence around them is thick for a moment, and then the girls burst into tears.

"I am doing the best that I can," she says over their cries. "Would you rather I went and threw myself off the mountain?"

Something flickers over his face—shame, maybe, but warring with anger and pain. Blood trickles from his temple. "I don't know what to say to you," he says. "I feel like I don't know you at all."

"I don't know myself anymore," she admits. They stand like this—frozen, not reaching out—until B looks down and notices the broken glass.

"I'll clean that up," he mumbles, and turns toward the kitchen.

"I'm pregnant," she says. As he slowly pivots to face her, she thinks back to when she told him about the girls—that awkward dinner, the fear and joy that leapt into his face. Another universe long, long ago.

There is no joy this time. B closes his eyes, then nods.

She says, "I don't know where that sack came from. But I don't care—I'll take it. We don't have enough food."

He opens his eyes and looks, for the smallest of instants, like the man that she married. "We'll find a way," he says. Then he turns for the kitchen.

She soothes the girls while he sweeps up the glass. By the time he comes back from dumping the shards outside, they are already tucked in their crib. He climbs onto the bed behind Heather and puts an arm around her.

"If none of this had happened," he says, "where do you think we'd be now?" A peace offering.

Where, indeed. Their old apartment, their old jobs, taking the girls to daycare, maybe the park. He'd worked with computers; his office had been a twenty-minute walk from their apartment. Before the girls were born, they had walked to his office in the mornings and stopped by a coffee shop on the way—latte for B, iced raspberry tea for her. In the latter stages of her pregnancy she'd been obsessed with the iced teas from that store.

"Please don't go up the mountain, or away," he whispers. "We can't survive without you."

She squeezes his arm, and says nothing.

The next morning, someone finds a sack of apples on the other side of the city, and two bags of flour and rice appear as if by magic on the doorsteps of the strip mall.

B does not ask her any more questions.

THE RIVER SPRITE

Once upon a time there were twin babies born to a woodcutter and his wife. Their mother planted herbs and kept a garden, and sometimes the neighbours from their village would come to her for medicines—tinctures to help them sleep, a salve to soothe the itchy red spots that came from mistakenly touching one of a hundred different plants in the forest.

The birth of the children also brought the mother a great sadness, and she had no balms to treat it. She had heard about this sadness and had hoped to avoid it by being prepared; she and her husband covered their lintel in birch sap, buried stones from the river at every corner of their house. Before the twins came—two girls, their hair bright like fire and their smiles just as holy—the mother made sure to go for daily walks along the river.

"The water will carry you," the river said. "Come back to the water every day and let your sadness float away on the waves."

After the girls were born, the mother went to the river, ready to give her sadness away, and instead fought the urge to throw her daughters into the water. She knew the girls belonged to her but somehow did not feel it. They were demanding and greedy, all primal emotions. Try as she might, she couldn't see herself in their tiny faces. Everything about them seemed alien, strange.

The river, to her surprise, told her that this was normal. She had given birth to changelings. When the mother consulted the old river sprite who lived beneath the waterfall, the sprite said much the same.

"You have been given children by the fairies," the sprite said. "See how pale they are? See how they scream when you yourself have always been so gentle? These children might look like you, but they are not *of* you. *This* is why you don't feel like yourself. These children belong with the fairies, and the fairies will come to take them soon enough."

"But if I have changeling children, where are the baby girls who belong to me?"

"The mountain fairies stole them," the river sprite told her. "You must ask the mountain fairies to bring your children back. Take these changelings into the forest and leave them on the forest floor. Turn in three circles and say *Give me my children*. If the fairies do not appear, take the children home and try it again the next morning."

The woman did this, but her babies did not appear, and so she took her changeling children home and put them to bed as if they were her own. The next day, she did it all again, to no avail. When she did it for the third time, she cried aloud into the forest air and begged the fairies to listen.

"I miss my babies!" she said. "I will not be whole unless you give them back to me."

The forest was silent; the forest said nothing.

In frustration and despair, the woman turned from the two babies on the ground and left the forest. When she had gone beyond the trees, three mountain fairies—one red-haired, one brown-haired, one with hair black as night—crept out from the trees and reached out for the babies.

"Come with us," they said. "We've been waiting for you. We'll give you halls full of golden toys and warm fires to lay by, and so many good things to eat."

The babies were cold and defeated by the rumbling of their stomachs. They held out their hands and the fairies scooped them away.

When the mother suffered deep regret and came back to find them, it was as if the twins had never been.

E stajfan is tired of watching the humans starve, tired of the city's dark
stink, tired of the despair that hangs around the buildings. The despair
that sits in Heather's bones—the slope of her shoulders, the lines on her
face. He is tired of it all.

But he is also tired of the mountain and its unrelenting calm—the
carelessness of the mountain centaurs, the cagey silence of his sister.
Petrolio's indifference.

People are starving! Estajfan wants to scream, over and over. *These
people are going to die!*

But he doesn't say this because he knows that no one cares. Not the
mountain centaurs, not the mountain, not even his siblings. Deer are
being hunted in the daylight; squirrels are being roasted over human
fires. The animals that live amongst the mountain trees are longing for
humans to perish.

The humans dwindle, weaken, disappear.

At last his brother offers to come down off the mountain with him—
to walk through abandoned human streets, to peer hidden in the trees
and see them starving. Petrolio comes to him after he has begun to drop

food at different points around the city. It isn't worry for the humans that brings Petrolio down from the mountain. It is worry for him.

Petrolio meets him on the mountain trail one morning, his blue-green eyes unsettled and searching. "Are you eating?"

Estajfan laughs. "*I'm* eating," he says. "*They* are starving to death. Like I've said a hundred times already."

Petrolio grasps his arm. "Estajfan—they're only humans."

He pulls away. "Does that mean they deserve to starve?"

"Humans had their chance," Petrolio says. This is what the mountain centaurs say. *Humans had their chance. Humans are a disease on the land. Humans no longer deserve to be here.*

"Heather is different," Estajfan says fiercely. "Heather is not like the rest."

"Estajfan," Petrolio says softly, "all of them are the same."

"How would you know?" He points a finger in his brother's face. "I don't see *you* off the mountain, do I. And yet you're perfectly happy to ogle that mirror when you think no one's looking."

Petrolio flushes. "Da told us all we needed to know," he says. "You know what they did to him. You know what they would have done to *us*."

Estajfan refuses to believe it. "Da also told us other stories. *He* went back down the mountain. *He* went into human cities. *He went back to our village.* Why would he do that if he hated them so much?"

"Why do you want to help them so badly?"

"Why do I need a reason? They need help. We can give it."

"If the ground magic is killing their gardens," Petrolio says, "how much do you think we can do?"

"I don't know," Estajfan admits. "But I can try. *We* can try."

"And if trying makes no difference?" Petrolio's voice is soft. "We go down and bring them food and try to help and still they starve? What happens then?"

You have a choice to make, Fox had said. *The world is no longer a place for in-between things.*

"At least we'll know we tried."

Petrolio watches him for a long moment, then sighs. "I'll help," he says. "Tell me what to do, and I'll go down with you. But honestly, Estajfan—I don't know what good it will do."

"It will keep them alive a while longer," Estajfan says. "Right now that should be good enough for all of us."

He hears the words as clearly as if Heather speaks them straight into his ear. *Right now, Estajfan, isn't going to last forever.*

In the dark early hours of the morning they run down the mountain like they did when they were young and then they run past the city, farther than Petrolio has ever gone. Day after day after day, they run through the foothills and into the flatlands. They run past buildings grown over with vines, abandoned cars like small green hills that rise up where the roads used to be. They go into abandoned cities and search the buildings for cans of food, sacks of rice and flour.

They drop what they find at different points throughout the mountain city. A bag of rice at the end of one street, a sack of apples gathered from the mountain trees at the end of another. Nuts and cherries, figs and pears. Estajfan is careful to be random, careful to avoid extra attention falling on Heather. Still, she pulls him into her orbit. He makes sure she has enough.

They travel under cover of the trees, under cover of the darkness, and the vines that grow over the ground muffle their footsteps. Yet, every time they run through the city, he waits for someone to jump out and see them. No one does.

They run through other cities; they take all that they can.

He finds her in the forest, walking with the girls. Every now and then she checks the sky and he knows she is thinking of snow—when it will come, *if* it will come, what will happen when it does. When he asks her how they are all doing, she only shrugs and looks resigned. "We might survive the winter. We might not."

"You *will*," he says.

But Heather looks away. "No one has come to help," she says. She blows gently over the faces of the twins, plays patty cake with their grasping hands. "We have hardly any gas left. There is no way to plow the roads and by the middle of the winter people will be too weak to shovel."

"We are bringing as much food as we can," he says. He doesn't tell her that they run later into the morning now and there are hardly ever humans around to see them.

"We?" she says.

"Petrolio," he tells her.

Heather takes this in. "And Aura?"

"Aura will not come down," he says.

She nods. "She's still afraid. I understand that."

She doesn't understand, not entirely. But he doesn't know what else to tell her.

The babies are not afraid of him. He watches them roll on the ground and giggle. He watches the way their eyes follow the swish of his tail. Later, when Heather is getting ready to leave, Greta reaches up from her sling and touches his flank, her tiny human hand like a fly against his flesh. His tail twitches involuntarily. The baby laughs.

"Come, Greta," Heather says, and she pulls her hand away. This might once have made her smile, but there is no room left in her face for laughter. No room left for joy.

He thinks back to the day, long ago, when she drew him the picture. She'd had joy then, even in her sorrow. She'd been excited. She had *believed*.

The girls crane their heads to look at him.

"Once there was a mountain," he says. He feels Heather go still. "Once there was a mountain that reached high into the clouds."

✳

They have been running for days—*like delivery boys,* Petrolio says with a half sneer, but still he comes—when they see the first human bodies. A woman and her child lying facedown by the road. It is still dark, very early morning—they almost miss them, half buried in the ditch. The child clutches a mirror in his small, dirty hand. His mother is bent over him. Already they are half covered in vines and dirt. As Estajfan watches, more vines snake slowly over the bodies, pull them deeper into the soil. He wants to look away but doesn't.

Petrolio comes to stand beside him.

"What happened to them?" he asks.

Estajfan lifts his hands. "Who knows," he says. "Maybe someone killed them. Or maybe they just starved."

There is another option, he knows. He looks at the flowers that line the borders where the road used to be. Orange flowers, green leaves. Dark berries. He looks back at the bodies.

The vines keep on coming. The mouth of the earth, green and hungry. He stands with Petrolio until the two are little more than humps beneath the green, and then turns to go.

✳

They bring down the food, they run farther and farther. They notice other bodies by the side of the road—some sinking into the grass and vines, others still fresh, glassy-eyed, looking up to the sky. It is winter, but still Estajfan sees the berries everywhere. Dark berries, white flowers, bright-orange bells that dip over the ground and smell so sweet.

When he asks the mountain centaurs what they think, they are evasive, unconcerned. "The humans are weak," they tell him.

"But they *aren't* weak," he says. Heather is strong, despite herself, and the doctor in the city—*Tasha,* Heather tells him—has not stopped in her quest to keep the city together. "They're fighting to survive."

"Humans had their chance," a black centaur says. He's tall and grace-ful, with a voice as deep as their father's used to be. "It is time for the world to thrive now."

There had been other mountains, other creatures, other parts of the world where magic was rampant and then died. The winged horses long gone now, the dragons of these mountains dead before the horses arrived. The mermaids and monsters of the deep all dead or disappeared. The humans alive and flourishing. Digging their holes into the earth and laying their roads where trees used to be. They multiplied like a disease. They built machines, smoked the air. They didn't need magic when they had airplanes and could fly. They forgot about the creatures that swam in the sea. They no longer listened to the voice of the earth, and animals around the world grew fewer, and died.

"I'm tired of everything dying," Petrolio says then—surprising Estajfan, surprising them all.

"Some things die so that others can live," a mountain centaur says. She has white-blonde hair and golden feet—the centaur who gave Estajfan his first warning months ago. "This is always what happens." She fixes her gaze on them both. "Do not go down the mountain anymore. We are not like them—we will live to see a new world."

Petrolio looks at her, and then at Estajfan. "*We* had a human mother," he says. "We might not be human, but we're not so different from them."

Beyond the other centaurs, Estajfan sees Aura listening.

The mountain centaur blinks. "Yes," she says. "But now your home is here. The mountain feeds you, the mountain shelters you from harm. Would you rather be without it?"

You have a choice to make. He watches the same realization dawn on Petrolio's face, followed by the same tinge of incredulous fear.

Aura, keeping watch, says nothing.

THE MOUNTAIN

Once there was a mountain that reached high into the clouds. On that mountain there lived a herd of wild horses. The ground magic was strong here, far from humans, and so were the horses. There were cougars on the mountain too, and mountain goats, and large brown deer with antlers that were heavier than gold. There were rabbits and foxes and squirrels that could fly, and all the animals could speak to one another without making a sound.

The horses were kind and curious, beautiful and grave. But they were also reckless—they were off the mountain as much as they were on it, eager to run down into the foothills and see what the rest of the world could tell them. Horses died in avalanches, horses fell into crevasses and were never seen again. But they were the mountain's children as much as the cougars and the foxes and the deer; the mountain forgave them their curiosity, and loved them without question.

The mountain was also a child of the earth. It had been born hot and red many millions of years ago, before there were oceans, when the sky above stretched out into green. Over the millennia, the mountain grew—earthquakes thrust it higher into the sky. The gradual creep of oceans brought it life. Grey-green lichen fed its insects, and low-lying trees fed the deer. The ground around the mountains softened into rolling hills and flatlands. The mountain, swathed in clouds, reigned proud and jealous over them all.

As is the case with most jealous things, the mountain had a favourite son. A black horse, the largest of the wild herd, a stallion with a star on his forehead. He was gentle and kind and beloved, but with a curiosity so great it dwarfed the mountain.

The stallion was faster than his brothers and sisters. But that didn't stop them from racing. Each day they ran down the mountains and far into the foothills, the other stallions and mares trying as hard as they could to beat the black. It never happened. He went faster and longer than they could match, running so far into the flatlands he lost sight of the mountain. Eventually the others stopped racing him altogether and the stallion went down the mountain alone.

One day, the stallion stopped by a stream. While he was drinking, a group of human women came down to the water, laughing amongst themselves. The stallion backed into the trees along the river and watched them until they returned to their village. He had never been this close to humans before. They seemed so tiny—quick and shining, there and gone.

The mountain told him that humans lived the way that comets shot across the sky—bright and burning, falling, gone. If you blinked, they disappeared.

The stallion didn't want to blink. The next time he ran down the mountain, he went back to that stream. Late in the day the women came down to the water again, and once more he hid from them in the trees and watched them laugh. Their joy seemed so impossible and fleeting.

After this, the stallion returned to the stream every day. He stayed hidden, but soon noticed that a young girl with blonde hair and blue-green eyes would always turn her head toward the trees. Could she sense he was there? He wasn't sure. But soon he stopped looking at the other humans and watched this one only. She never came close to the trees and he never ventured out, but every time he saw her, the ground magic shivered hard beneath his feet.

Then, one day, he found her alone. The stallion stood in the trees for a long time and watched her skip stones across the water. When she was finished, she came to where the stallion was hiding and gave him a gift—a flower chain she'd made. She put the chain around his neck.

"I see you," she said.

The garland felt so heavy and precious it might as well have been made of gold. As he ran back to the mountain that night, the horse was careful not to break it. When the other horses saw him wearing it, they looked away.

The woman met him every day after this. They would walk along the stream, or she would ride him, out into the flatlands, her hair flying behind her, her arms flung wide to the world.

The mountain felt the horse slip away and was powerless to stop the stallion as he ran to the woman. The ground magic was different in the flatlands—subtle, the magic of green growing things. It understood something about the stallion that the mountains did not. The stallion was already changing. He was already no longer the same.

By the time he climbed the summit on a night bright with stars, the stallion was a stranger to the mountain. He knew what he wanted; he knew what he had to do.

This is your home, the mountain said to its favourite son. *You belong here more than you belong anywhere else.*

But the stallion didn't want to belong to the mountain. Instead he dug himself a grave and laid down in it. He wished for the magic of green and growing things; the ability to bend, the resilience of moss and tulips. And the magic of green and growing things came to his call.

In the morning, he walked away transformed, and the mountain raged and raged.

— 8 —

Tasha is resting in the bedroom at the townhouse—a rare moment of silence and calm—when she hears Annie's footsteps clatter up the stairs. She hasn't bothered to take off her shoes.

"Someone left food on the outskirts of town," Annie says from the doorway. "And in front of the clinic."

Tasha sits up. "What do you mean, *food?*"

"Food," Annie says, incredulous. "A bag of apples, and some rice and flour."

"Who did it come from?"

Annie spreads her hands. "I have no idea."

"You're sure someone left it? Someone didn't break into our stores?"

Annie rolls her eyes. "Gee, I didn't think of that. Someone broke in and then left whatever they stole right outside."

Tasha flushes. "Well, what else are we supposed to think—it just came out of nowhere?"

When they get to the clinic, Elyse is standing guard over the food while a boy and girl sit nervously in a couple of the chairs.

"They brought it in," Elyse says, pointing to them.

Tasha goes to the children and crouches down, tries to remember their names. "Hello, you two. You found the food, and brought it here? Good job."

The girl nods, then looks at the boy, who must be her brother. "We just found the apples," she says. Nina. That's her name. She's seven, maybe eight. Thin and scrappy.

"The flour and rice were in front of the clinic," Elyse says. "I found them when I got here."

The apples are small and hard and green. They look wild. Tasha takes one and bites into it. The fruit is so sour her whole face puckers. It is indescribably delightful.

"You didn't wash that," Nina says.

Her brother, who is maybe twelve, thirteen, elbows her in the ribs. Frederic. "There's hardly any water for washing, dummy. Remember what Dad said."

Tasha laughs, then reaches into the bag and gives a fruit to each. "Your dad is right," she says. "But I think these apples are okay. See how they're not shiny? That means they haven't been sprayed with pesticides." Pesticides. She hasn't used that word in months.

They watch her, then each of them bites gingerly into an apple as though afraid someone will take it away.

"Can I have another?" the girl says with her mouth full.

Her brother elbows her again. "We need to share," he says.

Tasha nods, then reaches into the bag again and gives the girl one more. "Your brother is right," she says. "Take that to your dad, and tell him thank you." The children nod as one, then leave, the girl clutching the apple tightly in her small hand.

Tasha delves into the bag again and hands an apple to Elyse, and one to Annie. "What should we do with the rest of them?" she asks. "Go door to door?"

Annie shakes her head. "There aren't enough. Let's just keep them here," she says. "We'll add them to the stores we already have."

"Where did the food *come from,* though," Elyse says. "Why would someone just drop food here without saying anything to anybody?"

"Maybe it's from Joseph," Annie says.

But Joseph, when they ask him later in the day, has no idea. They've gone door to door after all, asking about these gifts. No one seems to know anything.

"Apples?" Joseph says. "Where would I get apples from?" He shakes his head. "Did you check to make sure they aren't poisonous?"

Tasha forces a laugh and tries to ignore the sudden drop in her stomach. "I don't think we're living in a fairy tale," she says. "I doubt anyone here has the strength or the malice to poison the food."

Joseph shrugs. "Probably not," he says. "Still—apples and flour appearing out of nowhere might as well be magic. I don't think poison is that far a stretch." There's a commotion at his feet and then a chicken pokes its head around the edge of his front door.

Tasha blinks, sure for a moment that she's hallucinating. "Hello," she says.

The chicken looks up at her, then retreats.

"You keep chickens in the house?" Annie says. "Do you know how dangerous that is?"

"They don't stay in the house," Joseph says. "They have the run of the backyard. I bring them in for company. Also—it's cold, Annie."

Elyse looks skeptical. She opens her mouth and is about to speak but Tasha rushes in, nods to where the chicken has disappeared.

"You have eggs?" she says.

Joseph's face goes dark. "They aren't laying anymore," he says. "And they certainly couldn't lay enough to feed the whole city."

"Well," Tasha says. "Keep an eye out. Let me know if you see any-thing . . . unusual."

He snorts. "Like a wicked stepmother? Okay." Then he looks at her. "If you find out who it is, what are you going to do to them?"

"I'm not going to *do* anything. No one's getting in trouble. I just want to know where it's coming from. And if we can get more. Don't you? Aren't we all in this together?"

Joseph rolls his eyes. "If someone is dropping food in front of the clinic, they've been hoarding all this time. So no—I wouldn't say that this person, whoever they are, is in with us at all." He looks at her, at Annie. "But then, you know all about hoarding." He shuts the door in their faces.

They drop in on Brendan next.

"Someone left food at the clinic," Annie tells him.

"Food?" he says. "From where?"

"That's what we're trying to figure out," Tasha says. "Do you have any idea where it might have come from?"

He blinks at her. "Sounds like someone's been hoarding food and feels guilty about it."

"That's what Joseph said," Annie says, slightly suspicious.

Tasha sighs. "All right. Well—if more comes, we'll add the extra food to the rest of the stores. If you see anything, Brendan, or hear of anything, let us know?"

He nods. "Why do you think more food is going to come? Isn't it better to assume it's a one-off?"

Tasha looks at him, surprised. "I don't know," she admits. "I guess I just thought—I don't know what I thought, actually."

Annie snorts. "You thought it was magic. You were ready to believe, like you always are."

"I was n—"

"Tasha." There is a long-suffering note in Annie's voice that shuts her up. "Don't even get me started."

Tasha smarts from this the entire walk back to the clinic. *Magic. Don't be ridiculous.*

But the next morning, there are more bags outside the door—cans of vegetables, rice and dried beans. Someone else comes running to tell them about a food drop at the edge of the city—this one out where Heather and Tasha both take their walks.

They gather the food and store it, put it all under lock and key.

The next day, there is still more food left outside—a random assortment of scuffed and dented cans that they store with everything else.

Not a lot, Tasha tells herself. *It's not a lot. Hardly magical.* But she cannot help it; she wakes every morning like a child, eager to see if more gifts have come.

*

In December, the first snow. They have prepared as best they can—indoor propane heaters looted from the hardware stores, propane doled out as carefully as gold. People congregate in the houses that have wood-burning stoves, the wood that they've all split for the winter stacked in the abandoned space next to Tasha's clinic, piled six feet deep.

They advise people to move closer to the strip mall, so that no one needs to travel very far through the snow. Once again, people bunk down in strange beds, on couches, on the floor. No one is a stranger to anyone else anymore. They shovel when they can, but the snow is heavy and wet; the paths around the strip mall are all that stay cleared.

As the days go by, the temperature drops. Some people stop coming by the strip mall for wood. Tasha leads a scouting party to Randall's house. He's an older man who lives on the outskirts of the city with his wife, and had refused to move. "We'll be okay," he had told her. "We've lived in this house our whole life. Don't want to say goodbye to it just yet."

When they get there, the place is dark and silent, freezing cold. They find Randall and Stella in their bed by the living room fireplace. The window is open and snow has dusted onto the floor. Tasha steps close to them, checks their pulses, and then looks away.

"Dead," she says.

Annie is too tired to be horrified; she looks around the room, then nods. "We should take the wood," she says.

When they return to the clinic, staggering under the weight of firewood, Tasha tells the townspeople. "Please everyone, stay close. We'll get through this together."

They are hesitant to believe her, she can tell. But no one disagrees with her, either.

✳

One night when Tasha is asleep on the clinic mattress, someone bangs loudly on the door.

"Tasha!" a voice yells, muffled by snow. "Tasha, please!"

The voice pulls her from sleep and dreams of fire. The man on her doorstep is Robin, one of the original residents who had helped her with the gardens. He's staying with a group of people a few houses down from Tasha's townhouse. Candice, one of the women in the group, is six months pregnant.

"The baby's coming," Robin says. Tasha's already pulling on her boots. Snow is thick and deep on the sidewalks; it takes forever to get there. "Go get Annie," she tells Robin, and he sets back off into the snow.

Candice lies labouring on the couch in the living room. The wood stove blazes fierce and orange, the room almost unbearably hot.

The baby is already crowning; when she guides it out, the child is blue, the cord around its neck a whitish-purple noose. She untangles the cord and stimulates the chest. Tiny hands and feet, tiny purple lips. A boy. The mother and the father—his name is Seth, she remembers—are both sobbing. The room stinks of blood and fear.

Noises at the front door, a gust of cold wind. She doesn't look up. She clears the baby's mouth with her finger, then gently turns him over and rubs his back, his arms and legs hanging limp. One, two, three rubs. A little movement. Not enough. When the child finally gasps in air, his arms and legs do not move. She turns the child over—he is so tiny, a crumpled fairy frog—then lays him down across her thigh, flicks a finger against his feet. Nothing.

Annie is beside her now, her hands ready. She passes the child to Annie and gets up to check the mother over. Candice tore, but only a little; she'll be okay.

She can hear people trying to be quiet in the kitchen. When she turns back to Annie, it's been five minutes since the birth; they tap the baby's tiny feet again and still he doesn't react, though his chest heaves up and down. They don't need to say anything to one another—instead Annie swaddles the baby and hands him to his parents.

They stay the rest of the night, keeping the wood stove alive, catching bits of sleep in turns in the armchairs. They try to feed the baby—first at his mother's breast, and then with some formula from the clinic. In the morning the baby is still breathing but is otherwise unresponsive. The parents are vibrating with terror.

"What can we do?" Seth whispers.

"He lost oxygen to the brain," Tasha says. "Because of the cord."

"He'll be able to move eventually—won't he?" Candice asks.

Tasha doesn't answer. She sees the mother swallow.

"He won't latch," Candice says. "I'm holding his head right up to my breast and he won't latch."

"He's three months premature," Tasha says, as gently as she can. "There is likely significant brain damage. He's not moving his arms and legs because he can't. He won't latch because he can't. We can try to give him more formula, but you should know that this is going to be difficult."

"Difficult how?" Seth asks.

"He's not going to have the life you wanted him to have," she says, slowly. "You can take a car and try to reach another city, somewhere with a hospital that might be better equipped. If you find one, they might be able to do more for him than we can. Take a car—we can give you some of the gas we have left."

"But what about the snow?" Candice's voice rises in panic. "What happens if we take a car and leave and don't find anything and he doesn't latch?"

By now, they all know the stories Joseph has brought them. Haphazard militia who prowl what's left of the highways, thieves who ambush families and steal their cars, leaving them to die on the road.

"We can give you more formula," Annie says.

"And what if that runs out?" Candice looks at them both, her eyes wild. "What if we run out of gas? What happens if there's no clean water or snow to mix the formula with when we're on the road?"

Annie, eventually, says, "You'll have anywhere from three days to three weeks."

The mother closes her eyes. When she opens them again, they are bottomless in a way that reminds Tasha of Heather. "It's so cold outside," Candice says. "I could take him to the mountain, like other mothers have. It would be just like falling asleep."

"What other mothers?" Tasha asks, her voice sharp.

Candice opens her eyes and stares at her as if from far away. "Mothers who leave their children in the snow," she says. "Mothers who leave their children on the mountain. Everyone knows the stories."

Tasha looks at Seth, at the people now huddled listening near the door to the kitchen. "Is this true?" she asks. How many mothers have taken their children away? She sees the bodies piled in frozen lumps at the base of the mountain, pilgrims on a climb to nowhere.

An older woman steps forward—thin like the rest of them, unbowed and tall. "It's an old story," she says. "Just something parents used to say to keep their children in line. Wolves who lured children up the mountain. Foxes who stole mothers away. My parents told me the same stories years ago."

"Stories," Tasha echoes. "Like the stories the others talked about in the fall? *Only* stories? You're sure?"

The woman laughs. "You've been here long enough, Tasha—the whole city is filled with stories like this. Mountain superstition—that's all it is. We can hardly get down the sidewalks. You think anyone is going to go near the mountain in the snow?"

"We're not going up the mountain," Seth snaps. "We have to try."

Candice blinks, comes back to herself. "Yes," she says, and nods.

Annie packs the car herself, loading it with as much food as they can spare, and all the formula they have. The other people from the house busy themselves clearing a path out of town as best as they can. Tasha gives the couple one of the flashlights from the clinic and a map—not that maps mean all that much anymore. She's marked the closest city anyway.

"Be safe," she tells them through the window of the car. They are terrified, almost babies themselves. The car creeps away down the road and disappears around a corner.

Three days later they come back, and they no longer have the child.

✳

Cans of stewed tomatoes, cans of corned beef and Spam. Bags of beans and lentils. The food that is dropped off at various parts of the town is just enough to keep their stores from dwindling into nothing. And yet as the winter begins to rage in earnest, even these gifts are not enough. It snows constantly. Soon the food drops are only on the outskirts of town. Deliveries go unnoticed, buried under the snow.

Sometimes there are footprints. Someone on a horse.

Brendan suggests putting a guard at the front of the clinic, to try to catch the "Food Angel," as some of the people have begun to say. Tasha vetoes this idea.

"Don't you want to know?" Annie asks her, incredulous, one night as they lie together in the clinic. Elyse is back at the townhouse, huddled in blankets, sleeping alone. They told her she could stay, but she refused.

"You've done so much for me," she said. "You deserve some time alone."

But this is what alone time with Annie means now—it's like lying on a mattress beside a stranger, the gulf between them growing wider by the day.

"Someone's been hiding food from us all this time," Annie presses. "Doesn't that make you angry?"

"Maybe it's not someone in the town," Tasha says.

"Who else could it be?"

Tasha shrugs. "Look—it's helping us get through the winter. Let's just stop asking questions for right now, and be thankful someone is helping at all."

"You're making no sense," Annie says. "You're the one who always wants answers to everything! Why are you letting go of this so easily?"

Tasha thinks about this. What else could it be? Some strange visitor, creeping through their city streets at night. Magic? She feels a whisper of something black and dark against her soul and tries not to shiver. If that's real, what else is real? What other stories might come to life?

"What are we going to do if we find them out?" she says, slowly. "Raid their stores? If it's someone from outside the city, are we going to keep them here, make them give us everything they have? Whoever they are, they want to stay hidden. And I don't think we can spare the energy to find out who it is. Things for the townspeople are already"—*broken,* she wants to say, but still she refuses—"bad."

Annie stares at the ceiling, silent for a moment, then says, "We could go, you know."

"What?"

"You and me. And Elyse. We could take a car and whatever gas is left and go find somewhere else."

"How far do you think we would get in the snow?"

"We walk out, then. We wear warm clothes. We keep moving."

"You want to take *Elyse* out in the snow? For days on end?"

"Randall and Stella's deaths weren't accidents!" Annie says, and Tasha goes silent. "They *chose* to freeze to death. I know that. So do you. I also know that not everyone is going to make it through the winter, no matter what we keep saying." She sits up, stares down at Tasha. "We need to go," she whispers. "We should have gone months ago."

"Things can be different here," Tasha says. "We just need time. We've prepared as much as we can for the winter. We'll be okay."

"What if we don't have that time? What if the propane runs out, what if we haven't cut enough wood, what if your magical Food Angel stops bringing supplies to top us up? I don't want to freeze to death, Tasha. We aren't even from here. Why stay? We got people away from the water. We don't owe anyone anything else."

So much in Annie's face seems different—frightened and small, not the Annie she remembers.

"We don't owe anyone anything?" Tasha says. "What about Elyse? You know she can't leave, Annie. Not in the snow. You don't even sound like yourself."

A short burst of silence, and then Annie jerks her hand away and laughs. "You can't be serious. *I* don't sound like myself? I haven't changed! I've been right here this whole time. Who was there when your parents died and you couldn't get out of bed and go to work? Who was there when you couldn't get up for the funeral? It sure as hell wasn't anyone from here."

Tasha thinks of Heather, and then of Joseph.

"We can't abandon them now," she says. "If we leave them to—to their stories, and the mountains—Annie, they'll all be dead by the spring."

"They aren't children," Annie snaps. "Jesus, Tasha—you make them all sound like they're from some backwater hamlet in the middle of nowhere. God complex much?"

Tasha shuts her eyes. "I didn't mean it that way."

"Well, that's how it sounded. And anyway"—there's that dark note in Annie's voice again—"you're one to talk. I see your face when they whisper those stories. When you talk to Heather. You're all *We'll get through* and *Let's focus on what's in front of us*, but you want to believe those silly stories as much as anybody else."

"Annie, I don't—"

"Yes, you do!" Annie cries. "You focus on *what's right in front of you* because everything else is too hard. You do this over and over again. Well, *I'm* right in front of you, and *I'm* saying that I want to go."

There is a long silence. Tasha stares stonily at the ceiling, then finally clears her throat. "I don't want to leave the mountain," she says, finally.

Annie opens her mouth, closes it. "What's that supposed to mean?"

"I don't know. It comforts me. And now, with—with the food—"

"You really think someone is up there, bringing food down?" Annie frowns. "Then why didn't we go closer when there was no snow?"

"I wasn't thinking about it as much when there was no snow," Tasha says. "I wanted us to think about the gardens and securing the food we had. And now—I think we're here for a reason. Maybe the mountain—or the stories that everyone is telling—maybe that's it." She thinks a minute, swallows. "I should have told Candice and Seth to stay."

"Tasha. That wasn't your fault. That was nobody's fault."

She can't speak; she only shrugs.

Another silence. "You've never even been here before," Annie says.

"I know."

"You didn't even know how to get here."

"I can't explain it. But I felt like we ended up here because we were meant to."

"For fuck's sake, Tasha. You cannot be serious."

"Why not?" Tasha tries to keep her voice calm. "It's the first city we came to that was still standing. That makes as much sense as anything else."

"It *called* to you," Annie insists. There's something else in her voice now. She sounds almost afraid.

"Yes? So what?"

"What did you do—tell yourself a story about it?"

"What? Of course not."

Annie launches herself off the bed. "You *always* do this," she says, again. "You tell yourself stories when you can't handle real life."

"I do not!"

But Annie doesn't waver. She stares down at Tasha, shakes her head. "You do," she says. "That's why you went back to work. So you could be a *doctor* and *save lives*. So you could make life into a puzzle you could solve. Beginning, middle, end. You made work into the magic you needed so you didn't have to be in your life. You think I didn't see it? I was there every goddamned day."

Tasha stares up at her, dumbfounded. "I didn't—Annie, I didn't mean—"

"And now you're doing it all over again," Annie says. She takes a step back from the mattress, swings her arm in a wild circle. "Maybe this *was* the first city we came to. Fine. But you've spent the past however many months telling everyone we'd survive. Telling *them* a story—one where you get to be the hero so you don't have to be the person who can't get out of bed." Her hands shake; she clenches her fists, stares at the floor. "Well, what about me, Tasha? What if I don't want to be the hero? What if I don't want to pass you your equipment and help you gather food and walk around with this goddamned key around my waist all the time? What if *I'm* not okay not knowing where our mystery food comes from? What if *I* don't want to wait here while we starve? What if

I want someone who will help me get out of the goddamned bed? Don't I deserve that too?"

Tasha stands and reaches for Annie's hands. "Don't leave," she whispers, and she brings Annie close, pulls her in. "Annie, I'm sorry. Please don't leave."

"Can't it just be us again?" Annie whispers into her shoulder. "I'm so tired. I don't want to think about taking care of all of these people anymore."

"There are no other doctors here," Tasha says. "If we leave the city, we leave them with nothing."

Annie straightens. "*I'm* not a doctor," she says. "I could leave tomorrow."

Panicked, Tasha reaches for Annie's hand again. "You'll get stuck in the snow even if you walk out. We have food here, we have shelter. I can't do this without you. Please, please, please don't go."

Annie's hands cup her face now, and she brings her lips to Tasha's, resting her forehead against Tasha's. She breathes slowly, in and out, until Tasha feels her own heart settle down.

After another long moment, Annie moves back to the mattress and pulls Tasha down with her, plants a trail of kisses that ends at Tasha's collarbone. "I'm sorry, Tasha, but I can't do this forever."

"We'll do more hunting," Tasha says. "We'll hunt, we'll dry the meat. Send groups out to scavenge as best as we can." She grabs a handful of Annie's hair and kisses her hard. "We won't do this forever. I promise."

Her promises are no longer enough. She can see that in Annie's face already.

✳

Still, it is not all bad. With the snow hemming them in, there is not much to do during the day, so Tasha converts a storefront a few doors down from the clinic—an old bank, the ATMs silent and useless and the floors heavy with thick carpet—into a community centre equipped with two propane heaters. People bring board games and play them for hours, sprawled on the floor. They boil water over the firepit in the back alley, stir in cocoa and powdered milk, then ladle the thin, rich liquid into mugs and pass them around. They tell stories, they sing songs. Everyone shares.

Sometimes Heather and Brendan bring the girls to the centre and Heather gets out her pencil crayons and teaches the children how to draw. Annie has salvaged colouring books and crayons from the grocery stores. Tasha can't draw but tries anyway. The children squeal with laughter at her attempts.

The children like to draw Tasha as a small stick figure with a black stethoscope around her neck, putting bandages on bleeding knees and stitching cuts together. In one picture by a little boy named Tom, she is sewing a severed arm back onto a body. When he gives it to her, she laughs and hangs the picture up in the clinic.

Heather draws on the community centre walls like a woman possessed—her movements quick and sure, a whole world tumbling from her hand in a matter of minutes. She sketches the children at various points on the wall—her babies, Tom and his older sister. Nina and Frederic. Other little faces in between. The children love her pictures. Brendan has told Tasha that Heather still goes for walks, though Tasha hasn't come across her in the forest again. (Tasha has seen her footsteps. She always sees her footsteps.) It is more difficult, walking through the forest in the snow. But not impossible.

One night during a blizzard, they cram as many people into the community centre as they can to share the warmth. Heather and Brendan arrive with dark bags under their eyes, the twins restless and feverish. Tasha takes one baby and Elyse takes another. They sing—Tasha sings as badly as she draws, but she tries anyway—until the girls are smiling, then they walk them until each twin is asleep. The strain in Heather's face eases a bit and she goes to where the other children are drawing, then slides down onto the floor beside them. Beneath the loose hang of her clothes, the soft curve of her belly is unmistakable.

She draws a mountain on the wall, and winged things that fly close to its summit. Fairies, Tasha sees, as she comes closer. Unicorns run down the side of the mountain, and still other beasts lie shadowed in the trees.

"What kind of mountain is that?" a child asks.

"This is a wishing mountain." Heather's hand doesn't stop. "It's filled with magic." She glances up and sees that Tasha's watching. She looks back at the mountain. "Magic that will make our world better."

"Is it like our mountain?" Another child—brown-haired, dark-eyed Sasha. She reaches up and touches a fairy's wing.

Heather smiles. "It can be like ours," she says. "It can also be different. It can be whatever we want it to be."

Tasha's breath catches in her throat. The twin on her shoulder coos softly in her sleep. Despite how delicate they are, the twins' heartbeats are strong. They don't know any different. This is their only world.

It might not be so bad, she thinks. Next spring they will plant again. In the meantime, they have the community centre, they have each other. Others might have much less.

Heather draws a bright thing, falling from the mountain. Then another, then another.

"What are those?" Tasha asks.

"These are fire-birds," Heather says. "They fall from the sky."

Tasha's heart thuds hard in her chest. "What did you say?"

Heather doesn't look at her. "Fire-birds," she repeats. She draws another one hitting the ground, a great gaping hole opening beneath it. "They burn holes in the ground, the way the meteors did."

Tasha tries to swallow. "Once there was a bird who was jealous of the sun," she says.

Heather looks at her, sharply. "*What?*"

"Once there was a bird who was jealous of the sun," she repeats. "No matter how high the bird flew, the sun was always higher."

Heather watches her for a moment, and then whispers, "Why should the sun fly higher than we do?" She holds her pencil crayon in mid-air.

"We work so hard to stay in the air but the sun sits up there and does nothing. It's not fair."

Tasha swallows. "How do you know that story?"

"My father made it up for me."

"My mother made it up for *me*," Tasha says. "When I was a kid, I had dreams about birds that burned holes in the ground. She made that story up so I wouldn't be afraid. How—how did your father know it?"

Heather puts her pencil crayon down, then shrugs. "My father once said that stories don't belong to anybody," she says. "He said they belong to the world."

"Yes," Tasha says, a little louder now. People turn to look at them. "But that exact story? Don't you think that's a little strange? Did our parents know each other?"

"I don't think so," Heather says. "My father never left these mountains. Did your parents travel here?"

Tasha shakes her head. "They wanted to. They always talked about coming. But they never did." She looks at the children, who have stopped listening to them and are back on the floor drawing their own pictures. "Why did your father tell you a story about birds who fly higher than the sun?" she says. "What were you afraid of?"

"*I* wasn't afraid of anything." There's a strange smile on Heather's face now. "My father, on the other hand. . ." She shrugs again. "He was afraid of a lot, as it turns out. I should have clued in when the birds in the story flew higher and kept burning."

Tasha frowns. "But that's not how the story ends."

"Isn't it?" Heather stands and reaches for Jilly. Again there's that flash when they touch—clouds and air, the high-pitched sound of screaming. Heather blinks and Tasha wonders what she sees—The smoke again? The fire?—but then Brendan appears by their side and takes Greta from Elyse.

"You can stay here if you don't want to walk home," Tasha says. *Stay. Stay and finish the story.* "You can have the mattress in the clinic, if you want. Or stay here with the others—lots of people will be sleeping here tonight."

"We're fine," Heather says.

Stay, Tasha wants to beg. *Rest. Let me help you. Please tell me what all of this means.* Instead she only nods. "All right," she says. "Just—hold on a minute." She moves to the doorway, then steps outside into the snow and makes her way to the clinic. She lets herself in and rummages through the shelves that Annie has organized so neatly in the back. She finds the bottle she is looking for and closes her hand around it, then walks back to the community centre. After Tasha stamps the snow off her boots, she holds the bottle of prenatal vitamins out to Heather. "For you."

Heather looks at the vitamins in Tasha's outstretched hand. "What good do you think those will do?"

"Who knows, at this point," Tasha says. When Heather takes the bottle, Tasha feels a small thrill at being able to help her, even a little, and watches as she and the girls and Brendan head out into the swirling white.

"You spend more time worrying about Heather than you do about Annie," Elyse says, beside her.

"What?" Tasha says, confused.

"Annie would do anything for you. And you keep pushing her away. Don't you know how lucky you are?"

"Elyse, I'm not pushing—"

"Yes, you are. You don't deserve her."

Tasha sighs. "Elyse, we're all tired. We're all working too hard."

"Heather doesn't even *look* at you. She doesn't care!"

"I just want her to survive," Tasha says, backing away from Elyse's anger. "I want *everyone* to survive."

"So does Annie," Elyse says. "But she wants you—the *both* of you—to survive most of all."

Tasha turns from her and goes back to draw with the children.

✳

Improbably, the old greenhouse thrives in the winter. As the snows blow, the amaryllis flush a deeper red. One day in early January, Tasha snow-shoes to the greenhouse and discovers that the vines have made their way out the door and are reaching to the dusty clouded sun.

She wrenches the door open and goes inside, and it is like stepping through a portal into the tropics. She has to peel off all her layers, sliding out of her coat and boots and shirt and pants until she's standing in her underwear, so awash in scents and vivid greenery, she's overcome.

It shouldn't be hot in here, but it is.

The greenhouse shouldn't be here at all, but it is.

Each time she stands in front of the flowers, her vision blurs and her mind is overwhelmed with despair—her mother in the fire, her father trying so hard to get her out, her father in the fire too. The people they left behind by the sea. Climbing the mountain that rises above them even though she's never climbed a mountain before. Climbing the mountain in the midst of a fire that burns down all the trees, the ambulance rumbling hard behind her. Water rushing over them, swallowing her air. Children that she's helped to birth and then, inadvertently, to kill. The people in the city who continue to starve. Poison plants that grow thick by the side of the road. She was not enough to stand between her parents and the fire. Her parents saved her, again and again, when she was a child, and in return she let them burn, she let them explode into nothing.

Her screams go on forever.

When she comes back to herself, she's curled on the ground, her forehead pressed to the dirt. There's a draft of cold air behind her—she turns, blinking slowly, and sees Heather outlined in the doorway. The twins watch Tasha with eager, interested eyes.

She stares at Heather, then clears her throat. "Did you hear me scream?" Her voice is hoarse and scratchy.

Heather cocks her head. "You weren't screaming," she says. "But I could hear you weeping as I got closer."

Tasha nods, wipes a hand across her face. "I'm so tired," she says.

Heather steps all the way into the greenhouse and pushes the door shut behind her. The cold air vanishes. She leans back against the greenhouse door and watches Tasha, not saying anything.

"Candice," Tasha says, finally. "And Seth."

Heather nods. "What about them?"

"I think they killed their little boy."

Heather doesn't blink. "Do you know that? For sure?"

Tasha wipes angrily at another tear. "No. But before they left, Candice talked about mothers leaving their children on the mountain."

Heather nods as though it's the most normal thing in the world. "Yes. I remember that story."

"I told them to go as far as they could. To try as hard as they could. I should have told them to stay here."

Heather hasn't moved from the door. "Sometimes people have to make hard choices, Tasha."

"What if that had been you?" Tasha cries. Then she stops, horrified. "I'm sorry. I didn't mean that. I meant—"

"You meant, what if my parents had decided to leave me on the mountain when I was born," Heather says. Her voice is so gentle. "But they didn't, and now I'm here. I understand."

"I didn't—"

"My parents had a hospital that functioned. They had help."

"I know, but *I* could have helped them—and Annie—for as long as we needed to—"

"My father used to tell me a story," Heather continues—looking at Tasha, but also not looking at her—"about a fox that wants children more than anything else in the world. The mountain tells her to go to the flatlands and turn over a rock and the rock will grant her children. But when she does this, the fox sees only worms, and she doesn't understand at first that the worms are meant to be her children. So she goes to another rock and turns that one over too, and the same thing happens, and it's only when she returns to the first rock that she realizes what's supposed to happen. So she welcomes the worms, and they go home with her at the end of the story. And she is very happy." She shifts her weight from one hip to the other, wincing a little. "I thought it was a beautiful story when I was small. I knew that my father was trying to tell me what it felt like to be the fox, surprised to find herself the mother of children who weren't what she thought they'd be. She was happy to have them, in the end. And the worms were happy to have her. They built a life together."

"And then my father died, and in the years after I came down from the mountain I couldn't think about that story without wanting to scream in rage. *Was I a worm?* I wanted to yell at him. *Was that all I ever was to you?*" She raises her hands and strokes the babies' red curls. "I was angry about that for years," she says, softly. "And then I had my own babies. And now

I just—these things are complicated, Tasha. It takes time to realize that your child is going to have a different life. We don't really have that time anymore."

"But we could," Tasha says fiercely. "We have to *make* that time. You're telling me if it had been you—you and Greta and Jilly—"

"I wouldn't have," Heather says instantly. "I didn't." But something flickers over her face and Tasha is no longer so sure.

"How do I show them?" Tasha whispers. "How do I show them that the only way we survive is by doing this together?"

"I think you have to understand that some people won't survive," Heather says. "Or that their choices will be different, and their lives will be different too, as a result."

"I can't accept that," Tasha says flatly. "There are enough of us here who can help one another. There has to be a light at the end. There has to be."

Heather watches her. "There will be," she says, finally. "But it's not going to look like what you expect light to be. You have to get used to that, too."

Tasha says nothing for a moment, finally aware that she's kneeling before Heather in nothing but her underwear. "You were right to be angry about that story. You're worth so much more than a worm."

Heather only shrugs. "I was angry at him for dying," she says. "For taking me up on the mountain when he probably shouldn't have— when he knew it was unsafe. And I was angry at myself for wanting to be the daughter that *he* wanted me to be. But I was also right, all those years ago, when I was younger. I knew what he meant, even if it wasn't perfect. Even if he didn't really understand it—or believe in it, totally—himself. He was trying to tell me that worms are beautiful too—that they shape the world in ways we all need. Without worms, nothing else survives."

Tasha sits with this for a moment. Then she reaches for her clothes. "Will you walk back with me?"

Heather shakes her head. "I like it here," she says. "We'll stay a while longer."

Tasha nods, then heads back to the city alone.

✳

January becomes February, becomes almost March. The food gifts come less and less. Wizened apples, dented cans.

Six families die over the winter. Flu, the cold, pneumonia. Tasha spends days and nights in the houses of the sick and dying and then, once death comes, she goes back to the greenhouse. She sheds her clothes and kneels in front of the jacaranda tree and lets the madness—grief, anger, despair, whatever it is—take her.

Except that as the months go on, the madness takes her less often. She does not weep, she does not scream. Her mind remains her own. There is no jumbled madness—just a long stretch of grief, which is familiar. A small and steady knot beneath her ribs. She lets the knot propel her as the days slide forth to spring.

They move the dead closer to the forest, away from the town. When the ground is warm enough to dig, those that are still able—Tasha, Annie, Joseph, others—bury the half-thawed bodies out by the trees and scatter quiet prayers over the soil.

The worms will eat them, she thinks. *And from their bodies, something else. From the death of one life, another.*

It wouldn't be possible without the worms, she thinks. *Just like Heather said.*

THE JEALOUS BIRD, AGAIN

Once there was a bird who was jealous of the sun. No matter how high the bird flew, the sun was always higher, and it made the bird angry.

"Why should the sun fly higher than we do?" he said to his fellow birds. "We work so hard to stay in the air but the sun sits up there and does nothing. It's not fair."

"The sun has always flown above us." The bird who said this was much older than the jealous bird, and had seen much more of the world. "This is how it has always been."

"Why should something stay the same just because it has always been that way?" said the jealous bird.

The old bird said, severely, "The sun is higher. We are lower. The sun warms us when we're cold and sends us light to see worms in the grass, and asks of us nothing in return. You should be grateful for this, not angry."

"I will be grateful when the sun sees how much higher I can fly!" cried the bird. He threw his head back and crowed, and many other birds, massed around him, threw back their heads and did the same.

"You cannot fly higher than the sun," the old bird warned. "It is foolish to even try."

But the jealous bird would not be swayed, for he knew a secret his mother had told him long ago: the birds themselves had come from the sun.

When he was a fumbling chick in the nest, his mother had said, "You have sunlight in your wings. All that we are comes from the sun. We are the same. Before the world was born, when we all spun round in the sky together, the sun's fire was also your own."

And so the bird gathered all those who were set on fire by his words and told them they would fly to the sun and reclaim their place in the sky. "We have the sun in our feathers," he said. As one, they spread their wings and lifted from the trees.

The birds flew high, and then higher still. They flew so high the air became thin; some birds gasped, but kept on struggling; other birds gave up and dropped back, far down to the ground. The jealous bird and a few close friends kept flying.

They flew so high the air was hard to breathe; they flew so high the sun began to burn their wings. One by one, the birds burst into flame and fell, screaming. When they hit the ground, the earth went black with mourning.

The jealous bird's wings burned too, but he held his mother's words deep inside and pushed on. He flew until the sky curved, until the great dark belly of the universe came into view.

The sun, the bird saw to his surprise, was still so far away. But the sun saw him, and knew who he was instantly.

"I have been waiting for you," the sun said. "I have been waiting for so long."

"I'm here to take my rightful place!" the bird cried. He puffed out his chest and waited for the sun to come at him, full of anger.

But the sun only smiled. "You know your rightful place," it said. "And your rightful place is far from here."

The bird opened his mouth to reply, but all that came out was air; surprised, he stopped beating his wings, and in a moment, he began to tumble, head over tail over feathers, back to the ground.

But I flew, he thought, dizzily, as he fell. *I flew all the way up to the sun.*

You are not meant *to fly as high as me,* the sun said, the words ringing deep in the jealous bird's chest. *Even if you can. For some, the world must not extend beyond the trees. I have seen this desire burn and grow in you and others. I have waited all this time to show you that you are wrong.*

But can't you help me? the bird said, still tumbling.

Why would I help you? said the sun. *You should have been content with how beautiful your trees are. That is your lesson, bird: your trees should have been enough.*

The bird heard this, and burned. And when the jealous bird hit the ground, all that was left of him were specks of soot.

9

"You shouldn't come here anymore," Estajfan tells Heather one day when the snow has almost overwhelmed her as she trudged to the greenhouse. "Let me bring you food in town."

He seems extra hard, somehow—all wiry dark-brown arms and body, blackened legs against the snow—but his eyes are the brightest thing in the forest.

He is not the centaur she remembers. When they meet under cover of the trees around the greenhouse, he is all business. Handing her the food he has managed to find. Standing ever so slightly away.

She is probably not the Heather he remembers either. She doesn't bring him drawings anymore and the only story she has left to tell is this one: they will survive today. Maybe they'll survive tomorrow.

Please, let them survive tomorrow.

"What happens when the food runs out?"

"There are still things that grow on the mountain," Estajfan says. He lets Greta pinch his arm, then makes a face. Her laughter flies higher than the trees.

"The mountain won't feed the whole city," Heather says.

Estajfan makes another face at Greta. "No," he says. "It won't."

"How many?"

Now he looks at her, only her. "You," he says. "I will try to save you."

She closes her eyes, takes a step back, a hand on each of their bright-red heads. "Greta," she says. "And Jilly." She swallows. "And B."

He doesn't speak for a long time. When she looks up at him, he only nods. "We'll go as far as we need to go to find you food," he says again. "I can run for years." Then he turns from her and goes back to the mountain.

At night, Heather dreams about killing the baby. She dreams about drinking poison tea, she dreams about climbing the mountain, about feeling the wind in her face as Estajfan lifts her into the air and throws her off the mountain's edge. She imagines surviving the fall, she imagines the pain. Crawling back into the city with broken bones and a belly that's bled empty.

No more, she tells B in the dream. *I won't have any more children. I won't. Don't ever touch me again.*

Awake, she says nothing. They are rationing so carefully it is a surprise to see her belly grow, but grow it does; the rest of her is so thin that the curve, though small, seems almost grotesque. Only one, this time. A boy.

("How do you know it's a boy?" B asks her, late one night as they lie on the bed.

"I just do.")

In another dream she's on the mountain, the baby in her arms. The wind blasts pellets of ice through her hair. Estajfan is there with her, shouting.

What do you want?

I don't know what I want. She holds out the baby, whose dark eyes watch her, unafraid.

Estajfan raises a hand and for an instant she thinks he's going to hit her. The ground wobbles beneath her feet and Estajfan is reaching for her. His fingertips brush hers. He pauses. It's only a fraction of a second, but long enough. She falls, the baby's scream loud in her ear.

She wakes up slick with sweat, curled over her belly. When she gets up, there is blood on the sheets.

B wants her to go see Tasha, right away. "The girls and I can come with you," he says. "We'll go together."

"No," Heather says. "I can go on my own. It's all right."

He's hurt. He's always hurt now, and she is trying not to think about it. She is trying not to think about anything. She cleans herself up as best she can and then sits with the girls while they eat wizened apples for breakfast. When B comes into the kitchen, he smiles at the twins. "You look so pretty," he says. It's true. They are beautiful and tiny, like little ruffled sparrows. Then he looks at her. "You're beautiful too," he says. "I don't say that enough."

Heather swallows the lump in her throat. "Thank you," she says. She crosses to kiss him on the cheek. The baby kicks as she straightens, and she takes B's hand and presses it hard against her abdomen. Another kick and a smile touches his face.

She blinks and it's Estajfan standing before her instead. His hand on her belly, his hand against her face. In his eyes she sees the mountain.

"Heather, are you all right?" B is frowning at her now.

She steps back and cups her abdomen, trying to quell the shaking of her hands. She manages to kiss him on the cheek again, and then turns on her heel and leaves without saying goodbye to the girls.

At the clinic, Annie is harried. Tasha, as usual, is unflappable and calm. Heather sits in the makeshift waiting room and listens to Tasha speak gently with a father and his children. Annie, at the front counter, takes inventory. She is always taking inventory now, watching their supplies dwindle day after day

"How are you?" Heather asks, surprising herself.

"I'm all right," Annie says, as though she's never asked herself the question. "Tired. Hungry. But aren't we all."

"And Tasha?"

"Tasha is Tasha." Annie shrugs. "One day she'll drop dead from a heart attack and all of this will be over, but until then, who knows."

After the family leaves, Heather follows Annie to where Tasha sits waiting on her chair. Annie pulls the curtain across and sits down beside her.

"Heather," she says. "What can we do for you?"

She tells them about the bleeding. Tasha frowns and gets up to check her belly.

"The placenta seems lower than it should be," she says, "though it's hard to tell exactly what's going on without equipment. Did you bleed with the girls?"

"A little," Heather tells her.

Worry settles into the lines around Tasha's eyes. "We'll just have to wait and see. But let me know if the bleeding continues," she says.

Heather looks at them both, then clears her throat. "What if . . . what if I don't want it to stop?"

Tasha blinks. "What?"

"What if I don't have this baby?" Heather whispers. "What if I *can't* have this baby? Can you help me with that?"

The women glance at each other. For a moment Heather sees strong emotion pass between them. Envy flickers in her heart. She's never looked at B like that. She's never even wanted to. She's only ever looked like that at someone else—and that, an impossibility.

"It's too dangerous," Tasha says, finally. "Heather—you're malnourished. I can't take a chance that something might happen."

She swallows, closes her eyes. "Isn't it dangerous to keep going?"

"Your body knows what to do," Tasha says, softly. "Trust your own body before anything else."

Her body. Heather lets out a laugh, and wipes a tear from her eye. "My body has always betrayed me," she says. Not strong enough, not *normal* enough. And yet still strong enough, somehow, to give her children, again and again.

"I would do it," Tasha says. "If this was any other time and we were in any other place. I would do it."

The sharp pull of the curtain. Heather turns.

B stands there, backlit by the light from the windows. She can hear the girls laughing in the waiting room.

"I wanted to make sure you were okay," he says. Something like terror in his face, something like hatred.

"Brendan—" Tasha begins, but he raises a hand.

"Don't talk," he says. "Please." He looks back at Heather. "Would you have told me? Or would you have just gone and done it?"

She stares at the floor. The criss-cross of cracks over the tile. "I *didn't* do it."

"But you want to."

"We're starving," she says. "You really want another child?"

B comes to her and grips her arm. She feels the other women shift, stand up. "I need you to have faith," he says. Angry, desperate. "We'll get through this. We will. The winter will end and we'll plant the gardens again—"

"And if that doesn't work? What happens then?"

"You're always so negative!" he cries, dropping her arm. "I've tried so hard and nothing is ever enough for you. Even before all of this." She looks up at him and then can't look away.

"No one wanted to touch you," he whispers. "No one wanted anything to do with you. I used to watch the way that people mimicked you at school. They called you crazy, you know that? No one wanted to be near you. But I did. I *do*."

She thinks, hazily, of the smirks his friends had shot his way after B came over to her table at the pub. The whistles that had followed them out onto the street.

"So what?" she hisses. "Am I supposed to be grateful you're paying attention to me now? Is that it?"

"Heather." Annie comes to stand between them. "Brendan. Look— this is all terrible—*everything* is terrible." She holds her arms out as if to push them away from one another. "But fighting helps nothing. Think about the girls."

At the thought of them, Heather feels her heart crack open. "I'm sorry," she says, and covers her face with her hands. "I just—I can't do this. It's too hard."

"You're not doing it alone," B says. "That's what I keep trying to tell you."

Heather lets her hands fall, then nods. "Yes," she whispers. "I know."

They walk back to the house together, each of them carrying a twin, the gulf that yawns between them growing deeper as they go.

✳

As the winter ends, the sky is blue—but never for very long, and not the blue that anyone remembers. The grass and trees are deep green, as though they've all kept on growing under the snow. The city is a daylight clock. The city is a shell. The mountains stand over them in shades of grey and green and blue.

There are no eggs from Joseph anymore. Heather no longer speaks to Joseph, apart from saying hello when they pass on the vine-ridden street. She doesn't really speak to anyone apart from B and the girls, who are babbling now—mostly nonsense, sometimes a few words of something only they can understand. They are tiny but fierce. They pull themselves up by the legs of tables and wobble around the house from one piece of furniture to the next. Greta is always first in line. Jilly, more timid when it comes to new adventures, laughs the loudest. Neither of them goes anywhere without looking to see where the other twin is first. Their eyes follow her everywhere.

Their backyard is soon a lush jungle of green. There is no in-between time, no in-between place. In the morning she cuts the vines back from the stairs and in the evening they have grown to overtake the porch again.

Look at the wildflowers grow, she hears people whisper. *Look at the lilies, look at the bushes that have come up almost out of nowhere. Look at all of it, so bright and alive.*

A week or so into spring, brightly coloured boxes arrive on their doorstep, holding new clothes for the babies and an invitation. *Please join us in the city square for a spring celebration. We would like to come together to celebrate the lives of those we've lost, and express gratitude for all that we've accomplished together.* It's signed *Tasha and the Council.*

"I don't know why it bothers you so much," B says, as they dress the girls in their new outfits. "The Council is trying to stay positive. Why is that so hard for you to get?"

"This is more complicated than just trying to stay positive. People *died* during the winter," she says, the words short and clipped. "Even though the Council did *so much*. It's eating away at Tasha, too, even if she's not talking about it. If it hadn't been for the Food Angel, we all might have starved."

"Fuck the Food Angel!" B hisses. "We survived because *we* prepared. Because *we* worked together. Because Tasha and Annie didn't give up. That's why. Not because some mysterious hoarder decided to be generous."

"But what do we do now—plant gardens again and wait to see if we'll have food for next winter? What happens if things don't grow a second time? Do you think Tasha—"

"What have you got against Tasha?" B yells. The girls watch them, transfixed and terrified. "She gave you *vitamins,* for God's sake." His face darkens. "She would have helped you get rid of the baby if she'd thought it was safe. Don't think I've forgotten."

How could she think that? The memory is in every shadow on his face, in every strained hello he gives her in the morning. "She's a doctor," she says. "That's her job."

"She didn't have to stay here, though," he argues. "They didn't have to help us gather supplies or build the greenhouses or get wood for the winter. They could have kept on going when they found out the hospital was destroyed. But they stayed. We're here—*you're* here—because of them. Jesus, Heather. What's your problem? Where's your faith?"

She laughs at this—high, almost hysterical. Faith in what? In centaurs? In other magical beasts that prowled the mountains around them long years before any of them were born? Faith in the ground that teems beneath them, in a world that chokes the food they plant and offers them poison berries instead? In the vegetation that creeps relentlessly in to drown the city?

Or does he mean faith in regular people, in the miracles they work with their own hands? They have survived one winter, yes. That is a kind of miracle.

But that was because of Estajfan. If they continue to survive, it will only be because of Estajfan. Tasha has nothing to do with it.

"I don't hate her," she says, finally. "But I don't trust her either."

It's B's turn to laugh now. "Are you serious?"

"Fine. I knew you would say that. Never mi—"

"You think she's got some kind of nefarious plan? That she's going to—what, hoard all of the food so everyone else starves?"

"Why is she here? Why *here*, B? Why spend the whole winter here and ration the goddamned food and practically take over a small mountain city no one cares about? Why not somewhere else?"

"Here is as good a place as any." He pushes the stroller past her, out through the front door. "And maybe she saw too many of us falling apart and figured she could help."

"Right," she says, pretending not to get the dig. "Because Tasha has no problems of her own and is taking perfect care of her own family."

"What?" He's genuinely surprised for a moment, then rolls his eyes and continues down the walk. "Oh, for Chrissake. You don't even *know* her family."

"I know you think she's strong and unflappable, but I see how she neglects Annie in favour of saving everyone else. And when she can't save everyone else—I've seen her in the greenhouse, B. I know what she does when she's alone. She's telling herself—and us—stories too. That we'll survive if we stick together, that everything will be okay if we just *hold on*. But what if she's wrong? What if things aren't going to be okay?"

"Won't they?" he says, exasperated. He doesn't stop pushing the buggy. The girls laugh loudly at the bumpy ride over the overgrown road. "How long do you think we'd survive all on our own? How long did Randall and Stella make it? Candice and Seth and the baby? We're only here because we stuck together. And we only stuck together because Tasha and Annie saved us."

"How is holding on to the idea of *pulling through* going to help us when there's no one left?" she says. And then, "Have you talked to Annie? Have you asked her how *she* feels about Tasha? Because I guarantee you Annie's not feeling the same saviour vibes that you are."

This time he does stop, and turns to her. "What is wrong with telling people that we'll survive if we stick together? What's the alternative—that we're all doomed? Is that it? Is that what you want us all to say? Because if it is—why bother eating at all? Why bother taking the girls out on those goddamned walks? Why bother anything?"

"Tasha's not looking after her own family—that's my point," she says. "I know she wants to help. But she's a fanatic. She's neglecting the person closest to her because she's hell-bent on saving the city."

He's beyond exasperated now. "And that's a bad thing? I want to survive. Don't you?"

"She wants to save the city because she thinks that's going to save *her*," she says, the words clicking into place like solving a puzzle. "And if—when—it doesn't, everything she's built will fall apart."

He starts walking again. "She almost died during the winter along with the rest of us," he says. "How is that saving her, exactly?"

"She's telling herself a story," Heather says. "One where she's the only one making the right decisions." He's pulled ahead of her—she speeds up to try and catch him. "You know about her parents, right?"

"Yes," he says. "They died in a fire. What does that matter?"

"I don't think she's over that," she says. "I think she's still trying to save them. I think *she* thinks that if she saves us, it will redeem her. Somehow."

B looks back at her, his eyes filled with loss. "We're all trying to save our parents," he says. "Even if we can't."

She reaches out to him, finally, wrapping her fingers around his wrist. "But that's just it," she says, softly. "We can't. We survive by moving on, and moving forward. She hasn't. She refuses to let go of things she can't control, even when they're already lost to her. And everything about that makes me nervous."

B shrugs her away. "Yes," he says. "Like how you moved on and forward by not talking to anybody for a year after your father threw himself off that mountain. Like how you move forward now by telling the children silly stories about magical mountains and queens who murder geese." He registers her shock. "You think I don't hear you telling those stories to the girls? My God, Heather—if that's your idea of *moving on*,

I think I'll stick with Tasha." He pushes the stroller ahead again, and this time she lets him go.

✳

As they draw closer to the square, they join a crowd. Little girls in faded dresses, little boys who run around, red scabs on their knees. Parents who look as tired and grey as Heather feels. At the square, people mill about, antsy and unsure. Someone has pulled an old wagon into the middle of the square and heaped it high with coloured boxes. Tasha is out front, greeting everyone, and as children shyly approach, Tasha's people—Annie and Kevin—climb on board and start tossing boxes out into the crowd. The children cry out with delight as they rip the boxes open on the grass. More clothes, some toys, more colouring books and crayons. Things salvaged and stored for months, it would seem.

"Where's Elyse?" Heather asks B when she reaches him.

He looks around. "Maybe she's resting. She's not well. Which you would know, if you'd been paying attention to anything else."

Of course I know, she wants to say. Instead she turns back to the boxes, to the scraps of wrapping paper that now litter the ground.

B sees the scraps too. "I don't remember storing wrapping paper."

She can tell by the look on his face that he doesn't remember storing clothing, or the other gifts that the children are unwrapping on the grass. Dolls and building blocks. Clay modelling kits. There is even chocolate—small bars that Annie pulls out of one of the boxes and tosses into the crowd.

Tasha approaches them just as B catches a chocolate bar. He can't keep the surprise from his face. "We had chocolate?" he says. "We had chocolate all this time?"

"I wanted to be able to save something special for all of us when we made it through the winter," she says. Always the same calm, knowledgeable voice.

Heather thinks of Tasha in the greenhouse—an animal crouched down on the floor, writhing and wild.

B fingers the bar, watching Tasha. *And what about the people who didn't make it through the winter?* he wants to say—Heather can see it in his eyes. Instead he unwraps the chocolate and breaks off two small pieces, squats down, and tucks them into the mouths of his girls.

"Here," Tasha says, and hands a bar to Heather. "How are you feeling?"

How *is* she feeling? At once stretched and lost—as though she is both a ghost and something more than herself.

"Any problems?" Tasha prods. "More spotting?"

She can feel B watching. "No," she says.

Tasha nods. "I'm glad to hear it. You know where I am if you need me."

"Yes." Heather says. "I know."

"Tasha," B says, and she turns to him. "How much food have you got hidden away?"

Her voice is still light, unconcerned. "It's mostly just the chocolate."

"And all these—gifts?" B moves his arm in a wide circle. "Just waiting for better weather while people died in the cold?"

Tasha flushes. "We had to make some har—"

"I know," he interrupts and looks away from her. He seems so disappointed that Heather almost feels sorry for him. "We've all had to make hard choices. I get it. But—people died, Tasha, while you sat on all of this."

She won't meet B's eyes now. "I know the names of everyone who died," she says. "Believe me, Brendan. I know. But I also knew that if we survived the winter we would need something . . . celebratory."

"And if we plant the gardens again and nothing grows?" Heather asks. "What kind of celebration will we have then?"

Tasha looks at her, but doesn't reply. Instead she walks back to the trailer and climbs up on it, then holds up her hands for silence.

"I am so glad to see you," she calls out when even the children are quiet. "To see each and every one of you."

The tired lines in the faces of everyone around them seem to lift a little.

"We've been through so much," Tasha calls out. "But we survived because we did it together. And we will *continue* to survive because we're doing this together."

There is a smattering of applause.

"We'll plant the gardens soon, and more—we'll create a proper farm," Tasha says. "We're clearing the vines from the roads and soon we'll send out scouting parties. If we've survived, other people must have too."

She continues to speak, and the applause grows louder. The faces around Heather and B begin to shine with something other than fatigue.

You can do it, Tasha says. Her eyes burn with hope and love. *We can do it.* The clapping becomes a cheer, becomes a chant. *Tasha. Tasha. Tasha.*

Heather feels the words lift around them and become something else. A legend, a story.

There once was a city in the shadow of the mountains. Then winter brought the cold, and many of them died. But with the spring came warmth and hope, and the strongest among them held hands out to the weaker and lifted them up to the sun.

We will be whole again, they said.

We will find others, they said.

We must believe in something larger. We must believe we're not alone.

She thinks of Tasha, weeping on the greenhouse floor.

"Where will the animals come from?" she hears herself call. The clapping dies down. "For the farm. A proper farm needs cows and chickens, at least. Where will they come from?"

"We'll find them," Tasha says. "The scouting parties will be looking for animals, too."

"And if you don't?" Heather says. "What then? What if there are no animals and the gardens don't grow again and we have to survive *another* winter—what then?"

"Maybe the Food Angel will come back," someone yells, in a voice that's only half joking.

"We can't rely on the Food Angel," Tasha says. "We have to rely on each other." She looks straight at Heather, her eyes so bright they look feverish. "The gardens will grow this year. They have to."

"You don't know that!" Heather cries. B puts a hand on her arm; she shrugs him off, steps forward.

Tasha opens her mouth to speak, but an outraged yell drowns her out. They turn, as one, to see Elyse walking toward them, half dragging what looks like a bundle of rags. As she gets closer, Heather sees that it is a bird, brown and mottled. A chicken. One of Joseph's chickens.

The yell comes again and now they see Joseph, striding up the road behind Elyse.

"Tasha!" he yells. "*Tasha!*" He begins to run, passing Elyse, making for the trailer. He is weeping, incandescent with fury. "You *fucking hypocrite.* You *goddamn murdering piece of shit.*"

"Joseph," Tasha says. "I don't understand. What's going on?"

"*She* killed one of my chickens!" he shouts, thrusting a finger at Elyse. Elyse lays the dead bird gently on the ground. There is blood splotched over her face, splashed up her arms. In her other hand she holds a knife; she sets that down on the ground too. She pays no attention to Joseph, staring at Tasha and Annie. "I did what had to be done," she says. "He won't let us take the hens for eggs, but we can eat them, at least."

Tasha looks troubled, and suddenly so tired. "Elyse," she says. "You can't do that."

"*He* can't do that!" Elyse cries. "We barely survived the winter. And he had chickens in the house that whole time!"

"Four chickens are not going to feed a whole fucking city!" Joseph yells. "*Three* chickens even less. What's wrong with you?"

"The rest of us are starving!" Elyse shouts. There's a grumble around them after she says this, a whisper of unease through the crowd.

"Elyse. Just stop," Annie says. "You're only going to make things worse."

"Why am I the only one who sees what we need to do?" Elyse cries. "We're going to starve if we don't make even harder decisions. You can't *celebrate* any of this aw—" She bends over and coughs heavily, her shoulders heaving. She stumbles forward, then rests her hands against her thighs and heaves again. Her cough is thick and wet, insistent. All-consuming. When she is finally able, she straightens, her face resolute. "It was just one chicken."

"She's not *just a chicken,*" Joseph says. His voice breaks. "She and the others are all the family I have left."

"Joseph," Tasha says. "I'm so sorry."

"This is all your fault!" he shouts at her. "I should have left months ago. We *all* should have left months ago." He gestures wildly to the dead bird at Elyse's feet. "You want that chicken? Fine. Take it. I am leaving this place. Fuck all of you." He turns and begins to stalk back to his house.

A man breaks away from the edge of the crowd and follows him.

Then another person, a woman this time.

Another.

Another.

"Joseph," Tasha calls. "*Joseph.*"

None of them turn around.

At last, Tasha turns back to the crowd still standing in front of the wagon. "We'll be all right," she says. "Don't worry. We have a plan."

But the spell is broken now. People begin to drift away from the square to their homes, leaving whatever else Tasha might have said to them unspoken.

"Maybe they should go," Elyse says, after most of them are gone. "That's more food for us, anyway."

Tasha's eyes rest on Heather, who has stayed with B in the square. "They'll come around," Tasha says. "You'll see."

The next morning, Joseph's house is empty. He and his chickens are gone.

The weather gets hotter. They eat a bowl of rice a day, topped with one can of beans, split between the two of them and the girls. They plant the gardens, and hope, as their stash runs out.

Sometimes Heather finds apples or other fruits in their backyard. B is too beaten down to ask about such gifts now; he just accepts them, and eats his share.

He still goes to the strip mall to help Tasha and Annie when he can.

But sometimes he sleeps away the day. Sometimes they all sleep, as the vines grow over Joseph's old house, choke it into memory.

On the days that B leaves, Heather musters the strength to take the girls to the greenhouse. One foot in front of the other.

Then, at last, one day Estajfan comes out from the trees when she grows close.

"Heather, please don't come to the greenhouse anymore," he says. "Save your strength."

"I can do it," she says. It is still possible—even with her belly, even with the girls. Delirium keeps her going now. These terrible, hysterical gifts.

"Heather." Estajfan comes to her and puts his hands on her shoulders. "Heather, stop coming here. Please rest."

"I rest here or I rest at home." She shrugs. "I'd rather be here with you."

He watches her face. "And your . . . B?"

She looks away. "All you have to share now is what grows on the mountain, right?"

"We still look," he whispers. "We go farther and farther, but things are harder and harder to find."

She closes her eyes. It is not hard to see. This abandoned city, that abandoned town. Large humps of green that used to be houses, smaller humps that might have been cars on the roads.

There are smaller humps even than those, almost imperceptible in the green. This one big enough, perhaps, to have once been a person. A child. The flowers that bend around them are bright and terrible—orange and purple and a brighter yellow than she's ever seen, giant half-moon traps that hang off the vines on other houses. Bushes with dark, juicy berries, soft white oleander plants that choke the hydro poles that stand still and useless, lining the streets.

She takes a breath, then opens her eyes. "You need to take us up the mountain."

He looks at her. "You should have left a year ago."

She laughs at this. "Well, I didn't. You really think I could leave?" Then she says it again. "Estajfan. You need to bring us up the mountain. Me. The girls. And B."

He shakes his head.

"Estajfan. Please."

Silence. She watches him clench and unclench his fists. Then he says, "I can bring you."

"Yes," she says. "And the girls. And B."

"Just you. The mountain is the centaurs' home."

She steps back from him, one arm around each of the girls, a hand half covering their ears as though they understand. She opens her mouth. "N—"

"*Heather.*"

She turns as Estajfan jumps back into the trees and disappears. The ground rumbles beneath her feet.

Elyse is coming toward her, from the field. She stops in front of Heather, breathing hard. "Heather?"

Heather digs her fingernails into her palms. The girls whimper, weak, against her collarbone. "What, the horse?" she says.

"That wasn't a hor—"

"You're tired, Elyse." Heather starts to walk back in the direction of the city.

"That—that thing—it was more than a horse!" Elyse lunges forward, grabs Heather's arm. When she tries to shake her off, Elyse holds on even tighter.

For a moment, everything around them stops. There is no birdsong, there is no rustle of the leaves. There is no wind.

"In the beginning," Elyse says, and she lets Heather's arm fall, "a horse fell in love with a woman."

"That's just a story." Heather resumes walking, her heart beating loud in her ears. She fights to keep from screaming. *Estajfan. Estajfan.*

"It's up there, isn't it?" Elyse says, stumbling after Heather. "On the mountain. My grandmother—she used to tell us stories. It's up there, and—" she coughs, ugly and painful, but keeps coming—"oh my God, Heather. Did he say—I heard '*centaurs.*' Are there more of them?"

She doesn't turn around. One foot in front of the other. Forward. Forward. Never back.

"What's on the mountain, Heather? Do they . . ." Elyse falls silent for a moment, and Heather can almost hear the gears working in her mind, pieces falling into place with terrifying precision. "Was it them who brought the food? Is there *food* up there?"

Heather keeps walking, willing herself not to cry. Elyse struggles relentlessly behind her. "No one has been up the mountain in years," she says. "There is no food. We all know that, Elyse. We've told stories about the mountain forever."

"You were there! You—" And then Elyse stops. "You knew," she says. "You've known this whole time."

"You're making no sense, Elyse."

"I'm making perfect sense!" Elyse cries. "You kept this from all of us while the whole city was starving?"

"*Is* starving," Heather mutters. She feels Elyse watching her. "We *are* starving, Elyse. We will continue to starve until it ends." The footsteps stop, and finally Heather turns to see Elyse half hunched over in the middle of the overgrown road. She and the girls are almost home; she has to shut this girl down. "You didn't see anything," Heather says. "I walk the forest all the time, Elyse—I know how the shadows and the light can trick you. Stop grasping for hope that isn't there."

"I know what I saw," Elyse insists. "And it *wasn't* a horse."

"What did you see?" It's B, on their doorstep, coming out to meet them.

Heather shrugs. She lifts Greta out of the sling and passes her over so that B's attention shifts to the baby. "Nothing," she says. "A trick of the light in the forest. That's all."

Elyse laughs. "The only one with tricks around here is you." She looks at B. "Did *you* see it too? Do you know about the creature in the forest?"

B pauses only for an instant, but it's enough. "What creature?" he says.

"Half man, half horse," Elyse gasps. "It was—Brendan, it was like something from a dream. Like the stories we used to hear when we were kids! But it was *real.* I swear."

"If there are magical creatures in the mountains," Heather says, trying to sound weary, not panicked, "don't you think someone would have talked about them before?"

"You did," B says. Low and unmistakable.

She glances at him. "What? I did not."

"Right after you came down, when your father died. You told the doctors there were creatures on the mountain. And no one believed you, so you stopped talking."

Heather swallows. "How would you know?"

"I went to school with you, remember? People talked. Everyone knew about your time in the hospital. Everyone said you were crazy. I said it too, once."

She looks away from him. The sting is so old it doesn't even hurt, but the panic building in her chest is something altogether different. "I barely remember you from school."

"Why would you?" he says, still in that strange voice. "You didn't talk to anybody."

She laughs. "And everyone remembered me anyway—because they said I was crazy? Because I walked funny?"

He doesn't deny it.

"They're up on the mountain," Elyse interjects. She has B now—soon she'll have the whole city. "Brendan—they have *food* up on the mountain. We have to go up."

He hasn't stopped looking at Heather. "Is that where the fruit came from? And the flowers?"

She doesn't meet his eyes. "There is nothing on the mountain," she says, again. "If we go up there, people will die."

"People have already died!" Elyse shouts. She takes one more step closer to Heather. "If you aren't going to do what needs to be done, then I will." She turns and starts to walk to the town.

Heather lunges after Elyse, all her careful resolve disintegrating in panic. B's hand on her arm is the only thing that stops her. He has Greta on his hip; Jilly, still in the sling, looks up at her, confused.

"You need to tell me everything," he says.

"You're hurting me," she says. She watches Elyse hurry away from them, then glances at his hand on her arm. He doesn't let go.

The ground rumbles beneath her feet.

"We can't go up the mountain," she whispers to B. "It isn't safe."

"Why isn't it safe, Heather?"

"It just isn't."

She finally wrenches her arm away, and he laughs—a short, sharp bark at the sky. "You can't really be serious. Half man, half horse? What kind of joke is this?"

"It isn't a joke," she says, dully. "But it doesn't matter. We can't go up there."

"Tell me," he says, and she knows what he means. "Tell me all of it."

And so she does—standing there in front of their house as the sky begins to darken and the breeze rustles through the trees. The day her father took her up the mountain. The songs he sang. The beasts in the trees and her father's explosive joy. The way he touched the palomino. His sudden stumble and fall.

"How could he do that?" B interrupts.

"How could he fall?"

"No—how could he take you up the mountain? On a path he didn't know was safe? A child like you who couldn't even walk straight on normal ground?"

"He helped me."

"What if you'd fallen? What if you'd gotten hurt? Would he have left you there with God knows what while he went down for help? Didn't he think about that?"

"He believed in me," she retorts. A reflex, her loyalty so deep it splits her in two. "I wanted to believe in myself too. To know that I could do it."

Help us, she remembers him saying. *Help my daughter.*

B shakes his head. "So—what—your father fell and this—creature— carried you back down the mountain? And then what?"

She thinks of it—night after night of hushed escape from the house. Estajfan, smiling as she drew him on the paper. Estajfan, telling her a thousand stories.

"I had no one else to talk to," she says, eventually.

"You had *people* to talk to!" he cries. "You didn't want to talk to any-body else."

"People wouldn't have understood," she says. "You don't know because you weren't there."

"I'm here now," he says. "I've been here for almost two years. And you've never told me any of this." B looks away, for a moment. He doesn't believe her entirely, she can tell. But who can blame him? They are all malnourished, weakened, beaten down by this disaster. What's easier to believe in—magic or despair?

"I've tried so hard to be good to you," B says. "But you never let me in. You'd rather believe in the stories you tell yourself instead."

"This isn't a story," she says, softly. "That's what I'm saying."

"Not just this," he says, surprising her. "Everything you believe about yourself is a story."

She blinks. "What?"

He sighs. "Everything. The mountain. These—centaurs. The way that everyone treated you at school." She opens her mouth to protest; he just shakes his head. "I know we weren't perfect. I know *I* haven't been perfect. But—people change, Heather. I've tried. Tasha has tried, and tried, and tried. And all you show us is a wall."

She swallows. She'd expected anger, not this.

"You might as well be up on that mountain already," he says. "You'd rather be in a fantasy world than here."

"Can you blame me?"

His face hardens. "I can, a little. It's like you believe that the only person who can change is you. You went into the forest while everyone else tried to keep the city alive."

"I had the girls," she protests. "I kept the girls alive."

"You did," he admits. "That's true." They stare at each other, and then he sighs again, and says, "So. These—centaurs—on the mountain. Is there food? Like Elyse said? Can we go up there and get it?"

"We can't go up," she says. "B—it isn't safe. People will die."

"People are already dying," he says, echoing Elyse. "If there is food up there, we have to try."

"B," she whispers, "no one can go."

"So that's it, then? They're going to let all of us starve?"

She doesn't say anything—her face says it for her. She watches the realization slide over his face with something like horror.

"Not all of us," he says, eventually. "Not you."

Heather swallows, puts a hand against his arm. "He said he could take me up. I said—"

He leans over and plucks Jilly out of the sling. "Go, then," he says. "Get the fuck up the mountain and leave us alone."

She is too shocked to protest. She watches him turn away from her as if in a dream. He walks up the steps to their house, carrying the girls, then stands for a moment, his hand on the doorknob.

It's a dream, she thinks. *It's only another dream.*

"Go," he says, and he doesn't turn to her. "That's what you really want, isn't it?"

"I have to warn him," she whispers. "I'll come back. I promise."

Beneath her feet, a steady *rumble, rumble,* in the ground.

✳

Estajfan is not at the greenhouse. She heads past it, toward the forest, pushing her way through the underbrush. Sweat pools in her collarbone and trickles down between her breasts. When she reaches out to push the vines out of the way, her hands sting where they touch the green. She stops to examine them—small welts rise and fade as she watches. *A trick of the light*, she thinks, and pushes ahead, ignoring the pain. She's good at that.

Another rumble hits—so hard and so loud she almost falls. When she rights herself, she's barely past the greenhouse. She retreats back against it, looks up into the trees.

"Estajfan," she calls. "*Estajfan.*"

"*Heather.*" Suddenly he's beside her, before her, everywhere. Mountain air and light and sky.

She wants to collapse, to cry, but she gets a hold of herself. "Estajfan, listen to me. They're coming up the mountain. You have to go—you, Aura, Petrolio. Please. I don't know what they'll do. They're—everyone is so hungry, and so desperate."

Estajfan shakes his head. "They can't come up the mountain."

"I know that—"

"No." He grips her shoulders again. "Heather—something deeper is wrong. I've been trying to figure out what the ground magic is saying—"

"Ground magic?" She stares at him.

An unleashed banshee wail shoots at them from all directions. Heather covers her ears and bends low. Low enough to see the lilies around the greenhouse open their petals like mouths and scream. The glass shatters. Vines crawl through the shards and loop around her arms. She yanks free but the vines wind tighter, pull her down to the forest floor. Tiny green tendrils burrow into her arms. A thousand tiny pinpricks, a thousand pictures in her head.

A father tucks his son into bed, lifts up the pillow, and smothers the child. Then he jumps headfirst from a third-storey window and his neck snaps like a twig.

A mother bursts into tears at a dinner table and stabs her daughter through the eye with a fork, then takes her own life.

Children face down in a filthy tub. The mother and father slumped against the sink, a gun on the floor, blood and brain matter splashed over the wall.

In their city. In cities far away.

Then her girls and B, dangling from a beam in the kitchen.

The screaming. The screaming. She's screaming with it.

The ground surges around her, green things thrumming in triumph. The air smells like the world has a fever.

Estajfan rips the vines away and picks her up. She turns into his shoulder and feels them start to climb.

Mama, says Greta's little voice inside her ear.

Da, says Jilly.

They are gone—her girls.

There are no stories that will protect her from this.

They are gone from her, forever.

– 10 –

Tasha is in the clinic, her stethoscope against a little boy's chest. She tries to concentrate on the heartbeat in her ears, but all she can see is Annie, pale and withdrawn in the corner of the room. When they woke up this morning, arms and legs tangled around one another, Annie had jumped away from her as though she couldn't stand her touch. She's been distant all day—even more distant than she's been recently.

Tasha tried to distract herself by seeing patients. Those who managed to drag themselves into the clinic today all showed the same signs—they were restless and weary, jumpy and odd, their eyes feverish.

Candice had come, complaining of a fever. Tasha brought her into the examination room and pulled the curtain across.

"Sleep," she said. "Sleep, and try to drink as much water as you can."

"There's no water left," Candice said, dreamily.

"Annie will give you some." Tasha glanced at the curtain. "Candice," she whispered. "What happened to your little boy?"

Candice blinked at her, the words seeming to come from far away. "He died," she whispered.

Tasha swallowed. "Did you—did you take him to the mountain?"

"I couldn't," Candice said. "I couldn't do it. We got stuck in the snow—I tried to keep him warm, but nothing helped."

Relief made Tasha dizzy; she reached out and held the other woman's shoulder. "I'm sorry," she whispered. "I'm so sorry."

"I would like to sleep," Candice continued. "I want to sleep and forget that any of this ever happened. But I just have nightmares. I never get any rest."

Tasha doled a few precious antibiotics out into Candice's waiting palm. "These will help," she said. She felt renewed and also weary beyond belief; when Candice stood up to go, Tasha hugged her, then let her move beyond the curtain.

As she moves through later patients, she notices they all say the same thing. A young boy comes in, trailed by his mother. She listens to his heart while his mother mutters something about strange dreams.

"Dreams?" Tasha says. *It's probably the flu*, she tells herself. *Delirium brought on by fever.*

"I just want food," the woman whispers. "But those damned flowers keep taking it away."

"What?"

A rush of wind outside the building brings the mingled scent of sweet flowers and dirty little boy to her nose. The mother only shrugs. "The vines eat everything, and give us only berries."

Tasha puts a hand on the mother's arm. "What have you eaten?"

Then, all around them, a scream.

The window shatters. The mother cries out and reaches for the boy, covers his ears. She begins to laugh—softly at first and then loudly—and then she screams, and her hands are around the little boy's neck and she *snaps* his head, and now he's sliding toward the floor, his eyes unseeing.

The mother stops screaming and whispers, "I'm not enough. We're all going to starve. I can't stop it." She lunges past Tasha and throws herself at the shattered window—her fingers scrabbling for broken glass. As Tasha watches, horrified, the mother slashes her own neck.

Tasha can't move. The screaming hasn't stopped. Vines snake their way over the glass in the window frame, slither toward her, across the floor.

She backs away and comes up against a cupboard, spreads her hands wide, sidles along the counter until she realizes she's looking for a phone. Futile.

"*Tasha.*"

She turns at Annie's call. Her wife's arms are bare. Something sharp glints in her hand. Glass.

"Annie." Tasha sidles along the wall. Annie stands between her and the door. Vines slither up her legs.

"I was never enough for you," Annie says. "I did *everything* you wanted. It's never going to be enough, is it? *I* am never going to be enough."

"Annie." Tasha raises a hand "Annie, please."

Annie lunges. Tasha kicks a chair in her way and scrambles along the wall, her hand reaching for the doorknob of the room that they've converted into a supply closet. She swings the door open and jumps inside, heaves it closed, locks the knob. Annie slams into the door and everything shakes.

"*I hate you!*" Annie screams. "*I hate everything you've done to me.*"

The darkness in the closet is absolute. On the other side of the door, Annie is cackling, mad. The sound goes on and on.

PART TWO

— 11 —

When she sleeps, Aura dreams about her mother—the same dream she's had since she was young: a house, a long window, a woman with blonde hair staring out. There is a man with her, flat-nosed and gentle, and then children, one by one. The woman dotes on her husband and her children with a love that's almost desperate. Slowly the woman's sadness lifts from her shoulders, but settles like cobwebs into the corners of her home.

The woman never leaves the village, although it could just be that Aura doesn't dream about her anywhere else. The children grow and Aura sees them arrive home from trips, from journeys far away. The mother is always at the door to greet them. When they tell her about their time away, there is a flash of something in the mother's eyes—longing, hunger, maybe guilt.

Sometimes the woman mentions events in the village. Small things, normal human things. Babies and weddings and death. These are the moments when Aura balls her fists in the dream. Sometimes when she unfurls her hands, she sees red crescent moons across her palms.

No one in her mother's house ever notices her. No one suspects that she's there.

But why would they? None of her half-siblings know the story of their mother's first husband. None of them know she exists.

As the village grows into a town, these children become town children, then town adults. They sail ships to the other side of the world and become teachers and, generations later, lawyers and doctors and accountants. And then they die. They all die. The daughters and granddaughters and great-times-many granddaughters are all, without exception, suffragettes. Maybe this is where the mother's passion and wanderlust has gone—passed down to the girls, who are strong-willed and difficult, mean and beautiful. They have the woman's eyes—Aura's eyes, and her brothers', too.

She tells her father about the dreams once, when she is small.

"She seems sad," Aura tells him.

Her father straightens. He is building them a treehouse, like the ones the village children play in, or so he says. The treehouse isn't really a treehouse—more like a platform that juts out from the tree—but Estajfan and Petrolio already know how to climb higher, to twist their legs and grip their ankles around the trunk. Sometimes they swing from one of the higher branches and do chin-ups.

Aura doesn't care about the treehouse. She cares about her father, though, so she climbs onto this half-built refuge and waits for him to answer.

"What does she look like?" he says.

She regrets telling him about her dream instantly.

"What does she look like?" he asks again.

"Like me," she says. The words feel like birds with sharp claws. She feels them push out all around them and draw the scene right there, like magic, and suddenly they are both standing *inside* her dream, inside the house. Her father turns in a circle, nodding. The plaster walls, the rough-hewn door, the scrap of bright cloth by the fireplace. "Yes, this is the house," he says and turns to her. "Do you want to see where you were born?"

She swallows, shakes her head. She just wants to leave.

"I think you should see it." He holds out a hand and she takes it. Her hooves touch spongy moss and floorboard all at once. They are still on the mountain, but they're surrounded by the house. She wants to run into the trees, but her father's grip is so tight it hurts. She whimpers.

"Be quiet," he hisses, and now she is truly afraid.

He pulls her to the back of the house—she's never seen the back of the house in her dreams; she's never wanted to be anywhere except where the woman is, and the woman never comes here—and steps through a doorway. There is so much light that at first it's hard to see. The windows are bare and the outside door is open. The room is so cold she shivers. She's never cold.

"The rest of the house doesn't feel this way," she says.

"No one comes here," her father says.

She doesn't ask him how he knows. "Why not?"

The ashes in the fireplace are cold like everything else in the room. Her father stares into them.

"There was a table here," he says, gesturing. "Our bedroom wasn't big enough to hold the doctor and the midwives, so they brought her in here and laid her on the table. She fell asleep, after."

He doesn't say after *what*, but Aura knows.

The floor is bleached white and the walls of the room have been whitewashed. Everything is bare, bare, bare.

"Why don't they tear this room down?"

He drops her hand and walks to the doorway. Aura wants to tell him to be careful, but she's not sure he'll listen. What if he *is* swallowed? Could her dreams do that—whisk him away to some in-between place?

He shimmers as he steps through the doorway. She calls out to him, and he shimmers back into place, instantly. It was only the light playing tricks. But when he turns back to her, he is sobbing—like someone's stuck a knife beneath his ribcage, like he can't breathe. The room shines with sunlight and something else. The bleached white floorboards, the blank walls—they pulse with forgetting.

Aura watches her father sob until she can't stand it anymore. She steps forward—her hooves clack against the wood and it's the first time in her life that she's been ashamed of her body, of how large it is and the noise it makes.

"Da," she whispers. "Let's go."

He lets her lead him. In the front room, she's suddenly terrified that the woman will be there, but it stays empty and she reaches for the front doorknob without letting him go. But when she tries to duck through the front door, he tugs against her, fiercely. His eyes are wild and animal in a way she's never seen. He twists, she loses her grip on him, and she feels the house hold him tight—the cobwebs of sadness that the woman beats back with her broom are angry now, hard and grasping.

You did this to me, Aura hears, and she knows it is the house talking. *You did this to her. You did this to us.* Her father moans—high and terrified.

The house is gathering him in. It will pull him into the back room and bleach him away. It will make him into nothing. This house and the ground it stands on—everything wants to forget. To pretend they have never been.

She grabs for him and pulls. The house *snaps* him away.

"No," she snarls, and pulls harder—she thinks of Petrolio and Estajfan and how they've teased her for being so much smaller than they are, but she is not small here, she is *not.* She digs her hooves in and pulls with everything she can, with her twin hearts and her love and her hot, hot rage. *No,* she says again. *No. No. No. Give him back.*

And then he is through the door and hers again. They are back on the mountain, and you wouldn't think that they've been anywhere except for the fact that their hands are locked together. They stare at each other, breathing hard.

"Don't ever leave the mountain again," her father says, finally. "I don't care if it's only in your dreams. Do you understand?"

"I can't control my dreams, Da."

"The house invites you, and you go in. Don't go in."

"But," she says, "*you* go down."

"If you get caught, they will kill you." He pauses. "They may be family, but they don't know you. They won't understand."

"No one even knows I'm there."

"The house knew I was there," he says. "The house knows you, too." She sees the effort he makes to calm himself. "You are not—*we* are not—meant to be."

The words hurt her so much she can barely breathe. "You'll never be safe off the mountain. Please don't go, Aura. Please."

"All right," she whispers.

He hugs her. When he lets her go, he says, "You be a good girl and go find your brothers."

The rage is back in her throat so quickly it burns. "I'm not a girl!" she shouts. "I'm not a girl, and you *aren't* a man!"

He nods, stricken. "I won't say it again." But he leaves her, frightened by her anger.

She would cry, except that crying will make her think of the house again, and she can't bear to be sad and scared anymore. Instead she runs and hides in the trees. Petrolio finds her, eventually.

"What happened to you?" he says, and he pulls her hair in the way that she hates. Like her, he is slim and blond, his four white feet always ready to run. When she chases him, she never wins.

Aura can catch Estajfan sometimes, but she's pretty sure he lets her do it.

"Nothing. Leave me alone."

But this is Petrolio, so of course he doesn't. "What happened? Aura, what happened?" *Whathappenedwhathappenedwhathappenedwhathappened. Aura, come onnnnn.*

She can't tell him. In the house, when her father let go of her hand, she understood that he was hoping the house would take him back, make him what he used to be. Or, failing that, make him nothing. *We are not meant to be.*

Her father still loves her, the blonde woman at the window. Their mother. He would be human again in an instant. He would rather be that than be all that they have.

Eventually, with no response from her, Petrolio gets bored and leaves her. She waits under the trees for some time, then heads for the tree-house and destroys it, tossing the pieces off the side of the mountain. When she's done, the tree is bare and trembling, the ground littered with broken wood, the air menacing and silent. The tree will be angry at her for a long time.

She turns to see her brothers standing silent in the clearing. She doesn't know how long they've been there. There is no fear in their faces, just curiosity and a mirroring grief. They feel her heartache without knowing what it is.

The next night, Aura dreams of the house and her mother again. She doesn't tell her father. She walks right into the house. The flat-nosed man is with her mother and the sadness in her face is gone. Aura watches them, invisible in the corner. She screams, but no one hears a thing.

✳

Many years later, when the meteors come, she is standing where the tree-house used to be. Petrolio and the other centaurs, the ones who were born from the mountain, have gathered in the clearing to watch. Her brother reaches for her hand. Estajfan is nowhere she can see.

The meteors fall on the city without mercy, without rhyme. They smash into the lowland trees. She watches fire hit the far-off river, imagines steam rising into the air, the riverbed dried up in an instant, all things lush and green burning away.

The mountain centaurs raise their arms and cry out with joy. Beneath her hooves, she realizes, the ground is rejoicing. Green things will grow again, tendril their way over human death. New seedlings will love the richer soil. They will love how much more space they have, the freedom to grow unchecked.

Petrolio squeezes her hand.

She doesn't want to think about the people in the city, but she does. Estajfan has told her stories. That *other* daughter, the one that they met on the mountain. She is down there now, buried somewhere in the mess.

It's been years since she dreamed of the house (she was a good daughter, in the end), but Aura thinks of it now as the world burns below them. Time passes differently here on the mountain; years since the last dream, longer than that since their mother grew old and died. Centuries? She isn't sure.

The mountain centaurs begin to sing. They are many but when they sing they sound as one—eerie and sad, angry and beautiful and triumphant as the city far below them catches fire. Aura and Petrolio stay quiet. The other centaurs don't care about what happens off the mountain. The mountain speaks to them in ways that it doesn't speak to Aura and her brothers. They aren't lonely, the original three—not exactly—but they're alone.

She casts her mind toward her mother's house, but doesn't see it. She imagines a fiery piece of the sky coming down to claim it—a gaping crater where their birthplace used to be, the bleached room gone forever.

It's a small, hard thing to be glad about.

THE DOCTOR AND
THE MOUNTAIN

The doctor walks for days and weeks and months, stopping in a hundred little villages along the way, and gradually the mountains come into view on the horizon. She grew up by the sea—she's never been to the mountains before. They seem higher than it is possible for anything to be, shimmering in layers of fog. Most of them are capped in white, but one mountain is green all the way into the clouds. The sea air tastes of salt. Here, the air tastes like the sky.

There is a city near the green mountain, nestled in its shadow. The doctor makes her way to one of its clinics and asks if they need help. The answer is yes. The answer is always yes. They give her a room in the physicians' lodge. The city folk bring her flowers as a welcome— great red bursts of amaryllis and shining white lilies. She puts them in her window.

The people are happy and fit and superstitious. There are a few houses built closer to the mountain but not many. Almost everyone lives clustered together. The elders sprinkle salt across her doorstep early in the morning on the first day of spring. For wealth, they tell her. Wealth and prosperity and protection from death. For a family, a man.

The doctor has no money except what the world gives her. She has a twin sister whom she sees several times a year, and twin nieces. They are all the family she needs.

And protection from death? She herself is protection enough.

When she isn't working, the doctor walks the streets and wanders out into the fields at the city's edge. Sometimes she walks in the evening, even late at night, when there are no other souls around. No one else in the city goes where she goes.

"There's something strange about that mountain," another one of the doctors at the clinic confesses to her, late one night over drinks at the pub. He too has come from away. "The people here tell all kinds of strange stories. Monsters and ghosts. Animals that talk, that kind of thing."

The doctor laughs. When her mother was thirty-seven years old, a man came to their house and called her a witch. His wife had run away with another man, and the husband was convinced the doctor's mother had helped her do it.

"She wouldn't have fallen in love if it hadn't been for you," he said. "She wouldn't have done that on her own."

The doctor's mother was also a doctor, of sorts. She grew herbs in their backyard that she made into medicine, and she delivered babies when she needed to and got rid of pregnancies when that needed doing. Sometimes a heartbroken girl or boy would come to her and demand a love potion. The doctor's mother would brew tea and sit down and tell them that you cannot make anyone fall in love with you. And sometimes people fall out of love, and there is nothing you can do about that, either. It will hurt. But while you can't see it now, that hurt is building a mountain inside of you. One day you'll climb that mountain. One day, your hurt will allow you to be and do great things.

When the husband came to her, the doctor's mother told him this same thing. But he refused to listen.

"I don't want a mountain," he said. "I just want my wife back. I *deserve* my wife back!" He was shouting like a madman, and the neighbours came to wrestle him away. When they were gone, the doctor's mother closed her front door and let out a long sigh of relief.

That would have been the end of the story except that a few days later, the man came back to their house in the night and burned it to the ground with the doctor's mother inside it.

The doctor had been ten years old at the time. She and her sister had been sleeping over at a friend's house. Her father had managed to get out of the house in time and never forgave himself for it. The guilt was its own kind of ghost.

So when other people warn her about ghosts on the mountain, about animals that hide in the trees—the trickster foxes, the river sprites that wait to drown you—the doctor shrugs and makes her plans. Ghosts don't lurk in the shadows, or in the places people are afraid to go.

One day, after she is finished her shift, the doctor packs her life into her satchel once again and makes her way to the foot of the mountain.

The climb is hard and slow, but the doctor is used to hard journeys. Heights don't scare her and she's slept in the rain countless times; she rests when she's tired. She hacks a little path as she climbs, switchbacking slowly up the mountainside. It's relatively easy—someone has been this way before.

When the centaur comes to greet her, she's only halfway up the mountain.

The centaur seems at once exactly the same and more alien than she remembers—like he belongs to the mountain and she does not. For the first time in her life the doctor feels bedraggled and foolish.

"Why are you here?" he asks.

How long has it been since that night at the house in the village—a year? Impossible, but yes. Weeks wandering away from the village, months spent in the city at the base of the mountain. It feels like no time at all.

"I wanted to see you," she says.

"How did you know I was here?" he says.

She has no real answer. "I don't know."

"No one comes up this mountain," the centaur says. "No one dares."

"Fear and strange stories won't keep people away forever," she says. "Humans climb. Don't you remember?"

"This is *my* home. Humans do not deserve to be here at all."

"Well, I'm here," the doctor says.

There's a loneliness in his face that she remembers from the last time she saw him. "Your children," she says. "Are they all right?"

Unexpectedly, he smiles. "They are beautiful. More beautiful here than they would be anywhere else."

"I'd love to meet them," the doctor says. It's been two years since they were born, but horses would be on their way to fully grown by now. Perhaps centaurs, too.

The centaur frowns. "Perhaps," he says. "One day."

"I could teach them, if you wanted," she says.

The centaur considers her for a long time, then shakes his head. "Not yet. They won't trust you. Give me time."

"*They* won't trust me?" she says. "Or *you* won't?"

"I could use your help," the centaur admits. "But not with the children."

"Anything." She feels—not sorry for him, but *something*.

"I want to teach them all I can about the world that they've come from, and their history," he says. "I want them to know about the things that the humans have made far below. I've been building a collection."

The doctor remembers the first time she saw him in this form, so striking and terrifying in that godforsaken room. He was beautiful then, but he is even more beautiful now, set against the backdrop of the mountain.

"I can teach them about the human world," she says.

"No," he says, his voice fierce. "I was human once. I remember. I do not need your help with that."

The doctor looks at the ground and then nods. "I could bring you things," she says, after a moment. "For your collection."

"I would like that." He looks down at her. "My children," he allows, "are rambunctious."

The doctor laughs. "Most children are."

"I worry about them. I'm afraid that they'll tumble down the mountain and hurt themselves. I'm afraid that they'll get tired of the mountain and run down to the land below and somebody will see them."

"*You* run down to the land below," she reminds him.

"That's different," he says. "I know human ways. I know how to hide. I am careful. They are . . . not."

"They could learn," she says.

"Yes," he says, that fierce anger back in his voice, "but the world will not learn, will it?"

She closes her eyes and feels the wind cool on her face. "Even so," she says. "You shouldn't hide them away."

"I'm not *hiding* them," the centaur says. "I'm keeping them safe."

It occurs to her—not for the first time—that the babies might have died after all. Maybe they died on the journey. Is she ever going to know? "Tell me what you need and I will bring it."

The centaur stares at her for so long the doctor wonders if she's hallucinating. Has she been dreaming this whole time? Then he nods.

"Thank you," he says. "I would like that. Bring me things that I can use to teach the children, and I will look forward to seeing you when you come back."

He doesn't say goodbye—he only turns from her, his black tail fanning the air, and jumps up the steep mountainside. The doctor stands listening to his absence for who knows how long. When she is absolutely sure he's not coming back, she turns and makes her way back down the mountain.

- 12 -

Petrolio and Aura are in the mountain clearing when Estajfan reaches them, Heather curled and silent in his arms. The mountain centaurs immediately gather around them, wary and stiff.

A mountain centaur with brown hair and their father's brown-green eyes confronts him. "She should not be here. You put us all in danger."

"In danger of what?" Estajfan looks at the mountain centaurs, who know, and his siblings, who do not. "What danger could humans possibly pose for us? They're all dead."

His brother and sister jump in shock. In his arms, Heather whimpers, and seems to come to, then moves to climb down from Estajfan's arms. Aura reaches out to her as Estajfan lets her down gently, until she is on her feet, her belly protruding in front of her. The other centaurs hiss.

"She should be down with the others," the mountain centaur says. "The world has decided—the time of humans is no more."

"Aura." Heather's voice is ragged with grief. If she hears the other centaurs standing around them, she doesn't let on.

"Are you hurt?" his sister says.

Estajfan sees the bleak mirth in Petrolio's eyes—*Of course she's hurt,* he can almost hear his brother saying—and addresses the question, and the other centaurs, at the same time. "She's alone," he says. "What do you think, Aura?"

Aura flinches again and balls her fists. "I'm sorry," she whispers. "Heather—I didn't know."

She didn't know, and neither did he—not until that moment of the scream, the sudden unleashed power of the vines and flowers, the world gone green and terrible. But he should have known. He should have *suspected.*

What happens when you choose a new life? You die to the old one, as their father had done so many years ago.

What happens when the *world* chooses a new life without you? He thinks of the months of going down the mountain and out into the cities far and wide—creeping through abandoned streets, finding food wherever he and Petrolio could. The slow grip of human madness the very thing that kept them safe. *What was that? Nothing. You're seeing things. That's all.*

He thinks of the small blonde woman down by the greenhouse. Elyse, Heather had called her. *What was that?* she had cried. And Heather, so determined to keep their secret. Elyse. Dead now, like all the rest.

Heather takes a step forward, almost falls, and Aura steadies her. "You're all right now," she says. "We will keep you safe."

"She is pregnant," another centaur hisses. "She cannot be here."

"She is my responsibility," Estajfan calls out, his voice carrying to the edge of the clearing. Countless green-brown eyes simmer with rage. "I will watch her. You are to leave her alone."

"She doesn't belong here!" another centaur cries.

"Where does she belong?" Estajfan calls. "Below, with the rest of the dead?"

The mountain centaur who protested moves through the crowd and spits on the ground in front of him. It's the palomino, the one who spoke to him those months ago. "You have betrayed all of us."

"I will watch her. I will be responsible for her. I want all of you to leave her alone."

"And when the child comes?" the centaur says. "What then?" She moves to strike Heather but Estajfan knocks her to the ground with one swipe of his arm.

"Take her to the cave," Aura says to Petrolio. Estajfan spares a glance behind him to see his brother gather the woman gently into his arms and carry her away. Heather doesn't look at Estajfan. She doesn't look at anything.

The palomino, still on the ground, snarls, "If you want a life with a human so much, then leave. Like your father did."

Aura bends to help the other centaur up, but the palomino pushes her away, her mouth set and furious. Aura addresses them all. "She won't stay here forever," she says. "For now, leave her alone."

Not forever, Estajfan thinks. *What does that mean?* When his sister turns to look at him, there's a warning in her eyes, and he stays silent as the mountain centaurs disperse.

"She is only one person," he says at last. "The mountain is not going to change because of one person."

His sister only smiles—a sad smile that makes her look, Estajfan imagines, like the mother none of them have ever known. "Change is already here, Estajfan. There is nothing any of us can do about it now."

Still, it surprises him how quickly they adapt to having Heather around. For the first few days she sleeps in the cave that their father had made ready for their mother all those years ago. Sometimes she eats what they bring her—mountain fruits, the nuts and berries that Estajfan has eaten since he was very small. Sometimes she curls against the wall and refuses to eat, or to look at him, or to speak.

Aura is Heather's shadow—guarding the door, leading her out now and then to walk among the mountain trees to relieve herself. Estajfan and Petrolio resume their runs down the mountain, this time looking for life instead of food. Carrion birds circle slowly overhead and the streets are empty. Estajfan and Petrolio bend through the doorways of house after house and find only bodies. Children on the floor and parents sprawled near them, dead of madness and grief. Plants have already wound through the windows and into the rooms, taking back the houses.

It is so strange to find the world of humans as silent as his mountain-top home. Maybe more so. There is, at least, no screaming, for which he's very grateful.

How had he not known this destruction was coming? How had he not seen it? The ground had been starving the humans out, yes, and he'd thought that was the thing making him so uneasy—the casual cruelty of it, the willingness of the mountain centaurs and the animals and the plants around them to let the humans starve.

You have a choice to make, the fox had said, and so he'd made it. He couldn't stand by and watch them disappear. And so he had done what he had done, had gone down and found food where he could and ensured that Heather and her family survived. Even that had not been enough, in the end.

Tonight he's in the mountain city, alone in the gathering dark. There is movement at the end of the street; he slinks into the overgrown space between two houses and freezes. Ahead of him, a deer, young and cautious, steps into the twilight. It is eating the vines that grow up the sides of the buildings. It stops to look around, then lowers its head to the vines again.

The blade is out of his hand and plunging into the deer's jugular before he has time to think about it. The deer drops, instantly. It makes no sound.

He tries to ignore the shiver of rage that rustles through the plants around him. How long has it been since deer ventured into the city? Years, most likely. He withdraws the knife, wipes it clean on the grass.

When he leans forward to lift the body, the vines have already begun to gather it in, green tendrils winding around the deer's legs and chest and heart.

No, he thinks, and pulls. The vines do not release it, and the body begins to decompose before his eyes. He slices into the deer again and rescues a haunch as tendrils and roots pull the rest of it into the earth.

You made your choice, he hears the ground whisper. The green things curl around his feet and pull at his hooves. He steps out of their clutches, then heads back up the mountain. The haunch stays fresh in his hands and does not rot.

✳

In the mountain clearing, under the moon, he gathers dead branches from the forest and lights a fire. The mountain centaurs mill about, suspicious as always.

"You killed it," one says to him.

Estajfan shrugs. "She needs to eat."

"The human has been eating," says another. A female. Green eyes and brown skin, silver hair. "Aura feeds her every day."

"She needs protein," he says. The mountain centaurs do not eat meat—they barely eat at all, from what he can see, subsisting on sunlight and anger.

He and his siblings haven't eaten meat since their father died.

The centaur glowers at him. "The animals will fear you now," she says. "The mountain is changing."

"The mountain was already changing!" Estajfan shouts. "I want to survive," he says. "And I want the humans—*her*—to survive. Is that so wrong?"

"Look what the humans did to the rest of the world," she hisses.

Estajfan sighs and does not answer. He roasts the leg until the smell changes to what he remembers from the days when their father cooked for them. Yes, he knows the stories. The way the dragons vanished, the way the sprites in the salt mines dwindled as humans dug deeper and deeper into the mountains, as they mined for salt, as they hoped for diamonds and gold. The ships that spread death in the water, the airplanes that belched death in the sky.

"They weren't all bad," he insists, to himself and to them.

The mountain centaur is unmoved. "Enough of them were."

Estajfan pulls the roasted meat from the fire and carries it to the cave where Heather waits, just beyond a copse of trees. Aura, keeping watch, takes the meat from him.

"Where's Petrolio?" he says, following Aura to where Heather lies on the bed.

Aura breaks off little chunks and feeds them to Heather, piece by piece. "Up in your spot at the top of the mountain," she says. "Hoping Da will give him wisdom."

He snorts. "How much wisdom has Da given us lately?"

"Not much," Aura admits. "But Petrolio is ever hopeful."

"What are the desks for?" Heather asks, as if she's just noticed them. She points to a corner of the cave, where three children's school desks sit covered in a layer of dust.

"Our father brought them to us when we were young," Aura says. "He liked us to stand in front of them when he was teaching lessons."

"I thought maybe they were for young centaurs," Heather says. "Though that doesn't really make sense, does it?"

"There are no children here. The centaurs have no young." Aura stands up and brushes the dirt from her legs. "Do you think you have the strength to come outside for a little while?"

Heather blinks at both of them, then glances at the desks. "None of this makes sense," she says.

"I'm sorry," Aura whispers. "I wish everything was different."

He watches Heather sit up, slowly, and brace herself against the bed.

"So they're really gone," she says. "It wasn't just a dream."

He's gone past her house, down in the city. He hasn't looked inside.

"Yes," he says. "But you're here."

She only looks at him, and her eyes are very far away. "Was it worth it? The mountain has the world now?"

To this, he has no answer.

She turns away from both of them and looks back to the wall.

Heather sees, and yet she cannot see. Long stretches of sleep pep-pered with even longer periods of lying awake, unable to get off the bed, unable to move at all.

Where are they, her girls? Far below her, hanging in the kitchen. When she closes her eyes, the image is imprinted on the back of her eyelids. Their tiny faces going black and green.

Come back.

Come back.

Come back to me.

They do not answer. They are gone.

She sleeps.

She eats what Aura feeds her, but cannot taste.

Estajfan brings her a plump avocado that Aura opens with a small knife she keeps tucked in her shoulder bag, her hands at once alien and also so human. The desks in the cave, the picture frames that gather dust. Everything is familiar and strange.

Sometimes Aura hums wordlessly and sometimes Estajfan hums along with her. Sometimes he sings the words. Heather hadn't known he could sing.

The walls of the cave are dotted with shelves and lined with cupboards and cabinets filled with surprises. Dishes and cutlery. A child's wagon, a butter churn. Lanterns, empty and dry.

A laptop computer sits on one of the desks, a small handheld video game atop it. On another are the paints and pencil crayons she gave to Estajfan those years ago.

The drawings she made for him are tacked up on the wall. There are more pencils and pens and sheets of blank paper and pictures torn from magazines, stock photos still in frames. Smiling children, smiling families. All dead now. All gone.

"Where did all this come from?" she asks them, in one of her lucid moments.

"Our father was a collector," Aura says. "And after him—Estajfan."

Heather looks around the space and tries to focus.

"This was for our mother," Aura answers the question before Heather can ask. "In case she ever decided to come see us."

Heather eases herself off the bed and moves slowly to the desk. She flips the laptop open. The battery is long dead, of course. "What use is all of this?"

"It's of no use." Estajfan looms dark in the doorway. "I just keep it to . . . remember."

"But you've never used a computer," Heather says. She crosses the cave and edges past him. The air outside is cold and starry.

"I haven't," he agrees. He comes to stand beside her. "There is no one, Heather. I'm sorry."

"No one," she echoes. Last night she dreamt of the girls again, and her father's face as he fell. She woke up alone in the dark of the cave, a moonlit shadow—Aura? Estajfan? She couldn't tell—outside the door.

When she fell back to sleep, she dreamed of her mother, who welcomed her into a room that was bare except for a butter churn toppled against the wall in the corner.

"Would you like some tea?" her mother asked. When Heather looked around, confused, her mother opened the window and plucked a mug off a tree branch. When she closed the window, leaves pressed against the glass.

"They want to come in," her mother said.

"Where's the baby?" Heather asked. "I left him with you."

"Oh." Her mother's kind face creased with surprise. "He's sleeping. Out there, like in the song. See?" Out the window, Heather saw him in the tree, embraced by the branches. When she reached for him, the tree would not give him up.

"He's for the trees," her mother said.

Heather turned to her mother. "Where are the girls?"

"They were for the trees too." She stepped forward, tucked a strand of hair behind Heather's ear. "Like you, Heather. Your life was always going to look a little different too."

In the dream her stomach dropped in mingled terror and rage. "But they could have done so much," she whispered. "Didn't *I* manage to climb a mountain?"

"Yes. And look what happened when you did."

Now, waking, she moves to the cave opening and steps out into the light. It's overcast, but she's been in the cave so long she needs to shield her eyes.

The mountain centaurs stand in a semicircle in front of the entrance, their faces stern.

"There is no room for humans anymore," one of them says. A male, tall and dark, his black hair falling down his back in careless waves.

Heather, weary, says, "Do you have anything else to say to me?"

"You are here only because of Estajfan," he says. "But he cannot protect you forever."

Estajfan shifts so he's partly in front of her. "*Nothing* will happen to her here," he says. The other centaur, unimpressed, moves away.

"Take me somewhere else," Heather says.

And he does. They climb another sloping path that ends in a flat space with three weeping willows. She moves slowly, weak from grief and pregnancy and trauma. She sits down with her back against a tree. Estajfan kneels beside her.

"Tell me a story," he says.

There are no stories anymore, she wants to tell him. But the stories find her anyway.

*

Once there were two little girls who were born as the world became new again. Their hair was red like the fire that destroyed the old world. At night, they curled into one another for warmth, their fingers laced together.

They were restless babies. Why sleep when you could keep your eyes open and discover the world? To soothe them, their mother put them in a sling and walked them through the ravaged streets out to the edges of the city, through the fields, close to the mountain in whose shadow they sat every day. They wailed and wailed and wailed.

As their first months passed, the girls cried less and less, and instead began to listen as their mother told them stories—of princesses who beat dragons, of girls whose tears could feed the trees.

"You can do anything," their mother said to them, over and over. "You can do anything, because you are so loved."

Greta, a few minutes older, liked to roll balls across the floor with her thumbs. Music made her laugh until she screamed. Jilly, the younger, liked to curl into her father's neck and whisper nonsense to herself. She loved birds. Greta was louder, but Jilly was the first to find words.

They grew, and were the best of friends. At school they sat together; at home they were never far from one another. Their parents joked that even for them it was impossible to tell the girls apart. They grew taller and slimmer and began to lose their baby faces, growing into their teenage skins. They had their father's eyes and hair. They had their mother's hands.

Since they had never known another world, they grew into this one the way tropical flowers grow from decaying trees. When their parents spoke of airplanes and music boxes that ran all the time, of lights that kept the city bright at night, it sounded like a dream. The girls knew only fires in the backyard and laundry done by hand. The water they bathed in was heated over the fire.

But the gardens were bountiful, and they always had enough to eat. They were loved. They were loved.

They remained restless, like their mother. It was not unusual for the girls to find themselves in the shadow of the mountain and not remember how they got there. They would stare at the mountain rising into the clouds and wonder what was up there. Was it magic, this mountain that haunted their days? Did it watch over them in ways they didn't know? What about the trees, their city, the sky? Did these watch over them too?

Sometimes, when they went out walking, they ran into their mother. She had been up the mountain long ago, the only one who had. When they asked her if she'd ever go up again, she shook her head.

"I like to be by the mountain," she said. "But my dreams are enough now. I don't really want to climb it."

When she was sixteen, Greta heard stories from travellers about a school far away where you could learn to be a doctor. She applied, and was accepted. Her parents packed her bags; her sister wept, but shouldered a pack for her as the family set out for the school together. Jilly, like their mother, was already an artist, her sketchbook filled with flowers and trees.

The world had been reborn a shadow of itself. They had no car, not even bicycles, so they walked to the school. At night, they slept beneath the stars. It took them seven days to reach the school, whose letter of offer had come to Greta by way of a man riding a horse, like all the other letters that passed from place to place. As soon as they got there, Jilly said, "Don't stay." She couldn't see a world without her sister. Would the mountain look the same without Greta there to see it? Would the flowers?

Greta shook her head. "I'm here for a while, and then I'm coming back."

Jilly opened her mouth to plead, but just then a hummingbird flew by them. She held out her hand. The hummingbird came to sit in her palm. She and her twin bowed over it in silence. They had never seen a hummingbird by the mountain, though they'd read about them in books.

"You see?" Greta said, her voice soft.

The hummingbird started, and flew away.

That night, over dinner, Jilly told her parents that she was also going to stay.

Her mother said, "Greta has a dorm room. You can't stay by yourself—you're only sixteen."

"Then stay with me," Jilly said. She watched surprise flare in their faces.

"But we've always lived by the mountain," their mother said.

Jilly had already drawn the hummingbird in her notebook. "Maybe it's time for us to find out the differences in the world?"

Their parents looked at each other. The twins had always suspected that something other than love lay between their parents—something that came close to love but wasn't quite the same.

"We'll think about it," their father said.

Their mother nodded, then reached forward and took their hands. "Magic will follow you wherever you go," she told them. Her copper-headed girls. The bright-haired twins who'd come out of her just before the world burned. "Even if we don't stay with you."

In the morning their parents had decided. They found a small house by the river. Near enough to Greta's school that they could visit, but far enough away to give her space. Jilly had her own room. Before long, the city began to clamour for her sketches. She drew flowers and humming-birds until her sketchbook was full, and then went into their new city and bought another.

She drew the mountain less and less, and then stopped drawing it altogether. They did not return to their old city. None of them ever thought of the mountain again.

The mountain, magic though it might have been, did not care in the slightest.

✳

"We should have left," she whispers to Estajfan. The words feel like a betrayal. "Right when it happened. I should have taken the girls and gone with B the day we climbed out of the hospital." The breath catches in her throat. "But I couldn't leave. You were here. I couldn't leave *you*."

"Heather," he says, miserable. "Heather, I told you you should go—"

"I know!" she cries. The words ricochet off the trees. "I made a choice. I made a choice, and I didn't even realize it. And now look what happened."

"You couldn't have known—"

She puts a hand against his mouth. "It doesn't matter. It still happened."

She lays her head against his chest and listens to his hearts. He lifts the hand covering his mouth and lets it gently drop, then strokes her hair. She reaches up and traces the angles of his face, the slope of neck that reminds her, for a fleeting moment, of B.

He smells of earth and sky and still the stars, but also something else now. Uncertainty. Her fingers touch his lips. He is here with her. He is here, finally here.

And her family is gone. Jilly. Greta. B. She whispers their names into his neck, his ear, his lips, the long dreads of his dark hair. He whispers back the names of those he's lost—his father, his mother, far away and long ago. The lives that weren't. The lives that could have been.

She takes their names into her mouth. He does the same.

"I want out," she whispers, and he freezes, unsure, but what she means is that she wants out of her body. One long seam from forehead to toes, split open, so she can march away from her old self like she was moulting.

Instead she presses against him. Her face is slick with tears as he breathes with her, as he whispers into her hair, as he lays her down into the dirt. She wants to dig her hands into the earth and bring up something new. She turns until she's face down, the ghost of B all around her and yet so far away, because it isn't B lifting her skirt this time, his fingers trembling but sure, his hands running around her hips and pulling her hard against the great bulk of him, lifting her off the ground and up against the trembling weight that could kill her. It isn't B above her at all.

Estajfan beside her on the mountain, Estajfan beside her in the city, Estajfan before her, at night, with the flowers. Estajfan here now, with her, above all other things. He has always been with her. She has always been here. He is inside of her and over her and somewhere else besides; they are breathing, they are one now, they are everywhere, together.

✳

The light fades slowly from the top of the mountain, throwing everything into deepening shadow. Her face is wet with tears.

Estajfan clears his throat. "Are you all right?"

She nods. She still can't speak.

"Heather—"

"I'm all right, Estajfan." Above them, the weeping willow rustles in the breeze.

What did she expect? What does happiness feel like when her girls are gone?

"How do you survive?" she asks.

"I don't know," he tells her. "It just happens."

They are silent for a time as the wind whistles lonely through the trees. "I saw a fox," she tells him, and he stiffens. "Foxes. A vixen and two babies. They came to me when we were under the hospital. They followed me for months as I walked through the forest."

His hand stills against her hair. "What did they do?"

"Nothing." She closes her eyes to remember. "One time I unwrapped the girls and put them on the ground. I was so tired." A long pause as she remembers. "I saw . . . a hole in the air, behind the foxes. It crept toward the girls and I knew it would take them away. I *wanted* it to take them away. But I snapped out of it. I got them back just in time." She opens her eyes and looks at him. "My father told me other stories. Mothers leaving their children. Things like that."

Estajfan swallows. "The mountain tells lots of stories."

"But the girls are gone now," she whispers. "I did that. I wanted it, just for that moment. And now it's happened. That was no story."

"Heather, I'm sorry—"

"Stop saying that!" She lurches unsteadily to her feet. "What are you sorry for? What can you do? Nothing. You could barely do anything for us when we were starving." She gulps a breath, tries to calm down. "You couldn't—or wouldn't—bring the girls up here. *You* said that. Fine. You were right—I should have left when the meteors came. And I didn't. It's my fault. You have nothing to do with it, with them."

He stands, and in the gathering dark he seems twice his size— magical and lonely, dangerous and beautiful. "I kept all of you alive," he says, hurt.

She laughs at this and spins around in a circle. "For what? *For what,* Estajfan? So that the trees could claim everyone anyway? So that I could stand alone on a mountain with a monster from the stories my father used to tell and know that the ordinary world is gone and magic is the only thing that's left? *I don't want magic. I want my girls back!*"

She screams those last words into the sky and they hang in the air like mist, clouding everything she sees. Greta, ducking behind one weeping willow. Jilly toddling after her, her small hands eager and outstretched.

Even B is hiding in the mist. His soft laugh, his smile. The way he'd turned hard, so defeated, in the end.

Her fault. All of it.

"Go," she whispers.

"What?"

"Go," she says, again. Even now, the fact that he's so near her feels like a gift. All these years and it's that same first night all over again, beautiful and wild. He is the only thing she's ever wanted. "Estajfan, please leave me alone. Just for now."

"But—"

"I can't bear it," she says. Greta. Jilly. B. She squeezes her hands into fists. She sees the worry in his face and shakes her head. "I'll be okay. I just—I need to be alone."

His face shutters, and he nods. Monster. She's hurt him. "All right," he says. "I won't—I won't be far."

When she opens her eyes again, a long time later, she is alone beneath the sky.

*

The stars hang heavy and bright overhead, brighter than they've been in a year. Three billion, one hundred and twenty-six million, four hundred and twenty-five thousand and one.

Who could possibly count the stars? Her father had been wrong to count them with her—wrong to take her up the mountain, wrong to fill her head with stories. But he had done it, and now here she is. The ground presses, rough, against her knees.

I want to be something else, she thinks.

No more sloping shoulders, no more awkward gait. No more dead girls or dead husband or dead parents. A new life here on the mountain. Four legs instead of two, family that will mirror her when she looks at them. She drops to her knees and digs her fingers into the soil, and it gives way beneath her hands, inviting her in.

"*I want to be something else.*" This time she says it out loud. She pushes her hands deeper into the earth and now she can feel it—the electric something that Estajfan called ground magic, thrumming and joyous, ancient, alive.

She digs and breathes and digs and breathes. The deeper she goes, the more the longing overtakes her, until it's a constant hum in her throat, in her chest, in her heart. *Estajfan, Estajfan.* She won't live in two worlds anymore. She won't do it.

She can't.

When the hole she has dug is deep enough, she scrambles into it and thinks of the horse that did the same all those years ago—what he wanted, what the mountain eventually made him be. Does she need a whole night? She looks up at the stars and pulls the dirt in close. She buries her feet and her legs—her human legs, the last time she'll see them—then the rest of the dirt falls in on top of her. She can't move. She can't move.

The ground whispers in her ear, incantatory and triumphant. She will become other, she will become more.

She cries out as the earth tumbles over her face and blocks the sky. When she screams, she gags on dirt.

– 14 –

Tasha doesn't know how long she's been locked inside. It feels like hours.

The mother's wild wave of grief, her plunge into laughter, the twisting of her hands, her boy's neck snapped. Annie's crazed voice.

What does it mean? What has happened?

"Tasha," Annie moans. She doesn't sound mad now, only heartbroken—but then she bangs on the door again and Tasha jumps. "Come out. I know you're in there. You can't hide from me forever."

Tasha gets up off the floor, silently, and feels along the shelves and through the boxes—gauze, bandages. Sanitary napkins, toothbrushes. On the highest shelf she finds what she's looking for, but loses her grip on the box, which topples to the floor.

"Tasha," Annie moans again. "You come out *now*." She starts banging on the door again.

Tasha scrabbles on the floor through clamps, scissors. She picks up a pair of scissors and unwraps them with shaking hands, then feels along the shelves again until she finds a small, heavy box.

Then she goes to the door and turns the lock slowly, hoping Annie doesn't notice.

One, two. Three.

She shoves the door open, pushing Annie back, brings the box up and smashes it against Annie's head. Her wife drops the scalpel she'd been clutching and as her hands go up to her head, Tasha kicks Annie in the stomach, then brings her elbow down hard against her neck. Annie falls and Tasha lunges for the scalpel, her fingers closing around it just in time. She climbs over her wife and straddles Annie's torso, holds the scalpel flat against Annie's throat while the other hand points the scissors at the soft knob of Annie's trachea. "Don't move," she hisses.

"Tasha," Annie whispers. "Tasha, I can't do it. Not anymore."

"They're only thoughts," Tasha says, her voice hard. "They'll go away." Her mad thoughts went away in the greenhouse. Despair faded, and became smaller. She has to believe the same will happen for Annie.

"They'll go away," she says again. Over and over. "They'll go away."

This time, the terror comes for both of them. She sees it sprout from Annie's ribcage first—an ivory creature with blood-red teeth, its wings all knuckled bone and raw, sinewy flesh. It moans at her, flapping its wings so that darkness brushes her face.

Look at what you did to me, it says.

Tasha whimpers. The creature slithers closer until it's nose to nose with her, Annie's fear and sadness staring her straight in the face. How selfish she has been. How selfish she has *always* been—desperate and arrogant, terrified and yet determined not to show fear. Telling stories. Telling nonsense.

"It's just a thought," Tasha whispers. She closes her eyes. "It's just a thought. It will go away."

But it's not enough, and her own creature crawls out of her ribcage— dark and silent, sticky with blood and lumpy bits of brain matter. It stretches its wings and makes for Annie.

"No," Tasha says. *"You're not real."* But the creature doesn't stop. Annie sobs in terror and now Tasha is sobbing too, shaking as she says the same useless thing over and over.

It's just a thought. It will go away. It's just a thought. It will go away.

The creature opens its mouth wide, showing its long, rotting black teeth. Annie screams and screams.

The creature bends, and Annie's face disappears.

Tasha screams, and faints.

✳

She opens her eyes. There are no creatures.

Beside her Annie sits up slowly, a hand pressed to her head. "Did I fall?"

Tasha shakes her head, sits up on her own. "Something happened," she whispers. "Do you remember what you did?"

Annie frowns. "I remember—the fire," she says. "I remember how you stayed in bed for days."

"Yes."

"I was in our house," Annie continues. "And you were there, in every room, and in every room you turned away from me. In the hospital, too—at work, at home. And then—and then we were here, and you were doing the same thing. Over and over."

She watches Tasha's face for a moment, then swallows. "Something came out of your ribs."

Tasha nods, swallows hard.

It's dark outside, maybe one or two in the morning. A gust of chilly wind blows on them through the broken window. Annie turns to look out the window and sees the dark shape of the body slumped over the broken glass. Her face alive with horror, she turns back to Tasha. "Who is that? What did I do?"

Tasha takes Annie's hands and squeezes them tight. "No. She did it to herself. But first—" and she watches Annie's eyes find the crumpled body of the little boy—"first she did that."

Annie covers her mouth with her hand. When she turns back to Tasha, they're both wondering the same thing. "The city?" is all she says.

Tasha closes her eyes. The screams, the long silence. "I think so," she says.

✻

In the morning they make their way out of the clinic, armed with scalpels and scissors.

The dead are everywhere, and already vines are growing over the bodies. The only sound a faint swoop as vultures circle overhead.

They don't go in the houses, just walk up and down the streets, finding no one.

"Are they all dead?" Annie says after some time.

Tasha wants to weep, but she's too tired. She also wants to be back inside—away from the living green that masses all around them, especially thick and lush where the bodies lie.

Annie touches Tasha's shoulder, hesitantly, as though they are strangers. "You need to lie down," she says.

"We *both* need to lie down," Tasha says.

"Let's go home," Annie says. "Let's go home and sleep and we'll see what we can do after that."

"What about Elyse?" Tasha whispers, shocked that she hasn't even thought of her. Annie has no answer, just takes her hand. When they reach the townhouse, the door sticks, and Annie has to shove it open with her shoulder. Tasha grabs her arm. "What if she's inside?"

They pause, horrified, but Elyse is not behind the door. They creep from room to room but there is nothing—no body, no voice, no shock of blonde hair. The house feels like a museum.

It is *a museum,* Tasha thinks. *A museum of a world that is never coming back.*

In the kitchen, everything has a faint greenish tint—the windows are almost obscured by vines. A handful of red amaryllis she brought back from her last trip to the greenhouse still bloom on the windowsill. Tasha checks the vase. It is bone dry but the flowers sit unchanged, deep and red.

She picks up the vase and smashes it against the tiles. Then she gathers up the flowers and throws them out the back door while Annie stands looking at her as if it's Tasha, now, who has lost her mind.

Tasha takes a deep breath. "I don't want them in the house anymore."

They climb the stairs to the bedroom, crawl into bed, and curl close together. Annie is weeping silently now. Tasha raises her hand and wipes her tears away. She falls asleep to the rhythm of Annie's heartbeat, firm and strong beneath her ear.

✳

In the morning they go outside, armed with scalpels and scissors. They walk up and down and up and down the streets, screaming names until they lose their voices.

Elyse!

Kevin!

Alan!

ANYBODY!

They retreat to the clinic, pry open a can of baked beans, share it between them.

"What do we do now?" Annie says.

"We leave." She closes her eyes and leans her head back against the wall. "Annie," she says, "I'm so sorry."

"We're still alive because of you," Annie says.

"Maybe that's why I'm sorry," Tasha says. "How long can we survive on our own?"

Annie clears her throat. "Well," she says. "We have each other. At the end."

Tasha reaches for Annie's hand. "Yes," she whispers, and she closes her eyes. "We do."

When she opens her eyes again, vines are slithering over the woman's body in the broken window and stretching out toward them. Tasha scrambles to her feet and pulls Annie with her.

"Out," she breathes. "We need to get *out* of here."

They lurch out of the clinic and into the stillness of the day. It is a stillness that feels different now—heavy, waiting.

"Let's go back to the townhouse," Tasha says, and they walk quickly. Everywhere they turn it feels like green things are moving, and yet everywhere they turn things are too silent, too still. Even the wind seems to be holding its breath.

"Run," Tasha says, suffused with sudden terror. "Run, run, *run*."

They take off down the street toward the townhouse—halfway there, Annie grabs Tasha and they both stop.

"Did you hear that?" she gasps.

"Hear what?"

But then Tasha hears it too. *Tap. Tap tap.* A faint rattle. Followed by a slow, almost imperceptible moan.

Annie turns her head. The vines and flowers—Tasha's not imagining this—freeze around them. "Where is it coming from?"

Tasha listens again, and then points. The screen door on the front of the house next to theirs trembles, just a little bit.

Tasha takes the scissors out of her pocket and walks slowly toward the house.

Get inside! a voice screams inside her head. *Get the fuck inside!*

"Tasha," Annie says. "Tasha, you don't know—"

She doesn't listen. She crosses the path to the house and climbs up the front steps. She takes a breath and puts her hand against the knob, then pulls.

Tasha drops to her knees, and Annie comes running.

It's Elyse, crumpled on the floor. She slowly turns her head.

"I heard you," she gasps. "I heard you call my name."

They gather her up, weeping, and hold her close between them.

15

He doesn't mean to go far. He doesn't. But he finds he needs to run, only stopping for a moment at the mountain cave to tell his sister where Heather is. "She's up with the willows. Go to her, Aura. I—can't."

And then he's past her, through the meadow, then on the downward path, his hooves hitting the shale and sliding, going down.

Heather. As a child standing before him on the mountain. As a teenager in the garden, her eyes lost and huge. Heather at the greenhouse. Heather on the mountain.

Heather, before him at the willow trees.

Heather, telling him to leave.

He'd been a monster that day when her father had fallen from the cliff. He hadn't meant to be.

She doesn't need help! he had wanted to scream. The child there in front of them, so sweet and open. The struggle of their climb had been written all over her face. She'd looked tired, and also guilty to be tired, as though her fatigue had somehow betrayed her father's dreams. He'd seen it all at once, had understood it instantly.

What monsters are these?

Get them away, get them away.

Help her, the father had said. The way their own father had asked for the mountain's help so long ago. *Make them like me.*

She doesn't need help! he'd wanted to yell at her father. *She doesn't need to be fixed!*

And so he had hesitated. Not for long, but long enough.

He runs. To the base of the mountain, past the city, through the foothills. The stars shine far overhead and the ground tells him nothing. There are no people. Not even animals bar his way.

When he stops, a long while later, he can smell the faint tang of the sea. He walks for a while until he reaches an abandoned beach village—old clapboard houses falling down, the centre street overgrown with grass and weeds. Two rabbits leap across what used to be the road and then disappear.

At the edge of the sea, he pauses for a moment, then he wades into the water until it's up past his knees, above his belly, until the ocean covers his back and he's just a torso in the waves. If someone saw him now, they would think he was a man. Only a man.

The waves push hard against him. Other things still live here, beneath the surface. He can feel them swimming far away. The ocean keeps on going. The mountain endures in a different way.

The green of growing things—that endures too, in a way he is only beginning to understand.

He stands for a while in the sea, feeling the waves, soothed by their roar. He isn't cold. The sky above him is shot with stars.

When daylight is still some time away, he turns around and heads for land. He stands dripping on the beach for one long moment and then begins the long run back home. He'll bring Heather here, he decides. He'll stay with her, he'll find them food. Whatever it takes.

He runs on a tangled road that leads him through one empty town after another. The buildings on either side are like dark hills with hidden eyes. They watch, but let him pass.

Then, suddenly, the start-up rumble of an engine. He freezes, alive with fear.

The headlights come from nowhere, and everywhere. The hard blast of a car horn burrows deep into his ribs. Lights come at him from everywhere.

A hot, sharp flash of something against his side—he cries out, stumbles, hits the ground.

He can't see.

He can't see. He can't see. He can't see.

THE DOCTOR
AND THE TWINS

The next time the doctor visits the mother's village, there are two new babies to see. Twins—like the doctor and her sister long ago, like the nieces who love her stories whenever she returns. The twins are healthy and big. There is nothing wrong with their lungs.

"And the birth?" the doctor asks, cuddling one of the babies—a boy, with large, dark eyes and a nose that already looks like his father's.

The mother has been smiling, but now her face clouds over. "It was fine," she says. "There was no trouble at all."

This is true; the villagers confirm it. No labour that stretched from one day into the next. No need for a surgeon's slender tools. The boy came first, and then his sister—the mother was up and moving around the house within hours. The entire village has been visiting the babies, playing the songs of welcome for days.

They are happy babies, which is just as well. Two babies at once is more than enough for anyone, the doctor thinks, remembering what life was like for her sister when her own two girls came into the world. An unending avalanche of crying and pissing and shitting and never enough sleep. The second husband holds the children like they are made of glass; when they cry, the doctor takes pity on him and reaches for them. He soon escapes outside.

"Surely he should learn," the mother says. She and the doctor are at the window, watching the husband retreat into the fields.

"Parenting is different for everyone," the doctor says. She's seen enough parents to know. "He'll get used to being a father, eventually. And you'll be fine."

"I thought I'd feel whole," the mother says. "But instead I feel . . . unfinished." She turns and grips the doctor's arm. "How are they?" she whispers. "How are my babies?"

"Your children are right here," the mother's mother calls from the front door. She shuts the door behind her and comes to stand with them. "See?" she says. "Look how beautiful she is. Look how beautiful they *both* are, and how perfect!"

"Yes," the mother whispers. She looks up at the doctor. "They're perfect."

The doctor stays for two weeks. She sleeps in her old room. The other husband, haunted and grief-stricken, does not come this time. There are no footsteps in the hallway. There is no dark presence on the other side of the door.

When the doctor is ready to move on, the mother insists on walking with her to the edge of the village, her twins in a sling. As the doctor says a final goodbye, the mother stops her with a hand on her arm, the same hunger in her eyes.

"Are they all right?" she whispers. "My babies. You never tell me how they are."

"I haven't seen them," the doctor says. "But I think they're all right."

"You *think?*"

"I hope," the doctor says.

"And—him?" she says. "Is he all right?"

"He is as all right as he can be."

The mother nods. "I knew he was different. I wanted my life to be different too. But at the time I didn't know what that meant. What that could be."

The doctor nods, and gently pulls her arm away. "We never do," she says.

The mother thinks about this for a moment. Then she turns back to the village without saying goodbye.

The doctor makes her way back to the city of her birth, where her sister still lives. At their house, her nieces run out to greet her.

"We've been waiting for days!" one of them exclaims, hanging on the doctor's arm. "Where have you been?"

The doctor laughs. "I could move as fast as the wind and it wouldn't be fast enough for you."

"Yes," her sister agrees, coming down the front walk to kiss her. "Nothing moves fast enough for these two."

Inside, the girls hang her coat up in the closet. The doctor carries her bag and her satchel to the guest room. She is barely unpacked before they're at her door and tugging on her hands, pulling her into the living room.

"Tell us about the centaur," they say. "Have you seen him? Have you seen the babies? It's been so long!"

The doctor lets the girls lead her to a seat before the fire. Her sister brings her a mug of tea, then sits in a nearby chair. She asks, "So *have* you seen him? Did you give him my thanks for taking those heavy, god-forsaken books from my shelves?"

As promised, the doctor had been bringing gifts up the mountain every time she passed by. Last time, she had given the centaur some of her old textbooks.

The centaur had loved them. He loved all her gifts.

"I've seen the centaur," she tells them. "He is as tall and proud as ever."

They delight in how intractable he is, how stubborn and rude. He is a puzzle that they've yet to unlock.

"Have you met the children yet?" her other niece asks. The quieter one, the one who reminds the doctor of herself. "Are they happy? Are they loved?"

"I haven't met the children." The girls and their mother sigh in disappointment. "Next time, maybe. Perhaps I should bring him a different kind of gift."

"Seems to me you bring the centaur everything. And the centaur brings nothing to you," her sister says.

The doctor looks down at her mug of tea. "He's lost a great deal."

"So have you." Her sister's voice is sharp. "So have we all."

"Perhaps. But how is he supposed to know that?"

"He would know if he *asked* you about yourself. If he spared one moment to think about *you*."

The doctor shrugs. "He has no obligations to me."

Her sister cocks her head at her. She has never been surprised—not when the doctor first told her the story of the centaurs, not later, not now. She is also the child of an almost-witch. She, too, lost her mother in the fire. She has survived all these years by turning her anger into love for her twins, her husband, and the sister she sees only a few times a year. Everything is magical and nothing makes sense. Everything could fall away at any moment.

"He has an obligation to you like everyone else does," her sister says. "If the centaur doesn't see that, then he's not worth your time."

That night, after the girls have gone to bed, the doctor and her sister sit outside. Together, they breathe the night air.

"You've lost weight," her sister says. "Are you eating enough?"

"What kind of doctor would I be if I wasn't taking care of my own body?"

Her sister snorts. "You. That's what kind."

The doctor chuckles. She always feels very young when she's with her sister, and tonight is no exception. "Do you miss them?" she says, after a while.

"Always," her sister says. "And I still see them everywhere."

The doctor nods. They often talk about this: how their dead mother sometimes seems to appear in a crowd; the way their father, who died last year in his sleep, still sometimes seems to come to them in the face of a stranger on the other side of the street.

"I keep running into the same stories," the doctor says. "Babies with no faces, extra limbs. Monster children that nobody wants." She leans forward and rests her elbows on her thighs. "The way that Mama kept running into people who wanted love. What lessons lie in that?"

"The centaur loves his children," her sister reminds her. "If what you say is true."

"Yes," she says. "But he doesn't want to show them to anybody. He keeps them hidden away on that mountain. And maybe that's my fault."

"Mama was not responsible for the choices that other people make, and neither are you," her sister says, sharply. "If he wanted an uncomplicated life, he should have stayed a horse."

The doctor laughs, and then sobers. "But what about his children? What kind of life will they have up there, alone?"

"Still not your responsibility. Didn't you say their mother has new twins? Human ones?"

"Yes," the doctor says. She can't keep the bitterness out of her voice. "*Perfect* babies. A boy and a girl."

"She's chosen her life," the doctor's sister reminds her. "And so has the centaur. You can't expect either of them to choose a different one. Perhaps that is the lesson you need to keep on learning."

The doctor looks away. "That doesn't seem a worthwhile lesson," she says.

Her sister sighs. "There are different kinds of magic. And there are different kinds of grief. One person can only carry so many kinds. You of all people should know that."

"And what if his children want to be in the world? What if they don't want to be hidden away?"

Her sister has no answer for this; they sit on the step in silence until a call from the house takes them back inside.

It's the second niece, awake. The doctor goes in to see her.

"Tell me the story again," she says. "Tell me what happened when the centaurs were born."

The doctor sits beside her on the bed and brushes the hair out of her eyes. She's told this story so many times they know it by heart. It is not, perhaps, the best kind of story for children. But it's the one they always want.

"Three doors for three babies," she says. "Three doors into the world."

— 16 —

JJ crawls behind the wheel and turns the key. Moira is beside him in the passenger seat while the others sleep in the back, piled on what blankets and clothing they've managed to scrounge. JJ turns the headlights on and there it is in front of them—a huge *thing* come to a sudden jerking stop, half man, half horse, all muscles and startled blue eyes. It raises its hands against the sudden flare of light.

"*What the fuck is that?*"

JJ is leaning on the horn, and Moira is screaming. She hears a wild shuffling in the back and then the clang of the back door of the U-Haul opening.

A shot rings out and the creature stumbles. Darby steps up beside Moira's window, the gun on his shoulder. The creature—the *thing*—looks toward Darby, its hands still up to block the light. Darby fires again. This time, the beast falls.

The impact shakes the ground around them. Moira and JJ sit stunned for a moment, and then they're both tumbling out of the truck. She gasps in the dark morning air, but only partly from the cold.

The creature lies sprawled in front of them, a dark splash of blood on its lower abdomen, the part of it that looks like a man. Before she knows it, she's on her knees by the creature, pulling the sweater from around her shoulders and pressing it hard against the wound.

"What the hell are you doing?" Darby crouches beside her.

"It's hurt."

"Of course it's hurt. I fucking *shot* it."

"What the fuck is it?" says Brian from Moira's other side. "Jesus Christ. Jesus *fucking* Christ. Where did it come from?"

The creature's breathing catches as Moira presses harder. She sees its eyelids flutter, then close as it passes out. "It's hurt," she says again. "We need to get it . . . somewhere."

"Sure," Darby snaps. "We'll take it to the next emergency animal hospital along the highway. No problem."

"Well, we can't just *leave* it here."

"Why the hell not?"

"Moira's right." JJ crouches down beside her. "We should take it with us."

"What the fuck for? You want to eat it or something?"

Moira tries not to shiver.

JJ doesn't answer for a moment. He just stares at the creature. "Are we dreaming?" he asks.

"Everything is a dream now!" Darby yells. "Let's just leave it and go!"

"JJ," Moira says. "It's *hurt*."

He slides his eyes over to her. He is so quiet, JJ. They know next to nothing about him. "Would you want to save it if it was a deer?" he asks. "Or would you want to eat it?"

"I can't," she says. "It's at least—at least *half* human."

JJ snorts, then stands up. "I know where we can take it," he says. "Put it in the back of the van."

Darby sighs. "Fine. Brian, JJ—let's just load the motherfucker in and go."

The beast is even heavier than it looks—the three men half drag, half carry it to the rear of the truck, then lift it in. Moira walks beside them, pressing her sweater against the wound all the way. Once it's in the back of the truck, she climbs in and sits beside it, then reaches for one of the flashlights they've stashed in the back and hands that to Brian, who climbs in beside her. From what she can see, there's a bullet lodged at the place where human skin gives way to fur.

Fur, she thinks, and suppresses a shudder. "Darby. Give me your knife." When he hands it to her, she reaches for the bottle of whiskey that Darby keeps in his pack. She opens it, then splashes it over the wound. As always, she thinks of Eric, who'd survived the scream and the godforsaken plants with Darby only to die from a blood infection, raving and delirious, a cut on his hand gone untended. He'd been halfway to death when Moira had found them. Now, whenever they stop, alcohol of any kind is the first thing Moira looks for.

"You're wasting good whiskey on an animal?" Darby grumbles.

She kneels in front of the creature and slides the knife into the wound, using her sweater to sop up the blood that wells, and gently pries the bullet out. It clatters to the floor.

As if he'd been waiting for her to be done, JJ starts the truck. Darby rolls the back door closed and Moira blinks in the sudden darkness, the flashlight wobbling in Brian's shaky hand. They move forward, slowly, into the dark.

Moira takes off her shirt and tears a strip from it, then douses the strip in more alcohol and presses it against the wound. The strip quickly goes red. "Tape," she says. Brian reaches into one of the packs and rummages around, then pulls out a roll of duct tape. Moira tears a piece from it with her teeth, the other hand still holding the bandage, and presses the tape across it. It sticks. She doesn't know how long it will stay put, but at least the beast won't bleed to death in the truck.

She hopes it won't, anyway.

"Dr. Moira to the rescue," Darby drawls. He and Brian snicker. Brian hands Moira another T-shirt from a pile in the back, and she pulls it on.

She says, "Tie its legs with something. What if it wakes up and thrashes around?"

Darby and Brian comply, using the rope that they keep by the door. Then they settle themselves on the blankets. Moira sits cross-legged in front of the beast and looks for the rifle, which is propped in the corner.

Odd, she knows—given that she's just pulled a bullet out of the creature—but it's good to know it's there, just in case.

"You didn't even seem that surprised," she says, after they've bumped along for a few minutes. She's looking at the shadow that is Darby, but he only shrugs.

"The world went down in fire and then in screaming," he says. "Nothing seems that strange to me anymore."

Life had seemed strange to her until the meteors had come and taken her sister away. It was a delightful strangeness—days that sparked in front of her, brimming with both routine and possibility. She could audition one day and find the part that would change her whole life; she could buy a lottery ticket at the convenience store and lift her whole family into another world. Every day was another day wherein *something* could happen.

Then the meteors had come. She'd been staying at her sister's place. Jaime had offered Moira her bed for the night, playing the good host, but Moira had said, "I'm fine on the couch," and it turned out to be true. She *had* been fine—the meteor had come through Jaime's bedroom window, demolishing the south side of the house and leaving the other half standing, practically untouched. There was nothing left of Jaime, not even bones.

She had expected to fall apart with grief, but instead the world became fuzzy, two-toned, monotonous. The collapse of things around them, the starvation—all of it unremarkable, all of it drudgery. She'd made her way back to her old basement apartment—her landlord was gone, or dead— and got used to living without power. One by one her neighbours left, and her friends disappeared. She grew potatoes in the backyard and was not surprised, come harvest, to find them stunted, almost inedible. She ate them anyway.

The other plants around her grew lush and green. Hollyhocks had bells as large as her hands and grew taller than her house. Tree roots broke the ground in the backyard. Berry bushes grew along the sides of the old roads, fruit hanging dark and luscious. For some reason, she did not touch those.

As the months stretched into fall and then to winter, she began to see small mounds on the roads when she went out in the morning—small green mounds with maybe a flash of red hair in one, a small curled hand in another. She didn't look too closely. Then the winter came and the snow kept her mostly inside, except when she had to salvage for food.

When the scream came, she was outside again, scavenging for supplies. She first felt a tremor of rage and grief shiver through her. When the big orange flowers around her opened their mouths and let loose, she backed into the first building she could see, an abandoned restaurant, and shut herself in the bathroom at the back. The scream became human, became a hundred different screams, became footsteps that ran around in terror. She thought dully about how the Moira of a year ago would have been alive in her terror, electric in her madness, desperate to hang on. There was nothing to hang on to now, so why be terrified? Survival was an instinct. Survival was boring. That was the secret, that's all it was. There was no hope, yes—but there hadn't been any since Jaime had died.

She sat on the toilet and counted the tiles at her feet. They were chipped and filthy. One, two, three, and four. Five. Six. One hundred and twelve.

See? She almost wanted to open the door and scream at them all. *See? You have it all wrong. Grief isn't painful—it's just boring. Boring as fuck. You can get used to it too.*

She sat on the toilet until the world went quiet and then sat until the darkness outside was absolute. Then she stepped out of the bathroom and around the bodies on the floor and went outside. She walked back to her apartment. Just like she'd done in the days after Jaime, she let herself in and crawled into bed, and slept until she couldn't anymore.

When she woke, it was late afternoon and the world outside had changed again, gone lush and thick, an even deeper green. For the first time Moira could remember since the meteors fell, it felt wrong to be inside. She changed into cleaner clothes and went out.

There were so many bodies. On the ground, slumped in doorways, everywhere. As she walked, vines stretched over the ground like twisted green snakes—slithering over the bodies, winding around the bodies, covering their hands and faces and hair in emerald green.

She avoided the vines as she walked. Eventually, even this felt ordinary, like she'd seen it all before.

— 17 —

Darkness, and then light. A force breaks her from the dirt. Air rushes at her face and she gasps in great lungfuls of it.

Blue-green eyes drink her in.

Aura.

Aura drops her on the ground, hard enough for stars to sparkle across her eyes. When her vision clears, Aura is all she can see.

"I should have let you suffocate," Aura says, her voice low and terrible. She yanks Heather up by the shoulder and stares her in the face. "I almost," and she squeezes Heather's shoulder so hard she gasps, "didn't get here in time. I almost didn't come here at all! If Estajfan hadn't told me to check on you—*Heather.* A few more seconds and you would have been gone. The ground was already smoothing over. There was almost no sign of you at all."

"I just—" Heather stares, her teeth chattering. "I just—wanted—to be different. I wanted my life to be—different."

"You *are* different," Aura says, and she lets Heather's arm drop. Heather backs up until she's leaning against the willow again. She feels the ground rumble and then go silent.

But she's not different—she's the same, Heather realizes. Covered in dirt—dirt in her clothes, stuffed in her ears, gritty in her mouth—but every bit the same. Her own two legs. Her own fragile human body. The baby kicks, fierce and alive. She bends over her belly and sobs.

"You can't trust the mountain," Aura says. "If the mountain can birth a centaur, it can birth all other kinds of lies."

"But it made your father different," she whispers.

"My father was already halfway into another world. You don't want that—you just want the world to know who you are."

Heather shuts her eyes and leans back against the tree. "There's no one left to know who I am," she says. "Everyone is gone."

"Not everyone," Aura says. When Heather looks at her, the moonlight shines behind her head like a halo. "You and Estajfan—" Aura makes a gesture with her arms, a half-circle—"I see you in his face. In the way he moves. I don't think even he understands it. The way our father kept seeing our mother long after he'd left the village and come back to the mountain. Your bond marks you both in ways that even the mountain does not understand."

There's another rumble beneath Heather's hands. She thinks it's the mountain, disagreeing, but then the rumble resolves into hooves striking the ground. Petrolio bursts from the trees, his face full of terror.

"Estajfan!" he cries.

"What?" Heather pushes herself up and stumbles to Aura.

"He's in trouble," Aura says, knowing instantly what Petrolio means. "The mountain"—her voice drops low—"the mountain won't let me see anything else."

Heather goes to the three willows and places her hand against a trunk, looks out across the land that stretches on and on into the dark. Foothills and flatlands and the ruins of so many cities. Far beyond that, the sea.

She couldn't see him on the mountain, but she can see him now. Below them, back down in the world that she knows.

"He's by the water," she says. "Or close to it."

"Is he hurt?" Aura and Petrolio cry together.

She closes her eyes and feels a darkened space, shadows skittering over the windows. The floor cold against her cheek. Against *his* cheek. The glint of metal. A rifle in the corner.

"People." It's the first thing she can say.

"What?" Petrolio grabs her free arm hard.

"He's alive." Dark silence, pressure against Estajfan's wrists and legs. He can't move. He's hurt. Around him, the reek of bodies that haven't been washed.

"Heather," Petrolio says, and she opens her eyes.

"He's in a truck," she says. "There are people with him. I think they're heading this way, but I'm not sure." She grabs Petrolio's hand. "We'll find him. I can help you find him. But we have to go down."

"Estajfan chose to go down." A new voice behind them. They stiffen in surprise, then turn to see a mountain centaur, tall and stern. Behind him, others in the trees. How long have they been watching? "Centaurs do not belong off the mountain. No one is to go down except for the human."

"I'm not abandoning my brother!" Petrolio cries, his eyes wild.

The centaur only watches him. "Then you make the same choice he made," he says. "And the mountain will dismiss you too."

Aura offers a hand to Heather, who takes it and scrambles up onto Aura's back. She wraps her arms around Aura's slender torso, then buries her face in Aura's hair.

Then Aura's hooves leave the ground, and they are running.

✳

When they reach the bottom of the mountain, Aura pauses for the tiniest of seconds.

"Where is he?" Aura shouts back to her. "Where do we need to go?"

The warm smell of metal; the tang of fear and fire inside her mouth. He still can't move, but they are *moving*. Heading north, toward the mountains. She was right.

"They're on the road," Heather says. "Turn south, and we'll meet them."

They run for what feels like hours—through the dawn and into the morning. When the road is blocked by sudden mounds of tangled vines—a buried car or two or three—Aura leaps over them, Heather clutching hard in panic, Petrolio at their heels.

As they get closer to Estajfan, a wave of pain rises behind Heather's eyes. She can feel him moving against his restraints, his fingers curling, his body flexing, getting ready.

The humans don't see it. They have no idea.

— 18 —

Snug on the bed in their townhouse, nestled between Tasha and Annie, Elyse is weak, but alive. They feed her carefully—canned beans, rice, tuna—until colour comes back into her face. The day slides into night. They sleep. They wake. They sleep again and dream.

"What happened?" she asks them, when the night has turned to day again. "What happened, outside, with the flowers?"

They tell her what they know, which isn't much. The scream. The long standoff with Annie.

When they get to the part about the grief and the despair, Elyse nods. "I was ready to give up," she says. "If it hadn't been for the coughing, I'd just be another body on the street. The breathing was the only thing that saved me." She told them about this when she'd recovered enough to speak—the scream of the flowers rising around her just before she reached their townhouse, the panic that had driven her to the house next door, which was closer, and then the default mechanism that had kicked in, the thing she knew to do when the air overwhelmed her, when breathing was hard. She'd learned it as a child. It went even deeper, now, than madness.

Breathe in until her lungs were three-quarters full. Then hold. Then out. Breathe in. Then hold. Then out.

Again. Again. Again.

Thinking back on it now, she manages a wry chuckle. "My banged-up lungs kept me alive, I guess. That's definitely a first. What saved the two of you?"

Tasha hears the brief whisper of wings. "I'd been around the flowers all winter," she says. "The greenhouse—I went there alone. It made me"—and she thinks back to those moments, her knees against the dirt—"delirious. Mad. I don't know. I felt the grief then too. But the more I went to the greenhouse, the less it affected me. Like I was becoming immune."

Elyse looks over at Annie. "Was it the same for you?"

Annie flushes, clears her throat. "I wasn't immune, or whatever you want to call it. If it hadn't been for Tasha"—she swallows hard, looks at her hands—"I don't know what would have happened."

Silence settles over them, broken by Elyse's ragged lungs. "Maybe Tasha was your breathing," she says. "The thing that kept you afloat—the way that the rhythm of my breathing saved me."

They sit with this, all of them, for a moment. Annie is the one who asks it first. "Do you think this means that other people survived too?"

"I hope so," Tasha says.

There is only one way to find out for sure. They do not talk about this, not yet.

The third night they are together, Elyse sits up in the middle of the bed so suddenly Tasha thinks she's having an attack.

"The creature," she says. "The creature on the mountain. We can go there, to get food." She coughs. "I should have told you that first thing."

"Elyse," Tasha says, carefully, "what creature?"

"The one I saw by the greenhouse. With Heather. It was part man, part horse."

Tasha and Annie look at each other over her blonde head.

Annie clears her throat. "Elyse, we've all had such a shock. Why don't you just lie back down and rest—"

"I should have said it first thing," Elyse repeats, frantically. "It's just—I was just—I was so tired! I saw Heather, in the forest. Just before the scream came. She was talking to a—a creature. Part man and part horse. I was on my way back to tell you when the scream came."

"Elyse," Tasha says. "This has been hard on all of us, and—"

Elyse shakes her head. "I know what I saw. Tasha—remember, the *flowers screamed,* and vines moved across the ground. You saw it too! Why couldn't there be such a creature?"

"We all tell ourselves stories," Tasha says. "Maybe it was just a man, someone who lives near the mountain. Someone we don't know, someone who's been living in the forest all this time."

"I know what I saw!" Elyse cries, again, setting off her terrible wracking cough.

They sit with her, in silence, until the coughing subsides.

"All right," Tasha says. She looks at Annie, who shrugs a little. "Elyse—okay. Maybe there is someone—some *thing*—on the mountain. Some person or creature or something that no one else has seen. But you can't climb the mountain. You wouldn't have been able to do it months ago—you definitely can't do it now."

"Then I'll stay," Elyse presses, "and *you* can go. The two of you."

Annie shakes her head. Her voice is low and soft. "We can't leave you alone."

"I'll be fine! I was by myself for *days* before you ca—"

"What would have happened if we hadn't heard you—if no one had come? You would have died on that floor, Elyse, and you know it," Annie says.

"So what happens when the food runs out here?" Elyse says. "You survived, I survived—only to shrivel away here in this house? This can't be how it ends."

Annie sighs, and Tasha knows what she's going to say in the instant before the words come out of her mouth. "I'll go. I can go up the mountain. Tasha—you stay here with Elyse."

Tasha shakes her head. "No one is going," she says. "Elyse—there's no path. We don't know what might be up there. It's too dangerous."

"So that's it," Elyse says. "We just stay here, and starve."

"No one said anything about starving," Tasha says, and the others look to her. She spreads her hands. "We find whatever food is left in any of the houses, and then we leave this godforsaken city. We go."

She can't decide what's worse—the relief in Annie's face, or the way that Elyse shuts down in despair.

✳

When Elyse is strong enough to walk, they go outside. Vines crawl under their feet and shift like snakes around the dead people on the road. Most of the corpses—if they see corpses at all—are buried, smooth mounds of green in the roads, the old town square. After a while, they stop noticing.

They search the houses that are still standing, but don't find much.

"We should go to Heather's house," Elyse says. "They might have more."

Tasha and Annie look at each other.

"Because of the creature?" Annie says. "You think it was bringing her food and Heather kept that a secret all this time?"

"I don't think," Elyse insists. "I *know*."

They walk to Heather and Brendan's house, stand silent before the door. Tasha pushes it open. The smell that comes at them is both must and decomposition.

They find the bodies of Brendan and the girls hanging in the kitchen. The green hasn't yet completed its work here, though it has pushed in around the window frames and the cracked and broken glass. Vines have crawled across the floor and up the chair that sits toppled underneath Brendan, wound around his legs, up to his waist. The girls are small green cocoons with black faces and bright hair. Annie goes to vomit in the corner.

Tasha pulls her eyes away. "Where's Heather?"

"I told you," Elyse says. "I *told* you she was hiding something. Otherwise she would be here."

"She could be anywhere," Tasha says. Even as she says it, she's thinking of their long walks in the forest. The greenhouse. The stories that Heather spun as she walked. "Maybe she was outside when the scream came."

Elyse crouches in front of the cupboards. She pulls out apples and potatoes, a bag of rice. She reaches into the back and pulls out lentils and beans. There are weevils in some of the bags, but others remain sealed and safe. "Where did all of this come from," she says, "if not from the mountain?"

Tasha shuts her eyes against her own memories. The flutter of wings against her ribcage. *Stories are never only stories, Tasha.* "Bags of rice don't grow on the mountain," she says.

Elyse sweeps an arm around the room. "Maybe *she* did this."

"I know you didn't trust her, but she wouldn't do this," Tasha protests.

"How do you know? Everyone went mad. Annie almost killed you! How do you know that didn't happen here?"

"I don't know," Tasha says, suddenly tired of it all. "I just—I don't think she could do that. She was already carrying so much."

Elyse won't let go. "Maybe that broke her, like it broke everybody else."

Tasha shakes her head. She looks at Annie, and then Elyse again, and she thinks back to that first day and the dark, bottomless pain in Heather's eyes. "Something broke her before all of this happened," Tasha says. "And she put herself back together in a different way. Maybe—maybe that's how we survived."

Annie is staring at her, head cocked. Then she takes a step closer to the window. "Heather might be out there."

The backyard is a jungle—even more so than the rest of the city. The vegetation is more than tall enough to hide a body.

Tasha shakes her head. "If she is, I don't want to know. We're done here. Let's go." Looking at the food they've gathered, she says, "We'll stay for one more week. Eat, regain some strength. And then we'll go south toward the water, and then east along the coast. The sea air will be good for Elyse."

Elyse does not ask about the mountain anymore.

Slowly, their strength comes back. The air begins to carry hints of summer. The plants outside continue to grow—lilies that mushroom into great orange giants, vines that thicken until they're as wide across as Tasha's arm. The women stay inside during the day and venture outside in the late afternoons, finding their way into each and every last house. They take what they can and ignore the green mounds that are everywhere. There is no sound, there is no change.

Still.

"Are you sure we're alone?" Elyse asks one afternoon. "I keep thinking that I hear things."

"Like what?" Annie asks, sharply.

"I don't know," Elyse admits. "It might just be an animal. Sometimes I feel like I hear something running down the streets." She looks to both of them, then swallows. "Something . . . galloping."

Tasha sighs. "It's probably just deer," she says. "There are probably so many more animals in the city now that the people are all gone."

Annie perks up at this. "If it's a deer," she says, "maybe one of us should try and catch it. We could use the meat."

"No," Tasha says. "No going out alone. It isn't safe. We can go a little closer to the mountain in the morning and see if we find anything." She tries to ignore the sudden light in Elyse's face.

"And then what?" Annie says.

Tasha watches the ceiling. "Then we get ready to leave."

Everything hurts. Dark shapes come into focus—a man, a woman, another man behind her. One has a gun at his hip; there's another gun in the corner where the woman is sitting. Estajfan remembers humans shooting the animals in their forest, terrified deer trying to get up the mountainside. His abdomen aches at the memory. No, not a memory. They shot him.

He tries to flex his hands—they are stiff, and barely move. He's lying on a floor that moves and jostles and bumps him—he recognizes the sound of wheels beneath him, that great whir and whine of machine.

The truck hits something on the road and his head bounces and hits the truck bed. He can't help it; he whimpers in pain. The woman crouches close to him, a worn boot near his eye.

"Is it moving?" a man says.

"No," another man grunts. "It's the truck, you fool. It's the goddamned fucking road. I told you we needed to keep cutting those fucking weeds."

"We can't fix all the roads," the woman says. "There's no one else left to do it, in case you haven't noticed."

The first voice sounds panicked. "It's moving. I can see it."

A hand on his head, suddenly, and the woman's face dips into view. Brown eyes, a sharp, crooked nose. "You've been hurt. You've got nowhere to go, so don't move. You hear me?"

"You're talking like you think it'll answer back." The drawl again, coming closer. A man's boots. "For all you know, it can't even talk."

"He can talk," the woman says. She crouches on her heels and looks into his face again. "He understands everything we're saying. You can see it in his eyes."

"So it's a *he*, now?" The man squats to stare at him, the rifle spread out across his knees. His muddy-green eyes remind Estajfan of the mountain centaurs; he has a tattoo of a cross on his left cheek. "Stop it, Moira. It doesn't matter if it can hear us or not. It's not going anywhere now, thanks to you."

"I wasn't going to let him bleed out," she snaps. The man only shrugs.

"But—but what if there are others?" The third voice again, younger, almost a boy. "Darby—what are we going to do?"

"We'll take this one wherever JJ wants to take it. Then we'll see what happens."

Take him where? Estajfan has lost track of how long he's been in here. How long have they been driving? He can't see outside but he can sense, from the way that the wheels jostle, that the humans are driving as fast as they can. It makes everyone nervous—he can feel it in the air.

Sure enough, there is a loud bang and they jolt to a stop. Everyone swears. There's a pause, and then the back doors roll open. The man called Darby steps to the back of the truck and jumps down. Someone outside is talking, but Estajfan can't make out the words.

"The engine blew," the boy says. The panic in his voice hasn't gone away. "*The engine fucking blew.*"

The woman stands and goes to the boy. She's afraid too—they all are. Afraid of him, of the road, of themselves. "We'll fix it. Darby and JJ will know what to do."

"JJ works with *bikes*, Moira—that's what he said! And it's already halfway through the afternoon. By the time we fix this, it will be dark."

"So we camp," she says, wearily. "We all need some sleep anyway. The truck has broken down a hundred times, Brian. It's not like we haven't done this before."

"But what if there are more of—*them*—outside?"

Moira shrugs. "Then I guess it's good I saved this one, isn't it? Maybe he'll be able to vouch for us."

She's half joking, but as usual, Brian doesn't get it. "How are we supposed to negotiate with these things? I mean, look at it. Him. Whatever."

Moira is silent for so long that Estajfan thinks she isn't going to respond. But then she bends toward him. "I'm looking," she says. She's talking to Brian but Estajfan feels the words go right through him. "I'm watching, Brian. There's nothing you need to worry about, at least not right now."

"Where did it come from, anyway?" Brian asks. "It didn't just appear on the road. It came from somewhere."

Moira shrugs, then locks eyes with Estajfan again. He hasn't blinked—he can tell that has unnerved her a little.

"JJ said he knew where we could take it," Brian says. "He didn't say he knew where it came from."

"Whatever. Go ask him."

The boy jumps down from the truck and shuffles away. Estajfan hears voices at the side of the vehicle, though he can't make out the words.

Moira walks away from him and slumps down against the wall, her arms resting on her knees. She stares at him. He blinks, slowly.

She saved his life, he thinks.

He flexes his fingers, and they move a little more.

A long time passes. Hours? Estajfan can't be sure. The light fades, eventually. Every now and then someone swears or bangs the side of the vehicle.

Then Brian appears. "We're spending the night," he says to Moira. "JJ says to get that thing out of the truck."

Moira rolls her eyes. "And how am I going to do that?"

"Not you," the boy mumbles. "I just wanted to tell you what was happening."

The other men jump into the truck. Together with Brian, they grab Estajfan by the legs and haul him toward the doors.

He can move more than his fingers now, but he stays limp as a fish.

"Jesus," says JJ. "This thing is heavy." As they tip Estajfan over the edge, his head thumps against the frame, hard. He fights to keep from grimacing in pain, but he can't help it.

"Hey," Moira says. "Did you see that?"

"See what?" JJ again.

"He hit his head," Moira says. "And I think he winced."

"So? Fucker's tied. He's not going anywhere."

They drag Estajfan away from the vehicle. When they drop him, his head hits the ground again, but he doesn't react. He's staring straight at Moira, who looks away.

"Is the truck fixed?" she calls.

"It's fixed, princess," Darby drawls back. "But we'll camp here for the night."

"Since when do we stop because it's dark?" Brian says.

"Since now," JJ snaps. "I don't want to have to fucking stop and fix the engine because we're driving over God knows what in the night. What the hell kind of hurry are we in, anyway?"

Moira points to Estajfan. "We just play prison guard until the morning? Why didn't we leave him in the truck for the night?"

"Sure," Darby says, slowly. "You can be the one to open the door in the morning, Moira, and see if it's broken free of the ropes and is ready to jump down and crush us all."

"I meant keep him in there, with us," she snaps. "No one's sleeping outside."

Darby thrusts his chin at the truck. "We'll sleep in there and leave him out here. You can take first watch. I thought you liked horses, Moira. Don't all little girls want a pony?"

"I'm not a little girl," she retorts. "And *he's* not a fucking pony."

Darby doesn't respond, just heads to the truck.

Moira stands looking after him, and then jumps into the back and retrieves the rifle. When she comes back, she settles down against a tree and scowls at Estajfan. "Don't go anywhere," she snaps. "If you even know what I'm saying."

There's a sadness in her face and eyes that reminds him of Heather, and makes him want to speak. But he looks away from Moira and stares at the trampled grass, the vines and overgrown weeds all around them. He digs his hands into a cluster of vines and pulls against the ties. The strands of rope weaken, give way. He waits until there's more commotion from the men—a clang, "*Fuck you, that was my finger, jackass*"—and when Moira looks up their way, he jerks and snaps the ropes, then lets his hands go limp.

He won't be able to get at the ropes binding his legs as easily.

Soon the daylight is gone and the dark is all around them. Eventually he hears the men swearing at each other as they settle down for the night, and then they grow quiet. Moira hasn't moved.

He looks up at the sky and tries to count the stars.

-20-

The tingle in Heather's fingers becomes a tingle in her hands, a warm flush that spreads from her shoulders down to her toes. As they run, she feels Estajfan come awake. He can move, and yet he doesn't. He can speak, and yet he doesn't.

In the early afternoon, Aura stops. Petrolio reaches for Heather—she almost falls, she's that stiff, but he has her, his hands gentle. He lifts her down onto the ground and holds her until the sleep passes from her feet and she's sure her legs will bear the weight.

"You haven't eaten," Aura says. She pulls her satchel over her shoulder and reaches into it, then hands her an apple.

"I'm not hungry. And anyway, you haven't eaten either."

"I'm not pregnant," Aura says. "If anything happens to you, Estajfan will never forgive me."

Heather bites into the apple, chews, swallows.

As she takes another bite, Petrolio comes to stand in front of her, swishing his tail back and forth.

"He can move his arms at least," she says, her mouth filled with apple.

"Is he being watched?" Petrolio asks.

She closes her eyes and sees flashes of the woman—brown eyes, crooked nose—the boy, the man with the tattoo. They are all thin and tired and angry.

"I don't know if they're watching him, but they've stopped," she says. "I think there's something wrong with the truck."

Petrolio nods. "We need to go now."

Heather drops the rest of the apple on the ground and lets Aura lift her up onto Petrolio.

They run.

*

Something shivers in the ground beneath Estajfan's ear. He knows, instantly, that they are here. He can feel Petrolio's beating hearts, the simmer of Aura's rage.

And Heather—he can feel Heather.

There's a rustle nearby and the man who is now on watch—Darby—sits up and cocks his gun. A twig breaks.

"Jesus, Brian. You're lucky I didn't blow your head off."

"I was trying to be quiet." The boy shuffles up beside the other man and props another gun against the tree. "Anyway. I'm here. You can go get some sleep." There's a pause, and then, "Did anything—happen?"

"With this thing? No."

He can hear Brian swallow. "Not just—the creature. The—plants."

"Brian, for God's sake—"

"You know they move! You've seen them reach for people. That's why we've been sleeping in the truck!"

"It's fine," Darby says. "Nothing happened." He stands and thumps the boy on the back. "Try not to get us all killed," he says, and he heads for the truck.

The boy clears his throat and leans against a tree. He's nervous. He's also very tired. Estajfan looks up at the stars again and waits for the boy to sit, to slouch, to nod off.

He almost doesn't want it to happen. He can feel the green things waiting, watching for a sign.

As soon as Brian relaxes and slumps to sit down against the tree, a slender grubby hand clamps his mouth, and the other holds something small and sharp against his neck.

"If you move," Heather whispers, "I will slit your throat."

The boy's eyes widen in terror, but he doesn't move. The rifle falls into the grass.

Petrolio emerges from the trees on the other side of Estajfan. He bends and slices the ropes that still bind Estajfan's legs.

Estajfan is on his feet almost instantly.

"We're going to leave now," Heather hisses to the boy. "Don't scream, or move, or I'll come back and kill you."

She retreats, slowly, and the boy doesn't stir. Then she trips over the undergrowth and the boy is after her instantly, grabbing her hair and her shirt, and now she's the one with the sharp thing at her neck as Brian screams, "*There are more of them! There are fucking more of them!*"

"*Go!*" Estajfan roars at Petrolio. He sees the other three scramble out of the truck. JJ runs to the front and turns the truck lights on and Petrolio cries out against the sudden blare of light, then turns and disappears into the trees. Darby plunges after him.

"Run!" Heather cries as Brian drags her back toward the truck. "Estajfan, go!"

Someone fires a shot; it whizzes past Estajfan's ear. It's Moira, coming toward them, her gun held high and pointed at his face.

Estajfan ducks and charges at the boy; Brian, terrified, drops Heather and falls backward onto the ground. Estajfan scoops Heather up and then he's rearing over Brian, and his hooves come down as Brian screams.

"*Stop!*" Moira screams.

Estajfan looks straight at her. "You saved me once, Moira," he says.

For a few seconds, she's stunned by the sound of his voice. It's all the time he needs. He turns and leaps and runs. Shots ring out, but they run and run and suddenly Petrolio is there, and Aura, and then they are all galloping, the shouts fading behind them.

— 21 —

M oira lets out one long, rage-filled scream as the creatures vanish into the trees. Then she goes to Brian, who lies panting and white-faced on the ground. His right leg is shattered, the tibia splintered white and ugly below his knee. She runs to the truck, jumps in, and grabs her makeshift medical supplies—rags, the bottle of whiskey. She tears a large strip of cloth and douses it in alcohol, then ties it as tight around his shin as she can to stop the bleeding.

He passes out, which is probably just as well.

"*Darby! JJ!*" There's a moment, a long one, and then they come back to her, out of the trees. Without a word, they carry Brian into the back of the truck.

"I need—sticks," she says. "Straight ones."

Darby goes to look while JJ dismantles the camp. Darby comes back carrying two large branches. Moira strips the leaves and gets the men to help her position them on either side of Brian's leg. She douses an old sheet in the rest of the whiskey and then winds it around and around his leg, over the branches, tying it as tight as she can to form a splint.

As she works, she sees how guilt-ridden and furious the other two are. She feels the same way. They had all pushed the kid around a little, but you had to be hard now to survive. Like JJ, so flint-eyed and dour and capable, holding a hundred different secrets, or Darby, who was snappy and mean and had panic-filled night terrors they all pretended to ignore.

They've known each other maybe two weeks at most. It feels like a lifetime.

"Okay," she says, when she's done the best she can. It isn't pretty, or particularly clean. Brian is mercifully still unconscious. She tries not to think about what will come later.

"I should have let him take the first watch," Darby says. "I would have—I would have let them go. I wouldn't have tried to be a hero—"

Moira pulls her hoodie over her head, grateful for its warmth, then rests a hand on Darby's arm. "At least he's alive." Alive, with a leg that's as good as useless. And no hospital in sight.

"We have to go after them," JJ says. "Both of you get in the truck. Let's go."

Moira and Darby both stare at him. "Why?"

"There was a woman with them," JJ says. "Right?"

"I think so," Moira says.

"Where there are people," JJ says, "there might be food. We need to follow them."

"How the fuck are we supposed to follow them in the dark?" Darby says. "We don't even know which way they went, for fuck's sake."

"They went north," JJ says, and he points behind them, into the trees.

"How the hell do you know that?" Darby says.

JJ shrugs. "It's just a hunch. A feeling."

"*I don't want to drive God knows where on a goddamned hunch!*" Darby shouts.

JJ remains calm. "They'll come back out on the road," he says. "Even they can't run through the forests forever—you've seen the undergrowth. They're heading north, toward the mountains."

Moira doesn't ask how he knows this. She thinks of the creature. How he'd reached for the woman and shattered Brian's leg in less time than it took her to inhale. How the woman had curled into his chest as though *she* was the wounded thing.

He could speak. He'd looked right at her when she held that gun in his face.

The rifle. She runs back to where Brian fell and finds it, already half covered in green. She reaches for it and is not surprised when the green vines and long, tangled grasses at her feet twine more tightly about it. She tugs, gently at first and then less so, and finally the green things let go and she stumbles back. As she rights herself, she notices something glinting at her feet—a small, delicate knife, a scalpel. She picks that up too. It is always good to keep what they find. She hurries back to the truck and hands Darby the rifle, then lets him hoist her up.

"What's that?" JJ says, pointing to the knife in her hand.

"Don't know," she says. "A scalpel? I found it near the rifle."

"What's Dr. Moira need a scalpel for?" Darby says, trying to make a joke.

She echoes JJ. "Just a hunch," she says. "A feeling."

JJ nods, then shuts them in.

As they bounce over the unforgiving road, she turns the scalpel over and over in her hands. She's never seen a scalpel like this—not that she's seen many scalpels at all. The handle is cylindrical and smooth, with tiny designs running the length of it. She slowly draws a line through the air with the blade.

Maybe it's magic, she thinks. *Like the creature.* Maybe she can cut a window through the air and step back in time to the years before any of this happened.

"What, now you're a doctor for real?" Darby teases. She lets him have his fun. They are three broken men and Moira, who is not a doctor, just someone who used to be on TV sometimes but has mostly been a waitress.

(It was the nose, her agent told her a million years ago. It was too sharp. *We want real but not that real,* he said.)

She wraps the scalpel carefully in some cloth and puts it in the pocket of her hoodie, then puts her head in her hands and tries to still her shaking mind. The truck rumbles through the dark and no one speaks.

She'd walked and walked and walked in those first few hours after the scream—moving out of her bathroom refuge and then down the street, out of her town, through the town after that. The sun had gone down, the stars had come out, and she'd taken shelter in an abandoned gas station convenience store, then woken to the sound of someone at the fuel tanks. When she went outside, she saw Darby trying to siphon diesel, the old U-Haul silent and waiting. Brian had been sitting in the passenger seat. He'd been the first to notice her.

Eric, already delirious, had been out of sight in the back.

"How do you know if there's even gas left?" she had called.

Darby had looked up, almost dropping his gas can in surprise. "I don't," he said, once he'd regained his composure. "But it never hurts to try."

She went with them—they asked no questions. Darby had rigged the truck up to work on vegetable oil as well as regular diesel, so whenever they stopped, they looked for both of these things. They didn't travel far. They found JJ a few days after that, waiting for something by the side of the road. Eric was dead by then and so it was only the four of them, swirling into place like a constellation. It feels like she's known them her whole life.

"Do you know how to set a leg, Dr. Moira?" Darby asks, breaking the silence. "For real?"

"Of course not," she says, staring at the floor.

Neither of them looks at Brian.

— 22 —

Annie has a pistol in her belt—they found it a few days ago, and it's the only gun they have—and Tasha has Elyse hooked around her shoulder as they stagger toward the mountain. It is harder going now than it had been during the winter—there is practically no path left, just an endless vista of green, with bright flowers that arch over them, glorious, unchecked. They take their time. The world is quiet save for birds that chirp unseen in the trees.

They smell the greenhouse before they see it, and are grateful the scent doesn't make them spin in panic. They creep forward to find the greenhouse door broken, its panes of glass shattered.

"Here," Elyse says between breaths. "The creature was *right here.*"

Tasha lowers her to the ground. Elyse still wears the Doc Martens, still has the black leather jacket. *Some things,* Tasha thinks, *have survived.*

Tasha looks up at the mountain rising above them. A mountain tall enough that one could climb it and reach the clouds. A mountain where mothers and fathers might have brought their crippled, disfigured young to die so many years ago.

The world is still beautiful, despite all of its terror and tragedy, and she understands none of it. Blood and brains and heartbeats? Things that grow and things that don't and stories about birds that fall from the sky? She tried so hard to keep them all alive—and for what? When her parents died, she was not there; the people in this city died around her even as she fought to stop it. And here she is, alive. After everything.

"I thought we could do it," she says then, staring off into the green. "I just wanted us all to survive."

"People believed in you," Elyse says. She coughs again.

"People believed in *stories*," Tasha says. She can't keep the bitterness out of her voice. "The mountain and its secrets. The Food Angel, whatever that was. There was nothing I could do about that."

"You were a story too," Annie says. "I told you that, Tasha—and you didn't listen to me."

Tasha nods. Her gaze drops to the trees—the green things that grow, the world that has turned away from them all. "I thought I would—rewrite it? Shift everyone's attention to things that mattered? I don't know."

"The Food Angel kept almost everyone alive over the winter," Elyse says. She points up to the mountain. "That's what the creature was. And that's where it *is*. I'm sure of it."

Stories are never only stories.

Tasha laughs, even though none of this is funny. "I guess it's going to remain a story now," she says.

"I know you don't believe me," Elyse says, "but it was there, Tasha. I know what I saw."

Tasha shrugs. "We should go back," she says. "We don't want to be stuck here after dark." She glances at the greenhouse as she and Annie help Elyse up. "No one told stories about the flowers," she says. "Even Heather never said anything about them—and she had them in her house."

Annie snorts. "I guess there's not much you can do when the world wants to starve you out." When they look at her, puzzled, she only shrugs. "It doesn't take a genius to figure out that's what's been going on," Annie says. "It doesn't even take a doctor."

As they move away, Tasha looks back at the greenhouse one last time. Flowers tumble from it, wild and happy. She felt no whisper of madness as they came close to it, no surge of despair.

It is only a greenhouse now, she thinks, *soon to be gone entirely. And these are only flowers. This is all they've ever wanted to be.*

*

They reach the city at dusk. They head straight for the townhouse. Around them, the same empty silence. The slow circle of birds overhead.

Tomorrow, Tasha thinks. Tomorrow the three of them will leave.

At the front steps, Elyse cocks her head. "What's that sound?"

They all listen—they hear birds, the rush of wind, and then a deeper rumble.

Annie breathes out. "It sounds like a car."

As one they move toward the sound—down the street, across the square and past the clinic.

People, Tasha thinks. *People.*

Beside her, Annie reaches for her pistol, then looks down sharply as she realizes it's not there. It must have fallen from her hip as they struggled through the undergrowth toward the greenhouse.

At last the vehicle comes into view, a filthy U-Haul lumbering over the green-choked roads.

It pulls to a stop in front of them, and the driver opens the door and swings down onto the ground.

"Tasha," he says.

It's a voice they all remember.

-23-

They run until Estajfan can't go on anymore. It isn't even Estajfan who stops—Heather makes them.

"Stop!" she calls out into the night. "We have to stop!"

Estajfan is wheezing, his stomach heaving in and out. Heather scrambles to the ground. "We have to rest," she says. "Estajfan—*you* have to rest."

He shakes his head. "They'll find us if we don't keep going."

"If you drop dead, they'll find us for sure." Heather pulls him away from the road and his siblings follow.

The trees are close, lit faintly by the moon. "Lie down," Heather says as she leads him a little deeper. Estajfan obeys. "Aura," she says, "you need to check his wounds."

They all feel Petrolio shudder.

"It's all right," Estajfan says. "Petrolio, I'm all right. The woman— Moira—she helped."

"She shot at you as we were running away!" Heather protests.

"Before," he says. "She took out a bullet." He gestures at the crude bandage that still sticks to his flank. "And I—I hurt the boy. I deserved to be shot at."

"You didn't deserve anything," Aura snaps. She kneels by him. Her hands are gentle, but Estajfan winces as she pulls the duct tape away. She inspects the wound as best she can and then pulls a small pouch and a tiny pot from her satchel. She takes a scalpel out of the pouch, dips it into the pot, and scrapes gently at the wound. Then she dips her fingers in the pot and smears grey salve over the wound before she covers it with a bandage.

"What would you do without that bag?" Heather murmurs.

Aura laughs. "It is helpful. Particularly when you have brothers who insist on getting into trouble."

Estajfan laughs too, then catches his breath in pain. Aura watches him. "If we see that woman again," she says, "I will thank her. If the bullet was still in the wound, you wouldn't have been able to run."

Petrolio stamps his hooves. "*Thank* her? If we see her again, she'll be lucky if I don't trample her into the ground."

"She was frightened," Estajfan says. "They all were."

"I don't care!" Petrolio shouts. "They shouldn't have shot you in the first place!"

Aura pulls another bandage out of her satchel—a long strip of gauze—and wraps the length of it around Estajfan's body. "That's what they do," she says, her voice soft. "Humans don't understand—they will never understand. That's why we are safe on the mountain in a way we'll never be down here."

"Not all humans," Heather says, hurt. She helps Estajfan shift so that Aura can reach beneath him and pull the cloth up tight, tying it in place. "Some of us have tried. *I* try."

Aura puts a hand against Estajfan's forehead. "Sleep," she says.

He shakes his head, tries to get up. "What if they find us?"

"If we hear something," Aura says, her voice firm, "we'll go. Until then, you need to sleep."

He looks about to protest, then sighs. Maybe it's her words, maybe it's her hand on his head, but soon he's asleep.

"Where did you learn to do all of that?" Heather says. "The scalpels, the salve."

"My father taught me," Aura says. "Sometimes animals on the mountain would get hurt and I would help him stitch them up." Her voice softens. "Estajfan kept bringing me things for my bag."

"So human knowledge is good for something, at least."

If Aura hears this, she doesn't let on. "Come," she says. "I hear water nearby."

✴

They find a creek, bubbling and swift in the dark. Not enough to bathe in, but Heather is able to wash her arms and face, to dip her head under and rinse the worst of the dirt from her hair. When she's done, she combs her hair out with her fingers.

Beside her, Aura stands pale and silent.

"I won't hurt him," Heather says. "I promise."

"That's not a promise you can make," the centaur says. "You don't know what it's like to be him, to be us—that's not something anyone can understand."

"But I can try," Heather says.

"Every time someone tries, *someone* gets hurt," Aura says. "It happened with our father and our mother. It happened with your father, the first time you came up." Aura shakes her head. "We belong on the mountain, Heather. I don't have to like that to know that it's true."

"And what about Estajfan?" Heather says. "What about"—and she's the one to make the gesture now, a wide half-circle, mocking Aura's earlier words—"whatever lies between us? You said that. Not me."

"I know. I don't need to understand that to know it's a danger." She waves at the copse where Estajfan sleeps and Petrolio waits. "We'll take you home. We'll see that you are as safe as we can manage. Beyond that—I don't think we can make any promises either."

When they rejoin the others, Heather lies down beside Estajfan, wrapping her arm over his chest, like she belongs.

✴

Sometime later, the truck passes. Aura is the first to feel the noise in the ground, willing the dark things around them silent and still. The faint beam of its headlights comes in their direction, then fades away along with the sound of the engine.

"Are they gone?" Estajfan says, from where he lies on the ground. Heather is still asleep beside him.

"I think so," Aura says. On her other side, Petrolio is tense, waiting.

"I broke that boy's leg," Estajfan whispers. "I didn't think twice about it. He didn't do anything to me."

"They captured and hurt you," Petrolio reminds him. "That's not nothing."

Estajfan nods. "Still," he says, "what are we going to do?"

"They've passed us," Petrolio says. "They don't know where we live or where we're going. Why can't we just go home?"

Aura doesn't look at Estajfan, but she knows what he's going to say.

"What about Heather?"

"What about her?" Petrolio spreads his arms out wide. "We came to rescue *you*, Estajfan. You're as much a part of the mountain as we are."

"But we aren't a part of the mountain," Aura says. "Not in the way that we want to be, not if we continue like this."

"Like what?" Petrolio cries, waking Heather, who sits up, watching them all.

Aura thinks of their long-ago life on the mountain, just the four of them, the wild animals, the sky. For a moment she's overcome with longing. *Da*, she thinks. *Da, you were right.*

But then, he'd also been unhappy. Hadn't she known that the best?

If there's no place for them on the mountain anymore, where else can they go? She pushes the thoughts away and addresses Heather. "They're heading for the city," she says. "What do you want to do?"

She can see the longing on Heather's face—except that she's not longing for the mountain. She wants her girls, she wants Estajfan, she wants all of it. She wants the life that used to be.

"I need to go back to the city," Heather says, finally. "I need to say goodbye."

-24-

When Brian wakes, sometime in the early morning, he writhes with pain. Since they have nothing to give him for it, Moira and Darby each take turns murmuring words of comfort in his ear, soothing him as best they can.

They can't see outside of the truck; they have no idea where they're going. They sleep and wake and sleep and wake again. Occasionally JJ stops and they get out to pee. The engine doesn't blow.

And then, finally, they come to a stop and hear the driver's side door open. JJ steps down and says something, but Moira can't hear what.

"Is he talking to someone?" she hisses. Darby is already at the back door. The latch sticks; he bangs it, yells.

For a moment nothing happens and Moira's breath catches. *This is it*, she thinks. *We've been ambushed. We're all dead.* But then the door unlatches and JJ stands in front of them. Beside him are three women, all as thin and dirty as they are.

Moira can't help it; she's so astonished to see the women she practically falls out of the truck.

"Easy," says the woman who catches her. She's tall and blonde. "Are you all right?"

"You're—you're real," Moira gasps. "You're alive." How many green roads have they driven down since the scream? She can't help it; she clings to the woman, sobbing.

"It's all right," the woman murmurs. "I understand."

When Moira finally gets herself under control, Darby is shifting from one foot to the other, and JJ stands silent, staring at the ground.

"Where are we?" Moira asks.

In answer, the women step back from the truck and point. Moira turns and there it is—the remnants of a city and beyond them, a mountain that rises into the sky.

She's never seen a mountain before, but right now she's more interested in the women. "Who are you?" she asks. "Does JJ know you? Is that why we're here?"

"JJ?" the blonde woman says. "If by JJ you mean *Joseph*, then yes."

JJ shrugs. "JJ is what my mother used to call me," he says. "My wife called me Joseph." He lifts a hand in the direction of the tall woman. "Moira, this is Annie. And this"—his voice is strained here—"is Elyse." Another blonde, small and gaunt, breathing with difficulty. "And this is Tasha," he says, motioning to the woman beside him. The smallest of the three, dark and silent. He clears his throat. "Moira, she's a doctor. Annie's a nurse."

"Help," Moira says, instantly. "Brian needs help." She scrambles into the truck, the small woman right behind her, to where Brian lies.

The doctor—Tasha—drops to her knees. Her hands move over his leg—fingers that know what to do. "What happened?" she asks.

Moira swallows. "He was—trampled." She motions to the makeshift splint. "I tried to stabilize his leg, but we were in a hurry and all I had were branches. . ." She's weeping again.

Tasha puts a hand on Moira's arm. "You did the best you could. You did an excellent job." She calls to the people gathered at the edge of the truck. "Annie, we need to get him to the clinic. Can you"—nodding to Darby and JJ—"help me lift him?" Then she reaches down and grasps

Brian's hand. "This is going to hurt," she says. "I'm so sorry."

The boy passes out again on the way to the clinic, but his screams linger in Moira's head like an alarm. She turns to face the doctor. "Is it infected? Is he going to lose the leg?"

"I don't know yet." The doctor is walking briskly after the others. "I need to see."

"Here," Moira says, running to keep up with her. She fumbles in her pocket. "I found this. If you need it." She hands Tasha the scalpel.

Tasha takes it gingerly and holds it up to the light, an odd expression on her face. "Where did you get this?"

Moira waves a hand back in the direction they've come from. "Back—there. Far away. It was just on the ground." She wills herself not to cry. "I took it—for Brian. In case I needed to use it."

Tasha stares at the scalpel in her palm for so long Moira starts to feel uneasy.

"What?" she finally asks. "What is it?"

"Nothing." Tasha shakes herself. "It's just that my mother told me stories about a scalpel like this. It's part of why I wanted to be a doctor." She puts the blade back in Moira's hand and folds her fingers over it. "Keep it. I have more. And you might need a weapon."

You might need a weapon. Moira suppresses a shudder. When they reach the clinic, Joseph is waiting for them.

"Did you ask her?" he says. "Have they seen it?"

"Ask me what?" Tasha says.

JJ is silent for so long Moira wants to scream. "We saw something," he says, finally. "Farther south, close to the water. I don't know what it was. Half man, half horse. We had it with us for a night, and then it . . . escaped." He sounds sheepish, and suddenly Moira feels it too.

But the small blonde has overheard them. She doesn't look surprised. "Centaur," she says, and the word slices into Moira, inevitable and perfect. "You saw the centaur."

✳

Brian doesn't lose the leg—at least not that night. As Tasha and Annie work over him, Moira watches from her perch near the front door, the night wind cutting softly through the broken front window.

She'd offered to help, but it's clear that these women have worked together for a very long time—they move in sync, the tools that Tasha asks for already waiting in Annie's outstretched hand. Her other hand holds a flashlight, illuminating the mess. Brian is delirious with pain and drifts in and out of consciousness. When he moans, Moira stirs at her perch.

"You can come closer," Tasha says, softly. "It would be nice for him to have someone he knows nearby."

She sits by Brian's head and takes his hand like she did in the truck. It's clammy, his forehead warm and damp.

"He has a fever," she whispers. "That's not a good sign, is it?"

The other women, intent on the leg, don't answer. Tasha is using a sponge to clean the wound and a pair of tweezers to remove tiny fragments of bone.

The leg is broken in several places.

"Anterior and posterior tibial arteries intact," Tasha says. She nods to Moira. "You did well to staunch the bleeding."

Moira squeezes Brian's hand and fixes her gaze on the collection of bone fragments that Tasha is amassing.

"Here," Annie says, after some time. "Hold this."

Moira takes the flashlight that Annie offers, then trains it back on Brian's leg. Tasha positions and grasps the broken bottom part of the shin bone, then slowly pulls as Annie braces the leg. Sweat stands out in beads on Tasha's forehead and for several long, impossible moments no one makes a sound. The bone slides into place.

"There," Tasha says, a note of quiet triumph in her voice. "Next one."

Moira holds the flashlight steady. The light doesn't waver. The light doesn't go out.

✳

When they are done, Moira leaves Brian bandaged and sleeping on the mattress at the back, his leg splinted and immobile as Annie and Tasha clean up.

JJ and Darby and the blonde girl, Elyse, sit in the clinic waiting room, half-asleep.

"He's all right," Moira says, and she watches Darby and JJ relax. "At least for now. Tasha says we have to watch for signs of infection but they still have some antibiotics, so hopefully he'll be okay." She plops down into an empty seat beside Elyse, then leans forward and puts her head in her hands.

"Here," Elyse says, softly, and when Moira looks up, the girl is offering her an apple and a potato in her outstretched hands. "When did you last eat?"

Moira can't remember. She takes the apple and bites into it as she rolls the potato around in her hand.

Tasha comes out of the back room and sits in a chair on the other side of Moira. "Joseph," she says, "what did you do after you left?"

"I biked as far away as I could get," he says. "Left the others almost right away—scrounged food where I could, slept in ditches. I made it almost as far as the water before—before anything else happened."

"And when the—scream—came?"

Joseph looks at his hands. "I was in bed," he says. "Some of the places I passed through were doing better than others. Ramshackle hotels, places where people were surviving without power. When I heard people screaming outside—" he clears his throat—"I saw my wife burning, and my boys, after the meteors came. Over and over in my head. I stood up, and reached out for the window, ready to break the glass"—he reaches a hand out now—"and there was a tree there, so close I could almost touch it. I counted a leaf, and then another, and another. I just kept counting. And the memories went away, eventually." He clears his throat again. "When the meteors came, that's what saved me then too, in a way. We'd gone on a road trip, and I was outside packing the van when the meteor took the hotel and the van with it. It missed me by inches. It was so hot

I couldn't stay there, so I just started walking away, counting my foot-steps as I went. I got to ten thousand before I came to."

"I counted too," Moira says. "When the scream came. I was in a bath-room, and I counted the tiles."

"And you?" Tasha asks Darby.

"I was buried when the meteors came," he says. A shudder goes through them all. "It took three days for people to dig me out. I spent most of the time thinking about going on vacation somewhere tropical and imagining the drinks I would buy, the things I would see when I went scuba diving. I've never been scuba diving." He shrugs, then laughs a little. "Happy place, right? That's what my therapist told me, years ago."

Tasha tells them about the greenhouse—the long walks she took to its warmth in the winter, the madness and grief she experienced there that left her shaking on the ground.

"It got bearable," she says, "eventually. As though the flowers . . . pre-pared me, somehow." She looks at them all. "The same way that your lives—the things your lives forced you to know—prepared you."

"So—what?" Darby laughs again, tiredly. "Only the broken survive? Is that it?"

"Nobody here is broken." Elyse's voice is fierce.

Moira only shrugs. "It's not that complicated. Grief is boring. You get used to anything in time—even that."

"But some people don't," Tasha says, glancing at Annie, who has come to stand in the doorway. "Lots of people didn't—look at how few of us are left. Annie and Elyse and I are the only ones left in the whole city."

At this, JJ—*Joseph*, Moira tells herself—stirs. "Everyone?" he says.

Tasha spreads her hands. "As far as we can tell. We've gone walking a lot. We haven't found anyone else."

"Anyway," Annie says, abruptly, "we're leaving. We should have left months ago."

"But what about the centaur?" Moira says. Everyone freezes, and she watches them all register this fact again—they've been so wrapped up in Brian they forgot. Her too. "You've seen him?"

"I saw him," Elyse says. "With Heather, by the greenhouse near the mountain. Just before the scream came."

"Heather?" Joseph gets up from his chair. "She was there? With the creature—the centaur—whatever it is?"

"Who's Heather?" Moira snaps.

But Joseph is looking at Tasha. "I told you that mountain was strange," he says. "It brought me back again. Twice."

"Who's Heather?" Moira says. "What the fuck is going on?"

Tasha hasn't taken her eyes from Joseph. "She died weeks ago, with the others."

"Tasha, I think she's alive."

✳

None of them can take in any more. Exhausted, they curl up in the chairs and try to sleep. Tasha and Annie sleep in the back room, near Brian, who is fitful. In the early morning Tasha checks him and finds that his fever has gone down a little.

"He'll need something to eat," she says, looking to Annie. "Let's get him something warm." The other woman nods.

They go outside and make their way to the townhouse, where they grab some rice and beans. They come back and light a fire in the alley pit behind the clinic, then take turns stirring the rice and beans over the fire. Annie is the one who brings it up again.

"Heather knew," she says. "She knew this whole time."

Tasha stares into the pot. "Looks that way."

"Did you—suspect her?"

Tasha stirs for a while before she answers. "I don't know what I suspected," she says at last. "There was something about her that drew me in. Like—oh, Annie, I don't know. Like she was family? Somehow? Or maybe I just thought she knew more about the mountain than she was letting on. But everyone else—there were so many stories. Foxes and murdered babies and people who disappeared. I didn't know what to believe."

Annie lets out a grim laugh. "I thought you were in love with her," she says. "I thought—I don't know what I thought."

Tasha shakes her head. "It wasn't that, ever. I—recognized her, somehow. She recognized me. That's what it felt like. Even though I know she didn't trust me. That's what I was trying to figure out."

They watch the pot for a few more minutes in silence.

"What happens now?" Annie asks.

"We're leaving. Same as before."

"Even if Heather's up there on the mountain?"

"Yes," Tasha says. She pours a bucket of dirty water over the fire and straightens. "We have the truck now—that's as good a sign as any we're meant to go."

As they carry the pot to the clinic, they both hear it—footfalls. Horses, galloping closer.

Annie's hands tremble; Tasha takes the pot from her.

Inside the clinic, everyone else is already crowded at the front window. Tasha sets the pot on a towel on the counter and checks on Brian, then follows everyone outside. They stand together and listen. Silence. Not even the birds.

Then, the sound of weeping. They shouldn't be able to hear it, but the rest of the world is so silent it isn't hard to make out. Hard sobs, thick and anguished. A voice she remembers, a voice she knows. She closes her eyes and feels the sudden rush of falling.

"Let's go," Tasha says, and she leads them all to Heather's house.

Heather slides from Aura's back onto the ground. There is no walkway to the front door anymore. She takes a few steps through the foliage and then drops to her knees. The vines and soft green things on the ground slide around her legs, but she pays no attention.

She doesn't want to go in. This is far enough. She bends down and places her forehead against the grass. Her sobs come hard and angry.

Greta and Jilly, snuggled against her in their sling.

Greta and Jilly, crawling on the grass.

B's hesitant smile.

All gone.

The centaurs stand guard around her and say nothing.

Then there's another cry—a human voice. The centaurs stiffen around her. She stands up, slowly, and turns.

She sees pale hair first, and the relief is so strong she's surprised.

"Elyse," she breathes. Beside Elyse, Tasha. And Annie. And *Joseph*.

And then she hears the unmistakable click of a gun. On the other side of Joseph stands a stranger, her gun pointed at Estajfan's face.

– 25 –

Heather is still pregnant, but even so she is thinner than Tasha remembers. She tries hard not to look at the centaurs, but this proves impossible. They are so large, so strange and beautiful—the brown-skinned one closest to Heather huge and tall, the other two pale and blond. Each centaur wears a golden cuff. Against the world's vivid green they're exquisite—a dream come to life that will fade if she blinks.

The darker one, she sees, has a bandage wrapped around its flank.

This is the one that Moira is staring at, her eyes glinting with fury, the pistol in her hands raised and pointing at its head.

"Moira," Tasha says. She wants to fall on her knees and weep, touch her forehead to the ground, pray. Something. She keeps her voice low, a hand outstretched. "Moira, put the gun away."

"I told you not to move!" Moira shouts at the centaur. "I fucking *told* you not to move!"

"*Moira!*" Tasha shouts, trying to snap her out of it.

"Brian is back there with a broken leg because of them!"

"Brian will be all right," Tasha says. She forces a steadiness into her voice that she doesn't feel, and takes a step closer to Heather. "No one else needs to get hurt today." She nods to Heather. "The baby?"

"Fine." Heather gets up, and looks from Moira and the gun to Estajfan and back. She moves to stand in front of him. "I think."

"Where did you go?" Tasha asks. "When the scream came."

"I was at the greenhouse. Estajfan took me up the mountain. I was going to come back—I only went there to warn him, to tell him to hide . . ." She looks up at the house and then back to Tasha. "Did you go inside? Did you see?"

Tasha nods. "I'm so sorry."

Heather wipes her eyes with her palm. "Were they—did they—"

"The plants came for them," Annie says, her voice gentle. "The plants came for everyone, in the end."

Moira is still holding the gun on Estajfan but Tasha can see something more than anger in her face now. Her arms slacken. The barrel dips.

"What are we supposed to do, Tasha?" Heather asks. "Where are we supposed to go?"

"I can answer that," Joseph says. "We're going up that fucking mountain!"

"Joseph," Tasha says, "we can't go up. It's too dangerous—"

"I don't fucking care! You heard Elyse—there's *food* up there. We've been starving for over a year!"

At last, one of the centaurs speaks. "The mountain isn't safe for you," the dark one says. "I do not—" and his eyes shift to Moira, and the gun— "we do not wish you harm."

"We just want to be left in peace." This from the blonde female, a bag slung over her shoulder and between her breasts. "That's all."

"But Heather went up," Tasha says.

The female nods and says, "She's not going up anymore. None of you are."

"You don't fucking get to tell us what to do!"

Tasha sees Joseph grab Moira's gun as if in slow motion. The surprise in Moira's face, the sudden splash of terror on Heather's. Elyse screams as Joseph shoots, Moira tackles him to the ground, something glinting in her hand.

"Let it go," Moira says, and as Tasha comes closer, she can see that it's the scalpel Moira showed her the day before. Moira's voice is surprisingly calm now. "Let it go, Joseph."

He stares up at her, anguished. "*Why them? Why do they get to survive?*"

To this, no one has an answer. When Moira finally leans back, Joseph pulls himself up to a sit, small and defeated.

"Moira," Tasha says. "That scalpel. You said you found it by the water?"

"No. In the forest. After we were—ambushed."

The female centaur steps over to them. "That's mine," she says, urgently. She holds out a hand. "That knife. Heather dropped it in the forest. Give it to me."

"It's mine now," Moira snaps. "Don't come any closer."

"Where did *you* get it?" Tasha looks at the centaur. She can feel Annie watching her, confused.

"My father gave it to me. It was a gift," the centaur says. "It's important to me. Please."

And Tasha drops to her knees after all. "There was a woman in my family," she says. "Long ago. My mother told me stories. She was a travelling physician." The centaur knows, Tasha realizes. Maybe she's always known. She takes a breath and says, "One summer, she delivered triplets in a village."

THE DOCTOR AND
THE VILLAGE GHOSTS

The second time she comes to the mountain, the doctor discovers that the centaur has cleared the path she'd hacked on her first climb. It's now free of brush, and in places the climb is so gradual it hardly feels like a climb at all. It ends exactly where they met. She finds him waiting for her there. She doesn't know how he knew she was coming, and doesn't ask. He is grateful for the textbooks. He doesn't take her to the children.

The next year is much the same—and the year after that, and the year after that. Every time she asks him if she can meet the children his response is the same: not yet, they aren't ready. He is grateful and polite but also closed to her. She continues to visit anyway.

Occasionally she travels to the wife's village. She has five children now, all thriving and happy. The mother is happy too, most of the time. She never mentions her other children now, even when she and the doctor are alone. She is afraid for the safety of her five children in the village; she doesn't like it when they're away from her, she doesn't like it when her husband takes them on trips. But she never goes. Once upon a time she had wanted a different kind of life; now the possibility of a different kind of life for her children terrifies her. The doctor knows that if the mother had her way, her children would never leave her.

The doctor has no children, only secrets.

The doctor brings the centaur medical supplies and history books and maps. She brings novels and books of poetry and mathematics texts that hold delicate equations; she brings dinner plates and wineglasses and cutlery.

She brings the centaur dried herbs and a mortar and pestle and shows him berries on the mountain that will help when his children have a fever; leaves to crush into a salve that will help with cuts and bruises. She brings him a surgeon's needle and thread and teaches him how to stitch a wound. She points out other plants that he should harvest and dry and use.

"For pain," she says, "and infection."

As the years go by, the doctor continues to travel—growing slower as her joints stiffen, but her heart and her mind as strong as ever. Eventually she begins to hear stories of a monster in the old village, and stories of another monster in the city by the mountain. The village and the city are far enough apart that no one would ever note the similarities, but the doctor does. She is tired of people who lie and are afraid.

The village monster, so the story goes, is tall and black as night. It sweeps through the streets in the early-morning darkness, stealing random things. A cooking pot, a toy that lies in a child's crib. No one can figure it out. What use would a monster—or even a thief—have for such things?

The monster in the mountain city is much the same—stealing furniture, coming and going like a ghost.

The city people tell her that spirits from the mountain come down to strike fear into the hearts of those who want to climb it. Leave the mountain alone, they tell her. As years pass, they tell her this more and more. People have gone up the mountain and disappeared, they say. It's best to stay away.

And yet despite the stories, the doctor can't determine if anyone from the city has ever actually gone missing. A friend of a friend of a friend disappears. A girl goes missing, a boy too. Perhaps they ran away together. People tell themselves all kinds of stories when they grieve.

One year she asks the centaur what he knows about the rumours.

"The humans are right to stay away" is all he says.

And yet he loves humans. He can't get enough of them. Doesn't he run among them and bring back their treasures? He boasts to her of all the things the children know—he's taught them their letters, he's shown them so much. Of the humans far below, he says, "They have only one heart," as if she doesn't already know. As if he, too, did not have only one heart himself long ago.

She brings the centaur blankets and jewellery, music boxes and more books. He never even tells her if the children have said thank you. One year a rich patient pays her with a series of handmade golden cuffs; she brings them to the centaur and drops them in a bag at his feet.

The centaur is struck almost speechless by this gift. He picks one up and puts it on his wrist right away.

"You're supposed to say thank you," the doctor says. Once more, she wonders if the children are still alive. Maybe there's no one on the mountain but him and a shrine of human artifacts to his first love.

The centaur says, "Thank you. They're very beautiful."

He is very beautiful, the doctor thinks—the cuffs look ridiculous on her thin wrists, but on the centaur they are an adornment for a king.

"I want to see them," she says. "I want to know that they're all right. I want to know that they are happy."

"They're happy," he says.

The doctor shakes her head. "I don't believe you," she says.

His face darkens; he looms over her, fists clenched. "*I am not lying.*"

The doctor stands her ground. In her head is a darkened room and a woman drugged and terrified on the table, three versions of a secret suddenly there before them all, screaming. "Maybe they *are* happy. But I would like to see. I brought them into the world; I deserve to know how they're faring."

The centaur is silent for so long that the doctor doesn't know what to do; she's hurt him, she thinks. All she meant to do was push. She wants to apologize but the words won't come out.

"If you feel that way," he says at last, "then perhaps you shouldn't have sent them—*us*—away in the first place."

"I was trying to *save* them! And you!" the doctor cries. "Surely you can understand that."

But the centaur turns from her. "Do not come back," he says. "I thought you were a friend, but you are no friend at all."

She watches him walk away from her. She doesn't follow him; she wants to, but she doesn't. As she makes her way back down the mountain, her head is full of sadness, her eyes blurry with tears.

On the descent it starts to rain. When she was younger, the doctor would have kept walking, but she worries about slipping now, so she shelters under a large overhang and sets up camp for the night. In the morning, the sky is clear and the warmth of the sun soon dries her clothes. As she makes her way down, she ponders his words over and over.

You are no friend at all.

In the mountain city, she stops and writes a letter to her sister. *I will be late*, she writes. *I have something to attend to here. Please give the girls my love.*

Is it a betrayal to want to see the children, to know that they're all right?

I only care about you, she wants to tell the centaur. *I only want to see you happy.*

She posts the letter and makes her way back to the mountain.

– 26 –

When Tasha finishes her story, Heather doesn't know what to say. She can tell that Estajfan and Petrolio don't know what to say either. Aura might know, but it's hard to look at her. There's too much in her face.

Finally, Annie clears her throat. "You knew," she says to Tasha, incredulous. "You've been lying to us this whole time. You knew about the mountain. You knew about—them."

"I didn't think it was *real*, Annie—I thought they were only stories."

"Stories are never only stories," Heather says. "Remember?"

Tasha shakes her head. "My mother told me stories about the mountain when I was small—she *made them up*, Heather, to try to help me sleep. Not because she thought that they were real." And then she is telling them all about her family's stories, fables passed down from mother to daughter, all the way back to twin sisters, and an aunt who was beloved. The doctor and her sister. The nieces, rapt in bed and listening to the words.

Estajfan says, "We never met the doctor. Our father never said anything—are you sure this is true?"

Tasha throws out her hands. "I don't know if any of it is true. But I thought you weren't real, and here you are."

Heather moves to stand beside Estajfan. "How does it end? The story with the doctor."

Tasha glances at Annie, and Annie looks away. "I have no idea," she says. "One year she went up the mountain and that was the last anyone ever saw of her."

Aura reaches for Tasha's hand. "I can tell you." In her voice is Tasha's sadness, magnified over and over. And beneath that, the resignation, the deep fear of facing that thing one hates the most.

Grief is inevitable. That doesn't make it any easier.

"Aura," Estajfan says. "What happened?"

"I need to take you up the mountain," Aura says to Tasha. "You deserve to see it—I will show you where she is."

— 27 —

And so it comes to pass that the centaurs and the humans make their way up the mountain after all. Aura leads them herself, following the path that her father carved into the mountainside—the same path that Heather and her father climbed those years ago. It is overgrown, but not difficult. They've left Brian back down in the clinic, with Darby standing guard.

As Moira climbs, she feels her anger at the centaurs dissipate. The light on the mountain trees is its own kind of knife, slicing her open. Jaime would have loved this—the clean air, the wildflowers that bloom at their feet. She sees the shadow of her sister everywhere—there her quick, slender hand, there the flash of her bright smile and face. It is so painful she almost can't breathe, and so beautiful she doesn't think of stopping.

There she is, just ahead, smiling at the centaurs.

Jaime's voice in her ear, or maybe just Moira's own. *They're impossible, I know, but here they are.*

Yes, she thinks. *Yes, they are.*

As they climb higher, she sees shadows coalesce around them that might be clouds but also might be people. A black-haired, black-skinned man, a woman with dark hair and a blue satchel. Another man who hovers over Heather and hums her a song. Moira wants to call to Heather to tell her to look, but the magic overwhelms her. Instead she looks to the others—to Joseph, who climbs with a face cracked with awe, to Elyse, who had been sitting warily on the back of the female centaur but is now silent and watching the sky. To Annie, grim and silent, who climbs beside Tasha as though she's stomping on her own heart.

She has no idea what to call this feeling that she has. It feels like waking up.

As Tasha climbs, she thinks of that long-ago doctor who was a witness to another kind of magic. The other doctor, who carried the birth of these babies with her through the years, and one year told the story to her sister late at night. A magical tale that was real.

The other doctor, she imagines, would have told Annie the story right away.

"I'm sorry," she whispers as Annie climbs beside her.

Annie doesn't reply, just puts one foot in front of the other.

Estajfan, the largest of them all, brings up the rear. Heather in front of him, limping and cautious but determined to climb.

Up the mountain, down the mountain, up and down and up again. The longest of goodbyes.

The world below them is a place he barely knows. He's only stolen from it—human things, human stories. He has been told his whole life that he doesn't belong there. And yet without the world below the mountain there would be no Heather; without the world below the mountain the centaurs wouldn't be at all.

They will leave. He and Heather. He isn't sorry.

He will run for her, he will go beyond the sea to find food if that is what she needs.

Wherever, he thinks. *Wherever you will go.*

✳

Heather climbs, and her father climbs beside her, breathing out of every leaf and twig.

The girls are not with her. It is as if they've never been.

Instead there is the baby, who kicks every now and then as they go higher.

She thinks back to those moments on the highest part of the mountain. The dirt that almost choked her, the taste of earth like copper in her mouth. The weight of it. She hadn't, as it turned out, wanted to be other than what she was in those moments. She only wanted to be herself, to be alive.

The baby kicks so hard she stumbles and falls, landing on the path on all fours.

Estajfan is beside her, his hand on her arm. "You're all right," he says. "You're safe."

She breathes in and out, her forehead against the soil. She shuts her eyes against the sting of tears. It hurts, climbing the mountain again. She doesn't want to climb anymore. The only mystery she wants to unlock is herself. "I understand now," she says. "I do."

"Yes," Estajfan says, and he bends to help her up. "I know."

She wants to ask him what he means, but the others are far ahead now and they need to catch up. She starts to climb again.

Some time later he picks her up. She wants to protest—*You've been injured, put me down*—but he doesn't falter.

I'm all right, she thinks. *I am safe, and I am climbing.*

✳

As she climbs, Aura thinks about her father—how kind he could be, how patient, and also how jealous and bitter. *Don't ever leave the mountain. The human world will break your heart and kill you.*

What would he do, she wonders, if he was still alive and waiting for them up ahead? Would he welcome these humans into their home or hide from them the way he'd hidden Aura and her brothers? Enveloping them in a magic made of love and pain and stories, weaving a net all around them that was hard to escape. *Humans will betray you. Humans will not love you. Look at your mother, look what she did.*

But look at the humans around them. Elyse, so sickly but so determined to hang on. The woman, Moira, who had saved Estajfan even though she feared him. Tasha and Annie, who kept the humans alive even as the ground tried to starve them.

Heather, always Heather, who saw a grief in the centaurs before even Aura herself knew what to call it.

Even Joseph, she realizes.

They've endured, these humans, in a way that surely even the mountain would understand.

Da, she thinks as she leads them past the place where Heather and her father had stopped those years ago. *Da, tell me what to do.*

He does not answer. He never does.

They climb for hours. They climb until the path stops in front of them, and then Aura crests the small cliff before them and sets Elyse down onto the ground before reaching down to pull Tasha up, and then the others. The other centaurs follow, one by one. Aura leads them down a path and around a little hill to a place where the ground opens into a tiny, improbable meadow filled with flowers. Forget-me-nots and larkspur and lilies. Black-eyed Susans that bend softly in the wind. Dark-red amaryllis that pop up through the grasses. Daisies, hollyhocks. A peach tree, an apple tree. Sunflowers that stand tall and proud. The plants here have none of the darkly beautiful menace that infuses the flowers down below.

In the centre of the flowers, there are two bare patches of earth. Aura turns around to face them.

"This one." She motions to the patch on her right. "She's here. Where the flowers do not grow."

Tasha takes a step forward and the others part for her. She falls to her knees before the grave.

"We came down to pick flowers," Aura says, her voice far away. "My father and me. That's when she came around the corner. He wasn't expecting her."

"What happened?" Tasha says.

But Heather knows. She sinks down in front of the other bare patch of earth. "He threw her over," she says. "He picked her up, and he threw her over the side of the mountain."

"Why didn't you tell us?" Petrolio is the first to break the silence. Sharp, raw, betrayed.

"He was afraid for us," Aura says. "I think that made him into something he didn't want to be."

"He forbade us to go down!" Petrolio cries. "But he went down because there were things there that *he* loved? He didn't tell us any of these stories. How could he do that?"

Aura nods. "When I looked at him after that, all I could see was her face as she fell. And he knew it—I think he saw her face too. I went down and found her body. I carried her here, and buried her. I didn't know what else to do."

"Your bag," Tasha says. "That belonged to her."

Aura's hands go to the old satchel slung over her shoulder. "Yes," she says. "I carry her with me wherever I go."

"And you?" Estajfan says. He is not as angry as Petrolio, but the hurt in his voice is deep. "What were you afraid of, Aura? You're the one who insisted we stay here."

"People have died!" Aura points to the graves. "Every time humans and centaurs come together, something happens, Estajfan. Someone gets hurt. The doctor wanted to help, but she died. Our father only wanted to love, and the house that we were born in—it almost took him. I was there. I *saw* it."

"You went down with him?" Petrolio says, betrayed.

"In a dream, or a vision, or—something." Aura shakes her head and her eyes fill with tears. "I *didn't* leave the mountain. We aren't meant to be off the mountain. And humans aren't meant to be up here."

"We aren't meant to be anywhere!" Estajfan cries. "We don't belong below the mountain with the humans—but we don't belong here, either, Aura, and you know it."

"Yes, we do," she whispers. "This is the home Da made for us. Da didn't think we were monsters."

"Da isn't here anymore!" he shouts. "It was the *mountain* that made Da into an in-between thing, Aura. It was the *mountain* that made it so that Da didn't belong." Estajfan clenches his fists. "And the mountain did that because it knew that he wanted a different kind of life."

"We're safe here," she says, stubbornly. "Look what just happened to you! We're safer here than we'll ever be down below."

"Aura." Petrolio steps closer to her. "The mountain centaurs—when we left, you know what they said—"

"I don't want to leave the mountain only to get shot by the side of the road!" Aura is weeping in earnest now.

"Yes," Annie says, surprising them all. "And I don't want to be in a world that's starving us to death. But it doesn't seem to matter what we want, does it?"

"I don't know," says Elyse. She's resting with her back against the peach tree. "I never thought I'd get up to the top of this mountain, and here we are." She laughs, and then doubles over, wheezing. When she catches her breath again, she locks eyes with Aura. "Here we are," she says, "no matter how hard the world tried to starve us. And you helped us up the mountain despite also saying that it tried hard to keep us away.

Maybe Tasha's right. Maybe there's a reason we're here. Us, and all of you, and no one else."

Heather laughs then, unexpectedly. They turn to look at her. "*Maybe you were ready to survive,*" she quotes. She looks at Estajfan. "Maybe we've always been ready."

In the silence that comes after this, Moira clears her throat. "There are two patches of bare earth," she says. "What is the other one for?"

Heather closes her eyes. "My father," she says. "This is my father's grave."

✳

The world behind her eyelids is swirling red and orange; Heather bends her forehead to the ground again and breathes in the smell of the mountain.

"I brought him here to be with her," Aura says.

Heather looks up. All around her is hazy sky and grey-brown stone and sturdy green lichens, fuzzy green moss. And the flowers. And yet there is no danger here that she can feel—only the colours, and love.

"He asked for help," she says. "When we climbed up. He thought that you could help me, that you could make me into something other than what I am."

Aura nods. "Yes," she says. "I remember."

"But I didn't need help," Heather says. "My body didn't do everything that I might have wanted it to do, but it was *mine*. I didn't want to change. I didn't want *him* to want me to change." She bites her lip. "I saw him stumble. I could have reached for him too, and I didn't. Not in time."

"Heather," Estajfan begins, "that wasn't your f—"

"I was so hurt," she says, talking over him. Her voice is far away, remembering. "Hurt, and so angry—but only for a moment. And even that moment was too long."

What if her father hadn't encouraged her to climb the mountain at all? What if she'd never felt like she'd had something to prove?

"He belongs here now," Aura says. "And so does she. The flowers wouldn't have come to them otherwise."

It's been so long since Joseph has spoken that nearly all of them jump when he says, "What—your mountain only likes humans if they're dead?"

"The mountain," a strange voice says, and they look up to see two more centaurs above them on a knoll, "does not care about humans either way." One male, one female. The female dark-haired, the male pale as Petrolio and Aura.

"We told you not to come back," the female says. "Aura, you should not have brought them up here."

"The humans in the ground?" Aura says. She places a hand on Heather's shoulder. "Or these ones?"

"Any," says the male. "Humans do not belong here. The mountain is only trying to keep us safe."

Tasha hears the whisper of a high-pitched scream in her ears, the crazy tilt of a world thrown open to the sky. She realizes only then that it isn't a memory. She reaches for Heather, understanding at last.

But Heather is not there. Instead it is the pale centaur, and Heather is in the air now, the centaur's hands strong and terrible around her, lifting. There is no time for Heather to scream, to even be surprised. Bright-blue panic in Estajfan's face, his outstretched fingers.

Sky over mountain over mountain over sky, and she goes over.

Estajfan reaches for Heather, misses, and then leaps over the side and is gone.

Petrolio crashes into the other pale centaur—they fall to the ground with a thud that shakes the trees. The dark centaur does not move.

Tasha, breathless, shouts to Aura. "Take me down. Take me down *now*."

Petrolio scrambles to his feet again. "I'll take you," he rasps. "Aura—get the others away from here." He bends and Tasha climbs onto his back—they turn to go but Aura shoots out a hand and grabs Petrolio's arm.

"Wait," she says. She pulls off her bag and gives it to Tasha. Then they are leaping over the knoll and down the path.

Elyse is on her knees, clutching her chest, her breathing hard and ragged. Annie bends over her, while Moira and Joseph stand terrified, still. The two mountain centaurs' brown eyes sweep them all.

"Leave now," the male centaur says as he climbs to his feet. "Leave now, or the rest of you will follow."

Aura goes to Elyse and kneels. Moira and Annie help the girl onto her back.

"The world is more than the mountain," Aura says, and she faces the mountain centaurs as she stands. "Green things grew around the graves here, even if the mountain didn't want the bodies. Change comes to the mountain, too, no matter how much we might wish otherwise."

She can't see him, but she knows that he's there—a small, slight man with dark hair, an easy smile, his fingers long and slender and stained with dirt. She buried him here all these years ago and he sank into the mountain. His bones became the dirt. His hands became the grass and trees, the flowers that grew up and blossomed. The vines that stretch up now and wind around the mountain centaurs' legs, shimmying up and rooting them to the spot.

The vines thread the mountain centaurs with green, shoot up their shoulders and around their necks, choke them, blind their eyes. Swift and greedy. The female centaur yells once in rage before she is silenced. In the space that was her mouth, a red flower blooms.

The humans stand frozen in horror.

Aura feels the unseen man smile at her, and ready himself. He has become part of the mountain but he, too, does not belong here. He is ready to go home, to follow his daughter back to the world below, now that she's come up to find him. Aura feels him sink back into the soil once more, and this time he is a river that runs through mountain rock, a starburst of energy that travels all the way down the mountain and back to the city.

He will be there, waiting for them, when they go back down. His unseen hands back in the soil again, coaxing the human gardens to grow. Already she can feel his hands brimming with seeds. The time for starving is over.

"Come," she says softly. There will be time to mourn her mountain home, but that time is not now. "We must go down." She makes her way back to the edge of the meadow and over the knoll.

The humans follow.

*

Heather is flying, falling, a great dizzied tumble. The same sequence that has haunted her dreams all these years.

Not her father's fall. Her own.

Then she slams into the earth—only it isn't earth, it's warm and close around her, *Estajfan*, his arms frantic to hold her.

The wind keening all around them.

He flails as he tries to right himself, get purchase on the mountainside.

The space around them endless and huge.

They tumble, they fall, they crash against the mountain. She feels him hit the mountainside and strain against the incline. A loud crack beneath them and he screams, and lets go. She hits spongy, leafy ground. Estajfan sails over her head, lands with an impact that shudders deep into the mountain.

The silence that follows is absolute. She can't hear her heart pounding, she can't see the sky. Her body is one long bell of pain.

But she's alive. She tries to breathe—it hurts, but she can do it. Vicious cramps hit her abdomen and she moans.

"Heather?" Estajfan calls. He's alive too. How can this be? "*Heather. Are you all right?*"

"Yes," she answers. Another cramp comes, and she whimpers. "Where are you?"

He cries out as he tries to move.

Another cramp, and another. Another. Another. It's too soon. It's too soon.

No, she thinks. *No, no.*

A face in front of her, calm dark eyes, dark hair. "You're all right," the face says. "You're all right."

Heather blinks. "Tasha?"

The woman shakes her head. "No." She puts a hand against Heather's forehead and takes a deep breath. The fresh scent of leaves flows into Heather's lungs.

"It's too soon," Heather says. She can't move her arm, she can't move her legs. Are they broken? Beside her, Estajfan moans.

Can he see the woman? She can't tell.

"It *is* too soon," the woman agrees. "But it is going to happen anyway."
She takes Heather's hand. "You'll be all right," she says. "Whatever happens."

"Who are you?" she gasps out. The woman only smiles.

"Breathe with me," she says. She touches Heather's forehead again.
"In and out."

How long do they do this? Heather isn't sure. Minutes, hours.

Something leaks from her, a warm gush out onto the ground.

"You're all right," the woman says again. "You'll be all right."

"*Who are you?*" Heather cries.

"I am the flowers," the woman says. Her hand firm against Heather's
abdomen, her other hand twining through Heather's fingers, squeezing
hard. "I am the flowers, I am the trees."

"Heather?" Estajfan calls. "Who are you talking to?"

"I don't understand," Heather presses. "Do you live here?"

The woman's face swims before her eyes. "I didn't live here," she says,
"but now I do. The mountain is my home; I will never leave it. Your father
has already left—he has gone to prepare the way." She nods to Heather's
belly. "He will come, your boy. We might have to pull him out."

"I can't do it," Heather whispers. "He won't survive." *I won't survive*,
she thinks. *The mountain will claim us all.*

The woman shakes her head again, and smiles. "No. The mountain
claimed me, but I survived. I came out of the ground with the flowers, and
so will you."

"I came out of the ground," Heather repeats, dizzily. "I didn't change
at all."

The woman leans in close. "Didn't you?" Her hand against Heather's
cheek, her expression gentle and knowing. "Heather," she says.

Heather. Heather. She hears the words as if from far away.

✳

"Heather?" Tasha calls. "*Heather?*"

"*There!*" Petrolio cries, and he jumps down the path to a large overhang. Two bodies lie crumpled and bleeding.

"Tasha," Heather answers, weakly. Tasha slides off the centaur and drops to her knees, then presses her hand against Heather's abdomen. Heather whimpers.

"How long?" Tasha asks.

"I don't know." Heather turns her head—she's looking around for something. "I don't know—how long—we've been down here."

Petrolio bends over Estajfan. Voices, another low moan.

Tasha leans in close. "He's breech, Heather."

"Yes." She glances over at the centaurs. "Help Estajfan, please."

Tasha nods. "His leg is broken," she says. "I think yours might be too. But we can fix that. Heather, look at me." Heather nods, meets her eyes. "He's breech," Tasha repeats. "I can't deliver him that way." She puts a hand against Heather's cheek. "Do you understand?"

"It's too early," Heather says again.

"I know. But we have to try." Tasha reaches into her medical bag and pulls out antiseptic swabs, then she dips into the bag that Aura gave her and pulls out a needle, small and sharp, a coil of translucent thread. The scalpel, smooth and cool beneath her fingertips. It sparkles in the setting sun, sharp and ready. The sun reflects off its surface and sends pinpoints of light over Heather's face.

"You'll take care of him?" Heather says.

"Yes." The word is like starlight in her mouth—impossible, unmistakable. "But so will you."

As they descend, Moira can't stop thinking about the centaurs that stand far above them, covered in green. She can't stop thinking about the way Estajfan jumped after the woman. Heather.

"Do you see them?" she calls to Aura and the others. They've been scrambling down for she doesn't know how long. No one survives a fall like that.

Beside her, she can see Annie struggling with the same thing. And if they find the bodies—what happens then?

"We're leaving," Annie says, as if she hears that last thought. "We get down from here, and we take what food we have left and go. We'll find other people somewhere. There must be others who've survived."

Others, Moira thinks. *Others who met their grief and faced it, or knew what to do with it.* She thinks again of Heather. *Maybe we've always been ready.*

"Heather and Estajfan have survived," Elyse says, with a conviction none of them feel. "We made our way up here. It means something. Nothing else would make sense."

Moira wants to laugh—*What about this makes any kind of sense?*—but she can't.

The sun crawls down the sky.

And then she hears a cry from Aura, and an answering shout—from Petrolio, Moira thinks. Petrolio, and Tasha.

They stumble down and reach the overhang. They *are* alive, impossibly. Aura kneels and Moira and Annie lift Elyse from her back, then rest her between them. She seems barely there and yet brighter, somehow, than any of them. Dazed and tired and still surprised to find herself there at all. And triumphant, somehow, in the knowing. Annie lowers her gently to the ground and settles beside her.

Moira crouches near Heather, then reaches for her hand and squeezes tight.

"Heather."

Heather. Darby. Joseph. Brian and Annie, Tasha and Elyse.

Aura. She whispers the names to herself. *Aura, Estajfan, Petrolio.*

Heather looks at her, eyes wide with fear.

"Heather," Moira says again. "It's going to be okay."

When Tasha cuts into her belly, Heather screams, but they are holding her down, Petrolio and Aura on either side of her, Moira at her head, Elyse and Annie behind her like blonde ghosts. Another shadow behind them—the other woman, brown-haired and gentle. Estajfan, reaching silently for her through the waves of pain and terror. And then there is a great wrench and something dark that blocks her view of the sky—her son, tiny and screaming as Tasha pulls him from her belly and holds him up. Heather sees four dark legs but then the light shifts and he is only a dark-haired baby boy, crying loud enough for the whole world to hear.

Tasha passes the baby to Annie and then begins to sew Heather up. It hurts, but not as much as she expected it would. After Tasha snips off the thread, she spreads the salve from Aura's bag over the wound and covers it in cloth, then Annie passes her son to her. He is still crying loud enough to fill the sky, and as Heather gathers him into her good arm she sees flashes of his life the way she saw her own fall from the mountain, the way she brought them to Estajfan, the way she saw Tasha and the flames. The long climb down, the even longer climb they will make to find food, to find others. The family they will become. The sudden blossoming of fruit trees and plants down below, a presence deep within the soil that she recognizes.

Her father has left the mountain too. He is waiting for her, down below.

Estajfan, she thinks. Estajfan beside her, around her, everywhere.

I survived, she thinks. *I came out of the ground with the flowers.*

The baby roots for her nipple like her girls did. Tasha cups his head and guides him to it, and Heather feels him suck at her as though he's been waiting for this, only this, all these months. It's an ordinary magic, but it's stronger than the mountain.

He is so small, but that is all right—he is here now. He is hers.

EPILOGUE

In the morning the doctor wakes up early; the sun has barely risen, the sky is still tinged with pink. When she exhales, her breath mists in the air. She shakes out the blanket that kept her warm through the night and then bundles it up and tucks it in her bag. For breakfast, a handful of berries and some dried meat. Not fancy, but she's survived on much less.

When she has eaten, she squares her shoulders and readies herself for the climb back up the mountain. Sleeping outside is not as nice for her bones as it once was, no matter how much mountain air she breathes.

As she climbs, she thinks about the babies. They had cried like all babies do, but in those dark moments when the wife was asleep and the husband stood in the corner of the room not knowing what to do, the babies' eyes had followed her. They might not have known who she was but they knew she was *somebody*. By the time she'd finished stitching up the mother and had turned her attention again to the babies, they no longer seemed unusual. Like they'd been born into a spot that had already been waiting. Like the world, whatever the villagers might have said, had been ready for their arrival.

She picked each baby up in turn and sang to it—old lullabies and holiday carols and songs about sunshine and love—then she wrapped each of them into a blanket and laid them on the table beside their mother. Then she turned to the husband and told him he had to go, and take the babies with him.

As she climbs the mountain these years later, the doctor wonders if that was a mistake. Should she have stayed there, in the village, and protected the babies? Had she acted too quickly in sending the children and their father away? The mother might have come around. The children were beautiful. It wasn't hard to see that.

They aren't monsters, the doctor might have said to her. *They're only different.* And perhaps the mother and her husband might have forged a way together. They might have had to move out of the village, but they could have done it, they could have survived.

Instead, this.

Higher, and higher still. The doctor pushes away the flowers that bob in front of her along the path. She thinks about the golden cuffs she brought him yesterday. An extravagant gift, but what was the harm— what was she going to do with golden bracelets anyway? When was the last time she'd had reason to adorn herself?

She's not entirely sure that the centaur will find a use for them either. What's the point of wearing golden cuffs if you live on the mountain and there's no one to impress? But he did what she thought he would do—he saw the gold and how it shone. He *had* been impressed—the human part of him, the part that measured worth in things like gold. Sometimes he was so human she almost couldn't stand it.

You are the best and most beautiful of creatures, she wants to tell him. The nobility of a horse and the sharp mind of a human, the strength of the mountain beating in each of his hearts. *Be worthy of that. It isn't hard.*

She reaches the last bend in the path before it stops. Beyond that there's a little hill; she's never climbed it because the centaur was always here to greet her.

It's so steep it's a struggle, but then she is over the rise, and there they are. Two of them. The father, dark and tall, and the girl, golden in the sunlight. Her long blonde hair shines almost white; her arms are tanned and muscled, and her shoulders slope in the happy way that children's do.

The girl turns and sees the doctor first. Her eyes are blue-green, like her mother's.

Far away, the doctor imagines that the mother stands up and listens.

She *looks* like her mother, the girl—the same face, the same scattered golden freckles. The same tilt of neck and chin. The resemblance is so strong the doctor almost cries.

I have a secret, the doctor wants to say. *I've been waiting all these years to tell you.*

Long years ago, on that second morning of labour, the doctor had reached into the mother and felt a leg where a baby's head should be. A leg that was not human—a tiny leg, an impossible hoof. She'd felt it with her fingers. She'd known it with her heart. She had taken her hand out and reached for her scalpel knowing full well what was to come.

She'd felt it, that centaur-shaped hole in the universe, and recognized it instantly. She thought the world would recognize it too.

That was a mistake. The doctor knows this now. She should have tried harder. With the father, with the mother. With the world below the mountain.

You belong here, the doctor wants to say. *You belong everywhere. You are not a monster.*

The girl looks about to smile, but then the father speaks.

"These ones, Aura," he says, then he looks up and follows his daughter's eyes to where the doctor stands.

And he is up, he is coming toward her in a blur of fury.

It's all right, she wants to call, and she puts her hand out, opens her mouth. *Aura,* she thinks. The sun comes over the edge of the mountain and sets the girl's hair on fire. *Aura. That's beautiful.*

Then his hands are around her and she knows in that instant that she was wrong about this, too. Sometimes there is no healing. His hands are stronger than the hands of any man she's ever known. He lifts her into the air like the feather she's always known herself to be.

She isn't sorry, even as the split seconds fall around her and she feels him let go. She isn't sorry. She saw magic all those years ago and there is magic here, too, at the end. She catches the eyes of the daughter in one last tilted moment and then she is flying, she is falling, and the mountain comes to meet her.

ACKNOWLEDGEMENTS

Thanks above all to Anne Collins, who took a chance on a wild idea for a story that then became a wild mess of a book. Under your expert hand, it has gradually become far less messy while also retaining its wild bones, for which I am so grateful.

Thanks to my agent, Samantha Haywood, for your faith and encouragement, and for always being so staunchly in my corner.

Thanks to the Canada Arts Council, the Ontario Arts Council, the Doris McCarthy Artist-in-Residence Program, Hedgebrook, and the Banff Centre, for your gifts of financial support and space in which to nurture this unpredictable story.

To Heather Cromarty, who read the earliest draft of *The Centaur's Wife* while I was still under the delusion that it was "almost finished" (LOL oops), and was so very kind.

To Sarah Taggart, dear friend and best reader, for your incisive and thorough comments. Thank you so much.

To Julie Gordon, bookseller extraordinaire and first cheerleader, who was there for me at countless bookish breakfasts at the Hamilton Farmers' Market and patiently listened to me worry about how this book was Never Ever Ever Going to Get Done.

To Piyali Bhattacharya, Vero González, Mira Jacob, Ashley M. Jones, Lisa Nikolidakis, and Yaccaira Salvatierra. Hedgebrook coven love is the best kind of love.

To Gary Barwin, whose words brought encouragement and strength when the writing of this book seemed impossible.

To Jael Richardson, #workwife and friend, who is a gift that lights my days.

To Ron Read, physician and medical expert, for fact-checking the medical details of an entirely unfactual novel and for automatically assuming (correctly) that the centaurs all have six-packs. Also, for rescuing Estajfan from a terrible death due to sepsis. I am grateful, and so is he.

To Cara Liebowitz, for your careful and considered thoughts on this book.

To the friends who've stood by and cheered, silently and aloud, during the ups and downs of writing: Elissa Bergman, Trevor Cole, Pamela King, Jaime Krakowski, Jen Sookfong Lee, Sabrina L'Heureux, Lisa Pijuan-Nomura, Stacey Bundy, Adam Pottle, and Ria Voros.

To Catherine Hernandez, my doula in the world of loss.

To my family—Raymond and Debra Leduc, Allison, Adam, Areyana, and Adelyn DiFilippo, and Alex Leduc and Aimee Leduc, for always being there with love and support and unbridled enthusiasm for reshelving my books in prominent bookstore displays and other guerrilla marketing tactics.

To Sitka, the Dog of Doom, who escaped her crate one day at five tender months of age and proceeded to tear apart, and then pee on, a draft of this manuscript, thereby inuring me to any and all future criticisms of it. (You were right; there was still much more work to be done. Thank you for exercising editorial judgement when I needed it the most.)

And to Liz Harmer, who told me that one short story about centaurs wasn't enough, that she needed to know more about them.

Grief is the hardest mountain I have ever climbed. I am grateful beyond words that I haven't had to climb it alone. Thank you to Richard and Jo-Ellen De Santa, Meghen De Santa Brown and Ken Brown, and Tim De Santa and Genelle Diaz-Silveira, for your love, laughter, and memories, and for opening your homes and arms to me as we walk this land of loss together. I cherish your fierce and brilliant hearts.

Finally, to Jessica De Santa. Dearest best friend and sister of my heart, who recognized me instantly that day in our St. Andrews dorm residence all those years ago, who believed in me before I had the strength to believe in myself. It was the privilege of my life to have you as a friend, and the dark howl that is life without you is matched only by the impossible, extraordinary grace of having known you in the first place. You were—you are—the greatest gift. Miss you now, tomorrow, always.

I hope I've done you proud.

AMANDA LEDUC's essays and stories have appeared in publications across Canada, the US and the UK. She is the author of the non-fiction book *Disfigured: On Fairy Tales, Disability, and Making Space* (Coach House Books, 2020) and the novel *The Miracles of Ordinary Men* (2013, ECW Press). She has cerebral palsy and lives in Hamilton, Ontario, where she works as the Communications Coordinator for the Festival of Literary Diversity (FOLD), Canada's first festival for diverse authors and stories.